Goddess Betrayed

William Laurence Grant

Goddess
Betrayed

Works by

William Laurence Grant

Goddess Betrayed

Goddess Revenge

Dance of the Wild Radishes

Follow William at:
www.williamgrantauthor.com/app/blog

Twitter: @wgrantauthor

Goddess Betrayed

by
William Laurence Grant

Aloha Pacific Books (2013)
New York and Honolulu

Printed in the United States of America

First Printing, 2013
ISBN: 0988939304
ISBN 13: 9780988939301

Aloha Pacific Books
Tompkins Square Station
Box 20201
NY NY 10009
www.alohapacificbooks.com

For Herb Kawainui Kane, whose art transformed Hawaiʻi's story and helped inspire this one, and for the Hawaiʻi which raised me like one patch of the multi-hued quilt of life … and for my wife and family, who are my heart.

Kaua'i

pua's hula school

koloa
plantation
menehune
fishpond

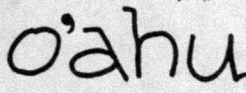

o'ahu

honolulu

hale nui
and
waikiki   birth
of dar

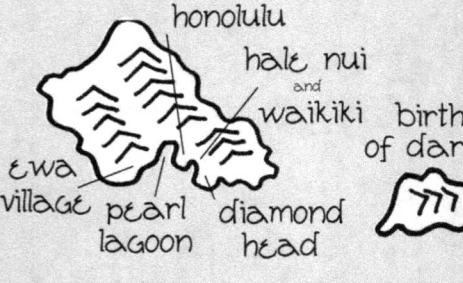

ewa
village   pearl
lagoon
diamond
head

gibson ranc

UA·MAU·IO·PA·O·KA·AINA·I·KA·PONO

hawaiian kingdom
1886

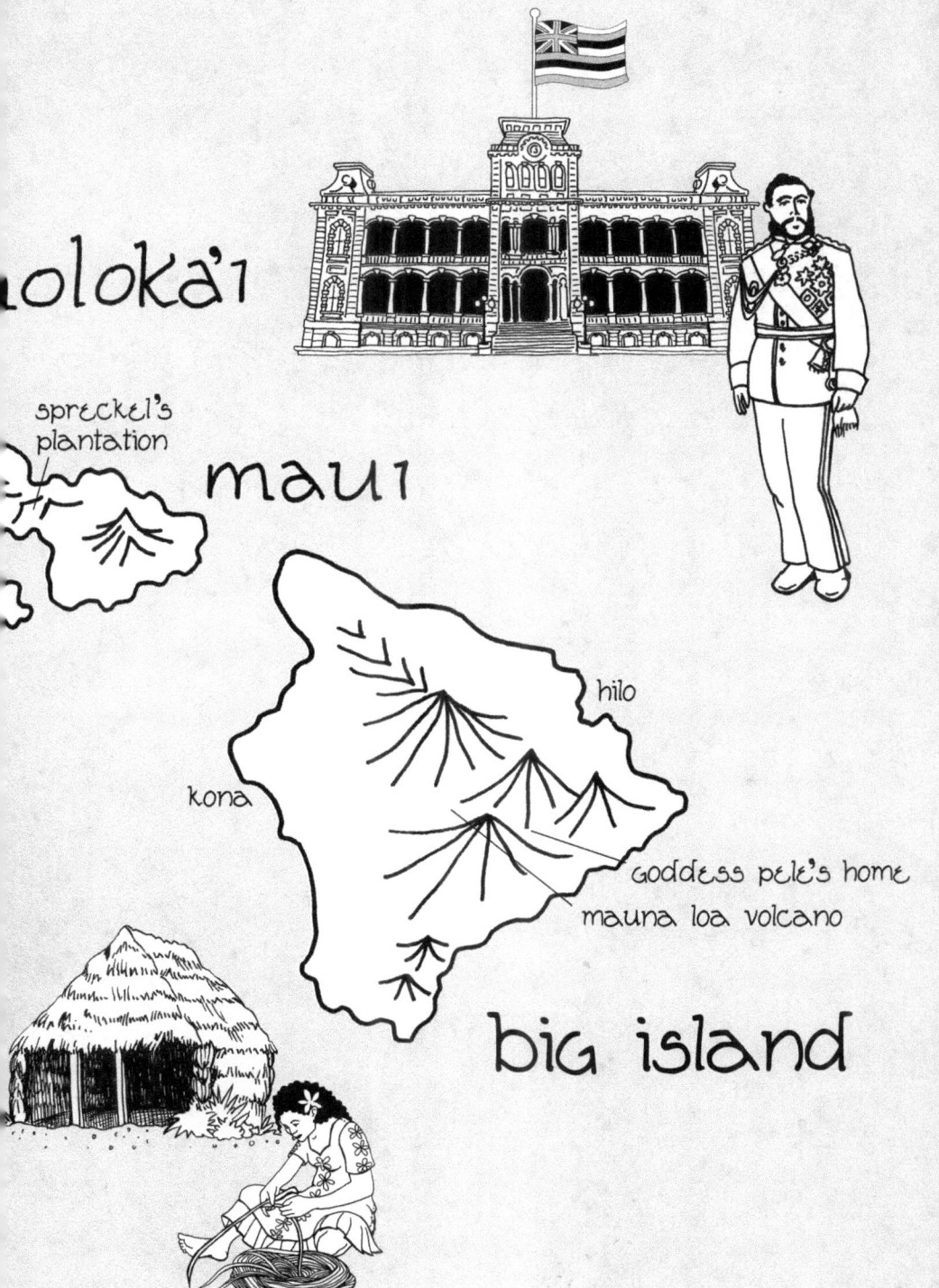

loloka'i

spreckel's
plantation

maui

kona

hilo

goddess pele's home
mauna loa volcano

big island

Principal Historic Characters
Kingdom of Hawaii

1886–87

Royals

King David Kalakaua	Monarch
Queen Esther Kapiolani	His Queen
Princess Liliu	His sister & heir

Supporters of the Crown

Walter Gibson	Prime Minister
James Wodehouse	British Commissioner
Claus Spreckels	German American industrialist
Chun Ah Fong	Chinese businessman
Chun Lung	His son

Opponents of the Crown

John Stevens	U.S. Minister
Sanford Dole	Missionary son, judge
Lorrin Thurston	Missionary son, legislator
William Castle	Missionary son, businessman
Volney Ashford	Commander, Honolulu Rifles

Common, Recurring Hawaiian Words

NOTE: Diacritical marks were not in common use in print Hawaiian during the 19th Century, so they may not appear in the text of this book.

Aikane [eye-KA-nay]   friend

Aloha [uh-LOW-hah]   welcome, love, farewell

Aumakua [OW-mah-KOO-ah]   clan gods, but not the high gods

Aue! [ow-WAY]   an exclamation

Awa [AH-vah]   a fermented beverage, lightly intoxicating

Hanai [HAH-neye]   the practice of fostering children

Hapai [Ha-PIE]   carry, slang for pregnant

Haole [HOW-lee]   Caucasian

Heiau [HAY-ay-ow]   temple

Hiki no! [HIC-ee NO]   Certainly! Surely!

Honi [HOH-nee]   kiss; traditionally done with the nose, not the lips

Hula [HOO-lah]   Hawaiian dance, had sacred roots

Kahuna [ka-HOO-nah]   priest

Kanaka [ka-NA-kah]   man; usually a Hawaiian man, a laborer

Kanaka Maoli [ka-NA-ka may-OH-ly]   The People; how the Hawaiians named themselves

Kapa [KAH-pah]   bark of the Mulberry tree pounded into fabric

Kapu [kah-POO]   sacred, restricted; system of taboos

Kumu [KOO-moo]   teacher

Lei [lay]	necklace of flowers
Luau [LOO-ow]	feast
Makai [mah-KEYE]	water direction
Makau [mah-KOW]	fishhook
Mana [MAH-nah]	spiritual authority; from inheritance & position, not achievement
Mauka [mah-OO-kah]	mountain direction
Menehune [men-ay-HOO-nay]	legendary race of small, dark people
Ohana [oh-HAH-nah]	family
O ia ho'i! [o-EE-a HO-ee]	That's right, So it is!
Poi [poy]	taro root, pounded and fermented into a staple food
Pono [POH-noh]	righteousness, morality, uprightness
Tutu [TOO-too]	grandmother; or older, non-related woman
Uhane [oo-HAN-ay]	soul
Uli [OOH-lee]	to steer; also the name of a sorceress
Wa'a [WAH-ah]	canoe; sailing canoe
Wahine [Wa-HEE-nay]	Woman

Please take these [lava] rocks and return them to the goddess Pele and ask for forgiveness for taking them. My husband and I went on vacation to Hawaii 5 years ago and he picked up the rocks not knowing about the bad luck. We have had the worst luck, loss of jobs, sickness, financial problems, and marital problems. Please kindly return the rocks and I will pray that my bad luck will go away. Thank you.

A&R, Philadelphia, PA

Pele the eater of land she devours with her flames. She rules the volcanoes of Hawai'i, and Mankind has no power to resist her. When Pele is heard from, her word is final.

Herb Kawainui Kane
Pele: Goddess of Hawai'i's Volcanoes

Prologue

All the gods died on the same day in Hawaii ... mighty Kane, whose black cape coated the heavens at night. Kanaloa, on whose broad watery back the ancestors migrated in their double-hulled sailing canoes. Lono, who returned each year on his beautiful cloud island bearing fertility to land and people. Ku, ferocious god of war ... and all the gods and goddesses, spirits and denizens to whom The People made offering and human sacrifice.

It was 1819 on the Western calendar, the day the great chief Kamehameha's warrior queen profaned the old religion. She served dog to the old chief's son after Kamehameha's funeral, then she peeled and ate yellow banana in front of all the courtiers, nobles and attendants.

The people were stunned, they murmured behind their hands, they shifted uncomfortably on their feet for it was so shameful. Only the woman was to eat dog, only the man permitted to dine on yellow banana. It was *kapu*, religious law bequeathed by the ancients. It wove gods, land and The People together. It made the Hawaiian who he was.

Violate *kapu*, man, woman or child, and you were bludgeoned. Priests broke your bones on the altar fire.

Hawaiians trembled. No mortal could lift hand against the queen. But the gods, what would they do? Where would they strike? How would The People be punished?

Priests wailed. They gashed their arms and broke their teeth.

Commoners and outcasts ran for the forests. They feared renewal of war and blood sacrifice.

... But nothing happened. Kane did not descend from his heaven. Kanaloa did not rise up from his wave.

For months the people wandered lost. Clans fought, wives were stolen, children enslaved and murdered. Commoners tore down temples and sold the effigies to Western traders and whalers, and they slaughtered the priest class. Nobles slipped into hiding.

Still nothing was heard from the gods.

Then in March the American brig *Thaddeus* arrived at the Big Island of Hawaii. *Thaddeus* had sailed from Boston 164 days around the Horn. She bore the first boatload of missionaries to the Hawaiian Kingdom.

The missionaries were young, some men had only met and married their wives days before embarking, and when they learned the old religion had died, they wept, praised and claimed the victory for their god. Jehovah had winnowed the mission field so they could plant the seeds of true religion in a pagan, wayward land.

The missionaries demanded native women clothe, native men go to work in factories and fields. They created a written language and introduced Western medicine. They built churches and schools, put a stop to *hula* and surfing, taught the chiefs about constitutional law and began a gradual takeover of the kingdom's economy.

The fire goddess Pele, aloof, demanding, smoked her pipe at her retreat high on the slope of Mauna Loa volcano on the Big Island, southern-most of the kingdom. She alone survived in the thoughts of her people. She saw everything, and she fumed. Her rage erupted in destructive explosions of fire and lava.

Still, only a few turned from the profane conduct of the West to honor her and court the old ways. What follows is the story of what they did next.

ONE

Saturday, October 2, 1886

Her skin glowed warm and gold like honey. The Moroccan sun had burnished it, he couldn't keep his hands from it. She purred against his ear while his fingers drifted along her exposed shoulders, dallied at her throat then slipped slowly down, just the tips lightly, as if tracing silken threads of glycerin, to tease open the drawstrings of her bodice.

She pressed moaning against him and he felt his belly relax. It was pleasure, pure pleasure. Hair flaxen, eyes blue, bluer than his, rose water on her tongue when it sought his, lilac rising out of her bosom. She sighed, breath moist. Pleasure, pure pleasure. He lolled in the peaches and greens of her satin boudoir.

She was young. The alarm went off in the back of his head. But she was French and taught him what she liked, a particular thing that shocked him the first time she led his fingers. Then he realized the effect and grinned through his eyes. Ah, the French. He loved the thrill of being with her, loved the risk, loved playing with the fire despite what was wrong about it.

He'd already been there, to the Viscount's villa. That's what was wrong. Already taken the man's wife. Already opened the safe, stolen the secrets, already escaped. What was he doing back? Even for the shade on her lips – he knew she painted them – the curve of her small breast in his hand, and the darting, teasing, daring of her tongue going everywhere, she laughing at him when he withdrew, put off by her boldness.

Except he could not escape her now. He tried his arms but they were pipes fastened down, immobile. His legs stumps, chest an anvil. Trapped. She had him. He panicked. No way to turn, no strength to pull away. Her laugh, calling his name, and the warning going off. Warning he'd ignored.

Warning now a pounding over and over. The door. Her husband, returned early. She knew, she was holding him there. Wanted him discovered, wanted the Viscount … He cursed her but his tongue was a fat toad. It wouldn't move.

He felt for the grip of his big Navy service revolver.

"Ramsey!"

The Viscount knew his name. She'd told him. Of course she had, pointed tongue flicking through the gap in her front teeth, smiling all the while at her husband, the minx. Of course she had.

He swung his feet off the bed. One still wore its boot. He had to escape.

"Ramsey! For God's sake, man!" The hammering resumed on the cabin door.

He stood, lost his balance and flopped back. The floor sloped unexpectedly. A bottle rolled across it, emptying whiskey.

The fumes turned his stomach, and the night rushed back at him. Not Morocco where he'd had to flee, but the steamship carrying him to safety. A poker game the last night before reaching port. He steadied himself by the cabin chair and pushed the hair off his face. The poker game. He, only an enlisted man up against ship's officers, he'd won the final purse. Thieved, more like. A slick manipulation of the cards.

He splashed cold water from the basin. It spilled onto his shirt front. He tried the looking glass, but his eyes were too bleary to see. Everything smelled anyhow. He stifled a foul tasting belch.

Voices in the passageway outside his cabin then the pounding again and screeching his name, and a ship's alarm joining in.

He should recognize the alarm but couldn't quite place it. He found the other boot. He'd stuffed his winnings into it. When did a man from the ranks put it over on ship's officers? The starboard watch helped him celebrate, stood him the first bottles. Then the anxiety again. It overwhelmed him. A new duty station, he had to impress, had to stay ahead of the investigators. He'd bribed the purser to open the ship's closet and drowned his anxiety in whiskey and rum.

"Ramsey!"

Face dripping, he cracked the cabin door. Instincts kicked in, he remained shadowed, pistol drawn.

"Goddammit, Ramsey. You the best the Navy has to offer?"

Stevens stood opposite him in the passageway, John Stevens. He knew the man, Minister to the Hawaiian Kingdom. Knew him from the dossier he'd studied in San Francisco. He'd been too young during the war but had fought Stevens' kind afterward, afterward in Missouri riding with the James boys, when they fought for the dirt farmers, the homesteaders and drovers and shipping clerks, and galloped off with saddlebags of silver taken from the government men who took it from the Confederate widows.

He squinted along the passageway, struggling to piece it together, the passengers milling, the ship's alarm rattling his brain. Why couldn't he place it?

"Look at you," Stevens said. "Need you to speak to the Captain, and you look like a scrub boy. You're a disgrace, Ramsey."

He narrowed his eyes. Stevens was short, wrapped in a smoking jacket, always his topper crushed on his head, a scrawny bird pecking with his stick. Two men he had shot. Both in blind, passionate defense of women he loved, so according to Blackstone's, they weren't murders, he'd looked it up. But Stevens he could kill. Coolly, professionally. Jerk him now by the elbow into the cabin, muffle the pistol report with a pillow. Slip his knife into the kidney like he'd been trained, use the rib cage as a guide. Who'd miss him? Stevens he could murder.

"Hear that alarm, Ramsey? Damn nonsense. Need you to get this boat moving."

He shook his head, trying to clear it. The alarm, he should know it ...

"What'd you say your billet is, Ramsey?"

"Attaché ... Hawaiian Kingdom." He pushed back the hair from his face. "Junior Naval Attaché."

"Government man, just what I need."

'Government man,' the words were poison poured down his well. But hide from the government in the government – best ruse. "What's that alarm?" he said.

"Forget the alarm. Native craft, that's all. A collision."

"Collision ... my God!" Ship going down, water closing over his head. He'd drown. All the Navy drills, he couldn't swim, not one lick. "My God, Minister! We've got to ..." The ship was heeling, decks aslant, he heard the bottle smash against the bulkhead in his cabin, it all made sense now. Water pouring below decks unstoppable. He'd sink, gagging, struggling, lost beneath the murk. He braced against the hatch, feeling his knees go. "The away boats, we've got to ..."

Stevens jabbed him with his stick. "Pull yourself together, man. You a sailor, are you? Get yourself to the bridge. Tell *Mariposa*'s captain get this boat going. I've business to attend, in Honolulu."

He slipped the pistol beneath his vest and struggled forward. The away boats were there. Stevens led him. Edison lights illumined his passage. Well-appointed, teak-framed cabins alternated port and starboard. *Mariposa* was civilian, he'd read up on her owner. Colonel Claus Spreckels controlled the Pacific sugar trade and much of the Hawaiian economy. He'd outfitted *Mariposa* to capitalize on the new occupation called tourism. Orders relayed about the ship, but there was not the muffled stamp of feet from sailors marshalling to obey them, no reassuring purposefulness of a man o' war's disciplined crew. The purser hurried by, the one he'd bribed the night before. "They sound lifeboats, friend?" But the man elected not to know him and disappeared down the companionway.

The ship's screws reversed and the deck tilted the other direction. It sent his stomach to his mouth. He grabbed a handrail and the door at his shoulder sliced open. It disclosed an attractive woman. Fresh young face, short auburn hair. Member of the opera troupe, he recalled, engaged by the Music Hall in Honolulu. She clutched a frilly wrap to her throat.

"Unholy – the conditions." He managed a bow. They could share a lifeboat. "I've an appointment with the Captain." He stifled a belch.

Her eyes widened, her mouth twisted in revulsion. He had a sudden realization of the sodden, smelly, unkempt image he must project.

"For God's sake, man!" Stevens held himself at the rising starboard rail and Ramsey, fleeing toward him, was suddenly face to face with the wind blown sea. Dawn's first touches had lightened it from ink to slate. Foam scudded across the chop, exercised by the remains of the gale that had roared out of the northeast during the middle watch.

Jacketless, wind tearing at his thin linen clothing, he lurched back for the passageway, wanting anything but the unbelted ocean.

"Up the stairs, man. Be quick about it." Stevens seized his sleeve and urged him toward the starboard ladder. He saw tree limbs, coconuts and household trash littering the surface, entrails of the island that humped on the horizon like a graygreen whale.

A figure appeared. "There's reason fer that alarm, gents."

Ramsey recognized the man, James Worthy of the starboard watch.

"… You keeps to yer cabin 'til you hears orders from the crew," Worthy said. "The Colonel's sure to be fierce as it is concernin' damage to his hull. Don't go fer passengers to gum up operations."

He noticed Stevens draw himself up. "I am a particular friend of Colonel Spreckels. I am the American Minister. Do you recognize me, sailor? The Colonel shall want his ship back on schedule."

Worthy spread his legs as the ship settled and fired his pipe. He appeared unimpressed.

"I have brought Mr. Ramsey with me, of the United States Navy," Stevens said. "We demand an interview with the Captain."

"O, it's you is it, Mr. Ramsey?" Worthy chuckled. "Me mates didn't expect we'd see you this side o' Madam Ho's, not after yester e'en's diversions!" He winked his one good eye.

"Ramsey is an officer and your superior, sailor. Tell him, Ramsey."

"That would be Petty Officer, your worship. Mr. Ramsey here's a Petty Officer, and bein' Navy he knows the Captain's goin' ter lend aid to the stricken vessel. It's rules of the road you might say, one sailor to another. Ain't that so, Mr. Ramsey?"

Ramsey struggled to take the anxiety out of his voice. "We just wanted to ... to take the report, Mr. Worthy. What's the damage? *Mariposa* – that is, is she sea worthy? Have you seen the other vessel?"

"Seen it? Was I raised the alarm. Take a squint through my watch glasses. It'll be clearin' *Mariposa's* hull just now, astern the freight donkey."

Ramsey crooked his arm to secure himself to the ladder then pointed the glasses astern. The white caps and sea trash leapt into view, but the circle of the glasses helped with the horizon line, so he lost all sense of motion and his stomach began to settle.

"I've got it," he reported, the breeze freshening his head. "Twin hulls."

"Yep," Worthy nodded. "A sailer."

"Fore 'n' aft rig," he said. "A beaut. The pirates rigged like that in Morocco. Quick as monkeys."

"Yep, saw one outrun a schooner once't, outside Maui. Sails close as a penny to the wind."

He scanned the craft with the glasses, the twin brown hulls, the carved, upswept prows, the sailing platform lashed between them and the outriggers port and starboard.

Worthy turned to Stevens. "You gents should feel the blessing running into one of them. Don't see so many this day and age, the big sailing canoes. Most natives, they've forgot how."

Mariposa was nearly full stop but her stern continued its slow sway to starboard. "It's sinking. Don't see a breach in *Mariposa*," Ramsey said, relieved, "but the sailer is down by the lees."

"There you are," Stevens said, "nothing to be done, poor creatures. They shouldn't have crossed the shipping lanes. There's laws in their country now. The native has to learn."

Worthy peered over the railing. "Like as not the storm blew through dismasted them. Took them off course. Put your glass on the masthead, Mr. Ramsey. Is she splintered?"

He focused on the sailing platform, saw the sail collapsed like a fan. The crew were pitching wooden containers over the side. He could make out faces, two of them, strong, chiseled, framed by coal back hair, set upon well-developed torsos. They were naked to the waist, bailing the hull with gourds. Their skin was bronzed, not African looking; not black like the Negro but Colored, definitely a Colored race. Not White.

He caught sight of a bearded native, a collar of green leaves about his shoulders. "Looks like the captain's roping the crew together right enough."

Worthy tapped out his pipe. "Nope, no captain – no officers as in yer White man's navy. It's one of their chiefs, more like. Or one of them hoodoo men. You'll see."

"Boy's got his hands full. Some goose in the way. Long hair, looks like a female – she's tattooed, by God. Around her shoulder!"

"You'll see many a strange sight in these waters, Mr. Ramsey ... why, they'll let a female act as chief, even a warrior!"

Mariposa's alarm rang out again, a different tempo, not the collision alarm, and her steam whistle blanketed the deck in a moist warning.

"What's that?" Stevens demanded. "Under weigh again?"

Worthy looked at him, surprised. "Why, no. Rules of the road. I explained that. The Captain's reversing engines. He's lowerin' the boat."

"Lowering the boat," Stevens cried. "You don't mean ..."

"Take the natives aboard, gents. O' course. Rules of the road."

Ramsey returned the watch glasses and glanced at Stevens. He felt as shocked as the minister. He appreciated marine protocol but did not believe it should extend so far, never would have in North Africa. They were natives and practically naked. *Mariposa* was filled with White women and children. They should not be placed in such proximity.

"Maybe the Captain's fixin' to throw them a line," he said. "Tow them in."

Worthy chuckled. "You don't know my Captain. He's Quaker. Don't come out his cabin of the Sabbath."

"But they're heathen!" Stevens said. "Not an honest, Christian man among 'em, despite the missionaries!"

"Bingo boys and layabeds, from yer barefoot *kanaka* to the King hisself. But my Captain won't rest 'til he's pulled every one of 'em from Davy Jones, mark my words. And seen 'em dried off and bedded down proper. We'll be trollin' out here 'til the next watch. Like as not he'll apprehend your bunk, Mr. Ramsey, seein' as you're government now," Worthy added with a twinkle. "You'll get a personal introduction to the Hawaiian, and won't have to pay yer tithe at Madam Ho's to do it!"

Stevens glared. "Well, you're Navy, Ramsey ..."

The sounds of the water surging against the hull changed as *Mariposa's* throttles clanged astern and she lumbered aft in the direction of the sailing canoe.

Ramsey grabbed the glasses from Worthy, took a quick look astern then sprinted aft. "Get to the Captain," he called over his shoulder. "Cavitation wave, tell him that. It will swamp the lifeboat and the canoe!"

He clambered down the same ladders and dashed through the same passageways he'd negotiated early on other mornings to keep fit. He'd had them to himself, save for the occasional crewman smirking at his diligence. Now he elbowed passengers aside and pushed through to the afterdeck where, fighting his nature, he pressed himself to the stern rail.

The sailing canoe rocked in the sea two ship lengths astern. *Mariposa* had severed one of its outrigger pontoons and splintered the nearer hull but the real danger arose from the steamer's wave. During a mission to South America he had studied the impact of cavitation upon torpedo performance and was surprised *Mariposa's* captain had not thought of it. The bearded Hawaiian had. He made out the man gesturing at *Mariposa's* approach. Her blunt stern raised a towering fold of white water. The crew sprang to their paddles and the Hawaiian pounded out the tempo like a coxswain.

Mariposa's hull shuddered as her engines ground to full stop. Worthy had gotten his message to the captain, but not in time. The steamer's hull slalomed aft on the white caps and seemed to push the wave higher. Two sailors on the lower deck shot lines to the Hawaiians. One missed but the other reached the craft.

He raised the glasses and nodded. The bearded Hawaiian was a seaman. He lashed the line to the one point where the angles worked to his favor. Then a head draped by a sheath of black hair filled the glass. He recognized the tattooed shoulder, it appeared like a slender gold leaf against the larger, darker man. The female steadied herself with a hand upon the mast stay and demonstrated wildly with the other. He could not catch her face but watched the drama unfold: the argument, the insistence then the Hawaiian in evident defeat, and the line released and cast back into the sea before it was ever secured to the sinking canoe.

He set down his glasses, stunned. It was his own solution, toss the natives a line, don't bring them aboard but tow them to safety. The female rejected it. *Mariposa* careened power off and nearly rudderless, building the cavitation wave taller than the canoe. There was no hope for them now.

He picked up the glasses. The Hawaiians braced on the tossing platform or bailed even more urgently. His stomach turned. It was the worst end, worse than shooting or hanging: choking to death in a dark, unmarked grave. He wanted to call to them, color be damned; demand they run, run fast as blazes, heedless action might save them, but stared mute instead, fixed.

Then two white-haired, frail-looking natives jumped over the side and sank to their shoulders in the murk. He recoiled from the sight, flung himself around the stern pole for security, blinked and gulped uncontrollably. Bolted to the deck, clamping his stomach and its illness, he forced himself to watch the men tread in the path of the wave and untie the damaged pontoon, cataloging this first encounter with the native people whose kingdom he was ordered to undermine and pull into American orbit.

Thirty-one years of age, doggedly conditioned and cleanly shaven, with blue eyes and black hair worn pomaded and combed straight back, John Taggart Ramsey was an intelligence agent, posted secretly by the Office of Naval Intelligence to the Kingdom of Hawaii. He'd held the Indian ponies for Jesse and for Cole Younger, covering their eyes so they'd quiet and couldn't give them away, and later carried a pistol which he never discharged except in the air, riding against federalism and carpetbaggers until he was fourteen. Then Jesse executed the Daviess County bank teller, thinking he was the Yankee officer who'd ambushed Bloody Bill Anderson. All of Gallatin, Missouri rose up, calling them thieves and killers, no better than government men, shouting they kept all the money they stole and never helped the little man anyway. He slipped out of camp with fifty dollars silver and worked his way down the river to New Orleans, and eventually into the Navy – the Navy, never the Army – which he used to leverage himself out of the South. At ONI he won a series of assignments ashore where he convinced his superiors he was nimble, precise, coldblooded, the right man to subvert a kingdom.

He watched the natives struggle like a family of ants stranded on a leaf in a pond. Though they appeared organized and disciplined they hadn't a chance against the inevitable. *Mariposa's* stern wave swept over them and filled the canoe to its gunnels.

He shut his eyes and turned his head.

Pua coughed up the water, spitting and retching, eyes stinging, throat aflame from its salt. The wave sucked at her as the sailing platform righted itself. She clung to the masthead, straining her arms against the pull. She'd never been in such deep water, never so far from shore. It terrified her. Another wave broke over her. She squeezed her eyes and ducked her head. It thrashed her against the planks, skinning her knees and tearing her hands. Blood in the water. Sharks.

She heard the bearded priest direct the men. She pushed the hair off her face and looked for him. His eyes, if she could catch his eyes ... She'd never pronounced a curse, didn't know how. She'd fought the black blood whenever it threatened. But he was just a minor priest, she was her mother's daughter. The black blood surged greedily in her. "*Ke ahi a Pele*," the people called it, goddess Pele's fire. She hated it, but it thrilled her.

The priest had driven her from her *hula* school using a stick. He wanted to avoid her eyes. She threw split bamboo at him and the double gourd instrument then reached for a *pahu* drum, at which he threatened with the stick and, her teacher offering no protection, she stumbled sobbing behind him down the muddy path to Hanalei, clutching her few things in a basket.

"You must leave Kauai island." The priest said this over his shoulder, not even turning so her eyes could catch his. "The movement needs you. Your mother commands it."

Her mother! The kingdom's High Chiefess, its most feared sorceress, a Kahu who commanded the Flying God. Her mother Luahine who abandoned her at age five for the dark arts – no noble family to care for her – then turned her knowledge to her own advancement, an unheard of violation of *aloha*. This was talked about at her school, this was known, it was seen. And she suffered the shame.

At Hanalei her heart rose. *Wa'a*, the double-hulled sailing canoe rode the breezes in the bay. He was the grand achievement of her people. His antecedents brought her antecedents like flying fish from the southern lands. His twin prows soared tall as the coconut. His woven sail surfed the god's own breath. On him, she could escape.

Then the demon ship emerged out of the mist like a monster. It belonged to the *haole*, the Whites, but breathed fire like

Pele herself. Its wail shattered her ears. She forced herself to stand up to it, chanting *mele oli* for protection. But the demon ship turned upon *wa'a* and, unbelievably, the priest took one of its tentacles aboard. It was a desecration. Her *hula* teacher would have struck her for less. She cried out in disbelief but the priest laughed at her. The black blood of her mother surged inside her then, and she turned upon the man. He cut the rope, though it was too late for *wa'a*. The canoe had been profaned, now the pride of her people dipped into the churning ocean in surrender.

The priest braced on the pitching sailing platform and directed the men as if desecration did not matter. Water fell from his curls and as she crept nearer, she could see beneath his beard the claw prints left by the *haole* disease. He was defiled. In the days of the ancestors when the people kept the old religion the defiled were enslaved, or they were sacrificed at the temples. Cursing him would help restore the land. It was her mother's undertaking, not hers. She wanted nothing to do with her mother. But the black blood boiled, and she loved it.

She felt with her toes across the planks. The wood was water soaked and slippery. Wavelets leaped between the slats as if to tease her. The soul stealing curse, could she summon it? She would free herself, free *wa'a* to carry her to safety. If she could catch his eyes … the Kahu must hook them, like a fish on the line.

The *haole* demon ship blasted the heavens with its fire breath and shrieked in triumph. She jumped, slipped on the plank and tumbled into the downed sail. She saw the priest shake his head, laughing at her. The *haole* ship shrieked again and he said over its voice, "Come, child. Into the canoe. *Wa'a* is sinking."

She struggled to her feet. Crewmen were hacking the lashings to free the undamaged hull. "No," she cried, "do not *hemo wa'a*! Do not cut him up! He must take me back to Kauai island!"

"You go to Oahu island, Pua."

"Take me to Kauai island," she begged one of the elders, his daughter a dancer, dead now from the *haole* disease. He would understand. "I am dedicated to the god Lono. Take me back!"

"Are you, child? Dedicated to the god Lono?" The priest looked at her.

She hesitated. The sailing platform wallowed beneath her feet. Ocean water lapped her calves. The elder climbed into the undamaged hull. It bobbed securely on its outrigger like a paddling canoe.

"Did you *'ai lolo*, child?"

'Ai lolo, the ceremony she yearned for all her life, the recognition accorded a sacred dancer. And no she had not, had not been served brain of the suckling pig, had not been admitted to the god's service. It was on account of her mother, she reminded the god every night with her prayers. Other girls examined the clouds to shape hands in dance. They watched the sea to sway hips. But she was drawn deeper and darker, to the volcanic talons that gutted the cloud so it bled, or to the sickness that caused the storm surf to vomit itself upon the shore. Her *hula* spoke of them, though she did not wish it, the under-things which were precincts of the sorceress and expressions of her mother's unbidden blood.

Under their spell her dance could never please Lono.

"Let me go back," she pleaded. "The god calls me. I must serve him."

The priest grinned. "The god speaks to you, does he?"

"I am *kapu* to Lono, dedicated to him!"

He took her by the arm. "The Jehovah god rules Oahu island, girl. Lono's voice will not trouble you there. And your mother, she speaks louder than any god. You go to serve her!"

... Outrage for a dancer to be touched! Her years of *hula* training, her *aloha* for beautiful Lono, she felt them fading. She pulled away.

"Daughter of Luahine, *hele mai*, come to me," a voice called to her from the canoe, kindly, but urgent.

It was the elder, the grandfather who comforted her on the voyage. He held up her basket.

No! The basket, inside she'd hidden the love token given by the god! She couldn't live without it!

TWO

W alter Gibson watched the deck gang secure *Mariposa* to the pier at Honolulu Harbor. John Stevens would be first to debark, he was certain, claiming his status as U.S. Minister. He unwrapped a peppermint to prepare his throat. He'd once inspired men to adventure and treasure with his words. Now his voice was a breathy whinny. It forced him upon wits and manipulation to defend the kingdom.

The sun warmed his shoulders through the material of his coat. He luxuriated in it for the moment. Diamond Head crater, haggard and dry, glinted to the east. Rippled peaks curved from it, battered by the explosion of foliage that vanished into the west; but not before his beloved Honolulu appeared, besotted, a sun-dappled dark green carpet torn by the roofline of Iolani Palace, masterwork of his king. West again ran the Waianae range, stark and volcanic. Between it and Honolulu undulated the plantations, a chartreuse tide of cane sugar tumbling north out of town.

How he cherished it, this perspective. And these islands. They were vestiges of Eden. Their sun sought his cares with pleasant fingers and soothed them, and they were many, his cares; the multitudinous cares of King Kalakaua's prime minister, the kingdom's most powerful *haole*. He sighed, following Stevens' struggle his direction through the crowded pier. A high rank, his as prime minister, which came at high cost.

Stevens raised his stick at a clutch of naked children begging at a vendor's cart. Gibson patted the head of a curly-haired boy who fled behind his legs, and gave him a candy.

"Well they were in the way," Stevens declared, pegging up to him. "What do they expect? – Just like that fool Captain! Do you know he kept us idling for hours? Insisted on taking all the division damage reports. Imagine, and my diplomatic standing meant nothing to him!"

He sucked his mint. "You collided with the sailing canoe of High Chiefess Luahine." He towered over the American Minister, and enjoyed it. "I'd have ordered the Captain to do nothing less."

"O you would, eh?" Stevens adjusted the brim of his top hat to look him directly in the face. "Well, let me be the first to inform you. The palace has more to fear than a few renegades in hibiscus flowers."

Gibson's eyes narrowed.

"It's Congress," the minister began then paused, savoring the impact of his news. "Congress, Gibson. It balked at the treaty."

He blinked, stunned. "The Reciprocity Treaty?"

"I told you it would. I warned you, your terms are too steep."

"Not – not read out of committee?" he stammered. How painstakingly he had strategized with the king. The kingdom depended upon reciprocity with the United States, it brought hard money to the islands. It was their only meaningful foreign policy. Its renewal would occupy the downtown businessmen for months. He needed them looking the wrong way while he made one more attempt at empire.

Dropping his gear on *Mariposa*'s upper deck, John Ramsey saw the two men huddle. He recognized the scarecrow-like Gibson from his ONI briefing, knew the subject of their exchange, another blow to the kingdom's independence. But he could not tear himself from the bawdy spectacle before him.

He'd known short ration days with his brothers clawing a yield out of the Ozark Plateau; learned the drover's itch to sleep light on the ground running outlaw; had stretched out the knots while easing into New Orleans' pleasure palaces, into the nimbus of her gentlemen whose manners he absorbed, and into more books than he'd thought possible to exist, books calling him like Sirens out of gleaming leather beds, their covers embossed with invitations to affairs delectable beyond imagination. Yet, there had been the investigation, and looking over his shoulder to elude the murder charge, and taking refuge in the Navy.

He inhaled deeply, feeling his chest under the constricting loops of his uniform, sinking into the musky green profusion. Finally, at this far-away duty station, which had nothing of dust and danger about it but promised verdant affairs of its own, he'd find safety and success.

"I shall follow my orders," he said under his breath. "I shall win my promotion. They shall not know me here."

Graceful brown coconut trees drew his eye, and from their shaggy heads to a herd of white clouds chasing above the valley. He breathed again, tasted exotic perfumes and imagined a shadowy bower, the moon at night and how a female might be inclined …

He caught sight of the pretty opera singer. He slicked and straightened, readied to present himself scrubbed and polished and looking shipshape. Then the friendly little breeze shifted. It blew offshore, carrying this time the overwhelming stench of man, of the Honolulu waterfront, of the discharge from a generation of western vessels and the refuse of its sailors rotting ashore. He recoiled, unprepared for it. And unprepared as well for the braying command which followed it.

"You there, Ramsey!" Stevens hailed him from the wharf. "Are you deaf, man? See to my luggage!" He pointed with his stick at the trunks stacking outside *Mariposa*'s hold.

Ramsey saw Honolulu loitering there, or greeting arriving passengers, or scuffing about looking for shade. Diamond Head lookout had relayed signals to the harbor master, so by the time *Mariposa* tied up, much of downtown had arrived at Fort Street Wharf, turned out as for a carnival. Society rolled up in buggies and carriages; Chinese vendors wheeled carts to hawk refreshment and curios. Mounds of cases and leather-strapped trunks appeared by drayage, and sugar brokers wandered the dock scavenging for news of foreign markets.

He shouldered his sea bag and descended into it. The excitement of a new duty station. The relief of a clean slate.

"Times have changed, Gibson." Stevens traced a line on the wharf. "You won't get the treaty renewed without you give something up. The furrow won't plow."

Gibson felt the cares return cold, impervious to sun. "It's the South, isn't it. Your Democrat president fears he'll lose it to the Republicans."

Stevens shrugged. "Reconstruction days, we could dictate to the South. But Reconstruction is gone. Grover Cleveland's the first Democrat in the White House in twenty-five years. He wants the South to vote with him, he lets Reciprocity die."

Sugar was the world's most competitive trade item. Fortunes were made on it, the kingdom built on it. Gibson coughed gently into his handkerchief, calculating the damage. Southerners wanted government out of sugar. Southern Democrats glowered as his king dazzled Washington in 1874, first crowned head ever to visit the United States. He was proud of Kalakaua for that. President Grant made much of his king at the White House and signed the first reciprocity treaty. It made Hawaiian sugar cheaper than plantation owners in Louisiana and Mississippi could grow it. One more sword thrust into the Confederates Grant had fought.

"Your President Cleveland has no gumption, Mr. Minister, not like General Grant. A Republican, wasn't he?"

"Gumption?" Stevens snorted. "It's politics."

"Well, it should be backbone, it should be moral fiber."

"It should be business," Stevens said, poking him with the head of his stick. "If you had any, you'd stand up to your own planters."

He had an idea for business, a sparkling gem of an idea, a godsend, truly. He would tend it in the shade of Reciprocity then watch it sprout tall, tall and wide to shield the entire kingdom. He removed his hat and blotted his forehead. "Our planters are missionary sons. They appreciate these islands are Edenic, a paradise you would despoil." He smiled benignly through his white beard. In removing his hat, he had released the lowering sun directly into Stevens' eyes.

"Give me what I want," the minister said, fighting the sun.

He sidled, keeping the sun in Stevens' eyes.

"You know what it is, give it to me!"

He knew: Pu'uloa, Pearl lagoon. Hawaiian kings used to oyster in it. Stevens wanted it, wanted it for Spreckels.

"Give it to me and you'll have the treaty," Stevens said.

The United States could take Pearl lagoon without asking. Everyone in Hawaiian government knew that. But his scheme countered it. It would be the adventure to cap all adventures, its realization the dream of a lifetime. Just the thought of it set Gibson's heart singing, as when he'd sailed *Flirt* across the world to Sumatra, and buoyed him so he could toy with the American minister. "Tush, Mr. Stevens." He replaced his hat. "Not content with Nevada silver or California gold? Your American Columbia must have a Hawaiian pearl upon her finger?"

"You're a fool, Gibson. We're remaking the Pacific, just as we remade the South. It's progress. We'll do more to benefit your precious native than you ever dreamed."

"'Those greedy for gain are robbed of life' – Proverbs 1 and 9, Mr. Stevens."

The minister leaned toward him on his stick. "You know well as I, your business element will put a pearl ring and more upon Columbia's finger, long as they can put Hawaiian sugar in her cup –"

"You'll not have an acre of our land, Stevens. Not while I am Prime Minister. It is sacred."

"Sentimental clap trap. Why don't you return to the mission fields."

His mouth opened, but he could not force a reply. He could not return to the missions, Stevens knew he could not. There had been a tragic misunderstanding when he presided over the Pacific field for the Mormon Church. He had presented the church the Hawaiian island of Lanai as a great center for missions. "The new Israel," he told the Elders, but they were not visited with the same angelic vision. They stubbornly demanded return of the money he'd invested, a demand he was not, most regrettably, advantaged to satisfy.

"You come between the sugar men and Reciprocity," he heard Stevens say, as from a distance, "and they'll measure you for a wooden habeas – not for the first time, eh, Gibson? And I'll hand them the nails."

The Royal Hawaiian Band muscled up, drowning any opportunity of response. Stevens stomped off, waving his hand dismissively.

Ramsey stood with his duffel in a long finger of afternoon sun as Stevens pegged up to him. "Useless twaddle," the minister said, brushing the notes away. "Look at them, natives every one of them, trussed like monkeys."

The band wore thickly crusted military uniforms. Red and yellow – the kingdom's colors, Ramsey read in his briefing book.

"That's the King for you, him and that German bandmaster he hired. Ridiculous." The minister stopped and looked him up and down. "What are you doing with that thing?" He poked at the string of white blossoms looped around his forearm.

"There's a young lady I thought I'd decorate, Mr. Minister. I bought it –"

"Get rid of it. It's an affront to the uniform. You sailors corrupt yourselves out here as it is. And see to my bags."

He felt his temper rising but fought it. A syrupy drawl often misled Yankee ears. He did his best to slip one on. "Whatever you say, Mr. Minister."

"The Hawaiian Hotel. You can find a coolie for my trunk, or one of the native loafers. They'll know the way – understand me, Ramsey?"

"Right away, sir."

"Have a drink at the hotel bar. Tell the barman you are my guest."

"Most congenial, sir."

The drawl wasn't too thick, it had worked before. But he saw Stevens' eyes on him, blinking, thinking. "What did you say your orders are, Ramsey?"

He smiled warmly as he could. "Why, commercial relations, sir. The Navy wishes to warehouse stores in these islands. The sailing ships weren't so dependent, but today's cruisers need their coal. And the supply officer must have his stores, as they say."

"I am aware of the Navy's needs, sailor."

"Yes, of course, sir. My orders are to survey the opportunities. Perhaps your office will assist me."

"Perhaps …"

"You'll point out the thorns in the thicket, as they say."

"Yes … Well, you'll find the local political situation a challenge, that's certain." Stevens circumscribed the wharf with his stick. "The native does not know how to govern himself, and the class of White man here is opportunistic."

"I shall be grateful of your assistance, Mr. Minister."

"Perhaps," Stevens said again.

The minister's words said one thing, but the eyes another. They flicked over him, prehensile, searching for weakness. His initial impulse had been accurate: a bullet, muffled, precise; or a blade, a slender calling card.

"Shall I see to your trunk, sir?" He saluted.

John Taggart Ramsey's first encounter with officialdom was the United States Army. At age eight he shot a trooper to death on the farm after his father left them. The Yankee's last words were, "Rebel bitch," spat out while buttoning his britches over his mother's fallen body. The trooper slashed him on the neck with his saber before tumbling face down in the mud.

He bent over the soldier in the rising silence that followed the explosion from his rifle. He wanted to be sure he was dead. If he wasn't, the hickory stock of his squirrel gun could finish off a Yankee, his brothers taught him, if you struck him hard on the head. His mother was dead, he knew that the moment he'd seen the trooper's saber pierce her consumptive chest and the blood erupt; the moment a scream tore from him like an animal, like a deer screamed when his brothers wounded it and cut out its heart.

He'd drawn the rifle from its secret place in the haystack, and blinking away tears, he'd aimed it at the man, whose face turned blank then infernal with rage. After the powder went off the soldier tumbled over in his sights like a rabbit.

Hiding behind the barn, blood caked in his buttoned collar, hugging his knees to his chest in the manure and trembling, he wondered if God would take a switch to him. The Yankee was a grownup, even if he was doing bad things to his mother. But after hours gone and nothing happening, he figured maybe God had seen so many bad things in the war, He was not at home anymore.

Orphaned in the March mud of Missouri in 1863 and sobbing uncontrollably, Johnny Ramsey joined the generation of Southern children who lost their childhood in the red tide of the war. Gone were the familiar guideposts, in their stead the pockmarked graves dug by artillery shells; headstones thrown up by carcasses of dismembered horses; and unnamed highways paved with corpses of faceless men in their blue, gray and homespun cloth. Having pulled the trigger carefully as his brothers taught him, he thought he now belonged somewhere, if only to the others the war had left behind, the ragamuffins who did anything they had to, to survive.

His neck wound turned into a fierce scar as he aged, his blue eyes grew dry and pale. He arrived in New Orleans just as Benjamin Morgan Palmer delivered his eulogy of Robert E. Lee. Lee was upstart Carthage to Lincoln's imperial Rome, was protector of the natural order, defender of life, liberty and property. But the federal heel had crushed the South's God-given rights like grapes in the press. Palmer's whisper carried through the St. Charles Theater, and men and women wept openly: the bruised wine was their communion, and one day it would restore the moral ideals of the nation.

Ramsey had never heard the Cause spoken of so nobly. The portrait painted in the St. Charles of fortitude in the face of over-reaching government, of gratification postponed in pursuit of an ideal, touched him. For a moment he wavered, but only a moment. He'd ridden too long with the James boys. They'd taught him nobility's limits in the new world of federalism and silver, and later, the Office of Naval Intelligence completed his education. Information was power, and once he moved beyond the saddle's confines into the post-war era of steam and international trade, he saw power could be had even if you were poor and orphaned. You simply had to be single-minded and self-serving.

Occasionally, you even had to eat very humble pie.

A round-faced Hawaiian trotted across the wharf with a hand cart. He was shirtless and shoeless and wore black calf-length trousers. "Where you go, boss?"

"Quarters of the U.S. Minister, friend. You know them?"

"Up Alakea Street." The Hawaiian was eager to help for the price of an American coin.

"How much?" Ramsey realized Stevens had left him nothing for the chore.

"Any size good." The Hawaiian's hair was black and curly beneath a billed cap several sizes too small. He was a big man, padded with flesh more than muscled, his skin darkened by the sun, but he moved lightly on his feet.

"And my sea bag there, it goes to the attaché's office."

The man placed it on the cart with the minister's trunks. "Which one? British-kine?"

He smiled. Honolulu was an international port. All the Great Powers were on station, even Japan. It would be an excit-ing venue in which to compete and win. "No, the American attaché. You know it?"

"Follow me, boss. I show you plenty – dis one, too?" He pointed to a black hat box. It looked well-traveled. A shipping label stated in faded ink, 'John L. Stevens, Minister,' and listed an address in Maine.

He hesitated. The thought of the minister stranded without his dress topper ... he'd allow himself to buck authority this last time. "No, leave that one. Just take what you have."

"Okay, boss. You come quick. *Wikiwiki.*"

He followed the native off the wharf and up the slope into town, anxious to report in and size up the station commander. He had to put him at his ease about ONI, secure his collusion in the cover story – negotiating commercial contracts – and promise loyalty above all. Then he could go about his real mission. Subversion.

He started to rehearse what he'd say – first impressions were lasting and he hadn't done it well in Morocco, chameleon that he tried to be – but the Hawaiian chattered on, interrupting his thoughts. He warned him away from a pack of wild dogs snarling and snapping over refuse then told him about a nut oil that was good for mosquitoes. "They only like eat you at night. The *haole* taste like good *kaukau*, plenty good foods!" he laughed.

Black flies swarmed thick as a carpet. He put a bandana over his nose against the open sewage and noticed a cart piled with lime, but no one grabbed a shovel to spread it. Seamen of every color loitered beyond the wharf, looking cast-off and derelict. Behind them huddled the splintered unpainted taverns and yellowed opium dens they favored.

He was astonished. This was not the sleepy, leafy tropical haven he'd envisioned. Honolulu looked dog-eared and commercial. Native beggars haunted its alleys. They were blank-eyed and pitiful, some wearing a discarded sailor's jersey or scarf, and others a frayed wrap or simple trousers that ended in shreds at the knee. He swerved from them. Leprosy was epidemic in the kingdom.

"No step deah!" the Hawaiian laughed.

He hopped over a festering mound of uncollected dung. They had crossed into what looked like the business district. Carriages and saddle horses wove in and out of one another with abandon.

"Dis Merchant Street. Den we go Alakea Street."

Merchant Street was a broad hard-packed avenue running up slope. It was treeless. Wooden sidewalks fronted the business establishments. They were busy with women, some of them dark-hued, in white tropical attire and parasols. Men, wearing straw boaters against the sun, occupied themselves with commerce or shared tobacco and in unrestrained voices, the latest news brought by the steamer. The natives, a better breed than he observed at the waterfront, made deliveries and swept red dirt out of the stores. The shops were overhung by second story balconies and rusted, metal sheeted roofs.

After dropping Stevens' bags at the Hawaiian Hotel, an impressive stone resort with wide, airy verandas, banana groves and spreading shade trees, he handed the Hawaiian a coin.

"No *pau* yet, boss. No finish. I take you."

"You have been the gospel works, friend. I'll find my way."

"Where you stay, boss?"

"I'm certain the Attaché has quarters for me."

The man made a face. "No more. Get big fire Chinatown. Everyt'ing *pau hana*."

He dismissed him but upon reporting in, regretted it.

"Where are my powders?" Commander Taylor shouted at the sailor who sat the desk in his outer office. He was suffering a terrible spell. Ramsey suspected a drinking bout the night before.

"Did the Navy tell you what I'm supposed to do with you?" the attaché asked after examining his papers. "Dreadful fire, it burned half the town a few months back. All of Chinatown. There's no quarters for you. And I sure as hell am not putting you up at the Hawaiian Hotel, or the Commercial."

"I'll find quarters, Commander."

"Your per diem will never cover it. The shore rats in this town love to fleece the Navy."

"My daddy taught me to be resourceful, sir." His daddy in this case was the admiral in San Francisco, who would approve any voucher that brought the Navy to power in the kingdom.

The hammering and sawing of Chinese work gangs reverberated through the office. The attaché rubbed his temples. "Get me those powders, sailor!"

"I made the crossing ..." He thought to tell the attaché about the American Minister's encounter with Gibson, but Taylor dismissed him with a wave of his hand.

Uncertain where he stood, he shouldered his sea bag and emerged into the evening. The dying sun ignited the clouds over Diamond Head. He took a breath. It was undeniably beautiful, golds and pinks even more vibrant than the sunsets at sea.

"Dis way, boss. Get quarters for you." The Hawaiian seized his bag and tossed it onto his cart. "Too much noise this side, now. Too much *pilikia.* My cousin get quarters for you, down Punch Bowl Street. Nice one."

It was a bungalow raised on low stilts against the occasional flooding. It had a sloping tin roof, screened-in windows and three rooms with open partitions that allowed the air to circulate. There was a corner post to which he could secure a small safe for classified documents. A monkey pod tree with delicate, umbrella-like pink and white flowers provided shade. Low hedges lent privacy, though the property next door was unoccupied. The remains of a native hut moldered on it and a grunting sow and her piglets had turned it into their mud hole. Back of the bungalow hens scratched and pecked near the privy.

"No rooster. I went *hemo* already!" The Hawaiian drew a thumb across his throat.

"Well I took you for a deadbeat, friend, but this will suit me, suit me just grand. Aces, in fact!" He grinned and handed over a thin stack of coins. "Tell your cousin I am obliged."

The Hawaiian bit one of the coins. "Good, boss. Tomorrow I come. Fix breakfast. Get guava now, and mango. *Ono,* taste good. Chicken egg and pork, jus' like British navy."

He shook his head. "Nope, don't require a houseboy. Sorry, can't afford one."

The Hawaiian laughed. "What you mean? Where you wash da uniform? Where you shine da boots? Get inspection, boss. You like pass, no?"

He laughed too. "Well, you got me there. Wouldn't know where to turn, would I? All right, we'll try it for a week until I know my way around."

"Okay, boss. Morning watch, I come. Sweepers, fore an' aft."

"Morning watch, that's grand, just grand. I'm up early."

The men shook on it.

"My name Manu," the Hawaiian said, raising his cap before he turned then trotted down the dusty street pushing the hand cart. Ramsey stepped into his new quarters, whistling.

Out of sight of the bungalow, Manu slowed and jingled the coins in his pocket. Plenty there for the man he'd stolen the cart from, and plenty for his cousin. He smiled with satisfaction. It had been deliciously easy. He was a spy. He spied for the Makahiki movement spawned by the native priests, the *kahuna*. They planned to unseat King David Kalakaua and place Manu's own mother, High Chiefess Luahine on the throne. Kalakaua was an accommodationist, he'd grown too close to the *haole*, local born and foreign.

Manu knew the *haole* better than anyone in the movement. He'd been taken as a cabin boy aboard a British whaler. He could speak English like a duke when he wanted. His years of polishing a brutal captain's brass, of mending sail and scrubbing decks for a deviant bosun; of canvassing the waterfronts of San Francisco, Singapore and Valparaiso had prepared him for this moment. Tipped off by an old shipmate, he'd accosted the Junior Naval Attaché on the wharf. He intended to work his way into the heart of official American presence in the kingdom.

He did not believe his people could hold out against the West, and he was not convinced they'd be better off with his mother on the throne. He was certain from his own painful experiences that she'd drive the harder bargain.

THREE

King Kalakaua built Iolani Palace – pillared, columned and turreted like a European import – despite the opposition of the downtown businessmen and the traditional priests among his own people. The thought still pleased him. He had concluded from his tour of foreign capitals that the improvement of the nation required an imposing stage from which to govern. He commissioned architects to design a weighty edifice, one that anchored his dynasty between the *haole* on the one hand and the *kahuna*, the native priests on the other.

The businessmen objected to the $350,000 cost. The *kahuna* protested that he did not prepare the ground with human blood. When he crowned himself at the palace he employed an elaborate Masonic ceremony which, he thought whimsically, split the difference between the two.

His guest sat in the Library Room, the glow of the oil lamp spreading over him. Chun Lung's father, held by the newspapers to be the kingdom's wealthiest citizen, would have appeared in formal, high-collared blouse, his queue heavy and graying down the middle of his back, but the son crossed his legs in a western suit and lounged.

Kalakaua stood in shirtsleeves at the sidebar. "First a cocktail then business, eh? Your father always declined a libation, but you are westernized. Punahou education here then Yale College, was it?" He hated having to toady to the Chinese, but he needed them behind his government.

Chun Lung nodded.

"Quite a feat of your father's, gaining you admission to the missionary school."

Chun Lung smiled. "I was the first Chinese at Punahou. Everyone else was *haole*. The missionary kids were a little surprised."

"I can imagine. You showed them up, of course. Though not an athlete, were you."

Chun Lung shrugged. "Baseball was all the rage. Seemed a little ridiculous to strike a ball with a bat after what I saw growing up in China. They were using bats to kill you."

He shivered, a monarch's revulsion for insurrection. "The horrid rebellion fomented by that Christian." He turned, a glass in each hand.

Chun Lung nodded. "Mind if I smoke?" He pulled out a prepared cigarette.

"Of course. – Now you have heard of the American drink, the martini. Try my version, more vermouth and I add a sliver of cane sugar. My gin is Boodles of course. There's a fair likeness of me in the London club by that name. Well, chin chin!"

Chun Lung stood. "Your very good health, Majesty. May *aina* the land prosper."

"It shall, once we loosen the grip of the *haole*. Missionary son or foreigner, they are throttling the nation." He drained the glass. "Rather smooth, isn't it. I call it 'Pulama,' which means torch, the symbol I chose for my dynasty. We must light many torches or the night of ignorance shall close upon my kingdom, do you see? Many torches, hey-hey! You must help me light another."

He turned back to the sideboard but Chun Lung declined a second cocktail. "My father is taken with your proposition, Majesty."

He felt chronically weary, siphoned by court life, but he could have danced at that. "Brilliant! – The Pacific basin a great marketplace, a breadbasket, you might say!"

"My father sees the possibilities for commerce with the East."

"Yes, if it is not plundered. We must protect the Pacific from the Germans and the Americans."

"And the British," Chun Lung added. "Even the Japanese for that matter."

"He will capitalize the project?"

"My father will consider it. He has a diviner who reads the *I Ching*."

"Fortune telling?" The king steered around his desk. "Doesn't he realize this is about fortune making?" He smiled at his own witticism.

"He will do nothing that is not propitious."

"But that is such superstition! Even my people have forsaken the *kilokilo*. One must preserve tradition, but when it comes to business you need quickness and intelligence. A little avarice, eh?" He fluffed his side whiskers. "The *haole* are right about that!"

"My father will not be hurried. Perhaps you must consult your great friend, Colonel Spreckels."

Kalakaua returned to the sideboard to hide his face. He could lose a small fortune at cards and call for another bottle, but when the gamble was the future of his people, he did not trust his self-control. "I am not certain the Colonel should be accorded another opportunity to profit by my kingdom. Make certain your father understands this."

Chun Lung stubbed out his cigarette. "This deal is likely to look more favorable to my father if there are certain changes at the palace."

"No Colonel Spreckels?" he said without turning. "The matter is already in hand."

"No Spreckels, and no Gibson."

He swung around. His eyebrows, leafy and effeminate, were arched in surprise.

Chun Lung spoke. "Your Prime Minister persecutes the Chinese for leprosy. We are faulted for enough evils as it is – everything from opium to seducing White women, even working too cheaply. We do not wish to be the progenitors of disease as well. That was Pandora, you recall."

"But the *pake* brought leprosy to the islands." He used the Hawaiian slur for Chinese. "Everyone knows it. Your field laborers brought it."

"I am *pake*, am I disfigured? Am I diseased? – If you want my father's money, you'll get rid of Gibson."

Get rid of Gibson. The king stood at the sideboard with his drink. For years the opposition press had hounded his administration. "The Three Kings," they named it, Kalakaua, Gibson, Spreckels. Nothing in print exercised him so. The Kamehamehas were never impugned for their *haole* advisors. Only his administration, his because he was dark – Negroid, some whispered; his lineage mediocre according to the nit-pickers among his own nobles.

But to be rid of them both, Spreckels and Gibson. He looked at Chun Lung. A kingdom built upon the colored races ...

A knock sounded upon the door frame.

"Majesty," said Walter Gibson. The prime minister uncovered a gray head, bowed at the doorway then entered unbidden and placed top hat and stick beside him on the settee.

"Ah, Gibson. At last. You know Chun Lung."

The two men nodded to one another. Chun Lung excused himself.

"I apologize for my tardiness, Majesty." Gibson unbuttoned his top coat. "I was late in receiving your message."

"I telephoned." Kalakaua loved to tinker – in his thirties he designed an iron clad, monitor-like vessel and petitioned the Emperor of Brazil for the funds to build it – and quickly adopted each new gadget. He gestured toward the box mounted on the wall. "Where were you? I wanted your help with Chun Lung."

"It is a pesky machine, Majesty." Gibson glanced at the instrument. "It has not sense enough of a man's privacy."

He nodded and lit a cigar at the lamp. "The spells again?"

"Like the devil since that wretch Stevens returned – your pardon, but the man gloats at our setbacks. He hasn't a diplomatic bone in him."

David Kalakaua was declared monarch in a tumultuous election – American marines and British tars landed at Honolulu to restore order – and Gibson, claiming he'd swung the vote by editorializing in his Hawaiian language newspaper, hitched himself to the young king's career. Together they delivered unprecedented stability and fortune to the islands.

"Never mind about Stevens," Kalakaua said. "We have more important business to attend."

His prime minister shook his head. "We cannot dismiss the man. He wants our land so frightfully, he would pull Honolulu to San Francisco with his own fingernails."

Kalakaua quaffed another cocktail. "I do not think the American public would appreciate Luahine in such close proximity. Can you imagine her sailing bare breasted through the Golden Gates, hurling curses like Jove?" He laughed.

"Pray God she remains on Kauai island. But I hear things, Majesty. My detectives tell me she has contacted the chiefly families on the Big Island. If she succeeds in healing the old wounds ..."

"It will never happen. I know my people. Her reputation as sorceress outweighs her *aloha* as High Chiefess. The Big Island will never accept her. Nor will the Island of Maui for that matter."

"If she succeeds in her movement, she –"

"Buck up, man! She would have to sacrifice her own blood to heal the divisions. Kamehameha alienated the chiefs when he united the islands. Luahine is his clan, she cannot bring them together, only politics can. They will respond to our plan, Gibson."

He made room for his prime minister at the writing desk. A scroll of parchment overlay it to the floor. "There, you see?" He inscribed a shape with his cigar butt. "From French Frigate Shoals in the north to Chile in the southeast, then Samoa in the southwest and back: as pretty an isosceles triangle as you could wish."

Gibson lifted his head from the map. "And your kingdom square in the center of it."

"You have craft, I give you that." He saluted Gibson with his glass. "'Pacific Primacy,' you named it."

Gibson lowered his eyes. "*Malama* the moon is but a pale reflection of the sun, Majesty."

Kalakaua looked at the map and his heart stirred. "The entire Pacific, all the islanders, united in one confederation – no longer a sponge for the bilge water of the world's navies."

"And you its prince!"

"Its own economy … not the stepdaughter of copra traders and sugar planters." The business he intended to capitalize was the guano trade, bird dung which supplied nitrogen for gunpowder and fertilizer for Europe's spent fields. It was lucrative as sugar. Wars had been fought over it, certain Pacific islands were thick with it, including French Frigate Shoals, which he claimed for the kingdom.

"Majesty, you have me on the foredeck of *Flirt* again!" Gibson's eyes glowed. "I am taming men and seas like the Christ himself! What won't the sugar men say?!"

"They shall say nothing. A government monopoly on nitrogen – my government monopoly. Hah! Let them haggle over who puts sugar in a matron's tea. We shall hold the key to war or peace!"

Gibson leaned both hands upon the map. His breathy voice turned reverential. "It's true, isn't it? The vital force has relocated to the Pacific, from the Old World to the New. O, I knew one day I'd be vindicated. But to be worthy, our sins must be expiated, Majesty. We must be forgiven our trespasses."

Kalakaua took Gibson's arm. "Ever the moralist, eh? It is the weakness of the Christian. But look: the triangle confirms me. The isosceles is perfection itself. There's a mathematic harmony to the world, the Greeks understood as much. So did my people, though they have forgotten. Hale Naua shall remind them, however."

Gibson shook off his touch. "Hale Naua? Your mystical society? But Pacific Primacy requires hard currency, not philosophy."

"Do you dispute me?"

"Majesty, it is only that a man, a man of action – why, even the Christ carries a sword. And Krupp steel is superior …"

"You would have me humble myself before the Colonel?"

"Colonel Spreckels will invest, Majesty."

"You have spoken to him?"

"He called on me. He is our largest creditor, of course I received him," Gibson said.

He threw his cigar to the rug. "I told you, never again!"

"But Majesty, without him –"

"Without him the Colored Race is lost? We are helpless without his charity?"

"No, without his capital we are lost. We are the Syrophoenician woman of the gospels, Majesty. We are condemned to the crumbs beneath America's table."

"Bah!" he exclaimed and wheeled away. He heard Gibson murmur, "I'll have to give the jackals Pearl lagoon. My God."

The king shrugged into his jacket. He started to speak but was surprised to find his prime minister seated without permission. He studied Gibson's back and saw not the man with whom he'd dreamed dreams, not the conspirator in government whose deviltry had kept the missionary sons off-balance for years; he saw a clothes tree with too spare a frame to drape its own garment.

"Come, Gibson," he said. "Where is your faith, man? Perhaps another séance with Mother Marianne, eh? I tell you, Luahine will wallow in the mud at Kauai island and cast spells over her pigs, so strong shall my dynasty become. And the Americans? They will hasten to trade with me, without demand for territory or concessions. Were you a follower, you'd discern it in the great Pythagoras."

"With respect, Pythagoras will not cast our net over the Pacific kingdoms. We must have capital."

It was a slight. He chose to ignore it. "You should know me better after all these years, Gibson. You have studied my people's wisdom, we were entrusted it by the gods. The monarch is its custodian. *'Mai pi'ikoi ka mano hae.'* I'll not strive for the shark when the mullet is at hand. No, I shall interest the bankers in London."

"I had rather you apply to the Chinese. They are surer." His prime minister sounded glum.

"Still unmoved, eh? Well, I tell you Chun Lung shall have his opportunity, never you mind. And the Colonel? In my kingdom, my new kingdom that I launch today, his only use is to lose to me at cards. Just now, I go to trump him." He raised his glass though Gibson would not, and saluted himself.

"Heed me, Gibson!"

FOUR

Her people loved Waikiki. She heard about it from her teacher. She wanted to love it, too. It was blessed by the gods. The nobles farmed and fished it, and the warriors healed their wounds in its sacred bathing waters. Graceful breezes cooled and kissed it, and out of its taro patches green tendrils unfurled like emissaries bearing fertility to the neighboring districts.

Then *makika* the mosquito arrived in the water cask of a western trader and took up residence in Waikiki's quiet ponds. Kanaka Maoli, The People were stricken. The district's terraced fields fell into disarray, their retaining walls crumbled and vast stretches declined into marsh and decay.

That was the Waikiki the bearded priest exposed her to. He would not let her see more or other, would not let her see it by daylight, would not let her absorb what her people once had accomplished.

"I keep you *kapu*, sacred," he said.

He moved her by dark from hut to hut tripping over roots. She cried to him about the Night Marchers, Oahu warriors whom Kamehameha, the islands' first king had butchered. They prowled after dark searching for souls on which to avenge themselves.

He waved his hand at her. "Your mother watches over you."

By day he stationed crewmen around her. She refused their food in protest, but she weakened and black blood tormented her, taunting with visions of the retribution she should visit upon her captors. She fought the visions with prayers to Lono, fingering his love token.

Finally, horses were delivered and she was taken on a long winding trail past a waterfall's roar and through perfumed layers of ginger, dozing in the saddle until they arrived at dawn at Ewa. It was a crewman's village, the elder who had befriended her at sea.

"*Hele mai*! Come to me, girl!"

A slender old *tutu* beckoned from under a swaying coconut tree. She was draped throat to ankle in the garment the *haole* liked her people to wear. Her hair was gray, piled atop her head, and she wore a *lei* of polished *kukui* nuts.

Pua pinched her cheeks to rouse herself and slipped from the horse.

"Your new teacher, Kumu Pakalana," the bearded priest whispered to her. "Keep Lono close to you."

Pakalana appeared more unyielding than her teacher, the *kumu* on Kauai. She trotted over and prostrated in the red earth at her feet.

"Is this one obedient?" she heard Pakalana ask.

"High Chiefess Luahine vouches for her."

The *kumu* snorted. "Show me the hands, the feet." She examined them then told her to stand erect. She poked about in her thick hair, in her mouth filled with white, even, healthy teeth; and stared into her eyes, which were hazel, clear and direct.

Then she examined her breasts and sniffed her skin. "This girl has her flow," she gasped. "I cannot teach this one the Hula Pahu! She has her *waimaka lehua*!"

The priest spun her around. "Is this so, child? You have your flow?"

She bit her lip.

So far as the school knew, she had never received *waimaka lehua*. She'd been cursed in retribution for her mother's curses – so the other girls said – a dry *kiawe* pod without a monthly flow. No one would *aloha* her, god or man.

It was a terrible shame, but she endured it. She even welcomed it. She pounded her *kapa* cloth, ground her dyes and watched the clouds bloom at sunset. She dreamed of Lono and stayed safe from her mother. She was happy.

"You have your flow?" the priest demanded.

"Lono visited me himself," she wailed, "the night of his moon!"

The god had come for her one evening when she, risking uncleanness, moped among the night creatures along the sand at Hanalei. She swooned, he pierced her with his dart – he left behind the long, slender cone shell as his love token – and she bled at last.

Pakalana laughed scornfully. "May Lono take you, send you back to Kauai, country girl! I do not care that you are daughter of the High Chiefess. You cannot dance."

"*Oia ho'i*, it is so! I dance the sacred *hula, kumu*! The god himself takes me!"

"Foolish girl. Your *hula* is nothing. It is Kauai *hula*. I teach Hula Pahu. Pele herself taught me at Kilauea, where her *lua* boils on the Big Island. It is the most ancient form of our people. It was danced by the gods at the temples of blood sacrifice. You dance to Lono, the half-white god. But Hula Pahu is Pele's, it is danced with her sacred fire in the womb. She alone must provide your bloody flow." She signaled the priest. "Take this one back. She cannot dance Hula Pahu."

Was she truly to be sent back to Kauai and safety? She glanced at the low lava wall edging the village. The crew were hacking the tops off coconuts and drinking the liquid. One of the men helped grandfather get his share. On the voyage he had been so grateful for her chant during the storm, so grateful for her *aloha*, and during her captivity he had shown kindness and respect. She hesitated. Perhaps *hanai* to him, family would fill her breast, leaving no room for her mother's black blood to rise.

"Kumu Pakalana," she began. She lowered her eyes in respect. "It is true I have my flow. I only just received it."

"You lied."

"I did not lie, *kumu*. I was not asked."

Pakalana looked at the priest. "I did not think to ask," he shrugged. "The High Chiefess summoned her."

The *kumu* sucked her teeth in disgust.

"*Kumu*, if I may," she pleaded. "I have dedicated myself to the gods. May I not be taught their Hula Pahu?"

"It cannot be done."

"I will make many sacrifices, *kumu*. I will fast many days."

"It cannot be done."

"But it is for Kanaka Maoli, The People. Perhaps Pele will visit me with her fire."

Pakalana laughed at her. "You do not know what you ask, Kauai girl. Only one dancer ever asked for Pele's fire. It drove her from dance. She turned to sorcery. Now she casts the flying curse."

Her mouth opened.

"Yes, Kauai girl, yes. Your mother Luahine. Do you think yourself like her?"

The *kumu* peered at her, as if she could see inside. As if she could see her pitiful flow and know that it was nothing, nothing compared to her mother, nothing compared to the flow of the mighty Pele.

"No one dares look upon Luahine. She lives like the outcast, she lives like the lepers on Molokai island. Can you follow her path? Can Kauai girl with her pretty *hula* become Molokai girl?" The teacher laughed again.

She could not speak.

"*E kali iki*," a deep voice said. "Pause a moment, *tutu*."

A light-skinned Hawaiian man with glistening moustaches and straight combed hair stepped in front of her. He wore a pale green coat, white trousers and his feet were covered – the *haole* custom, she'd heard. Her heart thumped excitedly as he leaned in. He lifted her face, looked into her eyes and stood back to examine her carriage. "Confirm that she is intact," he said.

"As you wish, Prince." Pakalana removed her from the men, ordered her to loosen her *kapa* girdle and probed her female place with her fingers. She winced.

The *kumu* stood and nodded to the prince.

"*Maika'i,*" he said. "This is good."

"You are intact, girl," Pakalana said. "But Aunty Pele will never visit you with her fire. You have not the *mana*. You will never dance Hula Pahu before the King, not as your mother demands. You have not the spirit. I, Pakalana say this is so."

"Yes, *kumu,*" she said humbly as she could and hung her head, the trick that always worked on Kauai. But she thought, "The King! With effort I may dance before the King!"

The *kumu* continued, "You may demonstrate your gratitude to Prince Koloa for your reprieve. He hails from your own Kauai island, is of superior lineage and *hanai*, foster child to Queen Kapiolani herself."

She threw herself upon the ground once more, but not so low as she had prostrated to Kumu Pakalana. She possessed woman's eyes now and kept them upon the prince. He looked fair as Lono himself and his beauty drove sorcery and black blood far, far away.

Koloa laughed. "She may not look upon it as salvation, *tutu,* not after you have introduced her to the training required to dance Hula Pahu! *Aue!*"

FIVE

*M*anu paused at Fort Street to catch his breath. Honolulu's telephone line bellied overhead and the late-October humidity squeezed perspiration over the aromas of red earth and sea spray. Dust swirled from the wheels of passing teamsters, dimming the luster on the tall boots held before him. He couldn't wait, so dodged among them.

Ramsey had ridden off on a bicycle at dawn. He was surveying the countryside in the Pu'uloa District near Pearl River. Pedaling rather than letting a good horse carry you was hard to understand, but it got him out of the way for many hours. As houseboy, the time should have been used to polish the boots into mirrors and align them heels out at the foot of the bed, as directed. Ramsey had his first state function, the king's *luau* and wanted to get it right. But an old shipmate did a better job and Manu had more pressing employment for his time. All hell had broken out between the king and Colonel Spreckels at cards. Soon as he confirmed the report, he crossed to Iwilei near Oahu jail where he released a flight of carrier pigeons to Kauai.

He puffed across a backyard occupied by a rabbit pen then skirted a grove of *hala* trees – very ill-omened, Luahine taught him as a boy – dragged himself up the four wooden stairs and through the screen door at the rear of the raised bungalow. He heard Ramsey stowing his equipment and cursed. He used a discipline from the art of *Lua* – he was the only master left on Oahu – to settle his breathing then bustled about the pantry in approximation of a domestic.

"You like I make chow, boss? Get *pua'a* the pig, *pake*-kine." Ramsey had picked up a few local words and phrases, so Manu used them to extend the ruse that he was just a country boy, a *kanaka*.

"Forget the chow, where's my boots, Manu? And what about my uniform? I expected you here, squaring away my gear."

"No worries, boss. Everything shipshape." He grabbed a dishcloth and poured the simmering kettle into the tea pot to steep then used the cloth to wipe the red dust from the boots.

"Where were you, anyhow?"

"Me? I pick up the pig. Get one *pake wahine*, one Chinee girl make *ono* – real good." He gulped. The cloth was damp, it had turned the dust into a red film.

"I don't pay you to loaf by the waterfront, Manu."

"You nevah pay me anyways," he shouted back, desperate for another cloth to wipe the boots. "Boss, you went pay the laundry, or what?"

"Nope, no pesos yet, I told Hop Sung."

"Hop Sung? Not Hop Sung, the name John Young!" He tried his pants leg, but it was soiled as the cloth.

"Well, I told that daughter of his, the pretty little one wears her hair in the bun."

"No stay daughter, boss! I went told you! Get the hair up, that one wife!" He tried the boots in the sunlight but the dull film was even more apparent.

"Anyhow, I told her it's my orders catching up. She seemed to savvy me right enough."

He sighed. John Young's wife spoke perfect English and taught it at the Chinese Church.

He propped the boots in the corner and dumped buns from Love's Bakery on a plate, and arranged everything on a tray. But distracted over the soiled boots, he dropped the tea cup – he'd passed too close to the *hala* grove after all – and stood for a moment, rolling his eyes. Then he recovered his persona, rounded his shoulders and shuffled in.

Ramsey was studying documents from the safe, still dressed in his cycling outfit. Manu knew he wouldn't remove any of it in his presence – the *haole* held unaccountable attitudes toward their bodies.

"*Beretania*, the British, dem guys pay good. Alla time on time. Watsa mattah you Yanks?"

"What's it to you, anyhow?" Ramsey said without looking up. "Everything you broke around here, you'll owe me money when it comes to settling up."

"Tea, boss." He tried to sneak a look at the documents.

"Put it somewhere. I'll get to it directly."

He cast around for something to keep him in the room. He found a brush and started working over Ramsey's dress tunic. "My cousin went tell me. He need the rent, yeah? Maybe the Commander fire you. Maybe you no get money."

"The Navy don't fire you, you're court-martialed. They'd haul me away in irons." Ramsey shuffled the documents. "It ain't the Merchant Marine you sailed with."

"Whale ship, boss. Work hard." He took a peek.

"Well, I had to quit my last duty station overnight, that's all. Tell your cousin he'll have his money."

"One *wahine*, boss? The husband went catch you, yeah?"

Ramsey looked up. "It was official business, Manu. I just had to – well let's just say I went above and beyond the call of duty. From your performance around here, I'd say that's something you know nothing about. Now bring my boots and leave me alone. Do something useful – and for God's sake, get rid of that red scarf."

He pulled the scarf from his neck. He'd been in such a hurry, he'd forgotten about it. "This nothing, boss. Hot outside."

"Nonsense. I know the *kanaka* wear them for Luahine. You're not one of her brood, are you?"

"I know her, boss." He turned his face moon-like and inno-cent. "Luahine one bad *wahine*. She one *kahu* witch. Stay away.

E malama o loa'a i ka niho," he said and crossed himself. "Me Christian-kine. Baptize, everyt'ing. I go Kawaiahao Church. Get the choir. Get the little *keiki* kids like sing. Luahine, she one *tutu* Pele. *Aue!* – she burn you up!"

"You attend Kawaiahao, yet you still believe in the goddess Pele, Manu."

The *haole* held his eyes, forcing him to turn away after a moment. "Too much confusion, boss. No make *pilikia* for Manu."

Ramsey stared at his houseboy's back as it receded into the bungalow. He wore the long white coat of his station, black pants rolled to the calf as the Hawaiians did them, and he padded on thick splayed feet that came from a lifetime without footgear. But the eyes that looked back at him had not been servile, had not been dull or ignorant. For just a moment they were dark and resourceful, had flashed with insolence and were the eyes of an equal.

He stowed the papers and removed his wool exercise costume. It was still damp. He had pedaled west in the direction of Pearl River, where the carriage track degraded to a trail then played out. His first order of business was to inventory the island's strategic resources – the admirals wanted to know what of military value would accrue to them from a revolution. But he'd only penetrated far enough to conclude that the island was so underdeveloped, any accurate inventory would require a significant commitment of time and equipment. His standard issue naval survey instruments would never do. He must manufacture his own.

He scrubbed all over with white birch bark as prescribed by *Dr. Gunn's Domestic Physician* then rubbed down with a Turkish towel. His flesh glowed with the stimulation. It was unmarked save for the scar on his neck and the raised welt from a bullet wound received during his last mission. His abdomen had firmed up with the cycling, and his thighs. Black hair populated them and his chest, which was smooth and well proportioned. Drying it, he thought of the punching bag he'd left in North Africa and identified the beam from which a new one might be suspended.

He poured water and shaved closely around his sideburns and combed back his hair carefully. Then he took a scissors to his brows and nostrils. He'd picked up grooming tips in New Orleans and, first state function at a new duty station, he intended to pass muster.

While examining his face, blue eyes those of a man who was not as he appeared, the conviction settled in. His houseboy was not the man he appeared to be.

He strode into the pantry to get to the bottom of it, and gasped. His dress boots stood in the corner streaked with red mud. Manu was gone.

In the rain forest behind Huleia Stream on the Island of Kauai, the kingdom's most feared chief collapsed quivering to her knees.

Huleia began its life as a bright sparkling strand of crystalline falls jack-knifing out of the island's perennially wet central highlands. Before it reached the coast, it aged into a doddering old flow that evacuated rotten waste through the broad leafed ferns and pulpy banana trunks hunched along its shoulders, and deposited the fetid red mud into which she sank.

The traditionalist encampment of seven neatly thatched lodges for the priests, four more under construction for her warriors, occupied an eastern-facing semi-circle on Huleia's upper reaches. The sun burned through Kauai's cloud cover there, seeming to smile upon the *kahuna* scheme to unseat Kalakaua. But here, where the sun could not penetrate, there was no encouragement to be found.

High Chiefess Luahine leaned her bulk against the trunk of a guava tree. Her breasts sagged over the top of her *kapa* wrap. The whale tooth pendant, symbol of high chiefly office which she had broken from her Big Island rival's neck, dangled between them. She had struggled through the muck to reach the sacred circle of fern, but settled for the tree rooted just short of it. She had her omen, there was no need to approach nearer. It hung from a twig behind over-ripe guava fruit. A slender black arm – she was certain she made it out – had slipped from beneath a feathery green leaf and drawn her attention to it.

The circle, made of carefully tended ancient tree ferns with gracefully arched limbs, had been planted at the exact center of the *menehune* district. What the elders told about the spells of the Dark Ones made hers appear insubstantial as sea foam.

She cupped the omen in her hand – two kits, a male and a female, born to *pe'a* the brown bat – and moaned aloud. The female kit was dead, smothered at the mother's breast. The female, not the male. She, not Kalakaua.

She shut her eyes and wept. "*Aue*," she cried, "*Aue* … ," wanting to address the Dark Ones in the fern circle, but struggling to find a form of salutation appropriate for *menehune*. They were small as children. Were they like older siblings or more like younger? Did they possess gender? She could not afford to offend them, so settled upon *aikane*, friend. She prayed they would take kindly to friendship with a chiefess of the people who uprooted their ancestors from the southern islands, then drove the survivors into the impenetrable nest behind their fishpond on the north island of Kauai.

"*Aikane*," she rumbled, "I, Luahine, High Chiefess of All the Hawaiians, beg you to hear me. Is this your prophecy for me?" She prodded the lifeless kit with a forefinger. She did not fear death; Kahu the Sorceress knew it in all its guises, from the wood rot and mud that became a potion, to the quivering flesh that desiccated under one of her spells.

She feared the manner of her death, feared she must offer herself to the lava that coursed toward Hilo Town. Unwelcome as she was on the Big Island, she did not know she could do it. Wasn't certain she could prostrate on *lauhala* mats as the lava drew nearer, didn't know she could chant the prescribed prayers while the fire first singed then set her hair ablaze, as it first boiled the blood then melted the skin from her bones. She'd led the return to tradition, to *kapu* and the former ways. She was convinced they alone could restore the people. But had she conviction enough not to run?

"*Aikane,* is my life required? I beg you, tell me it is not. Seeing Eye is weak within me. I have not my mother's *mana,* not her spirit and authority. She was Molokai island. I am only a daughter of Kauai."

A fern leaf gestured meaningfully – she had *mana* enough to detect that. "The goddess Pele rages over the faithlessness of the people. She combs her hair toward Hilo Town. The people cry to me as their mother. If Pele will halt her flow and spare them, they pledge to believe again. They will forsake the foreign gods and return to *kapu.* The *haole* erosion will cease. They will stand up as warriors once more. O, *aikane,* the priests declare I alone can redeem The People. I must sacrifice myself to Pele's fire."

Slanted black eyes blinked at this – she was certain Seeing Eye showed her truly. The *menehune* could have no more *aloha* for the priests than she did. The Dark Ones must be coming round to her. She felt a surge within and envisioned their darkness converging with the darkness in her. Perhaps the omen had another meaning, her life would not be required. She heard the rushing like storm surf dragging its claws along the ocean bottom. Darkness bubbled like Pele's own caldera. "Show me, *aikane,* show me the sign," she bayed, head swirling, daring to believe. "How is *kapu* to be restored, if not by my blood?"

Let Seeing Eye show me this, she prayed. I must have something to counter the priests … The fern leaf moved, she could just make it out. She bent over on her hands, the mud grumbling with the entirety of her weight. If only she could see …

"*Welina me ke* –? … My Chiefess? Are you …? I bring a message from Manu."

She goggled. The bearded priest. He'd ripped the vision from her. She turned back to the ferns. Nothing. No fluttering leaf, no flickering dark eye. "Manu …?" she asked, not comprehending.

"He sent the message by carrier pigeon. He urges us to action." The priest picked his feet out of the mud. "Spreckels is gone away in anger. Kalakaua seeks power like the *haole,* more power even than Kamehameha held. He would make himself chief over all the Pacific ... Come, My Chiefess." He extended a hand.

The darkness inside heaved. "For this you have interrupted my commerce with the *menehune?* For Kalakaua, and the white stork Gibson?" Curses welled up, competing to be spun. She was *kapu*, his head was not to be carried above hers. He should have lowered himself into the mud. "I should dispatch the shark goddess for your testicles! They are useless as the King's! How shall I discover the truth of the omen? You have driven the Dark Ones away!"

She reached for her *kapu* stick then gasped. A fused lump of hair and twiggy bone lay in her palm. She'd crushed the two bat kits. "*Aue, Aue!* What have I done?" She looked helplessly about, Seeing Eye of no service to her with this sign. "What am I to do?"

He helped her up and steadied her against his chest.

"*Aue! Aue!*"

"These are just signs, My Chiefess. In the season of the *haole* what merit have they? Come, the people need you. I need you."

He looked directly into her eyes. In the days of *kapu* she'd have fed his bones to the altar fires for the effrontery, but now, for the moment, she wanted to put it all aside. "What can I do?" She settled her cheek upon his chest. It was muscled and firm. His skin smelled of coconut oil. "The Big Island chiefs promise to join the movement if I sacrifice myself to Pele. The warriors side with me, but your *kahuna* urge me to it."

She felt his nose draw tenderly alongside hers, *honi* the kiss. His naked belly was warm against her breasts. "I will speak to the *kahuna*," he said into her ear. "Does your daughter not learn the Hula Pahu? Will Pele not accept her dance?"

"The girl learns nothing. Kumu Pakalana dismisses her."

"Pakalana dismisses everyone. When you were a student she said you possessed no more fire than the *opihi*, you remember?"

It felt good to laugh, deep and rolling like shore break. *Opihi* the limpet was tiny, its volcano-shaped shell the size of a fingernail. She pulled him into her, the sensation of his flesh making her feel young and free. Too long since she'd summoned him to her sleeping mat. "Perhaps Kalakaua will offer himself as sacrifice," she said playfully.

He touched her cheek and slid his hand lower. She opened to his touch. "The king would drink up the libation himself," he said. "Pele would never receive her share!"

"I would have to curse him first."

"You would," he smiled, tracing her nipple with his forefinger.

"A mighty curse. I would invoke the Flying God."

"Pule Kaholo, Prayer of Speedy Death?"

She felt him move against her. He had swollen. "O, no." She looked up through swimming eyes. "The Lingering Curse. Kalakaua must know the evil he commits with the *haole* ways."

He nuzzled her and bit her ear lobe.

She moaned, his beard brushing her cheek, then stepped back suddenly. Curses severe enough to overthrow a chief of Kalakaua's rank were rare. No ordinary priest could cast one. It required a Kahu who traced her ancestry to Molokai island. It also required the life of the spell caster herself, unless she possessed remarkable *pono* – unless her spirit were unclouded by greed or envy, or malevolence of any kind.

Her spirit was overcast and cloudy as Pele's own.

"I observed your daughter Pua as we sailed from Kauai – *Aue!*" He stroked her hair. "She is *wana* the sea urchin. The wary fisherman does not step upon her."

"I have not seen the girl since she weaned."

"I perceive her mother in her. I believe Aunty Pele would also. She is not a sorceress, she is a dancer. But she has *mana*, she has authority."

She grunted.

"You kept her *kapu* on Kauai. It was wise."

She looked at him. "Can I ask of my daughter the sacrifice I fear to give?"

"She is not your daughter. The people are your daughter. You are our mother."

"I carried her in my womb."

"You carry the nation in your womb. The people need you. They desire their High Chiefess on the throne."

"*Oia ho'i*." She nodded and chewed her lower lip, considering his words.

"Pua dances before the King tonight," he said. "Her *hula* will challenge him to return to the old ways."

"So Manu ordered."

"And Pakalana complained." He mimicked Pakalana's old-fashioned Hawaiian. "'The girl has no fire. The King will not be moved. He will have her seized and punished for her insolence.'"

They laughed together. He made *honi honi* again, but she pushed him back.

"We shall see," she said. "If Pakalana is correct, the King will arrest Pua and banish her from the kingdom. Then my daughter shall be safe from all this, safe from the evil done in secret."

"And if she has fire tonight?"

Her face darkened. "Then the King shall be driven away."

"This is better. Kalakaua vacates the throne. Let him make the sacrifice."

She shook her head. "You do not understand. When a dancer gives herself to Pele's fire, the goddess consumes her. Though she lives, she is the sacrifice. She is Pele's to command forever more."

He shrugged. "The daughter is sacrificed but you will rule the people, My Chiefess. This is the season of the *haole*. The movement requires it."

Luahine sighed deeply. She released him, turned and plodded toward camp, reassuming with each step the mantle of High Chiefess, sacred, fierce and alone. Her hair, black and unoiled, stuck out at angles. One cheek was tattooed in the old manner. The other bore the scar of a noble who had interrupted her once at table before she crushed his windpipe. On her breast lay the sign of office wrenched from the collapsing throat of the Big Island chiefess she'd cursed.

"No, the land is chief and man is *kaua* its servant," she said. "Me ... I am *kuapa'a*, its slave."

SIX

C ommander Taylor summoned him with a scowl. Ramsey, making his way over, renewed the vow to keep tucked in and behaving military no matter the provocation. The Chinese laundry had tailored his dark blue uniform coat snugly. He wore the insignia authorized for Petty Officer First Class, chevrons down beneath a spread eagle, carried his rating mark and had revived the shine on his boots. He thought only the scar peeking out of his collar marred the impression of porcelain perfection.

"Kalakaua knows how to give a party, eh?" The attaché embraced the king's *luau* with his glass.

"An improvement over my previous postings, sir." He saluted casually but appropriately for a social occasion.

The king's guests thronged around them at the royal boathouse, a long low structure jutting on pilings into Honolulu Harbor. The *luau* was dress rehearsal for Kalakaua's fiftieth birthday in November – the Jubilee, he'd styled it, after the approaching Jubilee Anniversary of Queen Victoria's reign – and the boathouse had filled quickly with the crowd and noise. Foreign military and dignitaries wore brilliant uniforms, their women turned out in splendid accents of red and yellow, the nation's colors. Island nobles in evening attire greeted one another with affection, their melodious Hawaiian bubbling like stream water against the clipped European cadences. Feathered *kahili*, totem of royalty, stood in stanchions, torches flamed smokily and pungent flowers clustered everywhere.

"I had a chance to look through your file," Taylor said.

"Unimpressive, I realize, Commander. I intend to be more productive in your command."

Taylor drained his glass and motioned to a waiter. The man, barefoot but dressed in the king's guard's uniform, carried a tray of champagne. "I trust you shall consider yourself *under* my command while stationed here." He handed Ramsey a glass.

"Of course, sir." He took a sip but kept his eye on the attaché.

"I have been privy to your dossier, you see – not just your official jacket, but your dossier. Regular Navy has its connections also, not just you spies at ONI."

Taylor's skin looked pale and blotchy. He wore his beard old fashioned and full, and his eyes seemed perpetually hooded from drink. He could not read the man's face and waited, alert for what card he would play.

"Dreadful business caught you up in Morocco," Taylor said.

"It was an ill-considered *affaire de coeur*, sir, an embarrassment. It haunts me to this day." He thought of his bullet wound.

"Nonsense. You undermined the entire French intelligence service in North Africa." The attaché's hand trembled as it stroked his beard. "How you learned the young mamselle's husband was slipping into the arms of Arab brothel-boys, I should like to know."

He kept quiet.

"You will not engage such conduct while under my command, Ramsey." Taylor, speaking under the rubble of sound in the boathouse, did not contain his emotion. "It is unbecoming the service, do I make myself clear?"

"Yes, sir." He sipped his champagne to seal his mouth shut.

"I uphold entirely the value of intelligence-gathering, it is honorable and saves lives. The Union deployed intelligence to combat the Rebellion. We saw it at Vicksburg."

"You were in Porter's command, sir?"

"I was. I had a gunboat during the siege. We discovered the rebel commander was holding a cotillion, so Porter had us douse our lights. 'Johnny Reb's dancing the quadrille tonight, boys,' he says, 'but he'll dance another tune tomorrow!'" He shook his head and chuckled. "Old Porter ... We slipped twelve gunboats right under the fortifications – that's military intelligence, Ramsey; outflanked the enemy without firing a shot."

He knew all about Vicksburg. It strangled the western campaign for independence, as Gettysburg did in the east. He tried to speak civilly: "Vicksburg turned into a blood bath. We fought to the last cartridge."

"Probably true," said Taylor. "General Grant needed the victory for Lincoln."

"But at what cost? Grant drove our women into the hills, defenseless women – and their children! They hid in caves, you hear about the cannibalism to this day!"

Taylor swallowed his glass and looked for another. "It was a dreadful campaign, son, no one was ever the same, I'll grant you that. But there was decency on both sides. We were comrades in arms, even if we were at war. Grant paroled the Rebel officers, gave them safe conduct, did you know? We had our protocols, we had our honor. – You there!" he called to a waiter. "Brandy!"

"Allow me, sir," he offered, wanting to get away before saying more.

"No," said Taylor. "I want you to understand this. You may be ONI but you are in my command. I will brook no disrespect of protocol or authority. There can be but one end to what ONI does, and it is the disestablishment of constitutional authority."

"I gather information, Commander."

"By any means possible, Ramsey, that is my point. By any means possible. If it requires compromising the affections of a young woman, you think nothing of it."

He was proud of his work in Morocco. It called upon all his craft, he'd been the toast of his peers, and it cleared the way for his transfer to the Pacific theater, a reassignment he desperately needed for his own safety. He felt his temperature rising.

"The world don't go according to Hoyle, Commander, not what I see. My brothers and I, we never knew the genteel war you describe. The Yankees came after us in Missouri? They shot first, pillaged your barn and wrote you a worthless ration chit after."

Taylor corralled another drink. "The exception, in my experience."

"Well, not in mine! Three brothers I had, three! Not one survived Yankee bullets. And the youngest was shot in the head at thirteen! At close range!"

"That's combat, son."

"Combat, hell, Commander. My brother Thrash was foraging to feed me and my sister. The Yankees took the winter crop then they took the mule for plowing. They came back and found the milch cow was hid, they took her. What was we supposed to do? Of course he was foraging! I buried Thrash then I buried my sister after the thaw. Behind the barn right next to my mother."

Taylor brushed his beard with his empty hand. It had steadied with the drink. "I see, John. Well, I am sorry. I didn't understand. Most unfortunate, of course. I apologize for my remarks. Thoughtless."

"There's nothing over our heads, Commander." At his last duty station a German diplomat's wife translated Nietzsche for him. She let him know her husband, away on assignment, did not appreciate as much as she the freedom the new philosophy conveyed. "No rules to protect us, no fairness, no God to keep your head dry in the storm. You keep your own head dry. I learned that lesson a heap of times, a heap." The words pushed to the front of his mouth. He didn't think, he just spit them out. "Military intelligence, it's not so we can have our polite differences then go home to our wives and children. The next wars get fought, they won't be about rightness, they'll be about power. Call me spy or agent, it's no matter to me. I deliver information. Information is power, and it is liberty."

Taylor appeared to have lost his stuffing. He finished his brandy. "Just don't embarrass me, Ramsey. I'm too long in the Navy. I will not be disgraced."

"Count on it, sir. I'm no lick an' a promise. I'm professional."

Taylor saluted him with the empty glass. "Now, where's the boy with that tray? You must be introduced to the native palate. Takes a stronger stomach than going into battle."

The attaché waded into the crowd, nodding right or left as he was greeted, and he followed, breathing deeply. He'd crept to the edge of insubordination. Another officer might have said he'd crossed the line, but Taylor had so weakened himself with drink that he quit the field rather than pull a gun and fight. He relaxed. This was a post he might turn completely to his advantage.

"I say, rather a devilish bit there." James Wodehouse, long-standing British Minister, indicated a mound of dried fish. "First go at the native fare, is it, Mr. Ramsey? Don't be put off. It only looks the pilgrim's salve!" Wodehouse shared a chuckle with Taylor over *poi*, the fermented paste they said was a staple at every Hawaiian meal.

He looked around the sideboard for cutlery. "O, you won't find any, old boy. Natives don't see the cause. Go right for it, don't you know, like everything they do. Just use the fingers. *Aut Caesar aut nihil* – all or nothing, eh?"

Ramsey abandoned the fish and accepted another glass of champagne.

Commander Taylor spotted the American Minister elbowing toward a table laden with tea sandwiches. John Stevens had kept his stick and used its head to force his way to the trays. Taylor tapped him on the shoulder. "May I present my new aide, Mr. Minister?" Drink had turned him expansive. "Petty Officer John Ramsey, a distinguished addition to official American presence."

Stevens surveyed him in his dress uniform. "Better turned out than I saw him last."

"So, you've had the acquaintance of the American Minister," Taylor said to him. "Perhaps he will extend the courtesy of his office to you." Taylor gave out his cover story. "Mr. Ramsey is posted here to negotiate warehousing with the government."

"Who's responsible for this imposter being assigned to my station?" The men dwarfed him but Stevens seemed to bloat with ill-humor.

The attaché began a light rejoinder. Stevens cut him off. "Your man left my hat box on the pier, Commander." Stevens jabbed with his stick for emphasis. "My hat box. With my beaver in it, not a silk topper, mind you, but my beaver. I've worn it at every posting on both oceans."

"Your hat box!" Wodehouse exclaimed. "Good God, man, it wasn't your dispatch case, was it. A hat box, there's hundreds after the steamer docks."

Stevens would not be turned. "My father's beaver, set on my head by his own hand, the occasion of my first posting. And your Mr. Ramsey here could not place it on the cart and deliver it to my rooms."

"Mr. Minister, I do not know what to say." Ramsey bowed and ladled his voice with honeysuckle. "I regret terribly the inconvenience. Your daddy's beaver hat, you say? I never had anything from my daddy, nothing except an ol' squirrel gun. They confiscated it during the war, never saw it again. I am aggrieved, sir."

"You are aggrieved? – I had to buy that beaver back, Ramsey. My own beaver, I had to buy it off a native grinning with it on his imbecilic head!"

The men kept very serious faces. Then he realized Stevens expected a response. "Mr. Minister, that is positively – I don't know what to say."

"A gold coin, the bandit would take nothing less."

"Mr. Stevens, my office would be only too happy –" Commander Taylor began.

"You will not, sir, you will not!" Stevens stepped back, a short man already wronged in a taller man's world. "Do you think I bring this to your attention for a coin? It is for the sake of the nation, sir. You have a man in your command that cannot be entrusted the simplest mission."

"Quite right, Mr. Minister. Quite right."

"Hideous sight that native presented, my father's beaver perched like a totem atop his rotund face. Had the audacity to offer me his sailor's cap in exchange. Said it had grown too small."

"The cad," said Wodehouse and turned quickly away.

Ramsey said abjectly as he knew how, "My deepest apology, sir." He added a bow to hide his face as he pictured Manu toying with Stevens, but it stretched his collar and exposed the scar on his neck.

"What's that, Ramsey?"

"Mr. Minister?" He straightened.

"On your neck. What's that?"

"O, my scar. Nothing, sir. I try to keep it covered. An embarrassment, I'm afraid."

"A duel? They are illegal."

"O, nothing so respectable, sir. No, just an accident on the farm back home. I was haying. It was the war, you know. No one to teach me proper. Nicked myself with the scythe. My mother like to whip the hide off me for being so careless, 'cept she was pretty far gone by then. 'Take your whole blame head off long as you're gonna do it,' she said, 'do it right.'"

"I see," Stevens said, and Ramsey realized he was now a document filed in the American Minister's dispatch case, and he would be studied.

There was an eddy in the crowd before a pair of ceremonial sandalwood arches and Commander Taylor took Stevens by the arm. "Come, gentlemen, the Queen's ladies have arrived. Shall we present ourselves to the royal family?"

Wodehouse craned his head above the native women flocking animatedly around the new arrivals. "I see Princess Liliu. Kalakaua has named her to the succession."

"The King should step aside for her now, there'd be sober government at last," said Stevens.

Wodehouse swept his glass at the untamed outbursts of flowers, the torches casting seductive shadows upon the walls, men overdressed for the tropics and perspiring freely, and the women working their fans upon yards of exposed flesh. "Egad, man, would you take all this on a tumbler of warm milk? Not I."

Ramsey made to fall in with the others but Taylor stopped him with a curse under his breath. "Professional, are you? – Embarrassed me with the Minister. The Admiral shall hear about this. You'll be on picket duty at the Alaskan coast in a month."

"Yes, sir." He took a glass of champagne from a passing waiter and swallowed it down.

The sun drifted into the Pacific and in the twilight, conch shells trumpeted over the heads of the assembly. The Royal Marshal of Household positioned himself alongside the sandalwood arches. The Hawaiian phrases with their triplets of vowels and soft consonants filled the boathouse, hushing it as the Marshal proclaimed his king's genealogy and titles: son of *ali'i* descended from Kane, God of Heaven; Generalissimo of the Forces, Sovereign Grand Master of the Royal Order of Kamehameha, Order of the Red Eagle First Class of Prussia, Legion of Honor of France, Order of the Chrysanthemum of Japan, of the North Star of Sweden and the White Elephant of Siam; *awa mo'i*, Father of the People and Protector of *aina*, the Land; Kalakaua the First, Monarch of All the Hawaiians.

The king entered through the arches followed by his queen, Kapiolani. Generous applause greeted them from the foreigners and falsetto trilling notes issued from the throats of the Hawaiians. Kalakaua saluted the assembly uniformed as Commander of the King's Guard, with embroidered gauntlets, sash, epaulettes and gold oak leaf clusters. At once the Royal Hawaiian Band struck up *Hawaii Ponoi*, the kingdom's anthem the king himself had composed.

Princess Liliu Dominis approached the queen on behalf of the chiefs, curtsied and draped her with leafy green vines of *maile*, addressing her the while in gentle Hawaiian phrases. Kalakaua made a short speech of welcome in Hawaiian. He translated for himself, the English as gracious, soaring and well-turned as any European monarch might deliver. He complimented his friends but was particularly effusive concerning his adversaries, the downtown businessmen who opposed him at every turn. He concluded with a graceful bow to his queen, and the party resumed.

"Kalakaua learned well on his world tour, don't you think?" Prince Koloa leaned in at Ramsey's elbow. They had met the week before at the reading club at St. Andrew's Cathedral, a mostly European social gathering frequented by the more cosmopolitan Hawaiians. Ramsey thought he could mine it for intelligence.

"There is not a sweeter tongue among us," Koloa said of the king.

"Your servant, Prince." He was glad of the diversion from Taylor's threat. He'd learned to accept Colored men of rank and education while on station in North Africa and bowed as protocol required.

"You really should study Hawaiian while you are stationed among us, Mr. Ramsey. It is a more generous language than yours. A single word conveys a host of meanings." Koloa's skin was only shades darker than his, and his hair just as straight, evidence of his White planter paternity. "You'd have noted what the Marshal left out of the King's genealogy."

"He is divine, is he not?" he said coyly.

Koloa smiled. "Of course. But so was our third king, and he gave away the kingdom."

Ramsey had learned about the Great Mahele. The missionary doctor Gerrit Judd worked his way into power in Kamehameha III's cabinet and organized the redistribution of the kingdom's lands. Since 1848 all but the royals had grown increasingly impoverished, while Judd's descendants and other canny *haole* became wealthy landholders.

"Genealogy does not signify parentage for us," Koloa continued. "So many of us shared parents in the old days. Sometimes it was difficult to say exactly whether a woman were your mother or your aunt. – I believe your familial arrangements were similar in the American South?"

He shifted uncomfortably. "I wouldn't say that, no ... we tried to keep things straight. It's different. You know, sheep from the goats. And we certainly didn't fight for those reasons. General Lee was the second Washington. We fought for liberty."

"Worth fighting for, a war that must come to our soil. Genealogy signifies for us whether a noble family has accumulated the *mana* to merit one's allegiance – in war or peace. This is not a matter only of bloodline but of association. The nobles of highest rank absorbed the wisdom and power of the families that went before."

"So the king is the superior man," he said, wanting to press back for Koloa's comment about the South.

"Or queen, in our tradition. I am *hanai*, foster child to Queen Kapiolani herself."

"And Kalakaua?"

Koloa colored. "I must test the point of your sword one day, Ramsey. Is it as sharp as your wit? A Navy man has been known to fence, hasn't he?"

"I prefer a Colt pistol in a matter of honor. But for exercise, I could meet you of an afternoon after duty hours." He gave a sidelong look. "Your Highness."

Koloa's eyes narrowed. "Yes, I believe it shall be an exercise when we meet."

"I shall uniform appropriately."

"You push me, Ramsey." Koloa straightened his tunic, the most brilliant in the room, splashed in British scarlet and piped in green and gold, a ceremonial dagger suspended at the belt. "You will come to respect this uniform. I designed it myself. The businessmen have the Honolulu Rifles. They are chartered as an honorary brigade, but the missionary party have usurped them. The crown has no military, nothing to counter them. They grow increasingly belligerent. I shall attract other Hawaiian men to these colors. I'll form a native militia. We shall not be caught napping, not like your South."

The band interrupted him. The Music Hall was featuring Verdi, and members of the visiting company launched into arias from *La Traviata*, followed by the third act chorus from *Nabucco*. Under the baton of Captain Henry Berger the Royal Hawaiian Band played march tempo better than Italian opera, and the singers struggled to keep up. Ramsey caught the eye of the auburn-haired soprano. She shrugged in a gesture of helplessness and plowed on to the end.

Koloa turned to him. "I was piqued, Ramsey. My apologies, it was ungracious of me. It's only – well, the subject of the Rifles … Perhaps you will review my militia when it parades."

He drew himself from thoughts of the soprano. "I shall be honored, of course."

"Well that's settled," Koloa said with a bow. "Now, Princess Liliu asked for you. She is interested in the Navy's agricultural project. You have been introduced? – You will detect in her the *mana* I mentioned."

"The superior woman. Not the same blood as her brother?"

"There you miss the point. She and Kalakaua were raised separately. Some believe her *mana* is superior to his because of the foster family that surrounded her. Though she married a *haole*, many Hawaiians would prefer to see her on the throne – of course, she is royal and next in succession."

They were making their way to the other side of the boat-house where the nobles conversed with one another in Hawaiian.

"In the South we say if General Lee had replaced Jefferson Davis as President of the Confederacy, we'd have our freedom today," Ramsey said.

"Yes, Lee had *mana*. The traditionalists say it is missing from Kalakaua's genealogy. High Chiefess Luahine uses their sentiments to her advantage."

"Do you number yourself among them?"

"Among …?"

"Among Luahine's followers," he said.

Koloa looked at him steadily. "I number myself among those loyal to the kingdom who oppose your government's insinuations into our affairs and will oppose them by force of arms, if need be. Perhaps a man of your genealogy understands our cause."

He looked aside rather than answer then Koloa stopped him before a short woman, dark and broad-featured like the king. Diamonds sparkled in her up-swept hair, finished by a bit of peacock feather. There was majesty about her, though majesty tempered by melancholy.

Mrs. Dominis presented her hand. He could not recall so direct a gaze by a Colored woman, nor had he ever bent over a Colored hand. But he'd been schooled, and he followed his training.

"Mr. Ramsey, I understand the United States Navy has a plan for industry in the kingdom," she said.

"Yes, Ma'am. The Navy believes both the kingdom and the needs of international shipping may be served."

She nodded. Ramsey's stated purposes were appreciated by the palace, always alert for new business opportunities. "One is aware, of course, that my people have served the needs of foreign nations in years past. Our own nation has not benefitted equally."

Petty Officer John Ramsey, Junior Naval Attaché, should have made a suave, diplomatic response. But John Taggart Ramsey, orphaned by war, denied the frontier, forced too young upon his own resources – by the same class of commercial man his grandfather, a highland Taggart had rebuked in fleeing kith and kin for America – could not. Arrested by the sadness in her eyes he was compelled to respond honestly.

"No, Ma'am. The sandalwood trade, of course. And now sugar whose control has passed into the hands of merchants, I believe."

"Some are of the opinion that we cannot be masters in our own home."

"In my home such persons were called carpetbaggers, Ma'am."

Koloa rendered the phrase into Hawaiian for the benefit of the nobles. They appeared to fix upon him with interest.

"You speak well, Mr. Ramsey," Princess Liliu said after a moment. "Perhaps *aloha* is not lost upon you."

"I confess your people's use of the term is a puzzle. I have heard it neighed by the thoroughbred and the nag, if you will pardon me saying, Ma'am."

She smiled. "One would in these days, but pray, do not judge our entire Race by what you see of the Hawaiian about town.

Aloha is among our noblest traits. – May I present my ward?" She signaled a lady-in-waiting who led over a thin, dark-skinned girl with a limp.

"Mr. Ramsey, Miss Hester Iolani. You may bow for the gentleman, my dear."

The girl did as she was told and was led away.

"She is not Hawaiian," the princess said. "From the continent of Africa, perhaps. She was abandoned by one of your commercial vessels, or she escaped. We do not know. She does not talk. Her teeth were broken away, and with her leg … our *kahuna* do not recognize the ailment but in Europe I believe it is known as polio. She cannot curtsy. Aboard ship there could have been only one employment for her."

Koloa spoke up. "You have named the girl, Princess? I had not heard."

"Yes. 'Hester,' after the Queen herself, and of course the name my brother conferred upon the new palace. *Iolani* means 'Royal Hawk,' Mr. Ramsey. We pray the child will grow into her name."

"You have adopted her?" he asked.

"I cannot do that, Mr. Ramsey. I cannot make her *hanai*. She is not Hawaiian and has not the proper birth. But I can extend her my *aloha*, my protection and sustenance. It is the obligation of the *ali'i* – the nobility, you would say. When the weak come onto our lands we must care for them until they are strong again. We extend our *aloha* to many – most of them our people, but too many of them Occidentals – your people."

He was surprised.

"O, *aloha* does not discriminate," Koloa said. "We take in many on my Kauai estate. You must visit. We adhere to the Law of the Splintered Paddle – our great king, Kamehameha instituted it. The paddle splintered when it struck him, you see. It spared him in battle. In return he said the strong must care for the weak. 'In my realm, even a woman or child shall lie unmolested in the thoroughfare.'"

Mrs. Dominis opened her fan. "Prince Koloa and his generation blame the *haole* for our problems, Mr. Ramsey. Many would agree."

"Well," said Koloa, "before the *haole* brought business to the islands, there was land enough to feed all the people. The elders tell the stories. All were cared for."

"By their families, you mean," Ramsey said.

"By their families, by their village, by their chiefs. They followed Kamehameha's law. The upper classes cared for the lower. 'From each according to his ability ...' Does the Navy permit you to read Karl Marx? My people were socialists before the Germans were a people. And we were strong. There is no Hawaiian word for 'poverty,' Ramsey. Think of that."

The princess placed a hand on Koloa's arm. "But we must admit it was we who put an end to the old ways – we, the *ali'i*. The elders ended *kapu*, the traditional religion is dead. We are Christian now. We must become good ones, before it is too late."

Liliu worked her fan.

"Ah, Princess, you have met my aide!" The attaché bowed clumsily and presented a red beaming face. "Shame on you, Ramsey, for denying me the honor of the introduction."

Ramsey exchanged a look with Koloa, but Mrs. Dominis extended her hand to the attaché. "You must not trouble Mr. Ramsey, Commander. I forced my attentions upon him. I believe your Navy has need of land for growing stores. You may consider the Pu'uloa District. Prince Koloa will make the arrangements. It was formerly in the administration of High Chief Paki, father to Mrs. Ruth Pauahi Bishop and *hanai* to me. Koloa will negotiate the lease and ensure that the United States Navy does not turn into – how did you put it, Mr. Ramsey? – a carpetbagger upon Crown Lands."

SEVEN

T he conch sounded summoning the king's guests to the *luau* in the adjoining room. Spread upon beds of green *ti* leaf were tier upon tier in gleaming sterling servers: pig, smoked fish, rounds of beef, crab, seaweed, *opihi*, chickens, roast turkey, stacks of duck and taro, sweet potato, and in great *koa* wood calabashes the *poi*, pasty and gray. Each place at the table was set with ornate dinner plates, trenchers trimmed in silver and gold and goblets of Italian cut glass in the royal colors.

He seated himself with the soprano, who laughed easily after a flute of champagne. Her hair was cut short – "better for the wigs," she told him – and she wore an emerald pendant, the heirloom her father placed around her neck in Ohio when she boarded the train to join the chorus in San Francisco. He approved of her, of it, and how he was allowed to enjoy its nesting place between her breasts. Brown-eyed and not more than twenty-one he guessed, her name tinkled on musical scales: Jessica Mornay.

"Have you tried this, Mr. Ramsey?" She peered into a calabash containing *poi*. "Do we dare?"

"Must I? I hear it is fermented tuber. We ate better during the worst of the war."

She peered again. "O, but I must. Mother will think me terribly wicked when I write her – dining like the savages. Won't she just faint with the shock of it!" She laughed.

"There is no implement, you realize."

"However does one ...?"

He gestured with his fingers.

"Ravishing!" she giggled and held hers before her, the *poi* gray and glutinous upon them. "I shall explain to Mother that my dinner companion was not a savage but a most connubial Navy man. That will relieve her!"

Wodehouse, on his way to the bar, stopped where they sat. "Go ahead, old man," he urged above the hubbub. "What's sauce for the goose, eh? Dig in!"

"Yes, Mr. Ramsey," Jessica chided. "Shan't I tell Mother of my courageous Navy captain? Dig in!"

They ate their *poi* together, made faces and laughed over the pasty, flavorless vegetable. "Got to hand it to the missionaries," he said, "they braved this out."

"At least they had pork," she said, enjoying the pig, which Wodehouse said was baked in the ground.

He asked her about *La Traviata.*

"O, *Traviata,* my favorite Verdi. It is terrible and sad, such a grand and noble sacrifice she makes for love ... She dies of course, after singing beautifully in the Third Act."

He looked at her and grinned.

"Mr. Ramsey, do you laugh at me?" She batted him playfully with her fan. She'd been edging closer during the course of the banquet.

"Well it's the same, ain't it? To say it's an opera then to say the soprano slumps to her death in the arms of her paramour." He slumped onto one elbow to mimic a dying heroine.

"O, you are a cad, Mr. Ramsey. Is love not the most beautiful thing? Does it not positively lift man out of his permission? Does it not soar him to greatness like flights of eagle's wings?"

He twinkled. Her butchering of words and phrases was part of her charm. "Beyond a doubt, Miss Mornay. Just don't want to pay dear for it, that's all, like the hairy man at a scalping party. Like to enjoy the lady's company after I've won her."

"I see someone shall have to educate you about love, Mr. Ramsey. How it inveterates Nature. Such a rendering I saw of the wild mountains at Yosemite Valley. In San Francisco before we left, the work of – O, I cannot recall the artist. Mr. Hall or Hill, or something. But extemporaneous, and a little frightening. Love must be like that, as if you stand on a precipice, untamed nature overwhelming you."

She fanned herself as if just the memory were extreme enough. He watched the color spread across the lovely white skin below her throat. "Perhaps I must find someone to show me that precipice," he said sincerely.

She glanced at him. "Mr. Ramsey, I don't know about you. Is the Navy always so forward? You should attend more opera. That will educate you, really. Stand on a precipice with you? – I'm sure I do not know what you mean. Now *Traviata*, that's how you learn about love. Violetta, that's her name in the opera. I will sing her one day and I shall die most divinely. You can read about her in the book Mr. Dumas wrote. He calls her Camille. Do you know it?"

She turned her eyes, brown and shining upon him, and he smiled. "Forgive my ignorance, I read what I can. The Navy does not encourage the consumption of fiction, I'm afraid."

She tittered. "O, Mr. Ramsey. How invective of you! Consumption, just the disease that brings Violetta her tragic end!"

He recoiled. "The consumption? Why, that was not my ..."

"When you sing her, you must hit your notes as though your very lungs are consumed. It is athletic, I can tell you."

"... Not my meaning at all. What's wrong with you? I had no idea – the consumption. Hell, you don't let fools in the barn with that. A woman with consumption? Fictionalized? – Judas Priest!"

She stumbled. "Mr. Ramsey, I – I ..."

He put a handkerchief to his temple and waved her off.

Before she could say more the Marshal of Household begged silence. "The King's Royal Troupe!" he announced.

Five dancers filed out. They were costumed in orange blouses with puffed shoulders and green skirts worn to the knee; were flowered and feathered, and sported ankle rattles and cuffs of shark's teeth and bone. Their hair, oiled so it glistened in the torchlight, was long, in ringlets.

The mood changed palpably as they lined up. The king's foreign guests had picked their way through exotic foods and tolerated the garlands and other foolery. The women in particular, though their pulses raced with the profusion of native perfumes, hoped they could flirt safely with the seductions of a pagan culture close at hand. But the dancers were too elemental, too unguardedly sexual for a White woman of any sensibility to sustain. They rose amid murmurs of fabric and headed outside toward the circle of carriages on the pier.

Jessica hesitated. Her companions from the opera troupe called from the doorway, but two diplomat's wives – olive-skinned South Americans – made a point of clinging to their husbands' arms and giggling loudly over their resolution to remain. She looked for a sign of encouragement from her dinner mate but he swallowed a mug of beer and stared straight ahead.

She excused herself primly.

One-eyed John Ukeke took the stage, to polite applause. He was Kalakaua's dance master, attired in orange shirt and white linen trousers. He'd woven vines about his head. He did not teach sacred *hula*, nor did he prepare the dance space beforehand or require his dancers to prepare themselves with fasting and prayer. He drilled them in the silken gestures that pleasured the court and chose *hula* danced to *haole* melodies. The dances weren't sacred but they entertained, and the king paid well.

Kalakaua's guests found places closer to the stage, poured port and brandy and lit their cigars. "Over here, old man!" Wodehouse called. "Ramsey! You're in for something now. Ukeke, he's your man. Puts on a show, knows how to feed the beast, what?"

He pulled himself together and joined the British Minister, the South American diplomats and their wives near the low apron of the stage. The captain of a Chilean frigate, eyes bright with anticipation, splashed brandy into a glass for him.

"Get on with it, Ukeke!" Wodehouse gestured to the dance master. "We've suffered through the entire night!"

The musicians began slowly and rhythmically on Spanish guitar and *ukulele*. The *hula* had been composed by the king and told a ribald story of the sea where it greeted the land, and swallowed the sweet waters of Waimea Falls on Oahu's north shore. The dancers took up the story, telling the words in the movement of their hips, the delicate formations of their hands and the naughty glances of their eyes.

The boathouse seemed to collapse upon itself, dense as it already was with male bodies layered in wool uniforms on a tropical night. Cigar smoke and alcohol sweated through open pores. Uncivilized impulses strained against the straps of convention. Mouths gaped. Eyes bulged. More than the dance of other Pacific peoples, the court *hula* of the Hawaiian Kingdom exercised the supple lines of the female body to greatest and most pleasurable advantage. Not a gesture, nor peccant switch of hip or twist of bosom was missed.

When the *hula* concluded, it was to an up-tempo chorus of rhythm and music that was unambiguous as to the outcome of land embracing sea. The chords of the *ukulele* quieted and the dancers composed themselves into the submissive gesture which ended the dance. For a moment just one sound filled the boathouse, the accelerated beat of the collective pulse of the foreigners. Then they broke into cheers and unbridled applause. Ramsey, pulled from his funk by the dance, joined them.

Ukeke bowed into it and was about to arrange his dancers for the next number, when a girl stole from the wings into the center of the stage. Her hair was parted in the middle. Feathery orange blossoms circled the crown of her head.

The dance master made to remove her then stopped short. An old woman appeared wrapped in Hawaiian cloth dyed brown and yellow. The king's dancers gasped and reverenced her then skipped off stage. The woman kneeled and set a tall drum before her. She collected herself then issued a wailing chant, the heel of her hand thrumming the drum head.

No one in the boathouse moved, or seemed to take a breath.

Kumu Pakalana thrummed the *pahu*, the sharkskin drum from her people's past when there were no monarchs, but priests and chiefs who conversed with the spirits at *heiau*, temples raised upon stone platforms. There the Hula Pahu was danced, so sacred and *kapu* that it spun the gossamer web in which were caught sea, land, gods and people.

She chanted and the voice of the *pahu* broke over the boat-house, speaking in a resonant growl to king and commoner equally. It dipped into the blood that had pooled under the moonlight at human sacrifices not long past; it spoke of the bones of an enemy defeated in battle; of the land lusted after as one would a lover; and of the endless, rhythmic rolling of the sea.

She peered around the drum. The girl should have sunk to the floor – a sitting *hula*, for she was not ready for Hula Pahu. The sitting *hula* was enough. There was no altar; she had not brought vines to connect the dance to Pele's *ohia* tree, nor had she a *koa* wood offering to place upon it. The sitting *hula* would suffice. The king would know the High Chiefess had called out to him, had warned him to return to the traditional ways. Queen Kapiolani and the court would understand as well. There was no need to put the girl's life at risk with Hula Pahu.

The girl should have sunk to the floor, but she stood rooted, head bowed.

She glared at her, willing her to dance. The girl's skin was golden brown, smooth and naked in the old style, her breasts bloomed with fertility beneath a *lei* of polished *kukui* nut – her own *lei*, lent the girl for this dance, and the strip of white *kapa*, stamped with her own clan pattern, sign that the girl was her school. She'd tied it herself around one arm before securing the *ti* leaf girdle about her hips.

Pua could not move. At the first rumble of the drum she should have uncrossed her split bamboo instruments and commenced her rhythm. But she saw the king himself. She identified him by the storied war cloak of Kamehameha. He was father of the nation and therefore her father. The sitting *hula* was an affront to him, she knew that. She saw him whisper to his queen and point to Pakalana. The queen grabbed his arm and urged him back to his seat.

She wanted to move as Pakalana taught. The *pahu* thrummed again, more insistently. But she could not shake herself from thoughts of the king. He was so beautiful-looking in the white uniform, his brow high, his hair curled above magnificent whiskers. Prince Koloa stood behind him, and at either hand were his retinue, the court priests and retainers, his palace guard and the feathered *kahili* and a rank of smoking *kukui* torches. A sea of *haole* faces tumbled around him, the Whites she had never viewed firsthand.

She feared the goddess Pele. Pele had long left her island of Kauai, was not well known there, nor well loved. The goddess had favored Kamehameha, had swallowed an army on the Big Island to protect him. Her ways were hot, impetuous, hard and final. Hula Pahu reproduced her in its heat and its rigid forms. Kauai, which Kamehameha never conquered, was closer to Lono, he who brought fertility and pleasure and traced with a finger the island's soft curves, as his white banner did its breezes.

She bit her lip, ashamed, and snuck a look at Pakalana. She could not help herself. Lono and his *hula* were closer to her heart. One day he would touch her again as he had at Hanalei. She was certain he, not Pele, must be closer to the king's. She could not dance.

Pakalana closed her eyes and prayed. Her hands moved as she did so, feeding the drum, serving Kanaka Maoli, The People.

The drum spoke without the girl. There was no mistaking its message. No dancer's motion was needed to translate. The drum became a molten force, both fire and water, the land and the sea shaking itself awake from too long a sleep. Pele had returned for her people, it declared. *Akahele* – Beware!

The nobles stirred. The voice awakened primitive longings and resurrected lost images of themselves. Some separated from the royal party. An older nobleman opened his throat and released a high-pitched keening into the night. A noblewoman plucked out her combs and shook out her gray-streaked hair.

She began to sway her hips and answer the drum with her own *hula.*

"Do you insult your King? I am your liege! I am your lord! I am invested by the gods, I am favored by the ancestors!" Kalakaua smashed a liquor bottle upon the stage. "Arrest that girl! Arrest them all!" He fled through the sandalwood arch, his party straggling in tow.

The crowd surged toward the stage. Ramsey struggled to keep his feet and his line of sight. He saw Koloa place his arm under the drummer's elbow and escort her out the back of the boathouse. A fleshy brown hand threw a cloak over the girl and hurried her after the drummer – not before the white strip on her arm slipped to reveal a tattoo, the very tattoo he'd seen when *Mariposa* collided with the vessel at sea. He fought through the crowd to the stage, but he lost her. The girl from the sailing canoe had disappeared.

EIGHT

F or the appointment his uniform was shipshape as he could render it. White Navy tropicals were frustratingly difficult to square away. He stopped on the stairs rising up from the Hawaiian Hotel's side gardens, dusted the red dirt from his boots with his kerchief and straightened his tunic. Mynah birds scolded out of a perfume-laden plumeria, two coconut trees swayed overhead in the morning breeze and the sun danced. He did not dally in it but crossed the hotel's wide, welcoming veranda and presented himself at the concierge cage, ten minutes early.

"There must be a mistake," the concierge said. "Management does not permit naval personnel upstairs, except flag rank, of course."

The cage had been crafted out of deeply burnished *koa* wood. It stood ten feet tall and was spacious enough to accommodate the concierge and the bell captain, one behind the other on stools covered in red plush. Its cornices were carved into towering *kahili*. "You would not be a flag officer, would you?" The concierge looked pointedly through the bars.

"Petty Officer," he said, "but the American Minister's expecting me."

"Ah, the American Minister," the man repeated, as if the words in conjunction explained everything. "Perhaps you would make yourself comfortable in the bar. The Minister can join you there, if he's a mind – Front!"

The concierge made to strike his bell, but he seized his wrist. "The American Minister was remarkably precise in his instruction, friend. I am to call upon him. He is not calling upon me."

The concierge winced. "The Minister is entertaining … in his rooms."

He attempted to recover his wrist, but Ramsey increased the pressure. Chinese dragons curled around the frontispiece of the cage. He placed the minister's card on the ledge formed by their intertwining tails and set a silver coin upon it. "Second floor, isn't it?" He stared into the man's eyes, seeing the pupils constrict.

"Yes, sir," the concierge said, surrendering. "Second floor." He recovered his hand but left the coin, a Kalakaua dollar, untouched.

One of the native boys in hotel uniform escorted him up the grand staircase. A long carpeted corridor dotted with pots of frilly green fern led to the minister's suite. Gauzy photographs of island scenes hung upon the walls at measured intervals.

He entered an airy high ceilinged room, its shades drawn against the morning light, and made swift mental notes: the disorder, the filth, the lack of security. Two high backed upholstered chairs thick with documents faced a heavily carved writing desk centered on the windows. A branch of candles had burned to the nubs, the wax pooled atop a layer of papers. Against one wall stood a round mahogany pedestal table, a dinner tray shoved beneath it. Upon a lace doily in the table's center, as though in the place of honor, stood the only personal item in the room, a small, oval-framed photograph. It depicted a young man, thin and pale-looking, not Stevens, holding a diploma.

He moved to the window. The cap of Iolani Palace was visible through it. Stevens' coat slumped to one side. A letter, unfinished with words heavily scratched out, lay beneath a stale-looking saucer of tea on the desk. It was addressed to Colonel Claus Spreckels in San Francisco.

The minister entered from an adjoining room. Cigar smoke eddied through before he shut the door.

"Mr. Ramsey," Stevens said and placed his hands on his hips, looking him up and down. "This is the way I prefer to see you attired – an ordinary seaman, almost a working man, you might say. Not the fol-de-rol of the other night."

"I wear the uniform of the day, Mr. Minister. As I am ordered."

"Sit down, Ramsey." Stevens pointed to one of the upholstered chairs. "Yes, uniform of the day. Though your dress uniform was a bit barren, wouldn't you say?"

He balanced on the lip of the chair so as to avoid the documents. "I have not worn a uniform in time of war, sir. My military career has been limited by the circumstances of peace."

Stevens remained standing and finished off the tea. "'The circumstances of peace' ... I rather like that, Ramsey. You can turn a phrase, can't you?"

"My father was a preacher."

"I see. But you've never let the circumstances stand in your way for long, have you? – War or peace."

"Mr. Minister?"

"I know all about you, Ramsey, all about you. Did you think ONI's presence here could escape my attention for long? I know about Morocco and I know about Valparaiso. You are a remarkably skilled operative, or you are damned lucky. Whichever, you are now mine, so let's drop the little charade and get down to cases, shall we?"

His eyes narrowed. ONI promulgated a clear chain of command for its men in the field. He reported to the admiral in San Francisco, was accountable to the station's naval attaché, but never took orders from civilian authority. "I can keep your office posted about the commercial contracts –"

"Commercial contracts be hanged!" Stevens gestured toward the door. "I have men in there would write contracts you could walk across, from here to California. I'm not talking about pieces of paper, Ramsey. I'm talking about land, land you can squeeze in your hands. Dirt and loam and mud, the only commodity of lasting value."

Stevens stared fiercely, and he said nothing.

"You do not share my passion for the soil, Ramsey. You are not a farmer, are you."

"I saw farming enough in Missouri, Minister."

Stevens snorted. "Missouri! – What, Boone's Lick? Little Dixie? Tobacco, was it? Or cotton on the Mississippi? Alluvial soil, Ramsey, you were spoiled. It infected you, infected your people, they caught that plantation-fatted, evangelical fever; led them into separatism and error."

He glared. "My people never saw a plantation. Never turned a cash crop. We sowed our own harrows, harvested our own crops – then your people come along telling us how to live our lives!"

"What are you telling me, Ramsey? You did your own work?"

"We did our own work, Minister. Then my daddy took a notion, run off to Kansas after Wilson's Creek, and we worked harder than ever, my brothers and me."

"He fought at Wilson's Creek?"

He shook his head. "He was a book reader. He set up a surgery out back. Both sides used it. We had one field nigger, my mother's, name of Hanky, he dug the graves. I had to keep an eye on him digging for three days after the guns stopped. Then my daddy took off north."

"You know what a pyrrhic victory is, Ramsey?"

"I'm not ignorant, Minister."

"Your boys won at Wilson's Creek but what did it get you? You controlled Missouri a few more years –"

"South of the Osage."

"South of the Osage, good," Stevens said. "But think about it. All the savagery you saw, all the limbs sawed off, all the young men lost, the widows made, what did it get you? You people stuck your head in the buzz saw of progress and lost it at the ears."

He couldn't debate Stevens' sentiments. He'd had them himself, curled in an armchair in New Orleans, learning the taste of twenty-five cent cigars and reading – reading and understanding.

"Come over here, Ramsey. I want you to see the outline of a victory that is not pyrrhic." Stevens spread a chart upon the desk. "This is what I want. Recognize it?"

"Pearl River lagoon."

"Best natural harbor in the Pacific – worth going to war over but you're going to get it for me without a fight."

"Hasn't been proved, Mr. Minister. The British started a survey but the natives drove them off. General Schofield took a look a few years back and told Congress we ought to seize it five miles into the interior, but nobody really knows."

"I want it, Ramsey, then I want the whole damn island, and you're going to get them for me."

Bent over the chart, Stevens was a caricature. His white hair slacked uncombed, his shirtsleeves were rumpled, and undersized as he was, he looked like a gnome. But he had risen after the war on the twin tides of industry and the Republican Party, and Ramsey could not dismiss him carelessly. "Permission to smoke?" he asked.

"Nothing really to smoke about, Ramsey. How to complete this assignment, that's all you should contemplate now. Should be nothing compared to destabilizing French intelligence in North Africa or to ferreting out Bismarck's need for gunpowder, as you did in Valparaiso. It is a government of natives, after all. Your success will restore my confidence in the Navy after the fiasco with my beaver hat."

"The Admiral issues my orders, Mr. Stevens, I think you know that."

"Didn't I make myself clear? You work for me now, Ramsey." He picked up his cap. "If you'll excuse me, Mr. Minister."

"O, I don't think you are walking out on me, Ramsey. You see, I know why you are in Honolulu – why you got yourself posted out here. What was it, this or Hong Kong? The Navigator Islands? Any duty station to stay ahead of the investigation?"

He replaced his cap on the chair.

Stevens hooked his thumbs in his waistcoat and rocked on his heels. "I see. I finally have your attention, do I? So smug, so arrogant. Thought you could dismiss me, thought you could play sixes and sevens with my daddy's beaver. Your kind think you are above it all, do anything you please. Tall, young, a regular Knave of Hearts with the ladies, the world's your plaything. It's quick as you please over the cobblestones or over the pebbles, devil take the carriage springs."

He sat and crossed his legs. "What are you talking about, Mr. Minister?"

Stevens walked to the chair. "O, I do enjoy calling a bluff." He leaned over and looked him full in the face. "Murder, Ramsey, of a Federal officer – New Orleans, 1874, the White League Riots. Only distinguishing characteristic of the assailant was a scar – dueling scar, somebody said, so for ten years they've looked for him in the Army, some Rebel seditionist hiding in the ranks with blood on his hands. Never thought to look in the Navy, because sailors don't use the sword. Haven't the sense of honor. But it wasn't a dueling scar, was it Ramsey?" Stevens grinned and jabbed him in the neck. "It was that, a miserable little farm accident befalling a miserable little Rebel dirt farmer. Nothing honorable at all. Nothing courageous." He stood up and returned to the chart.

His heart beat against his skin. His mind froze, refused to work. "I protected a lady's virtue," he said softly. "New Orleans was … it was hellfire, chaos. Couldn't believe it. The Federals, they were no better than the White Leaguers."

He had rehearsed the words so many times, running the explanation through his head like a schoolboy preparing his verses. He had tried out different words and phrases, imagining the variety of situations in which he might be caught up. Here in this place, not in a dingy courtroom with Army guards itching to get their hands on him, but in a sunlit suite at the very extremity of American reach, the prepared words sounded paltry, orphaned of any justification, and dusty in his mouth as uncombed cotton.

"Circumstances, Ramsey. They mean something to you, nothing to me."

"It was madness."

"You shot him in the forehead."

"I gave him a chance to run."

"You miss my point. You shot him in the forehead. Close range. You executed him. You looked right at the man. You saw him piss himself like an Irishman. You watched the light leave his eyes. You're a killer, Ramsey. I like that."

Ramsey bit the end of a panatela and spit the nub through the open window. Outside, the day still sparkled. To the east Diamond Head crater still presided brown and incongruous over the green landscape. The tops of coconut trees marked the boundary of the Waikiki District and Honolulu warmed itself in the sun, lush foliage broken by the grand, two-story residences erected by newly wealthy White businessmen, the crumbling native huts and bungalows nearly invisible beneath the leafy boughs.

He regained himself. "You'll never hang me." He struck a match. "I won't let you."

Stevens shook his head. "What are you going to do, run again? The investigation caught you up in Morocco. It caught you up here. This is the age of steam and telegraph, Ramsey. Think you can hide from me? Pickett stood a better chance charging the Peach Orchard. It will be just as futile for you and just as final. But you, no poet will extol. No teary-eyed panegyric for you."

Stevens lingered over the photograph on the pedestal table. "Do not believe because you have youth, you have time on your side, Ramsey. A man like you, I can help you. I'd like to, you possess traits. Just trust me. Time is a delusion, do not be fooled by it. – Now, I am going to summon my colleagues. I want you to listen to them. We're mapping the future of the Pacific. We're making a better world. You have a chance to be part of it, part of something significant. What's the Navy offer you? Trivialities, and an officer corps you don't respect – I know you don't, but you're forced to salute them anyway. I offer you an opportunity. Let's see if Wilson's Creek is far enough behind you to make use of it."

"And Commander Taylor?"

Stevens flicked his hand. "I am the American authority in the kingdom." He opened the door to the adjoining room. "Come in, gentlemen. I want you to meet Mr. Ramsey."

Three White men entered. Two were identically outfitted in white trousers and blazer jacket, sea blue tie and cap to match. The third was tall, older and dressed like a church deacon. A thatch of gray whiskers brushed his shirt front. "The Hawaiian League, Ramsey, or its three seeds. – The hope of respectable government in these islands."

Ramsey stood to the side and pretended boredom as introductions were made and the conversation heated up, but his head swirled. The men discussed re-ordering the Pacific under the protection of the United States. They'd install a White government in the islands and wanted the American government to turn its eyes as the Honolulu Rifles, the League's all-*haole* militia, was armed and prepared for revolution.

The plan was more radical than ONI's, which would retain the native monarchy as window dressing. The League intended to establish a White fiefdom in the middle of the ocean.

Stevens looked over at Ramsey. "I am certain the Navy will agree with me, gentlemen. The Rifles must be properly trained and led before my government ..."

The discussion turned passionate. One of the uniformed men – the two were baseballers, teammates on the Whangdoodles, whose members were downtown businessmen and graduates of Punahou School – claimed his rank as sergeant was sufficient to lead the Rifles. "I say we arm the Rifles immediately," he said, gesturing with a black, cylindrical bat.

"The Rifles?" William Castle, the other uniformed man, scoffed. "They are drawing room cadets."

"I drill the Rifles myself," said Lorrin Thurston, holder of the bat. Ramsey knew him by reputation. Younger than Castle, he was a legislator and incendiary columnist for the *Hawaiian Gazette.*

"I know you do. You take the rank of sergeant without the merit of preparation. I witnessed the American Civil War. It's a long way from writing about war to real soldiering, I can tell you. The Rifles have no training, no horse and precious little ammunition."

Thurston closed on Castle with the bat held like a foil. "Castle & Cooke should ship –"

"Castle & Cooke shall not import munitions to the islands. We've been through that," Castle said with determination, though he backed away a step. "I will not dishonor my father's name. He may have left the mission fields to establish a business in the Kingdom –"

"To advantage himself upon the natives," snapped Thurston.

Castle glared at him. "My father erected the Queen's Hospital. My mother held your hand through Punahou School. What would you do, fire upon Luahine's *kanaka*? Send native blood flowing in the streets? O, wouldn't her priests have a field day then! They'd call down every curse the old *kahuna* still remember. Not a thing would grow and the laborers would flee the fields."

"Gentlemen, gentlemen." Ramsey watched as the third man, Sanford Dole, waggled his hands at the wrist like a schoolmaster. "I remind you, you are Punahou men. You represent missionary interests. The Honolulu Rifles are not going to fire upon the Hawaiian. My heavens, the sacrifices of our forefathers."

"Not if we keep the Rifles disarmed, they won't," Castle said. "They are grocers and mechanics and plantation foremen. They are a danger soon as they uniform."

Stevens interceded and proposed a Canadian named Volney Ashford to command the Rifles. Ashford had fought with the Union Army, had recently joined his brother's law firm in Honolulu.

Dole said the Hawaiian League must be unified and quickly agreed. His whiskers switched from side to side as he embraced each of the men with bright, evangelical eyes. "Well, Mr. Stevens, it seems we are united behind a local militia – *haole* of course, led by the Canadian. So I for one see no use for the services of your Mr. Ramsey … He is a turncoat, is he not?"

"Let us say rather that Mr. Ramsey is a man for hire." Stevens looked boldly at him. "A mercenary, if you will – and I have his price."

The men turned to consider Ramsey. He smoked stonily.

"A mercenary? I see," said Dole. He closed his hands upon his lapels. "Mr. Minister, the missionary families share a profound love of these islands, perhaps you are unaware – rooted, I believe, in an appreciation for what Providence has wrought here. We have beat back native indolence and prurience of every sort. We have contained as well the excesses of seamen and merchantmen of every flag. It was a Protestant missionary, the late Mr. Richards, who stood between whalers and their lust for native women, for which his church on the Island of Maui was roundly cannonaded. Missionaries wrote the Hawaiian alphabet, cured the heathen of his nakedness and set him to honest employment, and changed despotic king into constitutional monarch. I cannot believe the march toward Christian civilization shall be abetted by one whose motive is so … ambivalent."

Stevens bowed in acknowledgement. "Well put, Mr. Dole, well put. But gentlemen, you misunderstand me if you suppose I would put Ramsey's talents to insurrection in the Kingdom. Those who hope for a formation of American Marines on King Street would better sow dragon's teeth instead."

"We had your Marines ten years ago," Thurston said. "It's tempting, when the palace broadcasts its latest nativist programme …"

"But it was a Republican White House then, Mr. Thurston. The current Democrat administration is not so interventionist."

Ramsey listened as Stevens bent the men to his ends. He was impressed. In his own work he used secrets to manipulate an adversary, but the minister appealed directly to greed. "No, gentlemen," Stevens concluded, "our future lies in Pearl lagoon. Offer it to my government and the Reciprocity Treaty follows. With reciprocity comes riches. You may achieve your ends without a shot fired!"

"Our Prime Minister will never surrender territory for the treaty," said Dole.

Castle sided with Stevens. "But this is the very pinch of the game! The Minister's not talking about the island – just the damn lagoon, a mud hole last time anyone looked."

Stevens drove home his point. "Precisely the need for Ramsey. He will determine its value to the Navy, and its value to the Navy will set its price for Congress. The Reciprocity Treaty counters

Luahine, keeps Kalakaua in line and maintains America as your closest friend and trading partner. I make it a 3-Spade bid, eh?"

The men said nothing. Ramsey, leaning against the sill, studied them to see who would make the first move. Then Castle gestured in Dole's direction. "Well Sanford, have you a counter? The Minister plays the strong suit."

"He does, but I am afraid a black heart trumps even a good hand." Dole lifted his chin and Ramsey felt his gaze, wide, unblinking, like owl eyes.

Stevens drummed the writing desk with his fingers. "Well, Ramsey? Do you sleep on duty? Mr. Dole calls your honor to question. Speak up, man. Can you assure us of service in your country's interests?"

He tossed the end of his cigar out the window. Stevens' question was an oakum stocking. It looked silk, but once tried on it was just hemp rope pulled fine. He wouldn't be serving his country's interests, he'd be serving Stevens and Spreckels, or whatever gang of industrialists the minister was beholden to.

He looked at Thurston, a conniver, dangerous once the Rifles armed. Castle would pick over the poke salad very carefully, but he would gladly take the profit. And Dole could burnish such words as to excuse even regicide. Had the Hawaiian League the sulfur to overthrow constitutional authority in the islands? Provided John Stevens supplied fuse and match, it did.

He stepped to the chart which displayed Pearl River. It lay due west of Honolulu Harbor and curled in the belly of Oahu like an embryo.

"Well? We shan't ask you to swear by the scar on your neck," Stevens said with palpable menace. "Just reassure the gentlemen you can be counted on."

He snorted. He had killed. The occasions had been moral imperatives, he'd been compelled to them. He felt they'd skewered his soul nonetheless, if such a quaint thing might be thought to exist. When next he had occasion to take a life – Stevens', say – nothing should prevent him from lingering over it therefore, savoring the exercise of power at its most intoxicating, enjoying it even, for the damage had begun so long ago.

"Gents," he said with a slight bow, "consider my services, such as they are, at your immediate and most perspicacious disposal."

NINE

Lost, alone, more alone than ever she felt at her *hula* school on Kauai, no mother, no aunties, no family – she found a way to live through it on Kauai. She dedicated her heart to Lono. He shone light-skinned like the moon. He took her in his arms, granted her womanhood, lifted her up. But here with Pakalana she had nothing. She saw no path for herself, nothing and no one to belong to. She'd failed, failed to do as she'd been told, failed to move when the drum commanded. She'd shamed the king, shamed her *kumu*, shamed her brother. She was empty, and in the emptiness the black blood boiled eagerly. It wanted to fill her, wanted to seize her belly, tear her female places away from Lono, take her heart, her hands, legs and feet, wanted to take over, fill her eyes so she saw only darkness, wanted to erupt out the top of her head.

Quaking, she waited eyes down in her teacher's compound. Pakalana sat cross-legged in the *hula* longhouse, stripping coconut fronds with a *haole* knife and weaving a basket from the green leaves. She retained the spine of the leaf, making the basket stronger, better for heavy carrying. Pua thought it had to do with her failure.

The day before, Pakalana sent her to Ewa village to fetch the cumbersome palm limb. Evening fell by the time she wrestled it back up the rutted trail. The day before that she cleared brown *kiawe* thickets from the bathing pool with a stone adze. The work was hard and tore up the lovely *hula* hands she'd thought so much of on Kauai.

She took it as punishment, though *kumu* told her earlier ranks of students worked also. They'd carved the compound out of the Waianae foothills with traditional tools. They built a kitchen area, a sleeping lodge thatched with *pili* grass, the *hula* longhouse and on the upland edge, the pool dammed with lava rock and granite. In the compound's center they piled red earth and packed it firm over the years with their bare feet. *Kumu* circled it herself with a necklace of stones carried from sacred places across the islands. A low altar stood to one side and behind it, nearly invisible in a glen, hunched the shelter for a female's monthly seclusion.

Earlier ranks worked but they hadn't failed. She had.

"Have you pounded the *poi*, Kauai girl?" Pakalana bid her enter, and she gave proper reverence.

"Yes, *kumu*. And I brought the wood for the fire. – Only, I ..." In the midst of her emptiness, Lono had appeared to her carrying the gourd of sacred Makahiki seeds. Her heart, instead of opening as a lover's should, turned cold to him. How could it not? Her heart was not her own now. Lono's gourd broke and the seeds spilled uselessly to the ground.

"So, Kauai girl, Lono visits you at his wet season of Makahiki?" *Kumu* looked at her closely. "He fears to lose you to Pele and the Hula Pahu."

"It is of no consequence. I – I must renounce him." This is what had welled up. She had finally accepted her fate, she was not reserved to sacred dance. The black blood made her unworthy.

"And his *hula*? The *hula* of your beloved Kauai island?"

She shook her head.

Her teacher raised her eyebrows. "Do you know what you ask?"

She hesitated. She wanted to pretend she did. Wanted to feel anything other than empty, other than alone.

"You do not know what you ask, yet you ask for it nonetheless?" *Kumu* set down her weaving. "Perhaps you have put yourself upon the path after all, Kauai girl."

On her knees she pressed her cheek into the palm of her teacher's hand. It felt leathery as pig's hide. "But I do not know where the path leads, *kumu*." She fought down a sob. "Do not know any –"

"Give no thought where the path leads, Kauai girl. Can you do that? Follow any path on the island long enough and it returns to where you started, so what does the path matter?"

She couldn't stop her tears. She'd believed herself favored by the gods. Could she submit like a commoner? "But the gods …"

Her teacher held up a hand. "The gods are busy. Or they sleep. Or they rut in the mountaintops like cattle. *Wa'a* does not know how he will be carried but he submits to the sea in order to arrive."

She wanted to do as *kumu* said, wanted to submit to her fate, let its waters carry her. On Kauai she was *kapu*, set aside. Here she could not be. She took a deep breath. "I pray only to Aunty Pele now, *kumu*. I pray to be worthy."

"You must pray to her sister Hi'iaka. She has charge of *wa'a o pele,* the goddess' canoe of fire. Even a Kauai girl must know the story."

She nodded. Everyone knew the story. It was Pele at her most frightening and unforgiving. She consumed her sister and a gallant Kauai prince, believing they betrayed her. Pele looked suspiciously upon Kauai thereafter, though Hi'iaka and the prince were mated forever in the *ohia lehua* blossom, first flower to decorate the goddess' ebony tresses after they cooled.

"Pele is jealous. She wants all your *aloha*. You may dance no more under the Lono moon."

She hung her head. It was not a trick this time. "I will do as you say, *tutu*, I will pray … I will pray for Pele's fire. She held her breath. She expected the black blood to thrash madly as she said it. She expected Pele's canoe to fill with the blood, to rise flaming like a lava field. Pele would seize her, flay her, love her, burn her, she didn't know.

But she opened her eyes and *kumu* still sat before her, and her lips moved, and she was saying, "… perhaps will visit you. And perhaps you will survive her, and live to serve The People. It will be your blessing and your fate."

She reverenced and turned to go. "I have my chores, *kumu*."

"You will go to Ewa village for fish, and go quickly as Big Island girl when she runs from Aunty's burning breath. We have visitors today."

Visitors? Company … news … excitement!

"And when you return, you shall bathe and wash your hair with *'awapuhi* blossom. After it dries I shall use the *haole* brush upon it. You will be beautiful as your name, Pua."

She trotted under the breadfruit tree, its green pods beginning to swell promisingly, and turned down the path to Ewa village. "Pua," Pakalana had said, first time ever *kumu* used her name, and first time ever her hair would shine from the *haole* brush. She lifted her head. *Pueo* the owl called to her from the grasslands. *Makani* the breeze kissed her cheek. What had so frightened her?

By the time she returned, skin moist from exertion, feet and legs soiled from the journey, the day had begun its decline and she heard voices. *Kumu* conversed with her mother's bearded priest, his head close to hers as they sat on mats in the *hula* longhouse. Its sides were open so their words carried into the compound. She built up the fire and prepared the fish for smoking. She rubbed it with sea salt, spitted it and tented it under green *ti* leaf to capture the smoke.

"She is a dancer from Kauai island," she heard the priest say. "I think Luahine hopes too much in her. My *kahuna* agree."

Her teacher sighed. "I am old now. Such things tire me. What does Luahine expect?"

"A Big Island girl, yes. One of the old families there. Or Molokai girl, if she had chosen a Molokai dancer, my *kahuna* could support her. Molokai island is home to the poison-tree goddess, a Molokai girl has the *mana*, she has the spirit, the authority."

"Do not think this girl has not the *mana*. She failed once because it was too soon. Aunty Pele already places her eye upon the girl, I am certain."

Pua looked up, surprised *kumu* spoke so forcefully about her, and caught the priest's gesture of disbelief.

"No," *kumu* said. "It is true. Aunty knows this girl already. Did she not, she would have consumed her when the *pahu* spoke at Kalakaua's *luau*. Aunty knows her already, as she knew Luahine at this age. – And she wants to love her, though Kahu is strong in her."

"So, what do we do? Pele sends her lava toward Hilo town, she burned a villager. The people cry, they know Kalakaua cannot help them. My *kahuna* say the High Chiefess must sacrifice herself to appease Aunty. Manu's warriors oppose it. It will split the movement."

"Faagh! Is the movement so weak? You do not know what you have in the girl. She is Kauai island, she is truly Kauai island. And Aunty Pele loves her."

"You know this?"

"I know this. It has not happened before, not a Kauai girl. Not within memory."

She heard the priest grunt. After a moment he said, "So, she could truly unite the people, Kauai in the north to Big Island in the south."

Not wanting to look, not wanting to dare, she lifted her eyes from the fire. She saw her teacher's nod. "*Pono*, righteousness from Kauai. *Mana*, strength and authority from the Big Island."

Her heart beat in her ears. If the priest said more, she did not hear. It was the dream of her people, embedded in story and dance, to unify the eight separate islands. Kings had attempted it with *mana*, but too often they ignored *pono*. It was like a dancer knowing the steps, her Kauai teacher said, but not preparing first with prayer and sacrifice. "*Pau ka pono, pau ka mana*," the old teaching, he made them chant it over and over. "Without righteousness, there is no strength."

And the movement wanted her to have a role in it. Abandoned, shamed, forced by them from her only home. They wanted her to help them.

"*Mana* from the Big Island?" she heard the priest ask.

"Aunty must accept her, but yes."

"And Luahine?"

Kumu snorted. "*E hoolohe!* Luahine has the *mana*, but not the *pono*. Let Aunty – what do you do there, girl?" Her teacher jumped to her feet. "Do you listen to the talk of your betters? Lazy girl!"

"No, *kumu*, I – it is only that I have finished, and I ..."

"Finished? And we have guests? Have you learned nothing? Fill the water gourd, go search for pigeon egg. Is this how Kauai girl shows *aloha?*"

She hurried away but by twilight had completed her chores. She unwrapped her *kapa* garment and with a sigh, slipped into the bathing pool. It was deep enough to submerge and swim underwater a few strokes. She pleasured in the coolness, black hair floating behind her in a cloud, feeling liquid like the monk seal.

She surfaced and broke open the stem of '*awapuhi*, working the sap into her scalp and down through the tips of her hair to her breast. The sweet scent filled her and in its perfume, in the sensations of water and hair and flesh, she tried to lose the words she'd heard. She'd left Lono, she understood that. She'd been torn from him by her mother's ambition. Pele alone was left to her, Pele to fill her emptiness. But in Pele, what was left her as dancer? Pele forced her so much her mother's way.

It was what they seemed to want for her, Pakalana, her mother's priest, even Manu. The joy she'd felt when *pueo* hooted earlier started to ebb. The owl was an ill-omen of Kahu the sorceress.

She worked the suds with her hands then massaged the shampoo into her almond colored skin. It felt good to touch her body, to be reassured by it, to put worry aside. Her body had responded to Pakalana's hard training, the hours spent in the bent knee stance, her weight settling through the hips down the backs of the legs, stomach pulled in. She felt the muscle and appreciated the long, trim lines as her hands soaped her sturdy arms and the downy hair under them, her round breasts, flat belly then along her thighs and calves, which supported her so securely in the dance.

She sank beneath the surface to rinse and reached for more *'awapuhi* to wash her female place. She wanted to serve The People. It was how she'd been trained. All the girls. Their *hula* served The People, served the land, served the gods. Served the beautiful light-skinned god ... served a beautiful prince ...

A voice stopped her. "Pakalana calls you. We will eat."

She wiped the water from her face and turned to the bank. Prince Koloa stood there. He wore dark *haole* trousers and a flower behind his ear. His torso was bare, his skin light, and out of his lean chest feathery black hair curled.

"Dry yourself." He stared at her briefly, frankly in extending the *kapa* wrap then turned for the *hula* longhouse.

She thought she'd faint! He looked at her! She looked at him! Their eyes met! It was like Lono himself! When the god found her at Hanalei, he'd granted her flow. She was woman now. What could this god give her next?!

She rushed to her sleeping hut. Her hair was thick with water but she twisted it into a knot and, breaking a stem of white plumeria with yellow centers, used it to hold the bun in place. Rivulets ran from it down her bare back. She changed to a *kapa* wrap she'd dyed golden with ground *'olena*, then stamped in the leafy fern pattern. It was her favorite. Pakalana frowned upon decoration, but she tied a triple *lei* of dainty brown *kiawe* seed around her throat.

Kukui oil torches flickered by the time she padded into the compound. She kept her eyes down and alert. Her prince was there, the priest, and Manu speaking to them both. Her brother nodded to her but she knew better than to approach the men. She went to the cooking fire and as Pakalana directed them to sit, she carried the smoked fish on two platters, one for the men and one for Pakalana and herself, and set them on a table smoothed out of breadfruit wood. They ate apart as in the days of *kapu*. There were calabashes of *poi* and sweet potato, and fresh coconut. Manu had brought spitted chicken and Koloa a sweet cake from town.

The priest poured *awa* into coconut shell drinking cups and the conversation quickened, but she kept her eyes lowered and listened. They joked, they laughed and it felt good to be inside such companionship, but she kept to herself and prayed not to hear her name.

They discussed their plan. The kingdom held its Independence Day festivities the following month, Makahiki season when it rained. Prince Koloa would paddle into the harbor in a single-hulled canoe fitted with the Makahiki pole. The pole was tall like a mast and from its crossbeam would flutter Lono's white *kapa* banner. Koloa would be helmeted in the gourd mask of the Lono cult, and with his light skin he'd send forth the call: return, Kanaka Maoli, return to the pure ways of old. Then they'd have the *kahuna* carry the Makahiki pole from village to village, island to island. The old families would rally to it. The people would rise up. On the surging *kanaka* tide the priests would demand Kalakaua's resignation and install the High Chiefess in his stead.

"*Hiki no!* Certainly! The plan is good!" they all said.

She started breathing again. They had not mentioned her, and her prince, he spoke to her only with his eyes.

"It is good," her brother said. "We put aside *pono*. We put aside *mana*. We take up the *haole* ways to combat the *haole*. We use 'power.' – Do you know this *haole* word, Pua?"

She shook her head.

"It is better she does not," her teacher said. "It is a word with no soul to it. *Pono* has drained from it, as it has from the *haole* themselves. A dancer has no use for such a word."

Manu chuckled. "Do you think the *haole* with their great ships and their cities – I have seen their cities, *tutu*, you could put Pearl lagoon in one, and it would be as a mud puddle."

"In London, Pearl lagoon would be a rain drop," Koloa said.

"Yes," her brother said, "so what does such a people care for *pono*? But the word 'power' means everything to them. They fear it, so we must show ours – the *kanaka* on every island, bound together no matter their chiefs or their clan. Put aside the old rivalries, Kauai does not contend with the Big Island, Maui with Molokai."

The priest grunted. "*Hiki no.*"

She saw her teacher spit on the ground. Then she said something in old Hawaiian, something she could not understand, then said, "You do not know the true *mana* of our people. It is this girl."

She did not look up. She refused to look up. But she felt the eyes of the men upon her.

"... A Kauai girl filled with Pele's fire."

"You match Pele's fire against the *haole* power?" Her brother addressed her teacher, but his eyes remained on her. They were not unkind. They probed, they reached wonderingly into her like the squid poked an arm under coral. Was anything there, this girl who had failed the *luau*?

Kumu sucked her teeth. "Only a man would ask such a question, a man who does not understand dance."

Manu laughed. "*Aue, tutu*! Then train her, train my sister. Train her to dance Hula Pahu before her mother. Train her to dance before the Goddess herself!"

Her teacher grunted. "I train her, but Aunty must *hanai* her."

Aunty! The black blood surged and she was helpless. It clouded her eyes, spun her head and beat in her ears so she could not think. A dark cloud spread before her and where it sloped, a canoe flamed, riding it like a wave. The canoe was tiny but grew as it surfed the wave, drawing nearer. The lone figure paddling it shrieked, and she quaked inside like the mouse in *pueo*'s talons.

TEN

Wet season arrived early, before Independence Day. It collared Honolulu, garroting the horizon in a noose of gray clouds and beat upon the banana leaves with liquid drum sticks. Water poured off corrugated tin roofs or swirled into downspouts to rain barrels which overflowed daily. Red rivulets coursed through the muddy streets carrying human and animal waste to the sea.

Ramsey scurried across Alakea Street to the attaché's office and shook out his uniform coat beneath the overhang of the wooden sidewalk. The rain continued as he reported precisely ten minutes early and was directed by the sailor at the desk to a leather divan. Above it were a rendition of the kingdom's coat of arms, gift of King Kalakaua, and an oil of the bald eagle in flight, painted by Commander Taylor.

He waited forty minutes before being called in. Taylor's office windows were shuttered and the dreariness of the afternoon contributed to the gloom. He realized any meeting with Taylor that occurred before 1600, end of duty hours, was not likely to go well.

"Why issue me a progress report that reports no progress?" The attaché stood with his back turned, arms crossed, looking at the shutters.

He came to attention before Taylor's desk. "You required a report, sir."

"I required progress, sailor. Reports are shit paper, do you understand? Shit paper!" Taylor faced him and leaned upon the desk, his arms trembling. "In the real Navy we stack them in the officers' head. And what do we use them for? – Go ahead, tell me."

"Would that be shit paper, sir?"

"Exactly, Ramsey. And I have plenty of shit paper in the officers' head as it is. Did I requisition more?"

"Not to my knowledge, sir."

"Not to your knowledge, very good. Not to your knowledge." Taylor crossed from the desk and transected his office. The flag of the Hawaiian Kingdom and the flag of the United States stood in wooden stanchions on either side of a comfortable looking, maroon upholstered sofa. Between them hung another of the attaché's oils, a painting of Diamond Head.

"So why in God's name, if Regular Navy doesn't requisition it, does ONI insist on giving me worthless shit?" Taylor whirled upon him.

"I am provisioning for another bivouac in one week, sir."

All of his attention had been going to the Pearl lagoon problem, since he felt far more vulnerable to Stevens than to the attaché. He'd established a base camp at Pearl and mounted two expeditions. During the last he had, secretly, spied Koloa illegally drilling a native guard at a makeshift firing range along the west bank.

Taylor gestured at his chest. "Wrong, sailor. You are provisioning for a bivouac starting tomorrow. Princess Dominis granted me this permission, I won't have you spoil it."

"The Princess granted me the permission, sir, as I recall." He immediately regretted his tongue.

Taylor's eyes bulged. "You are the most insolent jackass I have ever been saddled with! This is a command, Ramsey, and I am its commander. In time of war I'd have you executed for insubordination. I am going to enjoy failing your fitness report.

Now get out of here before I call the guard. Prince Koloa is escorting you to Ewa village. 0900 tomorrow."

The village *kahuna* was annoying. He was not of the rank that once advised the Kamehameha dynasty or now congregated about Luahine. He was a lesser priest, more of an agronomist and healer who shadowed Ramsey's every step, stopping him with a firm touch of his *kapu* stick and pouring out a stream of Hawaiian. His cant was taken up by Ewa's naked brown children who bubbled up everywhere and were endlessly underfoot. The priest was suspicious of the survey tube and appeared convinced that it drew off the sacredness attached to certain clumps of trees or folds in the land. Repeated stops were called while he prayed and awaited permission to enter a particular domain.

Ramsey stomped back to the village after the wind came up and dumped rain across the Waianaes. Ewa was an ancestral village, Koloa told him. Generations of bare feet had trod the red dirt path he followed. It descended from the foothills through tree-high green wild cane to the village's banana groves and taro patches, then to the village itself, and beyond its low lava rock wall half an hour's journey to the fishponds, which were in Pearl lagoon. Ewa had thrived until the missionaries arrived, and though its population had shrunk and half its habitations had been abandoned or their thatched roofs and siding had collapsed upon their wooden frames, the village was far enough removed from Honolulu to retain its native spirit. Koloa pointed out the paving of smooth stones and mortar from powdered shell within the village compound – "a tighter join than cobblestones, look here, Ramsey!"

But children, not men, maintained the paving now. And the shed originally woven to shelter the women as they beat *kapa* had been given to the repair of fishing nets, as most resources had to be devoted to food. The village felt proud that it could offer a *hale* – a grass lodge – and a share of the fishpond to Koloa, but it prayed that the prince soon would be satisfied and travel to a larger, more prosperous locale.

"I've got ten days! Ten days to finish this job!" he shouted at Koloa upon his return. "That fool priest keeps us waiting on a rock!"

He had to stoop to enter but inside the steep pitch of their *hale*, it was roomy and dry, pleasingly perfumed with herbs, and insulated against the damp by layers of matting atop a foundation of packed earth and cemented stones. He and Koloa had set up a field laboratory in one corner. There were desk, stools, specimen jars and a log book for charting their results. He was the more instinctual agriculturalist but Koloa was better informed, leafing through tabulations of current American principles and translating aloud a volume by Justus Liebig. He didn't care, but Koloa insisted the book was all the rage in Europe.

Koloa looked up when he entered. "That priest will get you into areas that are *kapu* even to me, Ramsey." He labeled specimen jars at the desk. His man Thaddeus assisted.

"We'll get nowhere if we have to worship every critter he takes a notion to. Yesterday he had me salaam a lizard like it was the Queen of Sheba."

"I'm not surprised. He's a little … I guess fretful is the word. It's the stars. We've lost a constellation, you see. Scorpio normally appears in the late summer sky. It's one of the rising stars used by the navigators, but it didn't rise this summer."

He put down his survey gear. "I swear, Koloa. Your people are about a half bubble off plumb. Can't see the stars? It's just clouds, ain't it? That volcano on the Big Island kicking 'em up like a dust storm – ain't that it?"

"I know what it sounds like. It's never happened before, that's all. Scorpio has the big hook? In our teachings the hook is actually the fishhook of the demigod Maui. He used it to pull the islands out of the sea. Makes us apprehensive when it doesn't appear – like we'll slip back down."

He shook his head. "He should have used it to pull y'all into the modern age."

Koloa chuckled. "I know we need science. I'm running my Kauai estate on scientific principles. Kalakaua says we've had it all along, had it before the European did. Science can't answer every question, that's all. Do you know your Shakespeare? – 'There are more things in heaven and earth, Horatio, than are dreamt of in your philosophy.'"

He did not know his Shakespeare. To bring an end to the matter he challenged Koloa about his progress. "What about the soil samples. Finish cataloging them?"

"I did, but there's nothing new. Still too acidic."

"You treated with the diluted solution?"

"Hydrochloric and acetic acids, yes."

He frowned. "Too red, too much iron in the soil. Mississippi Basin soil is dark as chocolate, you can plant anything in it. But your Hawaiian soil, I don't know, Koloa. Pretty to look at, but nothing will grow. That volcano goddess you set so much store by, she saw to that. I don't know how anybody survived before the traders came."

"I'll tell you how. Your people were ragged, scurvy-laden maggots when Cook landed. Our chiefs towered over them. You've read the journals."

He grunted. "Well, something must have happened."

"Something did," Koloa said. "We tried to become like you, God help us. Left our healthy diets and confined ourselves to your towns. You gave us syphilis and gout in return."

He made an exaggerated bow. "On behalf of all my people, O Royal Prince, please let me present you with something different – a thorough analysis of these lands. Only, I shall be denied the opportunity if your priest is not restrained. My daddy herded snakes was more cooperative."

Koloa sighed and pulled on his hat.

Beyond the village the rain had beaten down the *pili* grass, exposing the rust-colored earth in which it rooted. The water drained, sluicing into tributaries that poured down to streams, and by them to Pearl River and the sea. Birds, coming alive after sheltering from the drenching, shook their feathers dry as the sun strengthened. They flew off calling a warning when the survey party approached.

The priest led the party hesitatingly around a garnet-studded boulder then stopped once again. Koloa went to confer with him and Thaddeus began to fill Ramsey in on Makahiki. It was the god Lono's festival, when in the old days *kapu* was relaxed and the people engaged in every activity, ritualistic and otherwise, to insure fertility to the land.

"You make da kine, all you like," Thaddeus told him, illustrating with a gesture any sailor knew. "All kind *wahine*, all kind girl."

Chiefs of old had paraded Lono's Makahiki banner around each island collecting tribute. Luahine was resurrecting the custom, Thaddeus said. Her followers carried the banner from her camp behind the Menehune Fishpond to the south shore of Kauai island. The rural people flocked to it, bringing what they could offer. They were abandoning the churches and some swore they had sighted Pele herself in clouds and in sea mist, the forms she chose when not volcanic.

"You told me Pele left Kauai, Thaddeus. Thought she didn't like the island no more."

"Luahine get plenty *mana*. She bring the people together, make one big *ho'olaule'a*. She come Ewa side, she bring da warriors. This priest, he run like rooster. Plenty scared, yeah?"

"What about you, Thaddeus? You run?"

"Not me. I get this." Thaddeus pulled out the tip of a red scarf hidden inside his shirt. "She see this, she nevah curse me."

"What about Koloa, does he run?"

"Prince Koloa one *kanaka akamai*. Smart kine." Thaddeus winked. "He get red scarf, too."

Koloa ambled over. "Set up your tripod, Ramsey. The *kahuna* doesn't like the signs but I talked him into it."

"What'd you have to promise him, feathers and a bone whistle?" He opened his black instrument case.

"Some day you may grow to respect our traditions. You might learn something." Koloa took Thaddeus with him, and they walked the ground looking for sections to sample for the soil analysis.

The priest approached him and said something in Hawaiian about a stand of shrubbery near the large boulder. He appeared anxious about it but Ramsey shook him off. "Princess say *wikiwiki*," he told the priest loudly, and made the sign of a crown on his head. "Liliu say no more fussing like a wet hen. You savvy? Get a move on."

He set to work.

Standard-issue Navy field gear wasn't much and wouldn't have done the job he needed. He'd designed his own instrument and was proud of it. The brass survey tube gleamed in the afternoon light like the works of a well-run ship. Manu had turned up the craftsman who worked with him on the project, the beached armorer of a British whaler who dug from his sea chest a volume on the telescopes of James Short. Captain Cook carried Short's telescopes on his cruises on behalf of the Royal Geographic Society. With the armorer he mined the text for its discussion of optics and lenses, and together they produced the drawings, made refinements and produced an instrument with superior lenses and precisely calibrated refractions and levels. It was the finest survey equipment in town, probably in the entire Pacific, the armorer said.

He concurred. With it he could divide quadrants close at hand or identify foreign vessels far out at sea.

He exercised it now on its mounting, sweeping the horizon up to Diamond Head point where a frigate was just making its appearance. He adjusted the focus and the frigate sprang into bold relief, canvas blooming like clouds. Trimmed as she was, she had to be military, and by her rigging a Frenchman, most likely carrying the official delegation for the kingdom's Independence Day festivities November Twenty-Ninth. He made a mental note of her displacement and armor, and predicted she would water and resupply a week in Honolulu before carrying the Tricolor to the South Pacific and Tahiti.

There was a pull on his sleeve – a shirtless, school-age boy named Abner, slightly built, with shaggy hair that blew in the wind, and oval black eyes under thick dark brows. He'd taken him on as an assistant and they'd developed quite a partnership. The boy knew to move quickly, bring his survey stake into alignment with the azimuth then hold still while the necessary sightings were taken. His young cousins sailed their *lauhala* kites, tossed spears through hoops and generally got in the way, but he, proud to have a *haole* job, shooed them aside and got straight to work.

He directed Abner to the shrub which had been cleared by the priest. It rose skyward like a green diamond. Steam shimmered as the sun heated the damp grass at its base. He peered through his tube and signaled by hand until he found the target within the crosshairs. His instrument contained a true theodolite so it measured both horizontal and vertical axes, an advantage on the tumbling Hawaiian landscape.

He shaved his pencil carefully then pulled out a leather notebook. He'd ruled its pages into a neat grid. Numbers were irreproachable – you were either right or wrong, no guesswork – and he took care with the entries. The order imposed by the cage of lines, the precision of the numbers, and their steady march in columns through his book pleasured him. He smiled at the boy, confirmed his entry, and directed him beyond the shrub.

He caught Koloa and Thaddeus working toward the plot where Abner was setting his stake. Thaddeus dug and Koloa collected the samples in a pouch. At last, all the parts functioning, all in order. He'd been right to push Koloa, right to challenge the priest's superstitions, and right to demand the job get done.

He spit out the end of a slender panatela and flared a match off his thumbnail. The smoke vented in a lazy plume.

There was a sudden cry. He swung his head. The priest pointed his *kapu* stick in the direction of the boy. A boar charged through the diamond-shaped bush. It salivated and was enormous but bounded like a cat on its short legs. The boy, already standing still for the survey, froze. He was directly in the path of the lowered tusks. They were aimed to gore an artery and end his life. With a shout Koloa launched himself at the pig. It was just enough to throw off its attack. The beast veered to the right, brought up its snout and tore through the limb of the larger threat.

Ramsey sighted along the length of his left arm through the extension of his pistol. The trigger contracted without thinking about it and the weapon reported. He saw smoke drift from the barrel and, fifty yards away, saw the boar sink to its knees in mid-stride. He ran across the field. The pig grunted and struggled. Vapor rose off its wet hide. Its blood was beginning to coat the *pili* grass. He looked into its eyes. If it could gain its footing it intended to charge again. He pointed the Colt at the forehead but the priest stopped him. "*Mana,*" he said, and showed him the kill spot at the base of the skull. The boar's great spirit was to be respected.

Abner was untouched but Koloa's wound was bad. He lifted the shredded trouser leg. The tusk had opened the inner thigh. The blood was not arterial, meaning the femoral had been missed. Were they in Honolulu recovery was assured. In the country more than half a day's hard ride out of town, it was another matter.

"You see Ramsey, we're not so very different from you," Koloa groaned.

He removed his khaki jacket and placed it under the prince's head. "You mean your blood is just as red?" He raised the leg to slow the bleeding and slipped his leather belt above the wound to apply a tourniquet.

"I mean our gods are just as unfair as yours. You showed them no respect whatsoever. They should have taken your life."

"Why, your gods are discriminatin', Prince." He ladled his voice with syrup. "They took royal blood for a sacrifice. What would they want with a ornery Cayuse such as me?"

"I'll bear that in mind," Koloa said as he lost consciousness.

ELEVEN

Ramsey struggled with Thaddeus. "The damn savage will kill him!" But he was unfocused and emotional, Koloa's man strong, able to work him into the corner of the hut, pin him against the support pole.

"The priest pulls the tourniquet, Koloa dies! *Make* dies, you understand?"

He knew wound care from riding rough in Missouri. The belt he'd slipped around Koloa's leg staunched the bleeding but packing and suturing – real doctoring – were needed to save it and save his life.

"The priest like pray!" Thaddeus held him by the shoulders.

The priest had draped himself in green vines and started leaves burning. They filled the hut with an acrid repulsive odor. A pair of large half-naked women chanted in the corner, pounding a muffled rhythm with gourd drums.

The priest spoke sharply then Thaddeus said, "Come, Ramsey, we go. This one priest need quiet, yeah? Then the 'aumakua come. Then his magic work. Koloa mo' bettah."

But as he watched, the priest took leaves and fern from a *kapa* wallet, worked them into a poultice and stuffed it in the wound. Koloa, unconscious, groaned. He shouted and broke toward the prince. The two women leaped in his path and Thaddeus grabbed him and forced him out.

"It's plain ignorance, Thaddeus! That's just … it's filth! Filth, do you understand?!"

Thaddeus directed him into the village. "No worries," he said.

He stalked off.

"No worries," Thaddeus repeated and caught up to him. "The *kahuna* get plenty *mana*. No worries."

Thaddeus took him to the village *imu*, a pit dug in the ground for roasting. Two men were enlarging it to accommodate the boar. The village priest had put his *kapu* on the pig, on Ramsey, on the entire event, and the pig was being prepared with particular care. "See? The priest get plenty *mana* now. You get plenty *mana*, too, Ramsey."

Wherever they turned, children gazed shyly upon him. Elders touched him and smiled and maidenly girls turned doe eyes upon him with unmistakable frankness. "No worries, you nevah wait for Makahiki!" Thaddeus added with a grin.

By the time they returned to the lodge, gifts had appeared at the door: a roll of *kapa* cloth, a polished *koa* wood bowl and stone *poi* pounder, and chickens, squawking, hobbled together with coconut fiber.

Thaddeus supervised every order of the priest and told him he was satisfied, but he could not relax. That night he snuck in a bowl of clean water and a fresh cloth taken from his own kit, and managed to remove the poultice and wipe out the wound. But Koloa was no military man and could not contain his moans. The priest broke from his slumber and charged with his *kapu* stick, jabbering furiously in Hawaiian. He was shoved aside. The priest mixed a draught and poured it into his patient. Then a new drummer arrived. Through the remainder of the night the floor mat hummed and her chants resonated so supply that Ramsey felt them slip into his stomach, relaxing it, softening it with her rhythms. He leaned back on a mat and slept.

Koloa woke at dawn, drawn but fever down and on the mend.

"The *kahuna* thinks I tried to kill you," he said, supporting his head and giving him water. "I only wanted to remove that moldy wrapping. *Dr. Gunn's* prescribes cleanliness for every condition. Back in Missouri they'd of used the bullwhip on me if I'd stuffed moss in a gunshot wound."

Koloa examined the poultice and approved. "You really should learn our ways, Ramsey." His voice sounded weak but clear. "So much you do not understand."

"That female was here, Paka ... something. Everybody bowing and scraping. She played and sang all night."

Koloa brightened. "Was she alone? Did she bring the girl?"

"What girl?"

The prince settled his head back down. "You would know if she did."

"I think I should ride to town, fetch a real doctor."

"It's our Independence Day, isn't it? You'll never find one sober enough to ride."

"Manu will find one. He can find anything."

"Manu, yes – go, tell him what happened."

"You know my houseboy?" he asked, surprised.

Koloa gestured weakly before drifting back to sleep. "Everybody knows Manu."

Sweating from the muggy ride from Ewa village, the chestnut horse lathered and spent, Ramsey burst into his quarters.

"How come you back, boss?" Manu had taken over the bungalow in his absence. Foreign-looking native materials were scattered all about.

"Koloa's laid up, Manu. A boar. We got to get him some help."

Manu's eyebrows shot up. "How bad?"

"Bad. Jump to, you've got to find a surgeon – not one of those saw-a-bones off a ship, but a reg'lar cutter. We'll hire a wagon and carry him to the village."

Manu seemed to not comprehend.

"Don't you understand? Koloa's at the village. He needs our help."

"Koloa nevah come wit' you?"

"That's what I'm telling you."

"This no good."

"Find one will trade for his fee."

Manu shook his head. "No can, boss. Independence Day, nobody like work."

"But Koloa could develop gangrene! You know what that is?"

"The village *kahuna* stay?"

"He packed dirt in the wound, said a few salaams. If I hadn't applied a tourniquet …"

Manu shrugged. "Then no problem, boss. No *huhu*." He returned to his work.

"What is all this?" Ramsey asked, taking in the disorder that had befallen his quarters.

"Independence Day." Manu dug deeper into the gourd he was carving. "Tradition."

"Get rid of it, Manu. And see to my horse. We've got to find a doctor."

"No more time, boss. You too busy." Manu slid an envelope through the pieces of gourd. It looked official.

"When did this arrive?"

"Yesterday – I don't know, maybe day before. I no get watch. You nevah pay enough. The attaché, he like you in his box for Independence Day."

"I thought you couldn't read, Manu."

Black eyes blinked back at him. "Why too much *pilikia* for Manu, boss? The messenger tell me, okay? – You *wikiwiki* now."

Ramsey scanned the correspondence. "And he wants me to compete in the exhibition afterward. Ridiculous. What am I going to do about Koloa?"

"No worries. Get the *kahuna*, I tol' you."

"You don't know how bad he was hurt."

"You don't know how bad the attaché like hurt you. Then I nevah get pay."

He sighed. It was an order, Manu was right. "Well, there's no time. – Look, I'm writing you a message for Miss Jessica Mornay." He'd pursued her carefully since the king's *luau*, had sent flowers backstage for three days – a week would have been better, but he could not stretch his credit. Then he followed up with dinner. "She's at the Hawaiian Hotel. Think you can get it to her, or must I find a Chinese?"

Manu took the message and put on his shirt.

"See to my horse first then run that message to Miss Mornay."

"Me one aide now, boss. No can do horse."

"You're my houseboy, Manu, you'll –"

But Manu was through the back door before the words were fully out.

TWELVE

He thought if there was something to put your stock in, this was it. The Japanese were an inconsequential lot, horse-flies at best, weavers and painters and some old boys better at sword play than artillery and guns. That was gospel according to ONI.

But in the dignitary's box at the bottom of Fort Street, in the crowd pressed along the wharf and in the royal pavilion, not a soul kept his seat. Even aboard the ships riding at anchor, the foreign flags, the crews crowded the rigging.

Tsukuba was impressively outfitted and armed. At a signal from her captain ashore, her sailors cast themselves off the yards like swooping gulls … and were caught on the lower yards by their shipmates, or they grasped a stay and pirouetted about it, launching from mizzen to main, all choreographed like a waltz. His heart pounded for them. Faster and faster they went until the sailors looked like blue and white streamers arcing from yard to yard and stay to stay. He couldn't make out one from the other, the bosun's commands setting their rhythm like a dance master, the pace increasing until the crowd around him couldn't bear it. They erupted in shouts and applause and cries of "Huzzah" or "*Hana hou,*" and from the fringes pistols were discharged into the air. In a final flurry seemingly every man was in flight, and then all stood on deck perfectly aligned along the port rail, not a uniform amiss. *Tsukuba*'s bosun blew his whistle, her crew presented arms and the entertainment concluded in a cannonade of red and yellow smoke to honor the kingdom's independence.

"O, Mr. Ramsey, have you ever seen the like?! My heart has not quieted yet, it's as though I await my entrance myself. I thought I would faint when those sailors cast themselves into the air." Jessica Mornay had his arm as they stood with the attaché adjacent to the royal pavilion.

He had not seen the like. *Tsukuba*'s crew were well-drilled and fearless. The combination was deadly. It was something to put your stock in, even aspire to.

The battery of minute guns atop Punch Bowl Crater answered *Tsukuba*'s cannonade with a burst of red and white chemicals, colors of the Japanese flag, and the ensign aboard the frigate dropped and raised smartly in acknowledgement. He stood on tiptoes to get a better estimate of her captain. The man's uniform made his own look cheap and plain. The captain executed a crisp sword salute and Kalakaua, wearing a straw boater and white linen suit, Queen Kapiolani beside him in a shapeless white garment, nodded warmly. He began assembling his next report to ONI.

Another murmur rose from the crowd. Fingers pointed, elbows prodded but he was lost in his own thought.

In the harbor the wisps of colored smoke parted, the prow of a fishing canoe poked through. The curtain veiling the monarchy seemed pushed aside and behind it a symbol of ancient Hawaii appeared – the Hawaii of Lono and Pele and all the gods and customs and beliefs which had been covered over in the wholesale adoption of *haole* ways.

Ashore the natives pressed forward. Lono's white totem flew defiantly among the western vessels at anchor. The craft was but a speck compared to them, but to every heart that longed for what had been lost the canoe swelled until it seemed like the whitest cloud upon which Lono sailed to redeem the islands.

– Or if not the god, for the canoe's occupant was too dark to be the god himself, then certainly a priest of the extinct Lono cult. He was round, sturdy, paddled expertly one hundred yards offshore and wore the gourd helmet of the cult – though it looked too small on his head – a length of green vine trailing from its crown.

The *kanaka* surged to follow the canoe's every move. They pushed mindlessly over one another, rousting Ramsey from his thoughts. They wailed. Not western sounds, he noticed. Not the approving noises they made for *Tsukuba*. This was native keening, ear-piercing, heart-wrenching.

He watched the canoe glide toward the king. Kalakaua rose in his box unsteadily, rubbing his eyes as if to erase what they told him. The closer drew the canoe, the greater grew the hysteria around him. Then it swerved. The paddler drove it hard. It disappeared into the lingering smoke and the crowd sagged as if the vessel, in retiring, took its breath away.

"Spectacular!" Jessica fanned herself, the color flushing her bosom. "Like the swan boat in *Lohengrin* disappearing into the mist! – Such aplume the king has!"

He pushed through the Chinese vendors at the edge of the crowd. "I don't believe that was part of the program," he called over his shoulder, anxious to get away. He thought what would befall him if it came to Taylor's attention – or Stevens' – that the heavyset paddler was in his employ.

Along Merchant Street hay wagons filled with baseballers and spectators for the two-mile trip to Punahou Field. He lifted Jessica onto the hay, her pantaloons showing beneath a calf-length skirt, their ribbons the same shade of green as her parasol. He commented on her appearance, wondering how she could afford the variety of wardrobe. "An actress is always auditioning," she said by way of explanation then added with a twinkle that the trim was for the colors of his own costume.

At the attaché's insistence he had joined the Pacifics Baseball Club and wore their uniform. Its cost set him back but it looked handsome, a white suit with a green satin "P" sewn on the breast pocket, and straw hat circled by a matching green band. Their play had been an embarrassment but the club looked to show itself against the Whangdoodles at Punahou Field.

He enjoyed the game. Most men played it in a slow, courtly manner. He found he could streak from a base and steal the next under the pitcher's nose. The risk-taking thrilled him, a reminder of his days galloping from jobs like a mail rider, the wind whipping back his sombrero.

Jessica had not seen a match and with knitted brow said his explanations were "compounding." She understood the strikes but since the ball was already a ball, she wondered if another name couldn't be found for those pitches of which the umpire disapproved. As for stealing, was it really fair, and should children be exposed to an occupation which encouraged it in their elders?

As the wagon rattled off he answered her questions. Punahou School had taken up the game to exhaust its rascally young charges, missionary heritage being no seal against devilishness. A Punahou man first played close to home base to help his pitcher and manufactured a padded glove to protect his hand. When he told her the batsman called for the pitch he wanted, Jessica frowned and looked at him intently. "Do you mean to say the batsman dictates to the pitcher? I cannot understand you, Mr. Ramsey, really. What if I were to dictate my notes to the conductor? Can you imagine? You take invention too far."

"The Whangdoodles play a devious pitcher I look forward to facing," he said. "William Wall, a raggedy scarecrow of a man, he throws something called a curve. It's a big slow thing that looks like it will strike you."

"My goodness, should that be allowed?"

"Well the batsman don't have to call for the curve, but I plan to. Wall struck out seventeen men in a single game two seasons ago. Seventeen men! – It was the Honolulus. That boy will discover I'm no Honolulan. I am a Missouri mule, and I kick!"

His blue eyes flashed and Jessica loved it.

Walter Gibson had invited the royal box to an Independence Day reception at his home across the street from the palace. The king saw everyone down from their carriages at his prime minister's door, a short drive from the wharf. Gibson's daughter Talula and her husband Fred Hayselden greeted them at the top of the garden walk, then Kalakaua begged to be excused, kissed his wife's hand and departed. He dreaded Gibson's parties, which he found strained, penurious affairs not easily milked for diversion.

The palace compound was nearly deserted when he entered on foot via the King Street gate. Royal Household Guards stood their posts, their brass and ornamentation playing brightly in the afternoon light. His guards still hadn't the Prussian rigor he observed in the personal retinue of European monarchs – the Household Guards mutinied when Lunalilo was king – but the two on duty executed sufficiently with their rifles as he mounted the steps and entered Iolani Palace.

He had conceived the King Street approach to stir his subjects to an appreciation of majesty. Majesty in him bestowed majesty upon them. The grounds were walled and gated, the carriage drive paved in pink crushed coral leading to an enormous staircase. The palace flared away from the entrance into matching Italianate wings of buff stone, each finishing in a tower capped by castle-like turrets. Open balconies laced the upper story so the royal family might address its subjects, and these were separated from the living quarters by real paned glass. He had furnished the interior in London, purchased his royal scepter and robes there and ordered a crown modeled after the Russian Czar's.

He sighed deeply as he entered the Library Room. Either he had not built magnificently enough or his people were impervious to improvement. He had aspired like a poet to turn them to their souls, but their intransigence had forced him into undignified stratagems and compromises.

Chun Lung waited, smoking.

He mixed a drink and took a moment with it before he let his dignity slip a notch further.

"Were you at the wharf just now?" he asked. No, Chun Lung had not been at the wharf. "The Japanese were tedious. Who minds that they fly from spar to spar like monkeys? The captain was so impressed with himself. Lord, I shall have to entertain him at the ball tonight. Did quite like the man's uniform, I must say. Don't think your *pake* tailor has anything over the Japanese, my friend." This was business, so he spoke as he liked.

"What I have to do for my people," he sighed. "I toady to the Japanese government so it will send its peasants to our fields. Thank God they are arriving at last. Good workers, you know, better than your people. They're obedient. They stay on the plantations. Your people leave their contracts first chance they get and move into town. Then I have sanitation problems and Gibson pesters me for another thousand to do something about it."

He took his time with his drink. Chun Lung would wait.

He finished it and said, "There is a small problem with your father's bid for the opium license."

Chun Lung did not practice the courtesies of his father, the indirect talk, the deferring to tradition, the tepid progress via allusion. "Bid? You mean award, don't you? My father expects me to return with the license."

"Tell Ah Fong when the legislature voted last month he was the only bidder. But another *hui* has come forward. Junius Kaae represents their group. They gave him $3,000 earnest money."

"What did they bid?"

He shrugged. "Let's just say they think the coolies will smoke more opium than your father thinks."

"Who is this *hui?*"

"Tong Kee. You know him?"

"The rice grower – he doesn't have money. He loses his crop one year and he's finished. He must have investors."

"Well, I don't know." He detested the back-and-forthing that money required. So much better for the Crown to be well-footed financially; hence the Pacific scheme he and Gibson hatched. "It's a *hui*, he's attracted investors, I don't know who they are. I thought your father had Chinatown under control. This sort of thing should not be happening. Now I have to deal with Tong Kee and you."

"Perhaps you would rather deal with Luahine?" Chun Lung consulted his manicure.

He set down his glass. "I thought you were not at the wharf."

"Did you think such good news would be kept from me?"

He scowled. "What could be good about it?"

"Why, Majesty," Chun Lung laughed, "the traditionalists have left their calling card, the god Lono himself! You are like Tennyson's poem: Luahine to the left of you, the missionary boys to the right of you. Into the Valley of Death ride the six hundred – except you don't have six hundred men, do you?"

"It was a repugnant display."

"I do not care what kind of display it was. It weakens you, that I know. Which means you need my father's money more than ever."

He could not argue. "By Christ, I do not know what the Chiefess and her fool priests can be on about. Do they think to take these islands back to the Stone Age?"

"I thought you approved of *lei* and grass skirts. It's quaint."

"You trifle with me. Remember, I am King. Of course there should be dance again. And music. Our culture is a vibrant one. Could your people have crossed a thousand miles of open ocean to trade? Not in a thousand years." He glared. "We were the world's foremost navigators. We sailed by the stars and the slap of the current upon the bow. The European still huddled filthy and ignorant in his cave. But High Chief Poloa crossed the southern seas to colonize these islands. We are proud, strong. Kamehameha and his warriors towered over Cook and his men. They thought him a giant. He caught fifty spears thrown at him. We are brother to the Aryan, cousin to the Hebrew, we are ancient as the Chin. I will not give power back to the priests. Their *kapu* laws are a tumor that grows in my throat. It shuts me off so I cannot speak!"

He refilled his glass.

Chun Lung opened his pocket watch. "I am expected at my father's in Nuuanu. The Merchant's Association paid for tonight's pyrotechnics. I want to enjoy them with him."

He spun around. "You will depart my presence when I give you leave! We will conclude this business!"

Chun Lung brushed an invisible speck from his sleeve. "Of course, Majesty. Only, I thought you and Tong Kee had reached an accommodation. My father would do nothing ill-mannered."

He composed himself. "What is your father prepared to pay for the opium license?"

"$80,000," Chun Lung said without hesitation. "No more negotiations, no more buyers."

"Tong Kee offers more."

"Then may your Majesty smoke a bowl with him and enjoy it." Chun Lung stood up.

He grabbed his sleeve. "The specie must be gold – U.S. gold coin."

He'd minted the Kalakaua dollar, the kingdom's first coinage, but he would not take payment in it. He'd had Spreckels oversee the minting in San Francisco – the Colonel had taken a handsome broker's fee – and the coins had entered circulation, his royal effigy on one side, the Coat of Arms on the other. But the kingdom had no gold reserves so the Kalakaua dollar quickly devalued, was currently worth about eighty cents, and was the object of derision on the part of merchants and industrialists.

Chun Lung smiled. "My father commissioned a necklace of Kalakaua dollars for his number two wife. He said there wasn't a better use for them. They seem to hold their shine."

He smiled in return. "How soon can you make the payment?"

"New Year is when we Chinese traditionally pay off our debts. That will be February on your calendar."

His smile hardened. "O, but you are resident of a westernized nation, my friend. You'll retire your debts in accord with our calendar. That's December Thirty-First."

Chun Lung looked him over thoughtfully. "The funds must be a great need to you, Majesty. To capitalize the *Kaimiloa*, is it?"

The gaze discomforted him, lighting too harshly the dark corners he was forced to traffic. "An aperitif would be most thoroughly enjoyed," he countered. "You were properly educated in them at Yale, weren't you? Once you escaped the Calvinists at Punahou? – A liberal aperitif, shall we say the next week or so?"

Chun Lung bobbed his head. Not a respectful bow, he thought. More a sardonic nod. "Majesty," the man said, and departed.

He exhaled. The Chinaman was quicker of mind, but he was monarch and still held the keys to the realm.

He mixed another drink, the 'Pulama' martini he'd invented. He had successfully auctioned control of the opium trade for $80,000, a substantial price. The money would capitalize *Kaimiloa*'s voyage to Samoa, first step in erecting his Pacific federation. It would keep both Luahine and the Hawaiian League at bay – and, as monarch of the Pacific, he'd have allies enough to weed the *haole* from his administration. But what was he going to tell Tong Kee?

He carried his drink into the Throne Room. Chandeliers drooped like pearl clusters from its scalloped ceiling. Polished native and imported woods gleamed from the walls, thick draperies and hardwood flooring provided accents. There were chairs for the Privy Council and shining on the dais, the twin gold thrones from which he and his queen presided over their subjects.

He knew it was grander by far than anything the Kamehamehas envisioned. He mounted his throne and sat silently awhile with his drink. Unconsciously, his wrist oscillated from side to side, as though he held the hoop of the child's game, *pala'ie*. Rhythm was required, and a flexible wrist, and a mind that could hold disparate objects in creative tension, in order to pass the ball on its cord back and forth through the *lauhala* hoop.

At the Royal School the Kamehameha heirs, wealthy and titled, had galloped their horses, wrestled and drank, and caroused their way one after the other to the throne. David Kalakaua stood to the side. He could not match their aggressiveness. But when it came to the ancestral teaching game, as the Kamehameha princes tried to bull their way through it, he studied and learned. The hand that grasped reins – of horse or government – in the conviction of a divine right to command, was not the hand subtle enough to balance the competing forces and pass the ball through the hoop.

Since 1874 subtlety had been the hallmark of his reign. By not claiming too much for himself he'd kept the competing forces in check. As a consequence he'd ruled longer than his Kamehameha predecessors. But in launching *Kaimiloa*, he reflected, he was changing. He was manipulating *pala'ie* in favor of himself and his dynasty. It was his right as monarch of an ancient and noble people, and it would benefit them. But it had its casualties – Spreckels, certainly; Gibson to come? And Tong Kee … and Tong Kee was not a gentleman.

"God in Heaven! I need the Pacific scheme to pay off!"

His voice came back to him in the empty Throne Room.

THIRTEEN

R amsey drove the team mercilessly the final miles to Ewa village. The last reach was up a long rise from sea level on the western lip of Pearl lagoon. It had rained and the footing was sloppy. The horses spilled froth around the bit and were heaving when he reined in outside the village wall. He grabbed Abner and had him walk the team to cool them down.

"But don't unhitch them, son. We're turning around directly I get Koloa into the wagon. And don't ever drive a rig like I just did. Somebody'll horsewhip you."

He hurdled over the wall, anxious to find Koloa.

But it was a very different village from the one he'd left. Laborers had arrived, they were transforming it into a vast arena for the Makahiki. And with them, musicians, dancers, chiefs and families from the surrounding villages. Not the Honolulu native, he realized. These were a little overwhelming in their numbers and seemed to puff up in dimension. The totems of European clothing had been put away – not a top hat, sailor's coat or the missionary Mother Hubbard, not even a boot. They appeared effervescent and purposeful, and out of their brown sinews he saw men arise, proud and naked save for their loin cloths; and women, their sex narrowly contained by a twist of *kapa* cloth.

He threaded through them, returning glare for dark-eyed glare, hand on the pistol in his belt. The village priest stopped him outside the hut, shaking his head. Koloa had been made *kapu* to the night's ceremony. The priest glanced nervously over his shoulder. Behind him stood a stern-looking tattooed warrior, arms folded.

"Thaddeus?" he asked, and the priest pointed in the direction of the *imu,* where a knot of men supervised the pig. Koloa's man squatted among them on his heels but stood and greeted him warmly. He'd been drinking.

"No worries," Thaddeus said about Koloa and thrust a bottle of beer into his hand.

At nightfall torches flared atop wooden staves. Their light spread from stanchion to stanchion over the village wall and onto the *pili* grass and wild cane like a flaming carpet spilling into the dark. Then a chorus of conch shells throated nearby. Koloa tried to get up from his litter but Ramsey standing on one side, Thaddeus on the other, restrained him.

Everyone else rose solemnly. Mothers and aunties held up the babies, and fathers and uncles placed the youngsters on their shoulders for a better look. Only the very old had ever witnessed such a procession.

A rank of *kahuna* carried *kahili* feathered in beautiful red and yellow. Behind them marched a phalanx of warriors girded in white *kapa.* They were muscled, healthy-looking. After them came the bearded priest bearing a stanchion eight feet in height, a white banner fluttering from its cross beam. It announced the high chiefess.

When she came into view the people breathed as one. For a moment there was silence, deep, full and entire – not a sound from the bullfrogs, the geckos, any of the night creatures. She looked positively regal. Shoulder-high upon her palanquin and wrapped in purple *kapa* cloth, she was a mountain of folded, ropey lava rock, complete, self-contained and inert. Then the emotion breached. The people swept toward her, she who seemed able to absorb in her huge figure all their broken-hearted aspiration. Their wailing shattered the night, resounded off the

Waianaes and turned toward the moon itself. The warriors shoved the crowd back, priests called for silence and ordered the people to sit, and she was helped to her feet.

Luahine surveyed the people. She had never addressed so many. She was anxious. Perspiration beaded in the fine hairs along her upper lip. The people did not rally to her readily, they never had. She was feared but not respected, they never loved her. She fingered the pouch containing the bat kits. If only she could just cast a spell. She could not face what the *menehune* prophesied.

The torchlight showed the near ranks. They looked hungry, needy, even demanding, like squalling infants. They wanted her to feed them. Clapping erupted out of the darkness. It built rhythmically then died away. The silence was worse.

She swallowed and shifted on her feet. Bringing Makahiki to Oahu island was her idea. The incident of the giant boar was a sign, she said. The priests opposed her. Pele's fire was the sign, they said. It poured out of Mauna Loa toward Hilo town. She must go to the Big Island and sacrifice herself to the goddess.

But if her gamble could win Oahu with just a little blood shed this night, it would stop her own blood boiling later.

A child ran out of the crowd, through the legs of the screening warriors and scooted toward her. Nervous laughter tittered in the girl's wake. Luahine scooped her up and held her aloft. The child giggled, the tension broke, and she heard a rising storm of whistling, clapping and shouted approval.

She raised her hand, her voice a rumbling drum. The people were her children, as was the little one in her arms. She had arrived to care for them. It would be a night to remember. All the generations would tell *mele* of it, for tonight fertility would return to the land and the people. Compose yourselves and receive, she said.

The boar was laid before her on a ceremonial bed of *ti* leaves, the meat falling off the smoking carcass. On either side the sea turtles, chickens, calabash loads of *poi*, sweet potato, fruit and other foods cascaded away. She had Ramsey and Koloa led to positions of honor, the prince on his litter, then she and her party sat and she signaled the village priest for the prayer.

The village priest swept his *kapu* stick across the waves of people. They had known hungry nights in their lives, he proclaimed, but this would not be one of them. The families and clans would share what they brought in the great *kokua* of the *luau*, but more than that, they would share in the great *mana* of the High Chiefess and her Makahiki movement.

"*I mua, e na koa!*" he declared in conclusion, "Forward, warriors, forward!"

Luahine, who had been meditating on the pig and the great feast she was about to enjoy, glanced up with a frown. The Kauai priests resented her warriors. By sacrificing her at Mauna Loa the priests hoped to take the movement away from them. But if all were one, if every Hawaiian looked on himself as a warrior ... she nodded her head in agreement. "*I mua, e na koa!*" the priest repeated, thrusting his *kapu* stick into the air. The people replied in ringing waves of Hawaiian, "*I mua, e na koa!* Forward, warriors, forward!"

Their response thrilled him and the Ewa priest raised his *kapu* stick to start another round, but the bearded priest stepped into the circle of torchlight and elbowed him aside. He would not cede leadership to a *kahuna* from Oahu. He quieted the people and turned them to their calabashes.

The feast began, and with it the entertainment. Luahine welcomed story tellers and dancers from the villages to the dance floor, where they vied with one another to capture the notice of the seething crowd. When they flagged or their execution was less than perfect, they were pushed aside and the next troupe planted itself in the center. She rewarded particularly well-told *mele* or ribald dance with grunts of approval and a slab of pig. One very popular young man she clasped into the cavern of her breasts and gave him a *lei* from her neck, to shouts of approval from the crowd.

She would not address herself directly to Ramsey, a *haole*, but she introduced him to *laulau*, a medley of meats and taro steamed in a *ti* leaf packet, and leaned her fleshy hulk against him until he ate it all with his fingers and washed it down with a full shell of *awa*.

Awa, extracted from the plant root, was not overly intoxicating, but western alcohol circulated through the assembly. Drunken voices rose beyond the circle of torchlight and she grew concerned. The people had climbed into her canoe at last, she did not want to lose them. She clapped her hands and the entertainers retired. Her Kauai warriors helped her up and she stepped into the center. Pakalana folded herself to one side with her drum.

Luahine's voice sang over the night. It became the red earth, the sharp volcanic rock, the small growing things that poked out after the storm. It was the strong-limbed trees, *koa, kukui, lauhala*, which surrendered their livelihood to the people. These were the gifts left by the gods. The people must be grateful, she said.

The crowd settled as she chanted. Grandmothers pulled the *keiki* children onto their laps. Wives sat back against their husbands.

Then a man called from the shadows, "Where are the gods to protect us from the *haole* now?" He had been drinking the western alcohol. "Why is Kalakaua permitted to sell the land? Why do the chiefs abandon *aloha*?"

Her warriors gripped him about the arms and forced him back into the darkness, but he had lit a fuse. Other voices called out. The people were poor. They were broken and afraid. Their elders had died off. For two pitiless generations they had wandered aimlessly in their own land. The paradise described in the chants had turned into a hard country which the chiefs sold by lots to businessmen. The Jehovah god told them to look instead for the paradise *i ka make*, the paradise that came after death.

Luahine stamped her foot. Those nearby felt it like *ola'i*, the tremors that accompanied Pele when she walked the land. The chiefess raised both arms and summoned the people like a school of darting reef fish. She stamped again and began to move in slow, graceful *hula*. Pakalana's hands followed her on the drum.

She sang to the people in a low chant whose three repeating notes were intended to remind them of their sacred heritage. They were the Navigators, she told them, weaned from the breast of Kanaloa in far-away Kahiki. Eight hundred generations marked the passage from the first settlements to the Kamehameha Dynasty. These could be recounted by the priests whose chants recorded the lineage of the people, recorded as well the paths over the trackless ocean by which the ancestors had traveled from one moon to another in their sailing canoes.

On these islands, from Kauai in the north to Big Island in the south the people had prospered. They had kept *kapu*. They had followed their chiefs. They had obeyed the priests. At the temples they had sacrificed as the rites prescribed: first fruits of the land and sea, and also men – the blood surged red and hot out of the temples and coursed through the land, pumped by Pele's ferocious heart. Blood brought fertility. It linked *mana*, strength, with *pono*, righteousness. It separated the Hawaiians from the *menehune* and forged Kanaka Maoli, The People.

Then the chiefs strayed from the blood. They lost the way of righteousness. *Pau ka pono, pau ka mana.* They turned to the White god, the bloodless *Iesu* who had not the *mana* to die himself but demanded instead the death of all their ways. Her voice rose into her nose as she sang of how the chiefs had committed the terrible desecration of Ai Noa, the day of free eating seventy *haole* years earlier that ended the old religion. Pele had been affronted, she had hidden herself away at Mauna Loa on the Big Island and the people had suffered.

Here the wailing from the people drowned her out. They knew too well their suffering, felt like poison the shame of walking as strangers in their own land.

She quieted them. "I fear I must sacrifice myself on your behalf." This was her gambit. If doubters remained, she must lure them like *lalana* the spider. "Aunty Pele shows her wrath. She pours down upon Hilo town. I must give my blood to spare yours."

She saw the priests nod to one another. It was as she planned. They wanted her sacrificed, it would strengthen the movement and they would be rid of her.

But she'd sprinkled her Kauai warriors among the families. "No!" they cried, standing one after the other. "*Hiki 'ole*! Never!"

"What's this?" She feigned surprise, glancing sidelong at the *kahuna*.

"You are our Chiefess!" a warrior shouted. "We forbid it!"

"But Aunty is *huhu* ..."

"Let the *kahuna* sacrifice themselves!" one of them called out of the night.

"They grow fat from our offerings," cried another. "Aunty will eat and be satisfied!"

Those who dared, laughed.

She held up her great arms for silence. "Then my people, you must rid yourselves of the *haole* ways. Reclaim your souls. Abandon the Jehovah god. You are warriors!"

The carpet of torches convulsed as Hawaiians uprooted the stanchions and waved them, roaring in agreement. The guard who had been standing protectively over Koloa shook *pololu* his long spear, bellowed and ran to join the crowd.

"Follow your chiefs!" she cried, and more torches rose in agreement.

Thaddeus, sensing the mood of the village, pulled Ramsey behind him for safety.

"Worship the gods!" Luahine chanted, and was answered in return by her warriors: "They are mighty!"

"*I mua!*" she said.

"*Na koa!*" the crowd responded.

"*I mua!*" she repeated.

"*Na koa!*" they roared in unison.

"Return to the days of *kapu!*" Her voice soared confidently but there was no answering assent. "Return to *kapu!*" she called again but at this there were murmurs and eyes looking askance, and obvious currents of disagreement.

The warriors assigned to whip up the crowd hesitated. They looked back at the High Chiefess for direction.

She stammered and glanced at the *kahuna*. They squatted on the side grinning with pleasure over her embarrassment. *Kapu* was too far a reach.

The voice of the bearded priest rang out. "Celebrate the Makahiki!" He gestured in the torchlight with the Makahiki pole. Its white banner undulated in the flickering light like Pele's mist. "Make the land fertile again!"

The murmurs died down.

Luahine saw her way. "Make the *people* fertile again!" she crowed.

Heads swung her direction. Could the High Chiefess really mean to vacate the laws of the missionaries?

"Make the people fertile again!" she said.

Old timers winked at one another and the priests could do nothing to stop her. Makahiki had not been observed in generations. It was a season of unabashed coupling. For a fortnight all restrictions were relaxed and every class pleasured itself to the point of exhaustion. Luahine had the crowd's attention now.

"*Ua mau ke ea o ka aina i ka pono,*" she chanted, "The life of the land is perpetuated in righteousness." It was the kingdom's motto. To honor the old ways, to restore *pono* to the land and people, she would sacrifice herself ... or she would pluck the kingdom's most precious flower.

Once "flower" – *pua*, in Hawaiian – floated from her lips, she seated herself and signaled a party of torch bearing Kauai warriors into the center. When they parted there stood alone before the craning assemblage a single dancer, a girl, hair long and glistening in the firelight. A crown of white ginger circled her head. A green *ti* leaf skirt hung from her hips. Her shoulders and breasts were naked.

Pua's heart thundered. She couldn't breathe. In seclusion for days, fasting, praying, worrying, fighting her own darkness, she was blinded now by light. Torches burned everywhere she turned. A field of them undulated before her, an enormous gathering of her people.

She trembled, the dark blood threatening to rise. Had she managed to purify herself enough to receive the goddess? Could she, in her nervousness, keep Kahu the sorceress at bay? Pele could enter her, find her weakened by the blood ...

The *pahu* growled and she closed her eyes, recalling Pakalana's teaching. She must invite blessing but like a canoe in strong current, submit to her fate. "*Ho'opomaika'i ia mai,*" she prayed. "May I be favored."

The drum began its beat and she opened her *hula*. Where Luahine's dance had been of the earth, of majesty and history, hers was sinuous and light. It was the water moving in pulsating rhythm from the buried reef to the cresting wave. It was the sea foam spreading its hair upon the bosom of the shore, the breeze carrying the ocean's yearning for the land.

She scooped low to show the waves tumbling over themselves, and Ramsey devoured her. He could not restrain himself. She was breathtaking. She held her golden arms still for a beat and he spotted the tattoo on her shoulder. It dawned on him. This girl, this heart stopping girl, the one from the canoe ...

She bent her knees and he sucked in his breath. The movements and the syncopation of the drum released something deep inside. It was sexual and freeing. She was so alluring. Her shimmering flesh seemed to promise earth and sky at once. Her hands were strong and determined, lips soft and yielding, hair swaying in the torchlight as though alive. He had been offered native girls and declined them all. This one, God help him, against all nature he wanted.

He watched her dance his direction. Her leaf skirt parted, exposing her thigh muscle and calf on each step of the dance. Her light brown areola approached him, peeking out of the swaying tips of her raven-colored hair. His throat tightened. He couldn't swallow.

He felt Thaddeus elbow him. "You get plenty *mana* now."

Pua relaxed. The people stared up at her spellbound, appreciative. She swung around as the *hula* required and saw a large form hunched before her. It had to be her mother – her mother, and she wasn't frightened. She swung around again, dancing the Hula Pahu with passion. Pele's fire did not enter her, she knew it. The fire did not seize her. She was not changed. Pele chose not to dwell inside her, but she did still live. The goddess tolerated her dance though she herself was not yet an acceptable vessel.

Pakalana had warned her. "You must dance this time, Pua. Dance the Hula Pahu no matter what happens. You have learned well, so do not fear. Pele does not enter every time – even the most sublime dancer, she does not send her fire each time. The dancer is not consumed, she does not see the flames, does not hear the shrieks. Sometimes the goddess just prefers to watch and be entertained. *A'a i ka hula* – just dance!"

The *pahu* growled and she danced. She sank into the bent knee stance, hips steady, arms straight and strong as twin peaks. She felt heat, her own heat, rising out of her belly. It spread through her and filled each formal step of the dance with molten, sinistral, female power. Her hair swept across her shoulders alive, her eyes burst with light.

She danced, transitioning gracefully into second and third positions with scarcely a thought. Her body felt young, strong and quick. She swayed closer to Luahine and her party, as the *hula* required. The torches flickered and she made out Prince Koloa next to a *haole* whose eyes shot at her like sparks.

Ramsey wiped his brow. The dancer seemed to direct herself only to him. "*Mana*," Thaddeus said. He possessed it after the boar, more than another man. Makahiki, season to indulge … He imagined touching the girl. He'd touch her in ways he'd heard about, ways a White woman would not permit.

The girl drew closer, the dance mannered, formal, angular. Its rigidity, mixed with her succulence, made an irresistible combination. He could not divide the drum from the pulse throbbing in his head. She was shadowy, dusky. He wanted to enter her hidden folds.

She paused, smiled, and plucked a flower from her headdress. She held it out, her hand small, shapely and lovely. He swallowed hard. She had heard of his prowess. He struggled to sit up. But as he straightened his tunic, damning the fit which did not flatter him, the hand crossed before his face and tossed the flower to Koloa. The prince caught it, nodded his head and slipped it behind his ear.

Koloa? The girl was known to Koloa? He turned just as her hair fell forward like a curtain. A tiny smile dimpled her face.

Luahine's voice boomed and the chiefess was on her feet. Her Hawaiian flew rapid and imperious. He saw her thrust her *kapu* stick at Pakalana and Koloa. The dancer prostrated herself.

He opened his hands to Thaddeus. What is it? "*Ua pau ka pono.*" Thaddeus shook his head. "This one *hula make* dead. Luahine no like the girl make *moemoe* wit' Prince Koloa. His *mana pau hana,* no good."

Luahine embraced the people with her arms as she spoke.

"Luahine like *kapu* everyt'ing," Thaddeus translated. "She *kapu* this girl, give to the brother. This old style. Much *mana* for Luahine, the sister make *moemoe* wit' the brother. By 'm' by, she get more *mana* than the priests." Thaddeus shrugged. "Too bad Ramsey, you no can *kapu* this girl. But get plenty more, yeah?"

He was dumbfounded. "She gives her own daughter to sleep with her own son?"

"Get plenty *mana.* Old style."

"But this is ... it's so ... Who is the brother?"

He stared where Thaddeus indicated. The figure was round and familiar looking, but the torches lit him indistinctly. He couldn't quite make him out. Then the man stepped from the shadows clad in a white covering.

Ramsey gaped wide-eyed. "But that's my houseboy," he blurted. "He can't have this woman!"

The bearded chief took Manu by the arm. Luahine prayed over Pua then draped the two in orange *lehua* blossoms. Brother and sister were led off to a *kapa*-encased booth erected beyond the circle of torchlight.

Koloa got up stiffly and, leaning on Thaddeus' arm, disappeared into the dark.

The chiefess settled next to him with a grunt. She signaled for singers and musicians and pulled the cheek off the great head of the pig for him. Her breast crushed against his arm. She gestured that he should eat then laughed and pushed him playfully on the shoulder. She began eating herself, the food traveling to her mouth in an uninterrupted current. She swallowed, belched and continued.

The frivolity returned and the noise level grew. A stout *kanaka* with a shriveled left arm pushed his way into the circle of entertainers. The warriors sitting next to the chiefess stirred at the offense, but Luahine was working through a mound of *opihi,* tiny shellfish whose meat had to be sucked from the shell, and she took no notice. With a shout the *kanaka* lit torches and juggled them with his good arm and a foot until he had five going, and the people dared him to add one more. "*Hana hou!*" they called, "*Hana hou!*"

He seethed. He had not known Hawaiians were such a low Race. Incest – it revolted him that a man in his own keeping should commit it. The sin violated nature, it was like a White man taking up with the Colored. It happened with the Colored, God knows it happened, but you didn't encourage it. You passed laws against it. New Orleans was more liberal, but not where he came from. Where he came from the hoods came out. A man had to show restraint, it was gospel and right. It addled him elstwise, he couldn't stop himself. It addled his whole family. It was like a disease. It would rot you. He'd seen it.

He should quit the firelight he realized, and return to the hut. But the girl was so tempting ... so strong, yet so yielding; in her duskiness, the lure of the shadow, of the unknown. Manu would be investing himself upon her now, his own houseboy. The thought was unbearable. His throat turned dry imagining what must be found beneath her leaf skirt. It would be dark, mysterious and somehow transporting. He was strong enough to indulge but he would not succumb. He could sink into the dusk and still return. He could remain true to his Race.

The bearded priest strode onto the dance platform. He held up a length of white *kapa* cloth. Its center was scored by a red blotch. The people applauded and shouted their approval. They directed cries of encouragement toward the booth occupied by sister sacrificed to brother, to the end that *pono* was restored. "*Hana hou!*" they called, "*Hana hou!*"

Luahine examined the cloth. The blood was fresh, not much of it, much less than Pele would have demanded of her. Yet it was enough to bring the people to her and still the griping *kahuna* like lizards in the sun. She grunted, her labor accomplished and wiped the blood on her cheek.

Ramsey had enough. He found his way back to the hut, shouldering through arms that invited him in the dark.

Makahiki continued for days, and Kanaka Maoli found many ways to harvest its fruits.

FOURTEEN

Walter Gibson forced himself to remain on his knees inhaling the familiar incense, the sanctuary long emptied from the eleven o'clock Mass, his tired head resting on the pew in front, his boney frame angled and uncomfortable in the narrow space, the notes of the Advent Season hymns still settling in his chest. Intended to prepare the faithful for the birth of the Savior, their sentiments had splintered upon his unmoved heart.

He did not attend the church of the royals and blue stocking capitalists, Saint Andrew's; nor the church of the nobles and commoners, Kawaiahao. Nor did he attend the church of the missionaries and their upstarts which, after the Chinatown fire consumed Bethel Union, was Fort Street Church. He attended Our Lady of Peace, the Roman Catholic Cathedral located on Beretania Street.

It was the church of Mother Marianne whose Franciscan Sisters tended the lepers at the Kaka'ako receiving station on the edge of Honolulu. The nuns had been invited from America by Kalakaua, one of his ideas no one had challenged, and after his first encounter with her steady, no-nonsense black eyes, Gibson realized he loved Mother Marianne with all the ardor of a straw-haired youth.

He coughed painfully and glanced upward at the stained glass windows, a recent addition for which he had contributed a purse. His doctor was bleeding him, had prescribed cocaine and applied thapsia plasters to his papery chest. But no doctor could physic what ailed him now. Mother Marianne had been unaccountably absent from both Masses, and there was no solace for him.

He tiptoed out of the church.

Respectable Honolulu was quiet of a Sunday. In this the New England missionaries had succeeded in conforming Hawaiian exuberance to Calvinist mores. The waterfront's swatch of ramshackle storefronts did not close for God or man so long as a vessel floated in the harbor roads. But the upright citizens who identified their lives with the town *mauka*, to the mountain side of the waterfront – its low-roofed bungalows, its whitewashed houses of commerce, its foreign missions, seat of government, and big houses inland benefitting from the sanitation enforced by Gibson's administration – these citizens passed their Sunday mornings in church, their forenoons calling and their Sunday afternoons dining with family.

Such citizens were appearing now on the avenues as he made his way to the Convent of St. Francis. His path crossed Hotel Street then King then inclined toward the waterfront and Kaka'ako. He was recognized often and greeted each salutation with a nod and tip of the hat. Some constituents wanted his ear, a breach of Sunday manners, but more he would not give them. The image of an unblemished face, framed into a perfect oval by its starched wimple, quickened his step. The thought that it might be distressed in any manner was a distress to him.

Earlier in the day he had sent a boy with a fish pie and a pudding for the Sisters' dinner and a live turkey on a tether to be kept for Christmas day. There should have been a note of gratitude in her own hand by return. The very notion that his Marianne might be abed unable to enjoy her dinner, the notion that she might – God forefend – have fallen prey to the plague that had brought them together, the thought punished him without mercy. *"Ave Maria,"* he whispered, *"gratia plena."*

"Gibson!" A shay pulled by a light gray horse stopped at the curbstone. "Get in." John Stevens made room for him on the seat.

"Mr. Minister, I –"

"You go to the convent, I know. I'll drive you. Get in. There is a matter to discuss."

Stevens pulled the convertible over them for privacy and touched the whip to the horse's flank.

"I had not realized you were returned," Gibson said.

"Yesterday, hellish crossing from San Francisco. The *Lurline*, I missed the steamer. The Colonel insisted on luncheon with his wife."

"A formidable woman."

"If you prefer your Teutonic types."

He felt the barb. Mother Marianne, though she took the veil in New York, was German born.

"That damned volcano," Stevens went on, "it's still acting up, you know. Painted the whole skyline like some inferno. The Chinese crew refused to go up the yards, the heathens."

He looked at him questioningly.

Stevens slowed the gig as a pair of inebriated sailors tilted in front of them. "We got blown off-course. Never seen such a storm. Took the foremast with it. That ass of a captain was probably drinking. By the time we got righted we were off the coast of Hilo. He wanted to put in for repairs but I insisted. You could see the lava radiating. It keeps flowing, it will engulf the port."

"It will stop, I have every confidence."

"The damn *kahuna* are turning it into a test, you realize."

"I have every church in the kingdom praying for Hilo's deliverance."

Stevens shook his head. "I am a more practical man, Gibson. If Hilo burns the native will see it as a victory – punishment for the Colonel and every westerner who has an enterprise. It's bad enough the palace can't contain Luahine."

"What would you have me do? There's never been such a lengthy eruption."

"Build a wall to stop it, I don't know. I am responsible for American lives and property. My government expects you to do more than pray."

"Perhaps your government would invest the capital to protect its nationals properly."

Stevens halted the gig. "O, I like that, Mr. Prime Minister. I like that very much. My government invest capital? As you have gone whoring after capital in London?" Stevens laughed. "Do not look so surprised. Did you really think the Kingdom could approach the British for a loan and we not learn of it? I carry a letter from Colonel Spreckels." Stevens handed him a packet and urged the horse on. "I'll save you the trouble of having to read it of a Sunday. The Colonel has recalled his paper. Did you think you could go abroad without consulting him? Want to make the British your friends, he demands immediate repayment on all his notes to the Kingdom." Stevens laughed again. "I think that effectively bankrupts you, my friend. Unless, of course, you can get the local men of means to support your administration – Castle and Dole, and Charles Bishop. Bishop should help you, he's a banker. And the Kingdom's largest private landholder, is he not? Except, of course, his allegiance is to the Kamehameha line. He views Kalakaua as an upstart."

He turned the packet over. He recognized the seal. It was Spreckels' own.

"O, it is authentic, Gibson, never fear. When you read it you will hear the Colonel's voice. It is halting and accented when he speaks, but when it comes to a written contract, he is a locomotive under steam. I think you shall want to heed him." Stevens threw back the convertible. "Perhaps you'll prefer to get out here, eh? A stiff walk clears the head. I must find an errant sailor."

Gibson stepped down and did not look back. He could feel the man gloating. The news was catastrophic, Stevens was right. Spreckels had the power to bring the kingdom to its knees. Charles Bishop could extend a line of credit, but he doubted he would. The *haole* banker had received all the lands of the Kamehameha line when his wife, Princess Pauahi died. He mourned her incessantly and only had a mind for erecting a fitting memorial.

"Mistah Gibson."

He did not recognize the voice or the face. It was fleshy, Chinese and dark, that of the Hakka people. Chun Lung and his father, the fairer Punti Cantonese, detested them.

He had entered the hospital grounds where repairs were being made to the Kapiolani Girls Home for the Nonleprous Children of Leprous Parents. It was the Sisters' conception and he readily backed it. The Chinaman addressed him from behind a shoulder-high stack of lumber. He wore a gray soft hat that was not in fashion, and a dark western suit.

He held up his stick. "I have no purse to give you, sir, nothing!"

The man revealed himself. "The King, he like I bring this one chop chop. My name Tong Kee."

"The King? He is touring the Kingdom."

"Yes, he tell me Waipahu-side bring this one chop chop. You take him." Tong Kee placed a slender package on the stack of lumber. It was wrapped neatly in newspaper and tied with sisal. Gibson realized it was currency.

He had urged the king away from the palace to do what he did so well, rally the natives in the outlying districts. He spoke to them not as king but as *kanaka*, one of them. He sang the *mele* – many written by him or his sister, and set to western melodies – that recounted their proud heritage, and he poured plenty of gin and placed a calabash of Kalakaua coins in the midst of the *luau*. The tactic had won elections and secured a pliant legislature. He needed friendly natives now to counter Luahine's movement.

"You take him," Tong Kee repeated, tapping the package of money. "I take license. Sell much opium."

"But the license, the King already …"

Tong Kee placed a second and third package next to the first. "The King tell me give you."

The Chinese lifted his hat and walked away, leaving the packages on top of the lumber. He slipped them inside his coat pocket.

At dusk Ramsey let Stevens follow him to the waterfront. Then he turned quickly through a dingy alley – it was an escape he had practiced – and disappeared. Moments later he merged with the Sunday strollers and circled back for a quick stop at his bungalow.

The admiral's dispatch had arrived by the steamer the American Minister failed to catch. It disclosed the London loan application and Colonel Spreckels' intention to call his own bank notes. Spreckels wasn't breaking the economy, just turning Kalakaua to heel.

The particulars weren't his business, their effect upon Stevens was. The Colonel shopped the Pacific like a market stall. He stuffed mail service into his net, and steamship lines, the sugar trade and governments purchased with his loans. Stevens couldn't get his hands on them, only Pearl River, which turned upon the Reciprocity Treaty. The minister could squeeze profit out of that and was already the worst kind of hag, shrieking at the marketplace because the best deals were gone. He couldn't stand to hear more out of the man. He had his own deal he'd been nurturing.

Everything lay in order upon his cot next to an overnight bag: change of clothing, grooming products, rain cloak, bottle of champagne, orchid on the stem. He added a slim volume of love poems by Jose Maria de Heredia, which he could read in Spanish and had used to good effect since Valparaiso. He preferred mechanical books and biographies, and was largely self-taught – his mother's house slave Sarah could read and schooled him in his letters – but in New

Orleans he'd discovered how susceptible a certain class of female was to literature.

The champagne was warm as ice was a commodity in Honolulu, but two hospitality franchises located at opposite ends of Hotel Street, the Hawaiian Hotel and Madam Ho's, could be relied upon for their supply. He headed for one of them.

The fire that devastated Chinatown earlier in the year had broken out on a Sunday when laborers flooded the district from the plantation fields. A clutch of *mah jong* players in an upstairs room, drinking, gambling and arguing over their tiles, kicked over a brazier and the closely packed buildings went up like kindling. The fire blazed out of control and roared west from Smith Street toward Nuuanu Stream. China Fire Engine Company No. 2, financed by Chun Lung and his father, was quickly overwhelmed. The *haole* fire company responded, as did detachments of British sailors, while Kalakaua himself stood in the acrid smoke and storm of flames directing volunteers, but by nightfall what had once been the heart of the city below Beretania Street was a smoking ruin. Eight thousand Chinese were homeless.

Only two structures remained standing. One was the Temperance Fountain built amidst the saloons of old Fid Street, out of which zealots had for years hectored sailors on liberty from the world's navies. The other was Madam Ho's. Pundits claimed divine intervention had saved the one, the feverish workings of men had narrowly rescued the other – and praise the Lord, God had gotten to Madam Ho's first, pristine and unassailed as it was.

"John darlin', it's good to see you." He was greeted with a warm hug and wet kiss on the mouth. He smelled frangipani and ginger in a brew of transporting aromas. "*E komo mai*, sugar, come in and rest your ol' self."

Sienna Robichon was his favorite woman. He'd crossed swords with her in a Gallatin Street saloon after the war. She was petite and sassy, and the figure which had been hard and mannish, and which she'd plumped with scarves in New Orleans, had turned soft and womanly with age and Hawaiian food. Her hair was thick, wavy and auburn from an Irish ancestor somewhere, and her eyes green.

"Carl, fetch Mr. Ramsey's bag and champagne – is it a good vintage, John, dear? Take it upstairs and ice it, Carl, he'll have the Ilima Suite. Come with me into the bar, John, while Carl freshens your room. I want you to have the best tonight."

Sienna led him through a corridor into the salon, explaining it was part of the post-fire expansion she was engineering, and still under construction. More Persian than Chinese in decor, when finished it would cosset the girls on an enormous red ottoman, or in more cozy loveseats nestled beneath leafy green potted ferns. The walls were covered in gold fabric etched in green, and the carpet, also gold, had been laid, and the bar installed. It ran the length of the shorter wall, dark mahogany with a brass foot rail and tall stools covered in red leather. The back bar mirror, imported from Venice, leaned in a crate against it.

He looked around appreciatively. "Well, if this don't take the rag off the bush. There's more gold in here than Lafitte's, Sienna." It was the house in the French Quarter where she had set up their marks.

"My mama would have been horrified but the gents'll love it. You know what I always say."

He grinned. "Make a man feel good before you pick his pocket."

"That's right, cher. Somethin' for everybody that way. Otherwise you're just a damn thief, no better than a Yankee."

He laughed and hugged her.

Sienna was New Orleans Creole, French by way of her mother, who had a small estate in Faubourg Ste. Marie, and Spanish by way of her planter father, a refugee from the Haitian slave revolt, but she'd lost both in the epidemic of 1858. She fell victim to her surviving uncle's abuse, and during the war to his collaboration with the Federal occupation until General Butler's Order No. 28, which proclaimed that any young female persisting in public contempt of a Union officer would be arrested and charged as a town woman plying her trade. Since her uncle pressed himself upon her as though she plied the trade already, she thought to gain some satisfaction in it and therefore persisted in Union contempt quite publicly.

By 1872 she'd grown seasoned, and at twenty-five was still thought attractive enough to rule her patch of Gallatin and its swampy holes of lust, lice and licentiousness, though few on the street knew she snuck over to the convent when she could and helped the Ursulines educate the orphan girls. It had been her school during the better days and made her feel better about herself. White sat alongside Colored as she taught, no one the worse for it.

John Ramsey, when he wandered onto Gallatin one thick summer evening, reminded her of her charges. He was wiry and ragged and hungry for a better hand to play, but unlike the orphan girls, he bore a pocketful of stolen coins. His predilections gave her an idea and thereafter she teased information out of government men in bed, and he and his gang of highwaymen acted on it. Their business bloomed until the Federals closed the city when the White Leaguers rioted and seized New Orleans two years later. The Yankee major, crazed with bloodlust, who had her by the hair sick with fever and crying aloud for help, would have killed her had John not appeared, frantic while flames licked around the public buildings. He did not give the man a chance to run. He just sighted along the length of his extended left arm and the revolver exploded.

Sienna pushed leather scraps off one of the bar stools and sat him on it. "Drink?" she asked, reaching for a jug of bourbon.

He shook his head.

"It's Kentucky, John. I only carry the Tennessee because of the customers."

"I'm already stretched, Sienna, what's this night costing me?"

"That mountain pride, John, I swear. It's got nothing to do with us."

After the shooting he'd snuck her across the river by barge then held her a night, a day and another night in a hayloft, while she shook out the fever under a horse blanket. He cooled her forehead with his bandana and whispered in her ear, "You have to live, Sienna. You have to."

She slid a full tumbler to him. "Drink this down now. I took you on as family, you're my *lagniappe*, the nuns would say. Remember when we split up, ahead of the Blue Bellies? What we swore?" She tossed off her drink. "O, that's good. *Okole maluna*, cher. Drink up."

He swallowed the corn mash, savoring the charcoal and the painful trail when it sluiced down his throat. "That is good," he said. "So, you must be calling your own shots around here, if that Oriental lets you stock moonlikker like this."

"She's better 'n biscuits, cher. Moved to Macau a few years back. Sends her banker like clockwork though. Man works for Chun Ah Fong, you heard of him yet? Ah Fong and Colonel Spreckels bankroll the kingdom. Kalakaua cannot hold a dollar."

Madam Ho's did not start as a brothel. It was an emporium built by the widow of a merchant murdered during the gold rush in California. She named it proudly and eponymously like Madam Tussaud's, but discovered there was more profit in following the demands of the market – sailors on shore leave arrived at all hours, drunkenly demanding the whores promised by the name. In no time Madam Ho's made its owner a very wealthy woman and one of the celebrated denizens of an earthy, dappled Honolulu the missionaries could not rub out.

She had an eye for talent and spotted Sienna's many skills after she presented herself broke on the doorstep in 1877. Five years later the American was managing the house, and by 1884 the original Madam Ho felt comfortable enough to retire.

Ramsey gazed about the salon. "I should have partnered with you, Sienna. I'd be wealthy now, and prominent."

She laughed and poured again. "I don't know how prominent."

"I do. I caught word of you soon as I landed."

"Don't you know? A broke-down hooker is every gent's best friend. You'd be surprised the things they tell me."

"I am. And very grateful for what you pass along to me."

"Drink up, John. Enjoy yourself."

"Sienna Robichon, I just know you are tryin' to befuddle me before this evenin's very important engagement," he said, all magnolia and glowing.

She ran a painted nail along his scar. "A pistol shot would not distract a lady in your arms, darlin'."

He saluted her with his glass and swallowed.

"There is something I want to talk to you about." She led him by the hand to one of the loveseats. He brushed aside the fronds to sit. "You are playing with fire out here, and it worries me."

"Taylor?" He snorted. "Navy's full of men like him. Had his war, now he don't know what to do with his mean self. Should be put to pasture."

"I don't mean Taylor. I'm talking about the U.S. Minister. He frightens me, him and the missionary boys he goes around with."

He nodded. "Stevens knows about me, Sienna. I can't let him find out about you."

"Johnny, I could fly out of here like a good hurricane. I have money. I could go to Macau. But you –"

"It's a job, Sienna. We put it over on the Federals back home, we can do it again."

"There's somethin' disturbing about Stevens. He comes in here every so often. He's a looker, you know? A patron at the zoo, but won't feed the animals. Drinks his liquor, never touches the girls, sometimes Carl lifts him drunk into my buggy to get home."

"He thinks he's got my head in a noose, but I'm watching, Sienna. He'll make his mistake, then I've got him."

"I wish you'd quit all this, John. Come with me to Macau."

"I'm not quitting, Sienna. Getting out here is my chance. You 'n me, we've run from people like him all our lives. Or we've licked their boots. But no more. It's a new world out here. The Pacific, it's the next frontier. I aim to make something of myself. These boys will carve it up like they did the South after the war. But ONI, I play my cards right, I won't be sneaking through the back door to rob somebody's purse. I'll be sitting at the table this time."

At dusk he took a lamp and mounted the stairs to his suite. The corridor was shadowy and not quite finished, but his suite was everything Sienna had promised. It even had its own bath. The furnishings were contemporary: a chaise, upholstered arm-chairs, a Tiffany lamp and a pillar bed with posts capped by carved pineapples, symbol of hospitality. The windows looked west over the burnt hide of Chinatown where the lights of the workmen's camps winked. He stood for a moment before them, a hawk scouting the landscape, then pulled the drapes to block the sight. Tonight was for romance.

Carl, a tall Negro – he hadn't seen another in the kingdom – brought the champagne in a bucket, a bottle of brandy "compliments of the house, Mr. John," and a chilled seafood supper. Ramsey poured a finger of the brandy and just as he grew impatient, there came a faint knock at the door.

There she was, in his room. The low gaslights made her look fetching indeed. She pulled a thin scarf from her head – could she afford silk? – and smiled prettily.

"I hope I have the pleasure of Mr. Ramsey's company," she said. "It is so shadowy in this room, and a girl must be weary of her reputation, mustn't she?"

"Ramsey it is," he replied and poured her a flute of champagne. "United States Navy, ma'am. What could be more trustworthy?"

Jessica Mornay laughed. He thought it one of her best features. The vocal training turned her laugh into musical notes that tinkled down the scale like clear crystals.

She placed her things on the table. He had courted her – *a dozen red roses, and _dinner_, Mother!!* – and Jessica, a chorus girl with aspirations, wanted to believe him. A Navy man – he was a Petty Officer, certainly that meant something – could help her career, couldn't he? And he was charming, and those blue eyes when they darted down her bosom were oh, so exciting.

They toasted with the champagne and she told him eagerly about Nellie Melba, the operatic sensation from Australia. Miss Melba was a few years longer in the profession, her star on the rise. She had passed through Honolulu on her way to Europe where she would sing principal roles. It was inspiring to think that a girl from an ordinary background could aspire to the greatest stages and the most dazzling roles in theater. Jessica hoped with a little money and a little luck, one day her Navy beau might see her in the spotlight instead of the chorus.

He knew to be patient. They supped and drank and chatted. Jessica had learned to pick crab in San Francisco and dug in with the silver tool. If the adjacent rooms were occupied he did not know it, didn't think she did either. They were alone in the night.

After the supper and the wine she drew back the curtains. Even the remains of Chinatown looked romantic, an occasional lantern flickering in the blackness like a firefly.

He softened his voice and read from the poetry book:

> *Never have I so deeply felt as now*
> *The hopeless solitude, the abandonment,*
> *The anguish of a loveless life. Alas!*
> *How can the impassioned, the unfrozen heart*
> *Be happy without love? I would that one*
> *Beautiful, — worthy to be loved and joined*
> *In love with me, — now shared my lonely walk*
> *On this tremendous brink.*

Then he stood close at the window and slipped his arm around her. "The promontory, Jessica," he whispered.

When they kissed it was tender as a heartbeat. Jessica liked that his skin was smooth beneath his sideburns. She nuzzled the basin of his throat and recognized the smells: rose water and shaving soap and tobacco. There'd been a boy before this and he'd made promises after then disappeared. She'd had to leave Ohio. But John. John Ramsey was a man, he smelled like her father.

He liked the way she softened against him. There were places on a woman's body – he'd been schooled in New Orleans; they should be addressed, like you moved through interesting passageways from the outer courtyard to the inner sanctum. He took pleasure in the proper reverence paid at each stop. By the time he guided her to the bed her skin was electric with desire and her eyes pooled with each kiss. There were four layers of clothing to be removed and while she would not let him slip off the final one, it was flimsy and unstructured so as to mimic every yielding contour of her body. It was silk and pure white, and it matched the perfection of her sloping limbs and curving bosom. "Purchased it in San Francisco with my first earned money," she giggled and kissed him.

He kissed her back. He used his tongue inside her mouth the way the French girl liked. Jessica withdrew and he felt her body tense, surprised in his arms. He knew this was point of no return. She would submit to him, he'd have her his way. He pressed on her heavily with his weight, probed again with his tongue and she surrendered, he could feel it in her body, releasing from the top of her head to the soles of her feet, as though she'd exhaled completely into him, and her every breath now belonged to him. Her fingers knitted behind his head and she pulled his mouth deeper into hers, his tongue become the sex organ itself. When they separated so he could do other things with his tongue and fingers, she still had breath to groan, a sigh that escaped a reservoir of pleasure somewhere deep in her belly.

She lay beneath him, arms open, thighs akimbo, not only her will, but her body an invitation. He saw her nipples beneath the garment, hard, erect. Erect as he himself was. He squeezed them and she writhed, sounds like small beasts erupting from her. He circled his fingers toward the mound between her thighs. He could see her pubic hair press against the translus-cent material with every thrust of her pelvis. She had never been treated like this, he knew it. Had never been teased with release like a wild thing on a leash, never been stroked like her flesh was the gentle, vulnerable skin of a babe, never been fiddled like the subtlest and most musical of instruments. When his finger lighted there, the secret place the French girl revealed to him, she whimpered then cried, then cried out, eyes shut tight in the agony of pleasure, hands clutching his hand so when he took his finger teasingly from its home, she struggled with it to return it where she demanded.

He rose from her to strip down to his union suit. She was now in as much a hurry as he, but he slowed. Deliberately. She opened her eyes, cried for him to get on with it, but he quenched the cry with another deep, draining insertion of his tongue. When he stood again to remove his britches, she was limp, her own will now sapped, his to do with as he pleased. Except for the sheath she wore. From somewhere she was able to resurrect a last principle, and she pulled it down to her thighs when he lifted it so he could behold her, all of her, her flesh from pubis through panting belly to breasts like clouds to catch his head, all of it an undulating testament to beautiful, flawless, pure whiteness.

"No ..." she whispered, "please ... please come ... please."

She opened her eyes and they were liquid pools of desire, of heartfelt plea, of a soul begging to spill forth. It touched his heart. He sank into her arms and sank into all of her, deep and honest and straight as it was possible for him to be. And she folded around him like a flower both responding to invasion and relieved, so relieved to receive that for which it had hungered and was perfectly designed.

For Ramsey, the purity drove out Taylor and Stevens and Ewa village, and for the moment, all the demons which had cluttered his life since his eyes first filled with horror in Missouri so long before.

She stayed in his bed until dawn. They talked and dozed. He described the research for the Navy without disclosing his secret work at Pearl River. They made love once more and when she cried out on and on, she dug her nails into his back so he bled. Then she kissed him, pulled the curtain to the bath and cleaned herself, dressed then slipped down the stairs and out the Hotel Street door.

He fell into a deep sleep and when the knock came, it was Carl rousing him for breakfast.

"Downstairs, suh. In the sunroom. I'll have your coffee soon as it boils."

He washed his face, cleaned his teeth, prepared his hair and entered the sun room wearing white linen trousers, open collared shirt and a satisfied look, feeling far away from the Navy and duty. He expected Sienna to greet him with one of her brassy questions. Instead he saw Manu seated at the table in a shaft of sunlight sipping coffee out of a china cup.

"I suspect that is my Arbuckle's you are drinking."

Manu shrugged. "No *huhu*, boss. You like Carl bring you one oddah one?"

"You seem to know your way around Madam Ho's." He seated himself across the table.

Manu shrugged again and grinned.

"You're not really a houseboy, are you Manu?"

"Not exactly, boss."

"I didn't think so. And you don't have to torture me with that Pidgin English, do you."

"I thought you would expect it."

Carl brought more coffee, a sweet bread called *pan duce* introduced by the Portuguese laborers, and a mound of banana, sliced mango and melon.

"What do you want, Manu? I was expecting a more fetching companion at my breakfast – not a man who has relations with his sister."

Manu frowned. "Don't be ignorant," he said and helped himself to the *pan duce*. "I want you to do something – in your 'unofficial' capacity."

"I don't enjoy being toyed with, Manu."

"You've heard of *Kaimiloa*?"

"Of course," he replied. "Another of your King's excesses. Wants a navy, of all things. Honestly, Manu, have your people no sense at all? Stuck between grass and hay all their lives?"

Manu grunted. "It's worse than that. When *Kaimiloa* sails, she'll be carrying letters of confederation to the King of Samoa. It's Gibson's idea, first step in a plan to establish a Pacific empire."

His eyes narrowed. An independent Hawaii was acceptable to the Navy. A powerful Hawaii was not.

"No one knows about it. Not the Limeys, the Frenchies or the Krauts. And your government's intelligence service is, well ..." Manu sipped his coffee.

"I suppose you've been reading other people's mail again."

"Let's just say my organization is more highly motivated than yours. The survival of my people is at issue."

"Well I'm obliged for the information," he said. "It will win me a promotion and I can afford a real houseboy. But why have you chosen to bless me with this treasure? I tried to treat you miserably."

"You cannot believe how I tried not to, but there seems no other way. Koloa pulled away from us – after the *luau*."

He sipped his coffee, the phantasm of the dancer in the flickering torchlight replacing with disturbing ease the more immediate image of Jessica in his bed. "I'm not surprised," he said hoarsely.

"So I need your help to stop *Kaimiloa*. The monarchy led my people into poverty, think what a Pacific empire will do."

He shook his head. "When the Great Powers get wind of this, they'll seal off the Pacific to the Tropic of Capricorn. *Kaimiloa* won't get near Samoa or any other port."

"It can't be done that way, Ramsey. Not with the Navy. It will turn Kalakaua into a tragic figure, a heroic chief in the eyes of my people. I'm giving you the information in trust. We're sort of brothers, aren't we? There's a better way."

He did not want to accept a thing from Manu, not in a coon's age; not if the roof leaked, the creek rose and his was the last boat on earth. But the Hawaiian sat across the table because Sienna trusted him. And he trusted Sienna.

Kaimiloa sailed at the end of December with Prince Koloa and, as head of the delegation, J.E. Bush, a Hawaiian noble, Manu said.

"Bush? The inebriate?"

"Exactly. King Malietoa insists upon sobriety at his court. Says alcohol and syphilis are the only bullets the West ever needed."

"You want Bush drunk."

"Full as a tick for every high-level meeting. It will take Kalakaua by the lees and sink any chance of a Pacific federation."

He swirled his cup. "You have my admiration, Manu. But what's it to me? You're not getting me onboard."

"No. I want you to get me onboard."

He looked into the man's eyes. They were opaque and hard. He scratched a match and lit a cigar. "It's a Hawaiian ship. Can't Koloa do it?"

"I told you, my mother alienated him."

"Won't he oppose you then?"

"We're at sea, what's he going to do? Anything could happen to him, he's still knitting from the wound. Besides, he has hopes for my sister."

"You surprise me, Manu. You're as calculating as I am. Willing to intimidate a prince. I've done as much. Title seldom breeds character in my experience. Though I must say, I took a liking to Koloa. But auctioning off your sister like a brood mare? – You surpass me, I give it to you."

"My people have a combat art, Ramsey. We call it *Lua*. I am a practitioner. A warrior knew three hundred ways to break a bone or dislocate a joint. The *Lua* master could appear anywhere on the battlefield, and in any guise. – For the life of my people, I am on the battlefield, and I will assume any guise. Now, will you get me aboard that ship?"

"I must admit it is a pleasure having you nag me for something other than money. But how exactly does helping you help me? My people are not the Hawaiian."

"No, your people are not. You have no people, Ramsey, not really. You have your ambition. Why should you help me? I think you know why. And I think you have already decided to help me, else you would have left the table."

He grinned and nodded. "Yes, I'll get you aboard that ship. I'll get you aboard because I'll promise Commander Taylor I have placed a spy aboard *Kaimiloa*, who will leak to me everything that transpires on the mission before the palace first hears of it. – You will do that, Manu."

"Yes, I will."

"… But that only helps me a little. You must do me one more thing."

"Making you right with your boss is plenty, Ramsey."

"One more thing or the deal is off. Pearl River, I can't get in there. Something keeps happening. Koloa says it's got a spell. A White man can't get in without one of your damned bead counters."

"He's right."

"Get me in there or the deal is off. I want Pearl River."

"You want it for you or for Stevens?"

"What difference does it make?"

Manu pursed his lips. "So, you've become one of them, Ramsey. You've joined the Punahou boys. If you had a soul, I'd say you'd sold it."

"What'd you just tell me – you're on the battlefield, you'll wear any guise. What's a man's soul got to do with it?"

"I said I was doing it for my people, Ramsey. What are you doing it for?"

"Look, Manu, I'm through wandering around that swamp like a runaway nigger. Get me in there or the deal is off."

"*Ke hele i ka li'ula* – we have this saying, Ramsey. You chase a shadow in the twilight, you become the shadow yourself. Chase after Pu'uloa all you wish. I will not give it to you. It's sacred."

"I won't give you *Kaimiloa*, Manu."

"Fine. I'm a warrior. I'll find another way."

"Fine. You came looking for me, Manu. I didn't come for you. Now if you don't mind, I wish to finish my breakfast in peace."

Manu got up.

"And by the way, you're fired. Get yourself another houseboy job."

"You don't fire me. I quit."

FIFTEEN

Ramsey had no soft luggage of puffed up memories to haul into Christmas Day. He prepared to observe it in his bungalow, puzzling over his predicament at Pearl River. Stevens demanded results and he had none to show; their last meeting devolved into threats and counter threats, and had it not taken place on the hotel veranda he'd have garroted the man with his dinner napkin and been done with it. He was a hound off the scent. Instruments had disappeared at Pearl River, the leg of his tripod snapped, he'd taken a bad fall and he'd had to divert funds from Taylor's survey work upcountry to rebuild his camp along the lagoon after a heavy storm. He planned to review the few notes he had then dress and meet Jessica for supper at the Hawaiian Hotel.

The knock at his door was an intrusion, the invitation presented by the bicycle messenger even worse. Had the note not been from Sienna, he'd have torn it up.

Other efforts at cataloging Pearl lagoon had run aground before his. The Germans landed a survey party that disappeared, never kept the rendezvous. An American engineer, prey to a string of devilish occurrences, took the funds he'd raised and absconded to Tahiti.

Their failures only motivated him the more. That he seemed destined to join them in failure, and to remain further subject to John Stevens, fueled the rising irritation he carried into the dazzling new King Street entry to Madam Ho's. It led over a goldfish pond to a bright red lacquer door imported from Shanghai.

He was greeted by a Portuguese girl, in vogue just now, and an American whose family had disappeared during an Indian raid in the Dakota Territory. He suspected they were friendly with one another when customers were not in attendance, something Madam Ho had not tolerated but Sienna did. They were drinking already and greeted him with wet kisses and a plumeria *lei* then seated him on a fabric loveseat in the sun room. A sheaf of heliconia, red torch ginger and colorful bird of paradise stood in a corner vase, lending a festive air.

Sienna swept in. Her auburn hair was high on her head, her green eyes mirthful as ever, and she had applied color to her cheeks and lips. "John, you're here! Something to drink, sugar? Have an eggnog with me! *Mele Kalikimaka* – Merry Christmas!" She kissed him on the lips and called Carl to mix the drinks.

"What's this all about, Sienna?" he asked.

She seated herself next to him. The mauve empire line garment she wore did much to favor her bosom and hide her thickening waist. "Now John, it is Christmas Day. Put away that mean spirit of yours. Time for some enjoyment."

Carl brought the drinks in chilled silver cups. Nutmeg dotted the milky foam.

"Thank you, Carl," she said. "Have one yourself in the pantry. Here John, you'll like this. Carl makes them. None of that horrible Yankee rum. Give me hickory and smoke, the glands of an old possum and whiskey enough to know what you're drinking! *Okole maluna,*" she added, and they toasted one another.

"I have a gift for you, John. I think you're going to like it, though it comes with a price."

He looked at her guardedly. He and Sienna were closer than family. They never exchanged gifts. The idea seemed trifling after all they had lived through. "You realize I have nothing for you."

"John, I expected nothing different. You have done something extraordinary for that young singer? I am certain you have. What is her name?"

"Miss Mornay."

"Mornay, oh, yes. An attractive young woman, as I recall. But they all look so young to me! And what have you done for her?"

"I'll see her for supper this evening."

"Supper, is it?"

"I believe that is sufficient."

"'Sufficient,' is it? O, come, John, where is the dashing cavalier I know? What are your feelings for the girl, anyway? – Have an understanding with her?"

"Of course there is no understanding between us – that is, we understand there will be no ..."

"No future, John? You think she understands that, do you?"

"Yes, she understands. Her tour with the opera company will be over in a month or two, she'll return to San Francisco. And she understands I could be reassigned at any moment."

"Still the paramour, never the 'amour,' I see."

He looked at Sienna again. He was accustomed to the verbal jousts with her but this was unusual. "You have the bit between your teeth, Sienna. Where you off to with it?"

She got up from the loveseat and rang a little bell. "You have treated the singer well, John? You know how I feel about that."

"As well as ever I do. You know how *I* feel about that. – And I don't want another drink, Sienna. I have work to do, and yes, I want time to dress for Miss Mornay tonight."

"That wasn't Carl I rang for," she said. "I rang for your gift."

With a soft rustle of skirts the Hawaiian girl appeared before him. Her hair was thick, black and gleaming, and it hung to the middle of her back. She wore a pleated white long sleeved blouse with mother-of-pearl buttons, a dark skirt over bloomers that stretched to her ankles, and she was barefoot. Her single ornament was a red hibiscus flower in her hair. The aromas of ginger, fern and rainforest swam around her. She stood with head and eyes lowered.

He looked from her to Sienna. On reflex, he stood up.

"Your gift, John. Not from me, but from Manu. I sent him off. Pua is a young lady, I told him I wanted to speak to you about her."

At the sound of her name the girl lifted her head and looked frankly in his eyes. He had never seen them before, never been close enough to see how clear they were, hazel colored, how deep and innocent, how receptive they were.

"Manu has been a good friend to me," Sienna said. "I gather you have been your usual ornery self with him. I thought you were a better judge of character. You should be able to tell swamp gas from mist."

He glanced at the girl and squirmed uncomfortably. "He was my houseboy," he mumbled.

"And you treated him like a field hand. I know it, John. Don't try to argue. Now, he said you two have some kind of arrangement. You had the stronger hand to play, so he dropped off the girl – that's what he said."

He looked up, mouth open. "The stronger hand … ?"

"Don't you always, John? Now listen, Manu said you'd know what he expects, but I want you to know what I expect. Yes, she can work with you at Pearl River."

He was still off balance. "Work with me? I don't understand, Sienna."

"Well I don't either, John. Manu said you need help. Now, I know you don't hold no truck with the Colored. Maybe bein' out here has unbuttoned your collar a might, maybe it hasn't. But this girl will get you into Pearl River. She's got *pono*, as the Hawaiians say."

"I don't hold with all that voodoo talk."

"Suit yourself, cher. Manu just said take care of what you owe him. But I want you to hear what I have to say. The girl can work with you. It will help her English, she's picked up a little. You'll pay her of course, and you will treat her civil – civil, John. She's really unspoiled, never seen anything like it. She will stay here with me where I can keep an eye on her, and the girls can teach her about grooming. She don't know a thing, it's as though she's lived in the convent. Go ahead, John, speak to her, don't be an intimidating ass."

His throat was dry. "Good evening, Miss, uh, that is ..." He did not know how to address her.

The girl curtsied, the movement looking graceful and natural on her. "Happy meeting Mr. Ramsey. *Pehea 'oe?*" Her voice sounded shy and endearing. "*O Pua ko`u inoa.*"

"Use your English, darlin'. Remember how I taught you?"

She nodded and composed herself. "I am Pua, Mistah Ramsey."

"Pua," Ramsey said. "... Miss Pua." He bowed but did not take his eyes from her.

"'A gift,' Manu said, like for Christmas. I don't know what he meant by that, but I know what I mean. You need someone more than yourself to think about, John. It's good for you. Perhaps it will help you think again about poor Miss Mornay and your 'understanding.'"

When he last saw her the night was warm and close. Flickering torches lighted up the scene like a guttering inferno. The drum coughed a bestial pulse and the girl had been nearly naked, glistening brown flesh exposed by every slow movement danced to its beat. It had been an alien setting, a threatening riptide, a dark island of seduction adrift from the main. Now she stood clothed, motionless, in the daylight of Sienna's parlor.

There was no drumbeat. But he felt the same heat.

"And John, Manu tells me this girl's a virgin. She's still a flower, '*pua*' the natives say."

At the sound of her name the girl curtsied again. "*O Pua ko`u inoa*, Mistah Ramsey. I am Pua for you."

SIXTEEN

The last night of the year arrived emphatically. The afternoon grew overcast, the sun slipped below the horizon unnoticed and suddenly it was black, lightless night. It matched Kalakaua's mood.

He descended to the palace library early, an hour or more before he would present his queen at her birthday *luau*, and hours before Luahine would make her entrance. The chiefess would time it, he was certain, to maximum effect. In shirtsleeves he mixed a drink and stared glumly out the window. A bit of business more to transact before 1886 could retire.

There was much to boast of in the year: a trade balance unmatched by the U.S. or Great Britain – sugar the most of it, but also wool from Gibson's ranch on Lanai island, rice, coffee, bananas, beef and hides; Honolulu's alleys were largely cleared of wild dog packs and the prime minister's sanitation measures were reducing flea, tick and rat infestations; and he had reason to believe America's Congress would renew the Reciprocity Treaty. But the business that remained tasted *pilau*, sour in his mouth.

Through the palace window the King Street gate appeared unusually crowded with on-lookers. Word had spread of

Luahine's attendance at the *luau*. Most had tied red scarves about their necks.

He flexed his wrist. *Pala'ie*. The deft touch from the child's game was needed tonight to balance the tide of popular sentiment flowing toward the chiefess.

At 8:30 the Marshal of Household connected the switch and the palace grounds awoke in a moon-like glow of electrical illumination. The bulbs were suspended on flimsy wires strung between trees and when the wind sighed they pendulated, sending long skeletal shadows cavorting across the grounds. He stepped behind the curtain to observe his people's reaction. Those who had not witnessed the phenomenon were transfixed. A few crossed themselves. He shook his head. They were forever enthralled to the missionary god.

Soon the first carriages arrived. Kerosene wicks burned at their corners like running lights on black wheeled ships. The people jostled to see who rode in each. He could make out the shouted greetings when a merchant was recognized, or a noble.

He heard footsteps and turned from the window.

"Your Highness, we are prepared to conclude this business?" Chun Lung did not bow.

Breathing shallowly, he pointed to a chair. "We are."

Opium was the common ingredient in many curatives but Honolulu society was opposed to legalizing the drug. The Anglican Bishop published a sermon claiming it produced indolence and sterility. The missionary party, decrying the growing number of intermarriages with Chinese men, feared it was a devilish aphrodisiac that led White women astray.

He detested the habit but needed the money to send *Kaimiloa* to the South Pacific. The *Pacific Commercial Advertiser* advocated that the opium license be sold at public auction to avoid "the odium and suspicion of corruption." But he wanted to award it to a Chinese, and he wanted to award it himself.

He mixed another drink. "You are not dressed for the festivities tonight."

"No, with apologies to Her Majesty. My father is agreeable to helping the government with its finances. I think the figure for the license is more than generous –"

"In gold coin?" he interrupted.

"In gold coin, of course – so our business is *pau*. But my father's courtesy can no longer extend to the royal family. The landing fees are an affront and should be eliminated."

The current legislature had imposed a fee upon the Chinese whenever they docked in Hawaiian territory. A merchant paid it each time he returned from business in San Francisco or Canton Province.

"The legislature are always on the look-out for revenues," he said diffidently. He knew the legislature planned to raise the tax to ten dollars.

"The legislature are discriminatory."

He had to admit the truth in that. Only the Chinese paid it, no other nationality was taxed. "I'll see what I can do," he said.

"Contract laborers are treated like animals. The foremen, the *luna* use handcuffs and whips on some plantations. In Peru the coolies were caged. America has banned all Chinese immigration; too many of us in California, the newspapers say. I was called a nigger when I attended Yale."

"The *haole* are cruel."

"Not just the *haole*. My father expects change, real change for his money. So do I."

"Your father is being granted a lucrative contract."

"When you have money you realize a man's morals are more important. That's Confucian. Society should be in harmony."

"I couldn't agree more," the king said, feeling heavy.

Chun Lung got up. "My family have made a gift of silk fabric to Her Majesty. The queen will represent us in London? Perhaps she will have it sewn into a gown for her travels. The silk is *makana*, for her birthday." He added as he departed, "Once my father sees that a man's words are proved by his actions, he will reacquaint himself with the royal family."

He returned to the window. One more bit of sordidness remained in Eighty-Six. He had to woo Luahine. The thought was more repulsive than auctioning the opium license, but if he was to lead his people to independence …

"Do not lean too far forward, my King," his sister Liliu had said to him, gently but pointedly earlier in the day. He was taking the morning air with the queen at Hale Akala, the casual family bungalow adjacent to the palace. It was wood-framed and homey, a comfortable counterpoint to Iolani's stony formality.

He and Kapiolani reclined on deck chairs set in the garden. Tree fern screened them from the public and golden finches chirruped overhead. The queen had imported them from the Orient and released them in the garden. Retainers waved nets on bamboo poles to protect them from the squawking predatory mynah birds.

Liliu called upon them to give her answer. She would accompany Kapiolani to Queen Victoria's Jubilee, she said.

He stood and expressed gratitude. His queen did not speak English and would not represent the kingdom abroad without proper escort. Liliu accepted a rattan chair next to him.

He was reserved around his sister, their relationship strained. Conservative and Christian, she did not read the political situation as he did. She was friendlier to the *haole*. "If Victoria will receive you publicly, London's bankers are certain to favor our loan. The dynasty depends upon it. It is fuel for *Kaimiloa*'s voyages."

"*Nā holokai?*" the queen asked and caught Liliu's eye. "Voyages," he had said.

He sat and released a plume of blue smoke into the air. "*Hiki no*, certainly. Samoa first to our federation then other Pacific kingdoms. Tahiti of course, also the Loyalty Islands, and why not the Emperor again, Japan? But this time aboard our own flag."

He saw the women exchange a look. Kapiolani cleared her throat. "Ambition, My Chief, the elders eschewed it. It is not the way of The People."

They fastened their eyes upon him. They would not oppose him, not directly. They'd peck around the edges. They'd intimate, they'd remind, they'd hold up a wet finger to tradition, hope to modify, like a new berry added to a batch of dye.

He enjoyed the game.

"Ambition ... Chief Kaiana was ambitious, was he not?" He leaned forward, elbows on his knees. "*Pololu* his long spear brought Kamehameha his victories, until he fell under the gaze of the queen and became ambitious with another spear altogether. Perhaps I am only *ho'opiha*, ambitious that the spear of the islands should grow long as the gods will indulge it." He chuckled.

"You lean forward, Brother," Liliu said. "But *kiku*, is it not wise to lean back in the canoe?"

She invoked one of his favorite metaphors, but he was ready for her. "Ah! You see! The navigator leans back. The paddlers lean forward to catch the wave. '*I mua!*' they chant. Now is the time to lean forward. And you must paddle, paddle with me, send our long spear across the Pacific. Paddle hard!"

"And if the paddle splinters from our exertions?"

"Aye," his queen said. "A splintered paddle does not drive the canoe, then your long spear withers. Perhaps we must grow it another way."

Her eyes danced at him. She had not given him an heir, but he did enjoy their intimate moments. She was clever, and clever with her wit. "You distract me, wife. *Pono 'ole.*" He shook his finger. "Unfair!"

He reflected for a moment ... the kingdom's "Law of the Splintered Paddle," observed in the breach since Kamehameha instituted it, for few modern chiefs took care of the destitute. The law had to be updated. Self-reliance was called for now, not charity. Self-reliance to contend with the *haole*. "Consider," he said, "the paddle is only as strong as its splinters. Does the sailor not temper his paddle? He does. Each splinter of the paddle – the Hawaiian, the Tahitian, the Samoan – we must harden each splinter so the paddle drives the canoe of the Pacific before the wave. That, or the wave overwhelms us."

A retainer dislodged a particularly determined mynah, and it flew to the palace roof, complaining loudly of its lost chance at a golden morsel for breakfast.

"Perhaps we can no longer protect every finch, eh?" He pointed into the air and settled his boater over his eyes.

"But Brother, without protection can the Queen's poor finch survive? Can The People?"

He had tired of the game. In the morning sun, in the comfort of the palace gardens on the eve of his queen's nativity, the last day of the *haole* year, he felt secure in his stratagems. He would auction the opium contract. He would win Luahine to his cause. *I mua*! He would launch *Kaimiloa*, it was the tip of his long spear. *Pala'ie*, the child's hoop – he saw it tilting away from the *haole* and toward his people at last. The People.

"Sqraw! Sqraw! Sqraw!" he cried, scrabbling out of the chair and flapping around the women like the pesky mynah, while they shooed him from their bonnets and laughed, enjoying their king without the kingdom upon his shoulders.

Standing in the palace window, Chun Lung gone into the night, he sighed. The weight of rule sat upon him once more. Soon Luahine would flood his Throne Room for the queen's ball. He wondered if, once there, she could be removed. In the morning in the garden he had felt like the mynah. Now he wondered if he weren't rather the finch, his dreams a mouthful of golden feathers.

"*I mua*," he said half-heartedly and raised his glass to Eight-Seven. If he could not toast it in hopeful anticipation, he could at least drink to it.

SEVENTEEN

"He is so often at sea, Mother, My Brave Captain, how the Navy contends upon him – and the Nation!" 'Captain' was more easily understood in her letters than 'Petty Officer' – who had ever heard of the rank? – and Jessica was so certain of their future together. "Won't he solicitate Father at his next leave! You'll be so proud!" But she knew from theater that love benefitted from artifice, so she determined to powder it generously at her first royal ball. She wore the gown her mother did not know about and improved the cleavage with the rouge she took from makeup, and rehearsed her most coquettish laugh, all to entice Mr. Ramsey – or if not him then others, for competition had rushed more than one man to the altar.

Her plan opened thrillingly. She was announced on the arm of the Junior Naval Attaché at the Queen's Birthday Luau at Iolani Palace. They paused in the warm halo of lamp light on the veranda. Heady perfumes wafted out of the gardens below. It was a conspicuous location and she held her escort there. Her tinkling laugh – she rehearsed it – the cut to her gown and the maneuvers of her fan brought eager suitors for the cotillion after supper, and her dance card filled rapidly.

"I'll take the polonaise," she heard John grumble under his breath, but even that was stolen from him by the more determined Chilean ambassador.

"Shall I save you the waltz? Mother says an unattached girl shouldn't, it is so suggestive."

"Save me the waltz. But remember, I am working."

She worked her fan. He sounded terribly official.

Lorrin Thurston presented himself outfitted in the dress uniform of the Honolulu Rifles, moustache coaxed into martial points, long strands of brown hair arranged to cover his thinning crown. He handed her a flute of champagne, toasted her then had the waiter pour again.

She grew confident with the wine. A royal ball was nothing other than grand opera, it was curtsies and smiles and flickering wrists. "Who's bigger, Mr. Thurston, a baron or an earl?" She curtsied deeply and directed his eyes with the tip of her fan.

Ramsey watched her performance sourly. He had to keep alert. Kalakaua was meeting Luahine for the first time. How the king handled her would foreshadow the kingdom's future, and his own. His third dispatch to ONI had been a warning. A destabilized monarchy would not fall into American hands as the admirals hoped. It would be scooped up by businessmen – missionary sons and Claus Spreckels, or whatever cabal controlled Stevens. He had to proceed carefully, he wrote in code.

He had to proceed carefully because Stevens in power meant he'd never be free. He'd never escape the investigation unless he murdered again. His alternative was the king. The king had to manage Luahine skillfully, keep her close to counter the businessmen, but not too close.

"He's made his entrance at last. See? Always caparisoned like a black stallion." Thurston placed his hand on the small of Jessica's back and directed her attention to the king. Kalakaua had costumed gallantly and wore a great cravat in the green *mokihana* pattern, flower of Kauai, his queen's island.

"O, he is not his portrait," Jessica said, disappointed. "His portrait is attractive."

"He has lost his verve," Thurston commented.

"He seems sad."

Ramsey was concerned. Kalakaua looked off his feed. "It's just the torchlight," he said without conviction.

Thurston whispered noisily to Jessica, "Have you heard what they say about him?"

She drew closer. Thurston circled his arm about her waist. "Kalakaua is not a native. He's the bastard of a Negro blacksmith, Blossom was the man's name. You can see it in his brow."

She looked up at his moustaches. "But if he's not Hawaiian, how could he be made king, Mr. Thurston?"

"Just the question Mr. Thurston cannot answer." Ramsey took her arm. "Should we tour the gardens?"

"O, but I can answer," Thurston said. He did not release Jessica, and she hid her smile behind her fan. "It's the native himself. Knows no more about government than the Negro. Consequently a man sits the throne that is twice ignorant: he's an ignorant native, and he's an ignorant Black."

"I figure ignorance is color blind, Thurston. You're forcing the King to hitch his wagon to Luahine. No wonder the man looks done in." He did not move from Jessica's side. Her eyes glowed with the attention, and he saw the color which spread across her bosom when she grew excited.

"He does that tonight, Ramsey, and you'll see what my kind does about it. We won't allow the Kingdom to drive off a cliff. Our fathers sacrificed too much."

The band struck up the Mikado's entrance from the latest Gilbert and Sullivan operetta, and the king, appreciating the humor, bowed theatrically to the assembly.

"O, that's more like it!" Jessica exclaimed and applauded him. She hummed along, and the king noticed her. He dispatched Major Antone Rosa, the kingdom's Portuguese-Hawaiian Attorney General. "Delightful, Miss Mornay! The King loves a jovial tune," Rosa said with a bow.

Thurston cursed under his breath and wheeled toward the clique of businessmen, nearly overturning a waiter as he went.

"He ran like he was snake-bit, Major. You got some voodoo for him?" Ramsey drawled. "I'd like to purchase a vial or two."

162

Rosa smiled. "It's Luahine. She makes the *haole* a little *pupule* – crazy."

"They say she knows witchcraft," he said.

Jessica slipped her arm through his. "Can there really be such a thing, Major? My father is a doctor, you know."

"The islands are still a land different from your country, Miss Mornay, no matter what we may import from you."

"I trust the King's got some good voodoo for Luahine." He meant it.

Rosa smiled again. "We call it *mana*, Mr. Ramsey."

Kalakaua worried. Luahine nettled yet titillated him. She was a throwback, a throb of nature and a fierce warning. He was only a generation removed from *kapu*. Each upland swale and volcanic promontory still had its djinni – he had put many of them to music – and each tale connected his generation of Hawaiian not to a history but to a *lei* exuding the essence of Hawaii. It encircled god, native dweller and land in a necklace of *pono*, of righteousness – he was writing a book to that effect.

The *lei* sat lightly on the shoulders, he hoped the book would convey that. But governing was another matter. To govern in a *haole* world the *lei* had to be removed. All the nobles had to, and most prospered – in large measure from his policies. But they suffered, too. The nation's Father, he saw it. Each day when the sun rose upon the islands, its disc in transit erased more of their identity as The People. The lifestyle of *aloha* drained through their fingers like sand. It turned melancholy those of rank, despite their public smiles, for they were close enough to the past to know what was being lost. The *lei* of righteousness was dying.

Except when it encircled Luahine – that was evident the moment she appeared. His queen turned him from his guests, he signaled the Marshal of Household and a trumpet blared from the band to quiet the crowd. Then a conch sounded and her palanquin bore the chiefess before him.

She was everything he'd heard. Enormous, regal in her own right, imperious, a monstrous Kahu, a threat to everything he'd worked for ... and he needed her.

He watched the little play unfold. He'd choreographed it to the minute. Kapiolani greeted the chiefess with *mokihana* in honor of the Kauai heritage they shared. Princess Liliu draped her in strands of crown flower, a symbol of royalty and her own favorite. The marshal proclaimed her lineage, welcoming Luahine formally as *ohana* to Kapiolani and sister to Kalakaua. It wasn't true, but family was an elastic notion.

All according to plan.

Then the marshal took a step toward the chiefess and extolled her devotion to Pele. "You have reminded us of what we lost," he said.

He clenched his fists. This was not according to plan. He did not want Pele worship encouraged, it aggravated the missionary party unnecessarily. He glanced at the businessmen and saw Thurston react.

He intended to speak after Luahine. He'd balance whatever she might upset. But balance had to be restored now. He needed the *haole* asleep while *Kaimiloa* went about her work. He cleared his throat loudly and gestured the marshal aside. He fluffed his whiskers and announced the induction of the chiefess into Hale Naua. His all-Hawaiian philosophical society, the businessmen did not feel threatened by it.

High Chiefess Luahine was being granted the prestigious rank of Keeper of the Sacred Fire, he stated, the first to hold the office. It required her indoctrination into secrets more arcane than even Freemasonry possessed.

The nobles made noises of approval. Antone Rosa presented her with the blue sash and badge of office. Then the marshal approached holding two flaring torches. The torch was the symbol of his dynasty, Kalakaua said. With the torch of the High Chiefess burning alongside his, the shadows of ignorance, despair and oppression would vanish forever from the land.

Ramsey watched Luahine carefully. On her litter she allowed Rosa to settle the sash over her person, and she signaled her crier to accept the torch from Kalakaua. But she never changed her stolid expression, and he could not determine if she understood how thoroughly the king was using her.

He thought the king was doing well. He had stepped away from the business elite and given ground to Luahine without ceding anything substantial. If the chiefess wanted only recognition without power, she would be satisfied. Kalakaua would house her at one of his Oahu estates, place her on the royal payroll and she would pass the remainder of her days in comfort.

He saw Kalakaua finish by kissing the chiefess on both cheeks. Then the king mobilized the musicians to move the party along. Ramsey nodded appreciatively. Start the music and deny the chiefess a forum – a smart stratagem.

But Luahine was surprisingly spry. She uncoiled from the palanquin before the band leader could struggle to his feet.

At that, waiters stopped passing among the guests. Menials appeared from behind drapery and at doorways set ajar. He saw their faces glow as if absorbing the enormity of her, an *ali'i* belonging to them, fully in command in an alien setting.

The chiefess wore yards and yards of plain green *kapa* that finished below her knees. Her hair was oiled and long, her visage marred as if from combat, the flesh on her arms substantial and firm. Her attendants, sturdy warriors, scarred and wearing red *malo*, were at either elbow, but she stood a pace in front of them and spoke without moving, as though her tremendous size fixed her in place. Her voice filled the chamber. As she went on the walls seemed to dissolve, and her listeners were carried back to the islands the god Maui had dragged out of the sea with his hook.

She praised Kalakaua for preserving Hawaiian culture. Music and dance were sacred and had been bequeathed the people for the good of their soul. She called on the *kama 'aina*, the native-born to dedicate their children to the arts and to return their girls to the classical dancing schools. She sang a chant for Kalakaua: "*Ohia mai ā pau pono nā 'ike kumu o Hawaii,*" which urged him to gather up "every bit of the traditional knowledge of Hawaii." It was his obligation as Father to the People, she said.

It was already a principle of his reign, and Kalakaua nodded guardedly. Perhaps the chiefess had decided to paddle in his canoe after all.

Then she raised her arm.

E Pele, eia ka 'ohelo 'au;
e taumaha aku wau 'ia 'oe,
e 'ai ho'i au tetahi.

It was the traditional chant offering Pele the *'ohelo* berry made *kapu* to her. By reciting it Luahine declared herself in continuity with traditions that took precedence over any king or noble. The ancient practices coupled the people to Kumulipo, first husband and Po'ele, first wife, the two arising out of the slime by lightless night. From these first parents all else descended.

Thus in a breath Luahine unseated the Kalakaua dynasty and turned all her listeners, whether local or foreign born, into commoners and children.

With her next breath she began the story of the islands. Their birth was not gentle but violent, she said. The land exploded into life furiously and the ocean, far from providing a mothering womb, tore at it without mercy. Both were relentless. The watery god Kanaloa surged against the molten insinuations into his realm, and Pele just as ardently extended her fiery hair into the sea.

The impassioned, often destructive interplay of opposites was the Hawaiian's conception of life. It was a cycle without destination or meaning. It simply was, serene as the lap of a gentle swell upon golden sands, or monstrous as *kai e'e*, the tidal wave that destroyed a coastal village. Living so had made the people strong before the Whites, and very independent. – Too independent, Luahine said. Island refused to ally with island, noble family with noble family. They battled one another.

Luahine's rumbling tones filled the palace chamber. "To the god Maui was assigned the task of uniting all the islands." She spoke slowly so the translation was accurate; she wanted the

English speakers to understand her. "With his magic fishhook drew he them together, but Maui did not heed his mother Hina's warning. He was *maka 'eu,* his eye roved to the beautiful woman, and distracted thus, the islands slipped off his hook.

"Then Father Kamehameha set out to accomplish what Maui had not. Bereft of the magic fishhook, Father Kamehameha used instead the magic blazing trumpet belonging to *Beretania,* the British. From island to island sailed he his fleet, and the British trumpet blew its mighty blast, and the soil choked upon the blood of the proud warriors. Father Kamehameha succeeded where Maui failed, he united the islands. But he did so using the profane ways of the *haole.* His queen Ka'ahumanu abandoned *kapu.* Then she flew the banner of the Jehovah god across the land. She tore down the temples and slaughtered the priests. Ever since, the children have suffered. They are like *mahina hapalua hope* the waning moon, uncertain they shall ever return to fullness again.

"Then arrived the new dynasty, Father Kalakaua. He made promises. The people hoped. But he, too, is *maka 'eu.* His eye roves to the *haole.* The ancestors sent the magnificent sailing canoes which spread their *lauhala* wings across Kanaloa's back and rode the breath of the god like gulls, but he sends the *haole* vessel named *Kaimiloa.* It emits smoke like a sick dragon and must be fed the hard black stones like a spoiled child. It is not free. But this vessel, this vessel Father Kalakaua chooses to represent The People with the South Islanders."

Luahine looked about her. "Faagh!" she exclaimed and spit. "Today we call upon Father Kalakaua to restore what Kamehameha usurped. May he be *maka pa'a,* single-eyed. May he return prosperity to the land. Let *heiau,* a temple be erected in sacred Pu'uloa Valley. Let Aunty Pele's anger be cooled there. Let Hula Pahu be danced in her honor. Let the ways of the ancestors be restored so she no longer devours the people.

"Then shall Father Kalakaua be known as the Torch That Burns at Midday, *ho'oulu lahui,* to increase the nation."

When the last words of the translation died in the silence of the palace chamber, Luahine grunted and returned to her palanquin. She had spoken for forty minutes. No one had moved. There had not been a cough, a rustle, a clink, not even the scrape of wind along the outer wall of the palace. The enormity of her message settled upon the king's guests. In lieu of Pacific Primacy and *Kaimiloa* she stipulated the return to *kapu* and an end to *haole* ways. The *heiau* would be the first built in modern times. All eyes turned to the king.

"O, John," Jessica whispered. "Whatever can the poor man say?"

Kalakaua did not stir. He kept his seat and looked straight ahead. The silence grew uncomfortable.

"O, John," Jessica whispered again.

Kapiolani turned an inquiring face to her husband. The retainers remained rigid as he, the tension rising to breaking point.

Ramsey shook his head. The king had failed. He composed the report in his mind, how Luahine's triumph would ignite the businessmen. Stevens would incite them, there'd be revolution, and all his efforts on behalf of the Navy would amount to tissue paper. He'd lose his promotion and Stevens would own him.

He turned wanting to leave, needing to think. But Jessica held his arm and pulled him back. Then, incredibly, she began to sing.

The words to the kingdom's anthem spilled out of her haltingly: "*Hawaii ponoi, nana i kou moi.*"

The voice was off-key, the lower register not well supported. The king's guests heard her, an attractive young woman, evidently well intentioned. Perhaps she'd laced her corset overly tight, not expecting to perform. But by the time the band recovered its wits and struck up in accompaniment, the girl's dash into the embarrassing silence appeared less like foolishness and more like inspiration. They joined the final chorus, "*Makua lani e,* Royal Father, we shall defend with spears." The minute gun sounded midnight at Punch Bowl Crater, the fuse was lit to the pyrotechnics on a barge in Honolulu Harbor, and the words were buffered by the explosions that ushered in the New Year

– but the applause itself rolled on and on to cheer King Kalakaua and Miss Jessica Mornay.

The New Year's Day parade by the Honolulu Rifles was hastily organized. Where two companies would have turned out fully uniformed and armed, only a single company of grenadiers mustered, and no horse. Colonel Ashford assembled his men – twenty-five in total, all *haole*, the businessmen and their better employees – on the carriage track before Fort Street Church. Behind them stood the marching band, sons too young to bear arms but proud to measure the beat for their fathers with drum and bugle.

They had planned to step off promptly at one o'clock, but the unit was in such low spirits that the Ashfords – Volney in command and his brother Clarence the adjutant – found it difficult to collect the men and have them look military. Most were as hung-over as their commander and as badly in need of a pick-me-up. The Rifles' dress uniform only aggravated their condition. Its high round collar and dark blue, knee-length tunic strangled circulation, and the head gear – a braided metal helmet modeled after the Prussian Army – caused a man's head to swim in the mildest weather.

Deciding he could suffer the sun himself no longer, Colonel Ashford resolved to make do with what straggled before him. He blew his whistle and the troop came to attention. "Men," he said firmly as he could muster, "last night the palace rang with the kingdom's deuced anthem. Today, we put another ring to it."

There weren't the cheers he'd hoped for but the men swung into step and dragged themselves into the march.

Merchant establishments lined the street and the beat of the drums echoed off their wooden balustrades. One, two, then a small knot of idlers, then barefoot children running down the alleyways, and soon a cheering phalanx of supporters festooned the parade route. The band struck up *Abraham's Daughter*, a Union Army marching song. The Rifles put aside the black and blue fog of the previous night's excess, and to a man they straightened up.

> *O, kind folks, listen to my song. It is no idle story.*
> *It's all about a volunteer who's going to fight for glory.*
> *Oh! Should you ask me who she am, Columbia is her name, sir;*
> *She is the child of Abraham, or Uncle Sam, the same, sir.*

They sang the words at the top of their voices, and the voices came back to them, encouraging them the more and making the whole sound like a large boisterous regiment marching through the heart of the capital. Ashford put the men through their paces at the intersections, ordering them into quick step or into flanking movements so the Rifles were like a chevron negotiating its course up the street.

The onlookers swelled into a crowd and escorted them to the palace shouting encouragement, crying out the names of friends and family members. The Rifles smartened up as never before. Their alignment was true as any Prussian's, shoulder board to shoulder board, and they held their heads stiffly, eyes front until Colonel Ashford commanded, "Eyes, right!" as the unit passed the Hawaiian flag flying on the mast at Iolani Palace. Their heads swung as one, holding the palace in a moving frame, their eyes shadowed beneath the lip of their helmets as they marched by.

After circling the palace Ashford halted his men outside the King Street gate. The temperature was taking its toll and the uniforms had surrendered their crisp set, the brass and boots their shine to the dust. The men were wilting. Perspiration dripped from his own forehead and beard, and the wax no longer held in his moustache. But he would not be shut of the opportunity. Two of Gibson's native constables loafed nearby in the shade. A considerable assemblage – *haole* and *hapa-haole* – surrounded his men in a loose half-circle. Ashford glanced at Castle and Dole together in a buggy. Thurston in sergeant's uniform stood with his squad. Expectation hung in the air. It was Saturday, New Year's Day. In all likelihood Iolani Palace was empty, the king taking his ease at his Waikiki estate.

The Commander of the Honolulu Rifles made a decision. He called his men to attention and issued sharp orders to his sergeants. The sergeants pulled themselves up tall and straightened the ranks. The men shouldered their weapons smartly and broke into two squads. They conducted fifteen minutes of close order drill, snapping their rifle butts and answering the commands of their sergeants as if their lives depended on it. Then Ashford dismissed the formation and they ran to their wives and families while the band played martial airs in the bright sunshine. Food vendors arrived with carts, and the military spectacle dissolved into a carnival of laughter and gay spirits.

The bearded priest peaked out of concealment across the street. The Honolulu Rifles were a volunteer militia, more bravado than threat, yet today its message had been unmistakable. Had they carried ammunition for their Winchesters, the king's Household Guard could not have turned them from the palace gate.

Manu's warriors trained on Kauai, and now on Oahu. They would fight, but they were not ready to fight. They had no modern arms. The men on Kauai had resurrected the weaponry of their grandfathers – preserved in *kapa* cloth as curiosities, but now restored to their proper roles in service of the war god Ku. They replaited slings and collected smooth basalt sling stones. They honed their grandfathers' six-foot throwing spears shaped from *kauila* wood. They oiled clubs, replaced their shark tooth edges and restrung the stone adze that, in the right hands, severed an arm in a single stroke.

But theirs were not the right hands, the priest knew it. The men had no notion of hand fighting. He did, he'd brought adze and sling from Molokai, a few there still kept the practices. But most Hawaiians hadn't the constitution to wield native weapons, and Manu alone kept alive the art of *Lua*. The Makahiki movement required easier, western arms: rifles, pistols, sturdy naval cutlasses and plenty of ammunition.

That would take time, time the movement didn't have. The *haole* were plentiful as sand crabs, enough of them could flay even *mano* the shark. Luahine had intended to frighten them at the queen's *luau*. Instead, she angered them. More was now required, he saw. The movement needed her blood. It would unite all the factions. The priests were right; after her, there was always her daughter.

EIGHTEEN

The girl peered over his shoulder, her black hair mixing with his own as he floated in the canoe and rendered his drawings of Pearl River lagoon. She wasn't what he expected. She was so insistent and he didn't know what to do with her. His survey tube and plumb line yielded acceptable information – well within Navy tolerances, or any other civilized entity for that matter, he could name a dozen – and on his chart he painstakingly reproduced the dangerous physiology of the coral extrusions. Cupped in the placid waters of the lagoon, his horizon line lush, green, immobile and anchored by mountains, he hadn't the problems of the open ocean. His stomach and mind were steady, his pencil shaved fine and accurate.

Not accurate enough for her, she made irritatingly clear. She chewed the end of her hair and groaned as he worked, and when she could bear it no longer, she stabbed the chart with her finger and demanded change. She modeled the shape she wanted with her hand, turned by her training into a graceful, supple instrument. It was fascinatingly expressive and, he had to admit, remarkably accurate at reproducing the natural order.

He had absorbed a little Hawaiian – "*uli*" was one of the first. It meant "to paddle." The girl picked up a little English, but only enough to raise his temperature. Frustrated by equipment failures and sudden, immobilizing storms, he could not make progress and was certain Manu had keelhauled him once again in her.

"Ramsey, you no *kakau* like tree of coconut," she told him about a particular coral formation. "You *kakau* like *lau niu*, like him hair."

He held up his palm. This formation required particular attention. He needed a respite from her gibberish.

Pua fumed. She wanted to bite the hand.

Before he boarded *Kaimiloa* Manu instructed her to observe the *haole* Ramsey, report on his ways, but she was certain she wasn't to blaspheme her own. After a rip tide destroyed the plumb line, the *haole* Ramsey's drawings had deteriorated. He used a fathom pole but it was not precise. "You no *kakau* then get Uli!" she warned.

Pu'uloa was holy. Like the gestures of sacred dance, *kakau* drawings had to reproduce the shapes exactly. Otherwise Ka'ahupahau, the shark goddess who protected the lagoon for the people of Ewa village, would transform into Uli, a terrifying demon.

"Yes, yes," he replied. He dropped the hand and turned the page. Then he pointed the new direction he wanted her to paddle. "You *uli, uli* now."

"No Uli!" she shouted back, eyes blazing.

"Yes, *uli*! This one *pau* now!"

"Uli no *pau*!"

"That's what I said, girl! No *pau uli*. You *uli* now!"

"I no Uli! You one Uli!"

With that she tore off her missionary clothing, grabbed the pole and dove naked into the water. She kicked fiercely and drove herself to the bottom where she planted the pole at the bend in the coral outcrop. She surfaced for air, made certain he watched then dove again, outlining the sacred refuge where Ka'ahupahau rested her great tail.

He sat back, stunned, watched her pull herself into the canoe. She shook her head at him. Water coursed out of her thick black hair and along the slender curves of her body into a pool in the well of the canoe. She showed him the coral's depth with a finger on the pole, but he could scarcely take it in. As she bent over the chart to check his entry, her breast, glistening in the sunlight, slid along his shoulder. The sensation stopped his breath.

"*Hiki no*," she said, nodding her approval and looking in his eyes. Then she seated herself alongside her paddle, rubbed her shoulders and arms with *kukui* oil, glanced at him questioningly, and when he pointed the direction again and said, rather hoarsely, "*uli*," she slipped her blade sleekly into the water and pulled.

Next day she arrived from Ewa village without her western clothing. He stood straight up from his chair as though she were Empress of All the Russians in a sweeping gown. Her chest was bare, he didn't know where to put his eyes. Around her waist she wore a wrap of brown and white *kapa*. Later when the sun grew strong, she covered her shoulders while paddling, but as she was in and out of the water so frequently confirming his charts, the *kapa* was more often folded neatly in a basket, only a small flap across her hips. The sun mixed with the *kukui* oil to bronze her flesh.

When he lunched he offered food, but she shook her head. She brought foodstuffs from the village to maintain *kapu*, she said – guava, coconut meat, sweet potato – and shared with him, and they ate contentedly at separate tables in the shade of the camp during the heat of the day. At first he treated her like a servant, directing what she should do and expecting to be waited upon. But the more indispensable she became in the execution of the work, the more he let down his guard. She wasn't much use in the kitchen anyway, though she offered to pound taro into *poi* and chastised him for disposing of pig's hide before it could be dried and, with her teeth, chewed into supple strips useful for binding.

When she made ready to return to Ewa village one night, she hesitated, looking at him, and he, misunderstanding at first, returned her gaze, the flame, always a low burn, starting to quicken inside him, until he forced himself to look away. Still she stood there, saying something about *aloha*, a bit more urgently than he thought was required to convey "Good bye, until tomorrow," and so he kept replying "*Aloha!*" not knowing what else to say – what else he would permit himself to say – until it dawned on him that by *aloha* she meant it would be courteous of him to return the village's gift of roasted breadfruit with a gift of his own.

At dawn the next day he paddled the outrigger about the lagoon, scattering chum and looking for a fish he thought would please her. He enjoyed his increasing facility with the native vessel but could find nothing adequate. He paused at the lagoon's mouth where it opened dangerously to the ocean. He had never paddled into the swells. If capsized, he'd drown.

He looked over his shoulder in the direction of Ewa village. He thought of her conviction, how she was frankly herself whether on land or in the water. He took a deep breath and dug the paddle into the dividing line, where the lagoon's brackish water dissolved into ocean's tossing, living chop. The outrigger slid obediently ahead.

He fixed his eyes on the prow and discovered it provided him a kind of horizon as he paddled. It staved off the nausea. Then as he felt the thrill of challenging the peaking surf and gliding easily down the backside, he began to trust that the horizon was just as firmly anchored as ever, the mountains to port still deeply rooted despite the canoe's movement. He pulled harder, enjoying the workings of his muscles and the salty taste of the spray, and paddled to a promising spot near a meadow of seaweed. He scattered the last of his chum and dropped a hand line. In no time he hooked a yellowfin tuna. It turned into a fight, and he wrapped his neckerchief around his lead hand to protect it.

The girl, at camp when he returned, was impressed by the size of the fish. "*Ahi*," she called it, running her finger along the distinctive golden stripe.

It was a brilliant fish, plump and heavy, retaining its distinctive coloration even out of water. He presented it to her with a bow. "A gift for Ewa village."

She was taken with it. As she wove a coconut basket to carry the gift, she considered him. *Mana* drained through the *haole* soul – hence the empty color of White skin – this was talked about, this was known, it was seen, but she had not been contaminated by her contact with him. And Ka'ahupahu, the district's famous shark goddess had favored him with the *ahi*. Perhaps the hole in the *haole* Ramsey's soul was reparable.

Next morning, she arrived before sunlight at camp. She carried a container. "Ramsey," she called, "you come *wikiwiki*. Make sacrifice Ka'ahupahau."

She was in the habit of walking directly into his quarters. As he was still abed and painfully tumescent – he'd been dreaming wildly, vaguely, but distinctly pleasurably – he shouted at her to wait. "*Lua!*" he cried out, thankful to Koloa for teaching him the word. "Make *lua!*" She took no notice of sleeping quarters, but she did honor the privacy of bodily functions.

"You make *lua*, Ramsey. Then you *wikiwiki*. We go Ka'ahupahau."

He relieved himself, freshened up and slipped into his khaki and boots. She waited impatiently, calling out something about Ka'ahupahau. The goddess had to be placated immediately, the sun could rise no more than two fingers above the horizon.

She wanted to know where he'd landed the tuna. They crossed the knoll on which the camp was situated and followed a footpath to the ocean. He pointed to a brown stain several hundred yards offshore. He'd hooked the tuna there.

"*Hiki no*," she said and nodded firmly.

She unrolled two mats and withdrew from her basket a wooden platter, herbs, a piece of the *ahi* tuna, a basalt stone rounded and hollowed into a burning bowl, and a bone fishhook.

"You come," she said, kneeling onto one of the mats. "You look *makai*, ocean side." She pulled him down onto the other mat. The sun glinted off the unobstructed curve of the ocean, causing him to squint.

She placed the herbs in the burning dish. He made to ignite them with matches but she stopped him. "*Kapu*, Ramsey. No make Uli."

She took out her fire sticks and in short order had the herbs burning. Once they released their incense into Ka'ahupahau's waters, she began to chant. She lifted the offerings and her voice followed the eddying smoke into the goddess' lair. The ocean itself seemed to still where they knelt. Even the waves turned quiet and receptive.

He studied her. She sat on folded legs, the *kapa* girdle splayed along a muscled thigh. The position was not one of kneeling, not like the Catholics did it – not chin dragging, you'd say, but simply comfort. She was entering into communion with a world not so very different from her own, one in which she was comfortable, had relatives.

Her face was open, the light playing upon its features – not aquiline and classically formed, but generous, with an even nose and fleshy lips. Her hair was thick and black, shimmering with oil and emanating flowery perfumes. It cascaded over her shoulders and led his eye directly to her small, well-formed breasts. These had yet to be distended by milk and suckling infants but they gave every promise of comfort and sustenance. He had seen them enough to lessen their magnetism, but the duskiness so carelessly covered by the *kapa* cloth still caused his breath to hitch. He coughed and shifted his position.

She stopped her recital and glared at him. "You make *moemoe* now, Ramsey. No talk."

There seemed no clear way to educate a *haole*. He'd interrupted the chant, she must begin again. She had to perform the ceremony perfectly, only then might it work upon his soul.

In her training there was no separation between sound and subject. A chant did not describe a god, it invoked the divine presence. A *hula* did not tell a story, it was the story, its gestures sacred and learned over long apprenticeship. So powerful were these aspects of storytelling, of *mele* in materializing *mana*, that the chant had to be memorized perfectly – one chant she'd heard but not been allowed required a day to recite in its entirety. As she resumed she looked to see that Ku and Kanaloa stopped their endless wrestling at ocean's edge, the god Kane ceased his hectoring from the sky. Creature and creator must be caught up in the words. The words were the gods. They were bequeathed to the ancient ones like holy images chiseled on *makani* the wind by the tongue and glottal stops. They were passed to caretakers in each generation and treasured as the true heritage of The People, more valuable than the feathered cape and helmet of the chiefs or the shark-toothed club of the warrior. For that reason words were precious, spirit-filled and had to be spoken correctly and with *pono* in the heart.

She set the platter on the mat before her and bent over the incense to breathe it deeply. Then she turned and handed the *haole* the fish to eat. "You *ahi*, Ramsey. Make *ono kaukau*. You eat then give Ka'ahupahau." – By which he understood it was a piece of the tuna he'd sent to the village; in fact, it was the cheek, the most favored portion, and it was *ono* tasting. At her direction he cast the remainder into the water, an offering.

She picked up the fishhook. It was four inches long, curiously marked, sturdy bone with a deep eye to it. She held it before his eyes and looked intently into them. "*Makau*, Ramsey. This *makau*. You say it."

"*Makau*," he repeated. "Fishhook."

The gods could not be fathomed, the village *kahuna* had reminded her after he cut open the great *ahi* tuna and discovered the fishhook within. Ewa village had been in good spirits anticipating the distribution of the fish. The sun slipped into the sea, but the flames of its torch still licked the clouds over the Waianaes. The birds had not settled for the night, so continued their songs, and the families sat on mats outside their lodges and enjoyed the stars as they appeared, laughing and repeating the old stories.

Then the village priest discovered the fishhook. It was not ordinary, the elders agreed. It was the fishhook belonging to the god Maui. The shark goddess had risen up and swallowed the tail of Kopiana the Scorpion which contained Maui's hook, then delivered it to the *haole* Ramsey inside the *ahi* tuna.

"Do I return the *makau* of Maui to the *haole* Ramsey?" Pua asked.

The priest looked at her kindly. "Maui is a trickster, Daughter. You know this. What god, even Maui, would lend his magic to the Whites?" The elders murmured their agreement. "No, the fishhook is meant for you."

The grandfather who sailed with her from Kauai packaged the hook in *ti* leaf then placed it in her hands. "You must use its *mana* to draw the people together, Kauai to the Big Island. It is the labor of Maui."

She nodded. It was Maui's labor, but also her mother's vision. She fingered the barbed end of the hook, saw where something caught on it, anything – or anyone – would be secured and could not escape. She tasted for a moment the promise of it. Then the blood arose like black mist and clouded her sight. She heard the rushing in her ears, and her heart beat like a wild thing, scaring her. Her hand seemed to stiffen around the hook but she grunted and forced the packet into her *kapa* wrap and slowly, the black blood settled and the village crawled back into focus. It was her mother's vision but not hers. She did not want the hook. Ka'ahupahau had granted it to the *haole* Ramsey.

At the shoreline, Kanaloa rolling gently in the early morning light, Ka'ahupahau herself lolling in the swells beyond the reef, she showed him how he must wear the hook suspended over his chest. It would stitch together the hole in his soul, a priceless gift from the shark goddess.

Why had such a gift been granted the *haole?* She did not know. Perhaps he was to unite the islands. The gods could not be fathomed, they were fickle as the sea. But she saw with clarity her own task. Such a great gift was a dangerous gift. Misused, it would transform from goodness into evil.

She must help him. A good deed would keep Kahu the Sorceress from inhabiting her. It would tame the black blood, her heart would not seize her, beating wildly as the undertow … But what if she failed? What if she had no more facility for healing Ramsey's soul than for dancing Hula Pahu? What if she was no more than a Kauai girl, and not so favored a dancer after all?

Ramsey saw tears roll down Pua's cheeks. They glowed like pearls in the soft light. "The girl cries for joy of the gift," he marveled.

NINETEEN

Luahine had been hurried by the bearded priest aboard a war canoe – carrying just the priests, no warriors – and, rendezvousing with three other canoes off Diamond Head point, she'd disappeared into the morning mist. One of Gibson's detectives spotted them. The news was all over the Honolulu waterfront when Ramsey climbed out of his own canoe to pick up dynamite. He was shirtless, barefoot and stubbly, and extremely proud of himself. With Pua's help, and fixing the image of her full of life like a pup, he'd extended his excursions into the ocean until he was able to paddle the half day trip to Honolulu.

Gibson asked the Honolulu Rifles to corral the chiefess, and Thurston was deputized. He'd packed his squad aboard the interisland steamer for Maui. The waterfront rats hoarding their gin and opium bowls had their own estimates, and shared them freely while he tied up the outrigger.

"Maui? Ha!" growled one weathered tar, his backside squeezed into a bleached captain's chair, the sawed-off stump of his leg resting on the fallen trunk of a coconut tree. "That boiled-coat sergeant, he casts off peevish as Mahmood's camel, hammer an' tongs for old Luahine, or so he says. But what's the old girl going to do on Maui, I asks you? – Nope, it's Molokai for my money. She's gone there to take her seasoning, she has – that voodoo, you know. Spells an' such. The water cask must be filled."

"Yer a fart in the wind," his mate responded. "She h'ain't gone to no Molokai. It's the Big Island, sure as the sun come up. She's gone to palaver with Aunty Pele, she has for certain. The old girl's got a plan: Hilo town first then Kona. That's where the savages shanghaied Captain Cook, you know. Burned 'im and et 'im, as I heard it."

"Well, o' course she's a-goin' to Hilo town, what rum tiddler don't know that?" said one leg, who caught Ramsey's eye in disbelief as he secured the canoe. "Can you not take me punctilio? She fills her water, so to speak, at Molokai, which as every *kanaka* knows is the sauce pot for sorcery in these islands, and then, then she sails for Hilo town. She's not gonna go an' have no palaver with no Pele if her lamp h'ain't oiled an' trimmed, now is she?"

The seamen also reported the whole town was foundering with the death of Princess Likelike, mother of young Kaiulani who was heir to the throne after Princess Liliu. It had taken the natives hard, the men said. They lost their nobles one after the other – like geese, beak to arse to the slaughter. But the king took it hardest. She was no elbow relation but his own sister, and she had put the evil eye on him from her deathbed, said he'd gone the light heeled wanton in taking up with the West, and he'd be properly cursed for it.

The men meditated on their empty tobacco pipes after this turn in their discussion. "No denyin' the King's in a terrible scrape," said one leg. "That's a deathbed curse, that is. I've seen 'em, common natives, that is, chafe themselves over such a thing, take to bed and never rise agin. But Kalakaua, no tellin'."

Ramsey laid out a coin, thanked the men for their news, and left them ruminating upon Kalakaua's future. As for Thurston, he shared their assessment. Thurston had sailed the wrong direction.

He took his satchel out of the canoe. Thurston had run off to Maui like a horse in clover, his mouth full of bees. But so had he. He'd been too long at Pearl lagoon, he realized it now he was back. There'd be hell to pay with Commander Taylor. The strange fishhook lay with his gear. Pua had insisted he take it with him to Honolulu. "You bring, Ramsey." She patted his chest tearfully. His soul was too fragile, she said. Associating with the *haole* could tear it open again.

He didn't fight her on it. Things had changed at camp, he couldn't explain it. "You've given me a leg up, Pua. Like *lio*, the horse?" He made the motion of helping a rider into the saddle. "I'm making progress here, filling in my charts. Ain't home yet, but we're gettin' there, gal." He'd present Taylor an analysis of the soil samples from Ewa village, and he could assure Stevens of progress at Pearl River. What he needed next was dynamite to test his theory, dynamite the American Minister would have to supply.

He stuck his hand out, and she shook it shyly.

"When you come, Ramsey?"

"One moon, I'll be back."

She turned then and trotted with her remarkable vitality – obstinacy, he said at other times – up the trail to Ewa village.

He slipped the fishhook into his pocket and made a quick stop at his quarters to clean up before reporting in.

"I'm at war, Ramsey. At war, do you understand me?" Taylor made no pretense any longer. It was duty hours, but the desk drawer was open, the bottle upright and reachable. "I've got the businessmen on one hand. They want to unseat the monarchy. Insurrectionists and seditionists, they should be ashamed of themselves. And some of them U.S. citizens, so I have to protect them, God damn their greedy eyes. Then, I've got some wild-haired Chiefess stirring up the lower classes, making them believe in the gods and magic and who knows what. And their King, a man who should know better, he and his Prime Minister – a White man, no less – they decide they need a navy. They send a tramp steamer off to every backward, coconut crowned monarch in the South Pacific. And here I am in the middle of it, blind as a bat. ONI is supposed to be my eyes and ears, Ramsey, and you've been off fishing a fortnight with some native girl."

He was famished after the long paddle but ready to go. He had a source, a well-to-do fisherman on the other side of the island who owned two old sailing canoes himself. Against his will, his grandson had been impressed by Luahine's priests into their ranks. He would know her intentions.

"It will take me a day, Commander. I just need a good horse. You'll have your answer tomorrow. I'll know where Luahine is."

He watched Taylor refill his glass, appearing to think it over.

"By the noon gun, mister. *Zealandia* weighs in the afternoon. My report to the Admiral goes in her diplomatic pouch. I don't think you want it to go out as it stands now."

"No, sir."

"Then get a move on. Noon tomorrow."

He intended to stop first at Madam Ho's. Sienna knew the town, she'd help him make the arrangements cheap. But hurrying to her, he saw the window of Culman's Emporium. Jessica's face came at him like a ball of hot shot. Occupied with Pua and the bivouac, he had scarcely given her a thought. He dashed into the store.

"I'll require it made up attractive," he told the proprietor, "and the correct size, certainly. Pleasing to the female eye. The lady is in her bloom."

"A distinctive piece," the jeweler remarked. He was examining it through his loop. The smoke of a cheroot curled from his teeth. "You don't find many like it, rather dear when you do. Can't say as I've seen its like."

"Valuable, would you say?"

"I would, and a collector's item."

He nodded. "You encourage me, friend. I cannot call upon the lady just now myself. I wanted to send a fitting representative. You send the cream first then the milk looks just fine."

The jeweler smiled and weighed the piece in his hand. "You know, I wouldn't mind owning this myself. Might I interest you in something in exchange?"

"Tell the truth, I am in a peck just now."

"O, but I can show you some remarkable items from Towle of London. Just the thing to catch a young lady's fancy."

He shook his head. "Just make it up as I described."

The jeweler pulled out a display case. "I think I can offer you one of these pieces and a few Kalakaua's in the bargain. You could woo Cleopatra for that!"

He hesitated. He was short of money for the livery. No one liked the Kalakaua coins, but they'd accept them. He perused the case, had the jeweler show him several items, but made up his mind.

"No, think I'll stick with the cream I come in with. If you like it so well, the lady will think I'm Aces. – Here's my card. How soon can you deliver it? Boxed up grand, of course."

Hurrying around the corner from Culman's, he stumbled upon a livery. His hand ran to his chest. Good luck had not left him, even without it. He scraped together coins at his bunga-low, hired saddle horses and a *kanaka* guide with dispatch, but it was no use. Dusk drenched the twisting trail before they climbed the Pali, the man made camp and refused to go fur-ther ... Night Marchers, he explained, marauders, the spirits of Oahu's warriors King Kalakaua slaughtered when he conquered the island. They descended the Pali in search of souls to steal. It was *kapu*, no one crossed to the island's windward side after a certain hour.

Rain poured down at midnight, soaking him to the skin while the guide snugged in under his tarpaulin.

Next day he found the fisherman and collected the intelli-gence, but *Zealandia* had warped her iron hull out from the harbor hours before he, as beaten and spent from the trail as his horse, reined in at Taylor's office.

"*Bon voyage*, Ramsey." The attaché lifted his glass and saluted him. "You'll be leaving us before long – in irons, I have no doubt. '*Aloha*,' they say in the islands, '*aloha oe*.' It means, 'till we meet again.' But no Hawaiian will be seeing you again, Ramsey. There will be no fare-thee-well for you once the Admiral reads my report."

"But I have the intelligence, sir. Luahine sails for three islands. The priests are building a fleet. The warriors are opposed –"

"Intelligence?" Taylor laughed at him. "You have no intelligence. You're a spy, Ramsey, that's all. If you had intelligence, you'd have gotten yourself here before *Zealandia* made sail!"

He returned to his quarters, his mind working despite his fatigue. He'd have to outflank Taylor with the admiral – and an airtight case for Pearl River lagoon would do it. The lagoon could harbor every boat in the Pacific Fleet, he was certain of it, once the engineering difficulties were overcome. With enough dynamite, he'd demonstrate they could be.

He bathed and slept, and awoke the next day eager to put his problems behind him for a few hours. He breakfasted in his quarters, missing Manu on *Kaimiloa* and their jousts then prepared to call upon Jessica at her hotel. He shaved and combed, attached stiff cuffs and a fresh collar to his shirt and tied the stylish four-in-hand cravat beneath it, and slipped on his white linen suit. It was straight from Young's laundry.

Already hearing Jessica's musical voice and savoring her creamy skin, he stopped at the concierge cage and balanced his boater upon the dragon frontispiece.

"My advice to you, sir, is to call another day," the concierge said.

"I had Culman's send over a parcel," he explained. "I believe the lady will want to receive me."

"Ah, you are the gentleman. I see," said the concierge. "I recall Miss Mornay did appear quite pleased by the parcel, and it was Culman's, of course."

"It was."

"But you see, sir, the lady had a second parcel. It arrived this morning."

"A second? From Culman's?"

"Not from Culman's, no. It came from the palace. Official looking; a letter, actually. O, quite legitimate. We see them frequently here. Our distinguished guests, you realize, they often receive official correspondence."

"And ...?" The man was hinting at something.

"Well, the boy went upstairs with the breakfast tray. She's insistent about it. Wants it punctually at eleven o'clock. He ran back downstairs, tea service spilled, cap askew. Miss Mornay was uncommonly vexed. I'd even say heated, sir. Something about the letter ... or your parcel, can't be certain which. Had to send the house detective to her door. The other guests were complaining. There were shouts and the sounds of breaking glass. This is the Hawaiian Hotel, you see ..."

"My parcel ... ?"

"Can't say it was yours, sir."

"Still, if it was my parcel that set her off," he said, "perhaps I'm the one to reason with the lady. The hotel's reputation must be preserved."

He placed the last of his pay, a silver American dollar, on the counter top.

"Yes it must, sir."

He climbed the three flights of stairs to the hotel's top floor. Two bellboys loafed in the corridor, within earshot of the muted sounds that issued from Jessica's room. He nodded at them and knocked.

"Leave me alone!" Her voice came angrily through the door.

"Miss Mornay, it is John Taggert Ramsey." He spoke formally on account of the bellboys. They would report to hotel management.

There was a long silence.

"Miss Mornay?" he repeated.

The door swung open.

"You!" she said. "You! So you dare to show yourself!"

Her eyes were dark dots of fury, her cheeks flushed. Wisps of hair jutted at odd angles, and he saw the two top buttons had parted from the bodice of her dress.

"Jessica? I don't understand. You received my –"

"Your heathen wishbone. O, yes, I received it." She left the doorway and picked up the Culman's box.

He stepped into her sitting room. Two windows dressed with heavy lace curtains filtered the morning light. The bedroom appeared through a doorway on the right, its furniture overturned.

"Just what did you expect me to do with this, Mr. Ramsey? Hang it 'round my neck like a cannibal?"

"Why, Jessica, the jeweler said it's a rare piece. Whalebone, or something like. Scrimshaw, you heard of that? He fixed it up fine – that gold chain on it? That's the Simon pure, or I don't know cake from casket. Thought you could wear it, you know, when you call on native households. I do believe they'd appreciate the sentiment."

Jessica faced him with tears in her eyes. "Call on native households? Call on native households? They don't want me anymore! I got a letter from the palace, not even signed by the King. He refused me. Princess Likelike's funeral is just for the natives!"

"But nobody's going, Jessica. It's off limits 'cept to the Coloreds. Commander Taylor told me."

"Of course the King didn't invite you. Did he give you a mission? Did he ask you to help him? He asked me! Me! – And then I open the box from Culman's. If the King has rejected me, at least you have sent me … and it's a bone! A smelly old bone! What's wrong with you? A girl doesn't want a fishhook, she wants a ring!"

She threw the box at him. He reached for the fallen fishhook, but she threw the bolster at his hand then the lamp from the chair at his head. She reached for a plaster bust, and he closed the door behind him and descended the three flights to the lobby with as much dignity as he could muster.

TWENTY

Luahine's armada materialized out of the mist northeast of Hilo town and bellied up to the harbor like a scorpion on the flat back of the ocean. It paused in the green middle distance, carapace and legs and stinger disjointed and distended along the horizon, the double-hulled sailers, single-masted canoes and lean-hulled paddlers patrolling the Big Island's coast at their ease. Red pennants flew from the rigging and drums relayed signals across the fleet.

Onlookers crowded the shore, and young Hawaiians climbed coconut trees and shouted out what they saw. A few hundred people remained in the Puna District. They'd been herded by the lava – greatest and lengthiest eruption since the islands were united – into the shrinking cul de sac around the town. On the three landward sides the lava burned, oozing down-slope to the sea. Only the neck of the harbor and its *haole* buildings were still free.

A single dory pecked away at a knot of refugees huddled at the tip of Hilo pier. It ferried them and their baggage, snippets at a time, out to a ketch at anchor in the bay. The ketch was their last chance. They were the plantation superintendent and his Hawaiian wife; the clinic doctor, the saloon keeper and his children; and the owner of the general store, his family and his Chinese employees and their families. They had held out long as they dared, marrying their own petitions to the cloud of prayers sent up by churches throughout the kingdom. The vigils were well-intended, the fasts devoted, but they availed nothing. The last vestiges of western presence at Puna, the islands' volcano district, had tucked tail. The ketch would carry them to Honolulu.

– Except for one. The Reverend Horace Somers stood apart from the group, legs akimbo, hands deep in the pockets of his black frock coat. Behind him the lava haloed Hilo's two story wood frame structures, which were the business addresses of the men now stepping into the dory. Further removed, the landscape was ropey, charred and barren, everything green and alive consumed by the lava in its greedy descent to the sea: tree ferns and cane, taro fields and native thatched huts, as well as the *haole* buildings that had spilled inland beyond the packed lanes of the town itself.

The dominant remaining feature was the white frame New England-style church which stood between the lava and town. Somers had not built it, but he did serve it.

The clinic doctor hailed him. "Last chance, Mr. Somers. Get your family to safety."

He lifted his top hat in farewell. "We shall not quit the vineyard before harvest, Doctor! We shall not give encouragement to the pagan!" He had a barrel-like voice and knew his words carried out to the ketch, from whence they would be repeated in Honolulu.

"I know these blows, Reverend. There's no stopping a volcano!"

"There's no stopping the Lord, Doctor!" He replaced his hat and returned to town.

He had to stay. He had arrived in the islands to complete the civilizing work of the pioneering missionaries. They were the fabled first generation, they who had survived perils terrible to recount but had led the Hawaiian out of his night of ignorance, the most spectacular achievement in American mission history.

190

He, in following them, married the *kama☒aina* daughter of William Little Lee, the Harvard man who, shipwrecked in the islands, wrote the kingdom's first constitution. Somers sought a posting in Puna District, so volcanic that the country people clung stubbornly to their Pele worship, and devoted himself single-mindedly to converting their souls.

But it was not enough, never could be. He himself was not *kama☒aina*, was not local born; he was, therefore, not truly missionary. He was reminded of his status each time he saw them, the sons of that first generation. They had discarded the humble cloth for richer vocations and they clustered together at gatherings, sharing a fraternity of careless childhoods, sun-baked beach days and enchanted, perfumed nights. Despite the position conferred by his marriage, it was a fraternity he could never enter.

Therefore he had to stay. The missionary sons had not remained faithful to the call, but Horace Somers would.

He gained the knoll upon which the church stood and turned to watch the ketch run up her sails.

His wife slid her hand through his arm. "The children are frightened, Horace. So am I."

His marriage pleased him. Eliza Lee Somers was sun-flecked and gracious in the manner of the island-born children of the *haole* elite, the judges, legislators and counselors with whom Hawaiian monarchs surrounded themselves from the time of Kamehameha forward. She wore the loose Mother Hubbard, the *muumuu* imposed upon native women by Lucy Thurston and the other first generation wives. The costume permitted her to appear in public.

He patted his wife's hand. "The natives must witness our faith."

"But they are joining Luahine. The Bibles you passed out they dropped in the sand."

He turned to her. Soon she would deliver their fourth child, he felt every fondness for her. "Do you not see, dearest? It is as *Thaddeus* sailed 'round the Horn again. We are the pioneer missionaries. The pagan armies are ranged against us. We dare not fail the call. – Now, I have sent my deacon through town and down to the beach. There will be a cycle of prayer. Kindly have the maid prepare the children."

"She's aboard the boat. She says only the *haole* would be *pupule* enough to challenge Aunty Pele."

The ketch flew square topsails at her mainmast and was pretty to watch as she filled and heeled, the crew shaking out her mizzen quite readily despite the crowded deck. One of Luahine's big sailing canoes toyed with her, running up to windward and cutting off her mainsail from the draft, but soon as the crew flew all she could reasonably handle, the ketch got herself together and leaped out to sea, leaving Luahine's fleet in possession of the Hilo coast and the blue water that beat upon it.

Next morning when the chiefess put ashore at Hilo from her sailing canoe, Horace Somers was again at his station on the patch of green before the steps into his church. It was where he customarily stood to greet his members following services, but it also provided an unimpeded view of the harbor. He watched as Luahine was winched ashore using the steam derrick from the Spreckels warehouse. The priests settled her aboard a palanquin and then, struggling, lifted her upon their shoulders and carried her across the approach to the church into the plantation superintendent's house, most well-appointed in town.

Sienna Robichon spread the *Pacific Commercial Advertiser* flat upon the bar. Managed by Gibson before he entered politics and owned by Colonel Spreckels, it was the most favorable to the palace of all the English language newspapers. Four columns carried the story of Luahine's blockade of Hilo town.

Ramsey was unimpressed. "I told Commander Taylor three days ago, Sienna. He knew before anyone else in town. – Not that it mattered."

"I warned you to be careful out here, John. What's next? I don't like this talk of court martial. Major Rosa is the Attorney General now, we see a lot of him. He brings me all the latest."

He studied the paper then pushed it aside. "These editors will print whatever the hell they want. Look at this, 'Believed armed with mortar and cannon.' Luahine's got fishing canoes and sailing craft. If there's a Spanish musket aboard, I'd be surprised."

"Your court martial, John. Taylor's been braggin' about it."

"Taylor was pulled too green from the field. Know what this blockade does? Makes Pearl River more important than ever. The missionary boys know they need the Navy in here to keep the King from turning completely native. I got their backing. Stevens give me French leave, and grateful to it."

At first the American Minister refused the money to purchase the explosives then the ketch reached town with its report of native canoes from horizon to horizon at Hilo. Stevens sent over a draft on Bishop Bank and he had all the dynamite and equipment he could think of.

"Do not overlook Manu's sister, John. This must go well for you. You need her."

"She helps me, Sienna. I don't know what you're goin' on about."

"You know what I'm goin' on about. It's what you want to ignore."

"Damn it all, Sienna! I will not be flimflammed by all that nonsense. You been out here too long. Ghosts and gods, and the wind blowing through the trees. It's just plain ignorant."

"All I'm sayin' sugar, is hedge your bets. Who didn't have their voodoo, their little *gris-gris* for the hurricanes back home? Pua's got somethin', Manu wouldn't have sent her if she didn't. Protect yourself. Find out what it is."

He took delivery of the explosives at the waterfront and loaded up the canoe. He was testing different approaches. One was the standard mix of nitro and diatomaceous earth patented by Arthur

Nobel, now in general use for engineering. It ignited with a length of Velo fuse. The Navy was most familiar with this – he'd watched bored sailors fish with dynamite when stationed in Chile – but he thought the friction/static electric detonator, if it tested as successfully as it had in railroad tunnel drilling, would be safer than Velo for the large scale engineering the Pearl River project required. He also packed Nobel's blasting gelatin, made of gun-cotton to which was added a solution of the nitro – as much as 50%. The gelatin lent itself more handily to underwater demolition, but he was inexperienced at its mixture. He laid in blasting caps and ten foot lengths of bamboo, which would house the explosives in the test.

The canoe paddled unsteadily but successfully out from Honolulu Harbor and headed west along the coast. After laboring through rough water the better part of the afternoon, he beached once again at the campsite.

Pua had built a shelter removed from his but he could not find her. He swore aloud. She was as unreliable as her brother when there was fetching and hauling to be done.

He reset his field gear and at dark built a fire of driftwood over which he set a pot of fresh ingredients to stew. He sat up until the fire died thinking over Sienna's words. If there was Hawaiian *gris-gris*, he'd be a fool to overlook it. What had Nietzsche said about the primitives? – life-affirming, or something like. He yawned, bunked down in his tent and slept dreamlessly through the throaty noises of the night.

In the morning Pua kicked him awake. She wore her village attire, a short twist of *kapa* cloth. She brought Abner from Ewa. He desired to *hanai* himself to the *haole* who possessed such great *mana*.

The sky was lowering, the wind swinging around to the northwest and tumbling over the Koolau range bearing rain. He was anxious to get started nonetheless. With Abner and Pua to paddle, he was likely to finish up in a week. He pointed to his survey equipment and told them to *hapai* it into the canoe then stopped himself.

Nietzsche was the master and Sienna was never wrong. He took a deep breath. "Pua, I need your help," he said.

Before he could say more, rain splashed down like weights and they clambered into the tent. It was close and steamy inside and he was thrust up against the girl, her eyes tipped to his, hair perfumed with the valley, skin young and available. He swallowed, forced himself to think and asked Abner to translate. "Pua, you are so ... I mean, you know things, don't you. You're so ... that is, I see you at Pu'uloa when we're working, and you're so comfortable. You know, so natural. It looks so good, to be open like and, you know, so free, a fella might say. You're different, sure, but it don't make it wrong. I mean, a fella could ... you wouldn't mind, not at all, if – O, hang it all, gal! There's something I should do, isn't there? That's what I'm trying to say. *Pono*, I should pay my respects, shouldn't I? To somebody, you know, for you. You know, to Ka'ahupahau, or whoever y'all truck with out here. The chief god, the Uli, or whoever. They've been so – well, I guess I should say they've been generous to me, ain't they? They treat me good as you do. Kind, like. Not used to it, cuss like me. Don't want to go and step on nobody's toes. Hell."

The *haole* Ramsey could not be expected to discuss the gods properly as his soul was not fully healed of its great hole. He hesitated, he stumbled, his essence still leaked through the *puka* hole. But as he had made himself *hanai* to him, Abner wanted to present Ramsey in a manner that deserved the respect of the daughter of High Chiefess Luahine. After he burnished them in formal Hawaiian, Ramsey's words conveyed his deepest apology for violating the sacred ground of Pu'uloa and he begged the daughter of the High Chiefess for her indulgence. Would she cast her eye upon him and condescend to teach him the *pono* that would please Ka'ahupahau and protect him from the curses of the Uli? Though he had not the soul of a man, he beseeched her to pray that he set foot worthily upon the sacred land. He feared the burning *haole* afterlife.

Pua's heart burst. What *mana* the fishhook of Maui possessed! It was already advanced in its healing work!

She grabbed the chart with its inferior *haole kakau* and showed him by the shapes of her hands how to correct the errors in his representations. Ka'ahupahau must be drawn precisely like reproducing a traditional pattern on *kapa* cloth. Here her flukes, there her eyes, her magnificent teeth, the flourish of her mighty tail. The goddess was the reef itself, terrible if aroused, accommodating when approached rightly and humbly, but to protect sacred Pu'uloa, Ka'ahupahau would tear the bottom out of any foreign vessel.

He traced the patterns on the chart and saw the goddess take shape between the grid lines. Ka'ahupahau guarded the entrance to Pearl River lagoon. With Pua's corrections the route through the reef became evident. He could not contain himself. "You've done it, darlin'! You've done it!" He hugged her to his chest before he knew what he did.

Abner was surprised. The daughter of Luahine was *ali'i*. She should not be the familiar of a *haole*, even one with Ramsey's great *mana*. But she did not protest. She did not struggle out of his embrace, nor did she strangle him with the black curse of the Kahu.

Pua laughed, her face shining, then she clasped his hands in her dainty ones. "Ramsey, *hele mai*. You come. Make sacrifice now."

With all his *haole* possessions, Abner explained, he would make a most pleasing sacrifice to Ka'ahupahau.

They loaded the canoe with the bamboo and paddled into the lagoon. The rain had let up and the thick gray sky was keeping to itself.

He studied the chart and saw how it all fell into place. "This will put a spike in Stevens' wheel!" he crowed, relishing the freedom Pearl lagoon would give him from the American minister. "Won't we have a blow when this job is done?! Won't we?!"

He directed them to the mouth of the lagoon, checking bearings with his tube and filling in the critical missing numbers on the chart. The water was choppy but in the skilled hands of the Hawaiians the outrigger surged ahead. He crimped three blasting caps.

"Ka'ahupahau!" Pua cried and pointed to the shape of the coral outcrop they approached. He understood it now. It was

the outline of the shark goddess' tail that she'd insisted he reproduce so faithfully. She rattled off some comments to Abner. The
boy's eyes glowed at him.

He armed the first dynamite stick with a blasting cap and
introduced it into its bamboo tube. The wires had to hang just
so, he had to be careful with the clay tamping. It required all his
concentration. Pua jabbered at him but he shook her off. He
needed three bamboo torpedoes in all. He'd seat them in the
reef then fix the wires to the detonator. The coral was porous
and the tide in ebb so he thought they could conduct the entire
operation from the canoe.

"Tell her to hush up," he said to Abner, not lifting his head
from his work.

But she issued a stream of Hawaiian, slapped the surface with
her paddle and the canoe pivoted on its axis. He nearly tumbled
overboard.

"Pua!" he shouted, "Stop!" Squatting in the hull, he could
scarcely keep his balance. Abner and Pua drove the canoe back
to camp. He had all he could do to juggle the dynamite, the
blasting caps and detonator.

Abner leaped out of the bow onto the beach and disappeared
up a path. Ramsey turned furiously upon Pua, and she matched
him word for word in Hawaiian, jabbing him with the blade of
her paddle.

The boy returned with an armful of *ti* leaves and without
another word, she guided them back to the reef. Abner brushed
back his hair and picked up his paddle. "*Mana*, Ramsey, for
Ka'ahupahau. Daughter of High Chiefess say *haole* ceremony
pilau. No good. Need *mana* so Ka'ahupahau happy."

He armed the remaining torpedoes. Pua removed the ribs
with her teeth and secured the leaves like feathers to each
bamboo torpedo, chanting the while under her breath. He
reviewed his chart then planted the torpedoes in the reef, mark-
ing each spot carefully. Playing out the electric line, he directed
the canoe forty yards from the blast area. He knew the initial
wave would be convex, throwing a funnel of water skyward, but it
would be followed by an equally dangerous concave thrust that

sucked the surface waters into the depths. He began to link the wires to the detonator device, careful to keep the lines separate.

He noticed Pua had turned her back to him. "She no like, Ramsey. Still *pilau*. Shark goddess need big offering."

Pua began to sing a beautiful two-note melody. Abner picked up the beat on the blade of his paddle. It seemed to merge with the gentle rocking of the canoe as if a great submarine beast swished its tail in appreciation. "Daughter of High Chiefess pray for you, Ramsey," Abner said. "She tell Ka'ahupahau you one *haole*. The soul take time. She never know you also *ho'emi*, cheap. She pray the goddess like the little stink gift you make. Ka'ahupahau –"

Abner stopped. Ka'ahupahau did not answer the prayer. Kane and Kanaloa did. With a roar like thunder Kanaloa reached a watery arm up to Kane, and for a moment the two gods danced beneath the clouds. The wind blew like a storm and the outrigger tossed as though it would swamp. Then Kane rained upon them, Kanaloa twisted and boiled as though his stomach were upset, Ramsey cried out with delight, and Abner crawled to him shivering and quaking, and looking for refuge in the circle of his great *mana*.

Pua was speechless. What did the *haole* sacrifice mean? She looked questioningly at Ramsey.

"*Hoe wa'a*," he said, directing the canoe back.

The *ti* leaf offerings were gone, consumed. Where the *haole* Ramsey made his sacrifice, the water still churned and the silt and sand made it impossible to see the bottom. Was Ka'ahupahau weaving her great tail from side to side with the pleasure of the sacrifice?

Her heart racing, she held the canoe steady while Ramsey peered over the side. Gradually the bottom settled and when it cleared, he let out a whoop.

"The reef is gone! All *hemo*! All *pau*! It worked!"

Pua looked over the side … It was gone! Ka'ahupahau's sacred sleeping cave, the *haole* sacrifice had destroyed it!

She screamed. She had never seen such desecration. The *haole* Ramsey had not used Maui's fishhook for good but for evil! His evil would defile her – she'd never have *pono* to dance again!

Barking at Abner to paddle, she drove the canoe back to camp. When it beached she jumped out and ran for the village.

Ramsey, his mouth open, sat looking after her. He'd lost his detonator, gone overboard when the canoe leapt forward at the first stroke of her paddle.

Rain began to fall, cold and hard. He coaxed the boy out of the bow, they beached the canoe and lifting the outrigger, overturned it to keep the water out. They sheltered in the tent, crawled under blankets and eventually fell asleep on empty bellies.

TWENTY-ONE

E liza led the deacon through the chancel door into the church. Her husband had called another prayer meeting, larger than the first. The lava had not advanced beyond the low wall on the edge of town. He planned to claim it as proof that Jehovah had heard their prayers. The victory came after the High Chiefess arrived, he would point out. Like Jezebel thrown from the wall, so paganism would be thrown down by the Right Hand of God.

"Manny asks you not to preach that text, husband," she said, motioning for the deacon to present himself. He was a son of the old Puna chiefs and very respectful of authority. "He is concerned for what might happen."

Her husband glanced up from his writing desk. He was an enthusiastic naturalist. She appreciated the interest, it brought him closer to the land. "Not preach Jezebel in the face of the High Chiefess?" He shuffled his notes – from the look of them, a chronology of the current eruption. "Come forward, Emmanuel. What's this all about?"

Emmanuel sounded deferential but clear: "No make Luahine *huhu*, Ke Kahu."

"'Reverend Somers,' Emmanuel. 'Ke Kahu' is heathen. Now, what's all this about Luahine?"

"Luahine, she one sorceress, Ke Kahu. Much *mana*, get evil, like …" Emmanuel fumbled.

"Like Jezebel. Have you forgotten your Bible studies? – The cause for my sermon tonight. I expect you to translate. I take my text from Second Kings Chapter 9, make certain you study it first. It's where she paints her eyes like the brazen harlot she is – your pardon, Mrs. Somers. I am carried away by the subject."

Emmanuel shifted his feet and looked at her.

"Husband, what Manny is trying to say – that is, his daughter is in bed. I visited her last week. The doctor thinks it's polio. The captain refused to let her aboard the ship to Honolulu."

"Disgraceful. But you needn't worry for her, Emmanuel. Bring her to the meeting tonight. I will pray over her myself."

"But Horace, Manny's home is just inside the wall. If Pele surges …"

He looked from her to his deacon and back. "This is the reason? This is why you come to me?"

Her husband rose and she followed his gaze around the small chancel. It was unadorned. A simple brass cross, gift from a congregation in New Haven, stood upon a *koa* wood table. The pulpit was just to the side and forward of it. The people sat on benches, unpadded to keep them awake.

"We are on the battlefield!" he roared. "Do you not realize what tonight means? It is victory! Victory at last over paganism in these islands! What the first generation began I shall conclude – here, tonight!"

"But husband, she is a child. Our children, how can you put our own children at risk?" She spread a hand across her belly. "We should leave, and leave now. Ask one of Luahine's sailing canoes …"

"Ask Jezebel herself?!" He stomped away.

That night, the church full, her husband had their oldest boy open the shutters so people could stand outside at the eaves and follow along. He unlocked the pantry and revealed the shelves of dried goods that ensured the people would remain to the end.

He preached Jezebel who in his description grew into a monstrous, slovenly witch of a woman. She charmed the Hebrew king and led the people into every form of promiscuity and immorality. Fire was the sign of her god Baal, but Jehovah's righteous servant used fire itself to destroy her army of heathen priests on the mountaintop.

Sitting in her customary pew, the head of her youngest slumped in her lap, combing the child's hair with her fingers, Eliza glanced around. The Hawaiians were nodding in understanding.

"Fear not!" her husband continued. "Fire belongs to the Lord and only to the Lord! The fire that lingers outside Hilo is His alone. He shall use it to cleanse the people of their sins. Luahine and all her gods, and all who follow them, shall be thrown down like Jezebel and consumed by the mighty wrath of the Lord!"

As the service ended and the people departed with their food parcels, he intoned after them, from Psalm 91:

> *Thou shalt not be afraid for the terror by night;*
> *nor for the arrow that flieth by day;*
> *nor for the pestilence that walketh in darkness;*
> *nor for the destruction that wasteth at noonday.*

Next day Aunty Pele appeared to wake and stretch herself. Eliza saw the goddess did not tarry for her morning smoke, showed no appreciation for Psalm 91 or any of its siblings, but poured directly over the stones of the wall that protected Hilo town. Vegetation exploded. Contours disappeared beneath her red flow. Manny's hut lay directly in her path. Eliza caught sight of him running with his daughter in his arms, she screaming in terror. Pele sent her fire into a defilade, diverted it from the house and consumed instead the warehouse belonging to Colonel Spreckels. Next before her lay the sugar mill and her husband's church.

Eliza didn't hesitate. She packed up a few household items and herded the children in the direction of the waterfront. Behind them the *kiawe* sizzled and popped. Her husband lingered, but she hurried on. He had his notes, he said, the family Bible to collect and robes, and there was the door to the church. It must be locked.

She guided the children onto the pier that stuck into Hilo Bay and prayed the lava would not reach the wooden planks. Overhead the sky silted with ash and the air clotted with sulfur gas.

She began to tremble, the fear catching up to her.

"Smell that, pappa? Smell that?" Horace, Jr. tugged his father's sleeve when he joined them. "It's awful, isn't it pappa? Aunty Pauline says Pele makes that smell."

"Nonsense," her husband said.

"But mama, that's what she says. '*Enakoi*, Aunty Pauline says, like the horses after wet grass. She holds her nose and –"

"Quite enough, Horace," she said. "Quite enough now. Take Ruthie's hand."

At noon a steamer appeared. It was jammed with Chinese field hands, their pigs and chickens, and Thurston's detachment of Honolulu Rifles, dejected and completely outmaneuvered by Luahine. The men took one look at the encroaching lava and refused to debark. The steamer's captain ordered them to make room for the minister, but the household items had to be left on the pier. Waddling in the strong seas, the overburdened vessel cast off for Honolulu and safety.

TWENTY-TWO

W hen the sun was two fists from expiring in the sea, the
hour sacred to her clan, Luahine stirred from her
prayers. The packet containing the bat kit augury lay
before her. There seemed nothing else for her to do. She had
employed the soul stealing curse for her own benefit – she told
herself at the time, as she tore the totem from the throat of her
predecessor, that it was for The People – but so near now to
Aunty's fire, she had to speak truth. She had really done it to
unseat Kalakaua, restore the Kamehameha line and place herself on the throne. The old rivalry of the clans and chiefs was still
alive in her. She must offer her blood in sacrifice as the *kahuna*
insisted.

The bearded priest came at her summons. "*Ho'omakaukau*, I
am prepared," she said softly. "I have submitted to your counsel." He made to embrace her, but she waved him off.

He admitted the local delegation to the parlor and she
received them sitting cross-legged on her mats. The men surrendered their gifts to her, what they'd been able to scavenge in
the abandoned town, and lowered themselves immediately so
their heads would remain below hers for the interview. She
picked through a dish of coconut and salt fish while they spoke,

but their words were unnecessary. She knew the sufferings of her people.

Last to make his appeal was Emmanuel. "I strayed, My Chiefess. I forsook the ways of my clan. I served the *Iesu* god. My daughter was struck by the *haole* disease for it. But Aunty was merciful. She spared us."

The church exploded into flame at that moment. Fire ripped up the dry siding to the steeple and turned it into a torch that lit Hilo bright as noon. The men recoiled. There was immediate danger from the gas lamps on the street. Those that knew about such things began to murmur and look for an escape.

She put down her food. "*Kupuna,*" she said, respecting them as elders but understanding their motives. They cared no more for her than did the priests. She started a chant, favorite of the local chiefs, for it compared Hilo, beautiful Hilo, *Hilo halau lani* to a longhouse in the clouds. Mad shadows from the burning church cavorted through the room, prefiguring the scene she felt compelled to enter.

"I will represent you to Aunty Pele. It is my fate." She looked from face to face. Most were older, white-haired, scarred – not from a mourning wound as in the day of the ancestors, not a scar for righteousness or the sacred, but scarred by a mill accident, a fall in the fields suffered working for the Whites, or even – this on the face of an older man – the scarred eye lost to a foreman's whip. "I will bear these gifts to her. I will say the old prayers. I will ask pardon for the people."

The elders thanked their chiefess and started to leave. They could judge well enough from the beach whether Luahine had any *pono* with Aunty Pele.

"But you shall not depart," she said, her voice rising with intensity. "You shall remain here. You shall help me prepare. You shall gather up these offerings, and gin – I require gin for the libation, and red scarves. Your Chiefess does not appear empty-handed before the goddess."

The elders protested but she raised a beefy palm and stared them down. "You will pray for me here, or you will answer for my death to the priests in my fleet. They are more greedy for blood than is Pele."

Her attendants entered to ready her. They bore oils for her hair and a roll of red *kapa* stamped in the *lehua* pattern, Pele's own flower. "*Hiki no*," she gestured to the men, "and certainly, you will return to *kapu* to benefit The People."

By the time she trod heavily upslope night had come, the church had burned to embers and the sugar mill was in flames, the sweet residues caramelizing in the heat and sending noxious odors through the town. It was hot enough to break the sweat under her chin and down her breasts, which sagged outside the *kapa* wrap.

The bearded priest appeared out of the shadows, his face looking soft and compassionate. She sank into his arms. He struggled to sustain her but it did not matter. Death awaited up the slope. She wept onto his chest. "I am afraid. I do not know that I can do this." Her tears joined the beads of sweat. "What if I cannot prostrate myself? What if I flee from her?"

She no longer felt the High Chiefess. She had no command over her spells, and the spirit world, as if in reprisal, rose up to mock her. Stars danced overhead in the rising heat shimmers and the embers of fallen branches discharged spiteful showers of flying sparks. The chiefess was weakened, she had no more *mana* than a common *hula* dancer, they seemed to say.

The priest held her close. "Aunty only summons you, she may not require the sacrifice."

She stifled a sob. "You do not understand. The *menehune* showed me the sign. I have done wrong. I must go and say the prayers."

She leaned upon his arm and they made their way past the last wood framed structure of the business district into the tree-less, charred landscape. The birds had vacated long before, and in the hush only the volcano's distant cough could be heard. The cooled lava was blackened *pahoehoe,* a stiff basalt carpet taller than a man.

She stopped and embraced him. "Leave me now. Pray that I have the strength." She touched her nose alongside his. "And see to the elders. Tell them if they do not reform I will haunt them from the precincts of the dead. *Ho'o 'ino loa,* I will curse their children's children."

The priest reverenced her sadly. "My grief goes with you."

She felt his grip upon her arm, her muscle and flesh billowing over his hand. She thought he wouldn't let her go. No one within memory had been sacrificed to Pele, it was too horrible. He had a plan. They would flee somewhere. She would give up her title. Molokai island, they'd sail, just the two of them. They'd fish, they'd forget, they'd live.

Then he released her without another look and disappeared into the night.

She was alone, completely alone. Her heart pounded so she could scarcely breathe. She placed one foot in front of the other, forcing herself upslope. The eyes, the *menehune* eyes compelled her. What dark magic would they loose upon her if she attempted to flee? That fear swallowed even the fear of Pele's fire, and she took another step closer to the heat.

Where the lava flowed the land itself looked alive. Like an orange red demon it surged toward her then withdrew as its fiery heart exposed then covered itself with ash. She took another step. The heat grew unbearable, she thought it would set her hair ablaze. The ground tortured her feet. She could go no further. She dropped her stack of mats and collapsed on her knees. She reminded Pele, weakly, in the recitation of her birth chant, that she was not of Kalakaua's clan. She drew her heritage through Kamehameha, favorite of the goddess. Then as the glowing lava smacked its lips, she prostrated herself.

"O, Pele, daughter of Haumea the Mother:
Mai ka punohu a Kane,
Mai ke ao lapa i ka lani.
From the rising mist of Kane you came,
dawn dwelling in the sky."

She squeezed the ancient salutation out of her memory, reciting each phrase slowly and carefully, though flocks of other phrases competed for expression: the spell which warded off spells, the chant for self-protection, the dedication song of a priestess in the Pele cult, not uttered in a generation. All these cried for expression but she fought them off. Pele would see through them. The goddess would be satisfied only in the blood of sacrifice.

She raised her head and chanted aloud. Her voice had stopped chiefs and warriors, but it quivered now like a frightened girl before her mother. "Pele," she said, "Pele-who-eats-the-land …" She begged the goddess to accept her sacrifice and return to the people. Then she concluded with the traditional chant.

E Pele, eia ka 'ohelo 'au;
e taumaha aku wau 'ia 'oe.
O, Pele: here are your *ohelo* berries;
I offer them to you.

She struggled to her feet. The earth was blazing hot where she stood. It singed the hair on her arms. Her eyes watered so she could not see. She went through the motions of the offering. She removed *ohelo* berries from her hair and surrendered them to the fire. Then she took eight red silk scarves – one for each island that must be unified – and dropped them one after the other upon the lava. Sweat poured from her body. She took the gin and anointed herself head to foot. The remainder she emptied upon the scarves. They burst into flame, as did the gifts from the elders.

That should have been enough, but she knew it wasn't. She had violated the *kapu* she wanted the people to return to. She had cursed to death her predecessor, robbed her of her station and never atoned for it. There was, therefore, no *pono* in her heart. The ceremony had been motions only – empty, meaningless. Pele's fingers arched toward her.

She pulled the packet from her *kapa* wrap. She looked at its contents, the bits of bone and fur from the bat kits. She recalled how the female was stillborn. The omen had fixed this moment as surely as the sailing stars. She offered it to the fire, placing her fate entirely in the hands of the goddess. *Po'o* her own mind was empty now. She surrendered herself to Pele's fire.

"I wear my funeral robe, Sister. *A'ahu ho'olewa,*" she said and, overcome by the heat, she collapsed in a heap upon the mats.

The fire storm rose around her. She heard it, the voices of those consumed over the ages in sacrifice and in rage. Their pitiful cries licked her ears. Their twisted shapes agonized before her, their eyes, their mouths screaming black caverns in the orange red fury. Even in death they could not escape Pele's grasp.

The goddess drew closer. Luahine, her lids tightly closed, the Seeing Eye a useless, paltry thing, felt her heat. Aunty's fingers tested the fat of her limbs. Aunty's tongue slid along her body to her face. Aunty's hot breath invaded her. She gagged, unable to croak one last prayer as the burning vapor filled her breast then penetrated deeper and fuller and more ardently than a man ever had. It filled her loins, darted into every recess. It sought every female place. The heat built sensationally then burst into her blood, setting it to boil with a passion that seemed to drive her heart from her chest. She saw it rise out of her, saw a lithe, fiery hand grasp it. It began to pulse – not red blood, but blood red fire. The flames shot from her heart in great arcs. She was standing now, hair whipped from her face by the blast. Her heart danced among Aunty's waving tresses. She reached for it, attempted to wrestle it back. She was weak, she was no match for the goddess. She saw Pele's mouth open, heard her laugh in derision that she, a mere Kauai sorceress would contend so. Suddenly rage coursed through her, rage that tracked where blood had once flowed; rage that bounded along the pathways just traveled by Pele's breath, white hot rage which rose in her like a fountain of lava itself. She shrieked sounds she did not know, rising up as tall and wild as a volcano, ripping the disgorging, pulsating heart from Pele's hands, laughing in the face of the goddess, jamming the burning heart back into her chest, where with every beat, it filled her with Pele's own fire.

The priest carried an English watch. When its hands pointed straight up he could restrain himself no longer. He crept up the path. He found Luahine's enormous body snoring softly on the ground. All around her the lava had hardened. It had not advanced. The chiefess lay cradled in Pele's arms.

Faster than a *haole* steamer could travel, swifter even than the *i'iwi* bird searching for sweet *ohia* nectar, so flew the news. By signal to the war canoes in the harbor then relayed by torches from canoe to canoe positioned across the channel to Maui island; and so again by torch, runner and canoe to Molokai island, thence to the signal fire that blazed upward at Diamond Head on Oahu, where the grip of the Whites was the strongest. Finally to Kauai where the movement had begun: High Chiefess Luahine lives! Hilo is spared! The movement is blessed by the goddess herself!

Renew *kapu,* cried the messengers. Restore the gods. Drive the *haole* from the land. Kanaka Maoli, you are warriors again. *I mua, e na koa*!

TWENTY-THREE

He was not certain he needed the boy any longer, but when Pua did not return and Abner would not pry himself out of the ball he'd curled into, he tried to comfort him. He tousled the boy's hair as his sister once tousled his, and he pulled bananas from a stalk inside the tent and dished out tinned meat on a clean plate.

The boy looked guardedly from under pencil-dark brows and long lashes, mouthing soft words. "*Aloha*" was the only of them he understood. He recalled Princess Liliu's *aloha* for her ward, so patted the boy reassuringly on the back. "We're good as cream gravy here, son. Nothin' to fret over. Safe and warm, see?" He spread his arms to show how safe and warm they were, and Abner fell into them like a cloth doll.

He did not know what to do. He was surprised, but holding Abner felt tolerable. Then before he could think any more about it, his own words rose up quietly, fluidly, words winging in from his childhood before the war, before everything changed; stories of the hardscrabble farm on the shin of the Ozarks, stories of work – getting up by lantern light, drawing hand-me-down boots over bare feet; lugging the pails of milk with his sister, though his eyes were still thick with sleep; manure, straw and urine stark on the morning air – and stories of play, rough and tumble games with brothers much bigger and stronger. Then as the evening light waned, climbing into the loft to watch fireflies and try out tobacco. The more he, in telling of it, returned in memory to the South, the more his voice slipped into the rhythms of the Missouri he knew, which rallied against the Yankee incursion with ranks of straight-shooting frontier men, trappers and moonshiners, mule team farmers and cattle drovers waved onward by dry-eyed women in home-stitching, their Missouri Iron Brigade chasing the Blue Bellies in brilliant engagement after brilliant engagement, and at the surrender, famously riding into Mexico rather than strike colors.

He'd heard the tales time and again around a campfire or rough-hewn eating table, and though the words and images would not be recognizable, the sentiments in his voice seemed to comfort the boy, who settled his head upon his thigh and slept – and he sat up stiffly through the night so as not to wake him, and pulled his jacket over the boy's shoulders to keep him warm.

In the morning he took him back into the canoe and resumed his tests. Abner slipped his fingers into his hand, squeezing it at the blasts. But by evening of the second day he relaxed, saying that Ramsey's great *mana* extended even to Kanaloa's eruptions, and the boy took up a paddle to help.

He experimented with mixtures of the blasting gelatin, not permitting himself a greater than 30% solution of nitro. Its ignition without the friction/static detonator was more troublesome, requiring that he pack the gelatin, insert the primer and run Velo fuse from the shore. The Velo was of uneven manufacture so he resorted to cross-matching, a trick he learned from an old gunner. He split the fuse, inserted a wooden match stick, lit the head of the match, and it successfully ignited the fuse. Abner grew fascinated by the signs of a fire so powerful that not even watery Kanaloa could extinguish it.

He entered the figures into his notebook, satisfying himself as to the differing results of placement, mixtures of nitro, guncotton and the varying effects of explosives. His charts were filling with lines, numbers and calculations. For insurance, he made a second copy.

One night the boy assembled a *kukui* torch and went fishing with a spear he had fashioned. The fish swam to the light, he explained.

He sat alone with his thoughts, boots propped on an empty dynamite case. Outside the campfire the darkness seemed watchful, no longer friendly as when Pua stayed late and they taught each other new words. This night was starless, the sky so low that even Honolulu was blanketed, and he could not orient himself, north, south, east or west.

He lit a cigar. He had every reason to feel satisfied. Pua had caused him to see the reef as a thing alive, and the work progressed as a consequence. Pearl lagoon had never been charted to such an extent, nor had the engineering been explored to demonstrate the feasibility of dredging it into a harbor. The obstacles that defeated others he had overcome. He sat on the shore of a first-rate military facility, demolition in more experienced hands would make it so. This was intelligence of the highest order, of interest to his government and to governments around the world swinish for the Pacific. It was intelligence only he possessed and its possession was power.

Should he entrust it to his government? – that was the question. The government used its power to despoil his homeland. It taxed and abused and invaded. It would do the same to the Hawaiian Kingdom, of that he had not a doubt. Do it to the Hawaiian Kingdom which, unlike Southwest Missouri truly was a paradise, a paradise where a man might make a second chance.

He sighed deeply. Pistol, sextant, ruler, normally he held each contentedly. Each drew a straight line that inscribed its own truth, nothing to quibble over. Nietzsche made him comfortable with their finality, their lack of ambiguity. Ambiguity was the province of priests and politicians. It had nothing to do with the purity of power well-exercised.

The pure case was simple. Make his case for Pearl River, sell it to the highest bidder then disappear into the Orient with

Sienna and put a bullet in Stevens if he got in the way. Power well-exercised.

The longer he stared into the flames, the more complicated the case became. There was not a straight line to connect the points, and when he dug around for an azimuth he came up empty. He was empty within. He blinked rapidly at the sensation. Telling Abner stories of the farm in Missouri had brought it back.

"It's only Melancholia," he told the flames and threw his cigar butt into the fire. Vigorous exercise followed by a good sweating – that was *Dr. Gunn's* prescription. The accumulation of bile, nothing more.

But this night it did feel like something else, something deeper. So many accomplishments, yet only emptiness, as if there were a hole, as if everything slid through him like wet sand, and not only was he empty, he was nothing. When the chips were down and it was place a bet or fold, he had nothing for the hand.

His thoughts turned to Jessica. He did not love her, not in the newfangled way the poets were writing about, but he did feel tender toward her. Their private hours had grown pleasurable and satisfying in a self-serving manner for both. He had pushed aside the notion that she would expect a ring and marriage from him, expect such tokens of normalcy. There was little normal in his life – had not been normal since the first year of the war.

After the Confederate victory at Wilson's Creek he hid behind the door while his father settled the argument that tore their family apart. Pulling on his traveling britches, he packed his leather books – "witless dreamer," his mother sneered, calico, scornful, consumptive; his father grabbed nigger Sarah by the arm and loaded her white-eyed and terrified into the wagon. He wasn't leaving her in sin a moment longer, he declared. The Lord vouchsafed to continue the South in its iniquity, he would lead her poor soul to the promised land up north.

His father held the team, expecting the boys to jump in. But his brothers assembled in a phalanx before their mother, who hurled words he'd never heard out of her until her feathery lungs gave out. "That nigger's my property!" was her final protest. "My wedding, momma give her to *me*!"

In the phantom light of the fire he saw his mother steady herself by clutching Hanky, still unwashed and stinking from the graves. His brothers shifted uneasily, his sister bawled and he, the youngest, tugged on her hand, asking why she cried, why?

"Well, one or two of the pups is coming with me!" his father roared. He'd grown his beard like John Brown and it terrified him. Handing Sarah the reins, his father grabbed for him and his sister.

His mother shrieked, upsetting the team. Sarah fell from the wagon into the mud. She struggled through it until she could grab his father around one tall boot. She refused to let go.

The noise, the cries, the confusion – he remembered, looking back, he wanted to scramble up the wagon just for safety. Winter of 1855, year of his birth, was cruel. Sarah delivered a child, a boy the month before him, light-skinned, the color of sorghum his brothers told him once, meaning something by it. But the cabin she shared with Hanky was damp and drafty. She lost the boy but kept her milk, and when his own mother was dry, too resentful to produce, his father settled him in Sarah's arms alongside the fire, "where she shoulda been all along."

He took a step toward the wagon but Sarah held his eyes. Her eyes had always comforted him. He took another step and she shook her head, no. Hanky, quieting the team, spoke slowly but forcefully to his father.

"But Sarah good as raised the boy. Good as raised the both of 'em," his father protested. "Get out the mud, Sarah. Get out. Hanky, you stay here, take care of the spread. The youngsters is comin' with me. Want 'em to meet Mr. Lincoln." He'd traveled all the way to Alton, Illinois to hear Lincoln debate Douglas in Fifty-Eight, and swore he could recall every word the great man spoke.

"Take me!" Sarah cried. "Take me, but not them! Don't you know? Don't you know what's bound to happen?"

She knew, and Hanky knew, and his mother knew, and at last they got his father to know. Through miles and miles of state militia and vigilantes and slave holders along the Missouri, and the Jayhawkers and Redlegs who knew no order beyond their own causes: an addled White man traveling north with a slave woman, he was likely to get shot, she'd be sold and the children indentured before ever they met Mr. Lincoln.

Sarah turned on the wagon seat as his father snapped the reins. She hugged a patchwork shawl around her shoulders and held his eye. He did not understand. Whatever was taking his father away, whatever was hurting his mother, she had to be the cause of it. Copying his brothers he tossed a clod of mud far as he could at her.

He couldn't say, but it looked like she cried at that.

From a slave's dark eyes to Pua's — in the rose glow of the embers, it seemed not so inconceivable a journey, though the Hawaiian girl's held a different, uncramped light. It was an animation he did not detect in his own and it was so enticing. He wondered what it must be like to have such eyes, to be filled with what lit up those eyes.

Next day he attacked the last challenge the lagoon presented, a large coral head two hundred yards into the center of the loch. It was broader than the beam of a steamship and silted half way up the formation by runoff from Pearl River. On Pua's drawing it formed the very tip of the shark's blunt snout. Its polyps bearded with green seaweed were visible just below the surface at high tide. Its demolition would prove the feasibility of blasting a channel through the reef in lieu of quarrying out the lagoon's muddy bottom.

He prepared his charges carefully. It was his first use of the gelatin full strength. He'd have preferred dynamite but feared the silt would implode the charge. And he regretted more than ever the loss of the friction/static detonator, as he was short on Velo and could pay out just fifteen yards of line. It placed the canoe within the blast zone.

He told Abner he'd have to remain ashore and watch.

The boy was as quick a study of English as Pua. "I come, Ramsey," he said.

"No, too dangerous, Abner. Too much *pilikia*. You stay."

"My *mana* strong like *haole mana*," he protested. "*I hoe waʻa* for you."

"Sorry, Abner. You can't paddle for me this time. You have to stay. This blast, it's too strong, I'm going to be so close to it. I can't chance ... son, if you was to ... here, take my glass. You'll see everything like you stood on the reef yourself."

He showed the boy how to focus the survey tube then struck off toward the final obstacle. The sun, herald of a pristine Hawaiian day, sent warm rays through his shirt as he paddled, coddling the muscles of his back and shoulders. Pua had taught him to "*hana*" the water by squeezing his abdominals and pulling the paddle toward him. He pleasured in the work, in the sweat that beaded beneath his bush hat, and in the grace with which the canoe skimmed over the surface of the lagoon, its outrigger steadying it to port. He backed water when he drew alongside the coral head – "Pohaku Uli," Abner named it, for its wicked beard of black seaweed – looked back at camp and raised his hat. He could just make out the boy waving an arm in answer.

Low tide occurred at noon, and though well into its ebb at mid-morning, it was still floating the fringes of seaweed that hung from the uppermost stories of the *pohaku*. Crabs scurried across its face and disappeared into its alleys when he tied up. He placed the charges then paid out the line. The Velo uncoiled quickly. Fifteen yards was an undistinguished, and as he looked at it now, an unsafe amount of fuse to put between himself and so significant a measure of explosive. He had chosen to mine the rock at mid-ebb so as to stay out of the water, but in doing so, he sat in a flimsy canoe exposed to a looming mass of coral raised above the waterline. He lit a cigar and smoked up all the patience he could find, watching the waterline decline until it occurred to him that in order to retain his hold upon the fuse, he actually was decreasing his distance from the *pohaku*. He crosshatched the Velo, took a breath and started the match with the tip of his cigar. Once the fuse flared into burn, he dropped it and dug his paddle into the thick water.

The village at Ewa Point had grown accustomed to the thunder that roared periodically from the lagoon. The initial curiosity of the inhabitants was quelled by the horrifying story Pua told them when she fled into their midst. So fearful were they of an aroused Ka'ahupahau that they remained in the village, did not venture into the water to fish and subsisted solely on the product of their taro patches and vegetable plots. Pua's personal dilemma – having defiled herself by contact with the *haole* Uli – was beyond the resources of the elders to resolve. They allowed her the seclusion of the purifying hut on the far side of the village. The *wahine* offered their family chants in rotation outside the hut, while on the inside, Pua fasted and prayed, burning *noni* leaves and sweetgrass for cleansing.

The thunder that erupted from the lagoon before the sun peaked caused everyone in the village to stop. The ground trembled beneath their feet. Sleeping babies started into wakefulness and cried. Dogs yipped and howled. Men working the taro dropped their digging sticks. Women ceased weaving and pounding. A cascade of water blossomed overhead like *'ohai* the rain tree then plunged back to Kanaloa. The Waianaes returned the thunder, sending it back to the sea.

The villagers tensed, anticipating the next as the *haole* Ramsey was known to continue his sacrifices into the afternoon. But there were no other sounds.

After the sun crossed its peak Abner arrived breathless and frightened at the village. He was wet and smelled of seawater. The words tumbled out. Ka'ahupahau … she had struck the *haole* Ramsey … his *mana* had not been strong enough … he was bleeding everywhere from her teeth … Abner had pulled him out of the water, clinging to the outrigger …

The elders looked at one another. Ka'ahupahau had spoken. Perhaps they could return to their fishing grounds again.

Pua broke into their circle. "Ka'ahupahau has eaten the *haole* Ramsey," Abner repeated. He looked helplessly from one to the other.

"You cannot go," the village *kahuna* warned her. "You will be cursed forever."

"The *makau* of Maui," she demanded of Abner, "does the *haole* Ramsey wear it so?" She drew a finger below her throat.

The boy shook his head.

"*Aue!*" the villagers exclaimed. The shark goddess had taken back the gift of the fishhook. There was no hope. They began to walk away.

Tears welled in her eyes. *Uhane* the soul that had been growing in Ramsey must have flown away.

"Ramsey *hemo* the *makau* of Maui," Abner volunteered. "He take away."

Pua's eyes flashed. Ka'ahupahau had not taken back her gift! Ramsey had done something with it – perhaps he was not cursed after all! She could touch him and not be defiled!

She raced down the path to camp, Abner at her heels. There she found Ramsey as far out of the water as the boy had been able to pull him. He was bleeding from multiple gashes to the abdomen and upper legs. He was unconscious but breathing. Together they carried him into the tent and laid him on his cot. Abner searched for Ramsey's knife and cut away his clothing. The *makau* of Maui was not around his neck.

She washed out the wounds with fresh water. Ka'ahupahau had seized him in her great jaws and mauled him but he had the power he worshipped, he fought back. There were jagged pieces of the goddess' coral teeth embedded in him, and she picked them out and pressed the wounds to force them to bleed. Ka'ahupahau's bites were known to cause the skin to stink and ooze like *wana* the sea urchin.

She made a poultice of *noni* and layered his body then burned incense and sat with him hour by hour. His eyes were closed, his English words splashed about like a mountain stream. She laid a compress across his forehead to keep the fever down and dropped sweet coconut milk between his lips.

The old grandfather arrived from the village and examined the canoe. The coral had torn holes in the hull. He called Abner and they plugged them, sealed the plugs with *kukui* gum and refloated the canoe in the lagoon. It leaked but was seaworthy.

When Ramsey opened his eyes the first time he saw Pua. She filled his field of vision and took his moment of consciousness to drop more coconut milk between his lips and to follow the liquid with a smattering of *poi* placed on his tongue with her finger.

When he woke again he saw Pua. She smiled and chattered at him in Hawaiian, her voice as soothing as her touch.

When he woke the third time, she sat him against her and placed a piece of fish in his mouth. He tried to serve himself but she shook her head gently and said, "No, no, Ramsey. I eat you." He was too weak to correct her English.

Abner crept close and sat on the foot of his bunk. A *tutu* from the village fanned him with incense from a burning bowl.

"Ramsey," Pua said, "him Maui fishhook. You take?" She placed a hand on her naked chest, hoping he would understand. He could not heal without it.

"Jessica," he whispered. "Honolulu."

She bit off a Hawaiian word with her teeth and set him down on his cot more roughly than she had picked him up. He heard her issue instructions to the *tutu* and glimpsed her dash out of the tent with Abner as he dropped off to sleep once more.

TWENTY-FOUR

T he stay of the opera company had been a savory diversion for Honolulu, pointed as it was by tea dances, brilliant soirees and delicate liaisons, many adumbrated in the social columns of the *Pacific Commercial Advertiser* and *Hawaiian Gazette.* But as society was wound increasingly tighter by the militant turn in events, the company packed its trunks and anticipated its return to San Francisco and reliable American republicanism – all save three of its members: the second violinist who had been enticed by an orchestra to Maui; a portly baritone reported to be ill with an embarrassing disease; and the young chorister with the enthusiastic voice, Miss Jessica Mornay.

Its eagerness for the boat notwithstanding, the company accepted the invitation of the Honolulu Rifles to a farewell gala at the Hawaiian Hotel.

The band's music and an undammed river of illumination poured out of the hotel's open windows. Pua and Abner stood outside in the shadows. Within, the shapes swirled back and forth, males mixing with females in the *haole* manner. Theirs had been a difficult, time-consuming paddle from Pearl lagoon, the canoe leaking and Abner bailing with a gourd. They did not reach Honolulu until well after dark, whereupon they changed into western dress and girded themselves with the *ti* leaves they brought for the seriousness of their purpose. They hung the leaves in a loose chain about their shoulders and Pua, stripping the rib, fashioned herself a headdress.

They'd gone first to Madam Ho's.

"Sienna," Pua demanded, but the Chinese doorman did not recognize her.

"Missy busy now."

"Sienna," she repeated, a difficult word for her to pronounce.

"You go *wikiwiki*, *kanaka* girl. No more *kanaka* whore now, okay? You come back by 'm' by."

They went next to Ramsey's bungalow. No one else locked their doors, but he did. She boosted Abner through the window, and he let her in. A metal box sat on the floor. They could not open it, but they went through the desk and every drawer looking for *makau* the fishhook.

"Faagh!" she exclaimed, turning her face away in disgust.

She had opened a drawer and removed a packet of papers with the *haole* signs on them. They were tied together and odorous.

She thrust the packet in Abner's face. "*Kaka*," she said, indicating a strong, disagreeable odor. It was the smell of the female Ramsey knew.

Abner examined the lavender writing paper. He read aloud the address: "Hawaiian Hotel."

"Humph," she grunted. "Kaka Kamahine!" She seized him by the arm and dragged him off in search of the female, the "Stink Girl."

They mounted the steps to the lobby of the hotel.

"Come here, girl!" the concierge commanded. "What is the matter with you? They expected the entertainment an hour ago. You natives, you still can't tell time!"

He rang for one of the dining room staff and a tall, formal-looking *kanaka* reported to the desk. He wore a cutaway coat, flowing cravat and glistening shoes.

"Take them into the Monarch Room," the concierge ordered, "and remind Colonel Ashford that the Rifles' purchase upon it expires at midnight."

The Hawaiian nodded and beckoned the two to follow. The room was a riot of sound, color and movement. The party was well-advanced, the Rifles a great success with the theatrical company. The women were outnumbered, the men clustering around them, preening, offering plates of food, glasses of champagne. The women, their feathers aflutter in the heated currents, tittered and laughed, and pushed away and flirted back with light-filled eyes. A great gaslight candelabra bathed the room, and sconces flickered on the walls. There was a head table at which sat the officers in dress uniform, hands gloved white, ceremonial swords unslung and hanging over the backs of chairs. Behind them rose a small platform for the orchestra, most of its notes lost in the hubbub.

Pua, so much in the country over the last month, shrank from it. Abner hid behind her. The big Hawaiian smiled comfortingly and led the two onstage.

"Ah, at last!" Volney Ashford exclaimed. He called for a flourish from the band and commanded the room's attention. "Ladies and gentlemen! We could not permit our dear friends to return to America without one final draught of native culture. May it bring a flush to every cheek and lure our more venturesome guests back to us soon!"

Loud "Huzzah's" echoed through the room.

Ashford nodded to the big Hawaiian, who ushered Pua center stage. The band members vacated and the percussionist, assuming the boy was the dancer's accompanist, led Abner to his drum kit.

The room quieted, all the faces turned toward the girl standing before them. She fulfilled most expectations: open, even-featured face, flowing dark hair decorated with wild plumage, necklace of leaves. But Rifles in the habit of attending the king's more aboriginal exercises expressed disappointment in the attire, which covered throat to calf. Ashford silenced them. The Mother Hubbard was in keeping with the hotel's decorum, he said.

Pua was terrified. Had Kaka Kamahine somehow found her out? Was she an Uli of frightening powers? Looking over the *haole* faces she found her on the right, laughing with one of the men. She prayed to Hi'iaka, raising her arms.

First one *haole* started to clap then another, then the room erupted into rhythmic applause. The big Hawaiian walked over. "*A'a i ka hula,*" he said, "just dance." He smiled encouragingly.

Pua stamped her foot. Her words floated out over the heads of the onlookers. It was the opening sentence of her dedication song. She would not perform a sacred *hula* in so profane a setting, but she could educate the *haole* with the story of Hi'iaka.

> I am above Waipio,
> My eyes look sharply down.
> I have gone along the path
> By the sea of Makaukiu,
> Full flowing like the surf.

She began by telling of Hi'iaka's great battle with the dragons that inhabited the coastline of Maui. Her hands created the movement of the surf, her arms the sinuous coils of the demons Hi'iaka fought bravely, refusing the temptation to call on the powers of her famous sister Pele. Abner picked up the beat on an upright drum, and the clear tones of her voice, rising and falling in the plain notes of the chant, sank into its rhythms as the sounds and the movements of the *hula* expanded to fill the hall.

She ended her dance with *kar'apuni,* circling on her left foot while rotating her hips, before bowing with arms extended and head lowered.

The notes of her chant faded and Abner finished with a diminishing rattle of the drum. The room fell silent for a moment then it broke into jeers. The Rifles were not pleased. This was not the *hula* they had ordered up. Lyrical sashaying back and forth was what they wanted, hips moving, hands suggestive, eyes enticing. The dancer's curves were scarcely noticeable beneath her costume. The accompaniment had been a tepid meter tapped out by the boy on a single drum. It was a disgraceful conclusion to a brilliant evening.

The Rifles hooted and howled, thrumming the floor with their boots. Pua looked at the big Hawaiian in terror. He strode onto the stage, cleared his throat and began to sing. The lyrical falsetto raised high in his nose quieted the audience. They hushed one another as their ears tuned to the notes and the lyrics. It was "Aloha 'Oe," the love song written by Princess Liliu Dominis. The melody was European and pleasing, the words familiar to many of the listeners, as the song was popular in American concert halls.

> *Aloha 'oe, aloha 'oe*
> *E ke onaona noho i ka lipo,*
> A fond embrace *a ho'i a'e au,*
> Until we meet again.

He sang the chorus then entered the second verse, which described the sweet memory of the departed one, whose image was locked in the heart.

Pua took up the story. "Aloha 'Oe" had not been danced before. She created the movements as she danced, the strong male voice painting the images of heartbreak and longing. She seized the words with her hands, lent them rhythm with her hips, and wove into being a heart-wrenching story, familiar to all, of love lost.

By the third stanza the band had returned to its instruments and the entertainment concluded with everyone in full voice, the theatrical troupe feeling deep in its heart the pathos of the curtain descending upon its Hawaiian tour.

Pua's bow was greeted by a crash of applause, whistles and cheers.

Jessica had determined not to return empty-handed to her mother. She must remain in the kingdom and make something

of herself, a good marriage at the least, and the prospect frightened her. So when the Rifles offered the cast one final taste of
island hospitality, a party in the Monarch Room of the prestigious Hawaiian Hotel, she accepted calculatedly. Their ranks
contained the town's brightest lights.

She wore her most fetching gown, the peacock with feather
trim in case she were invited to sing. At the affair's conclusion
she shook it out so the fabric fell neatly over the bustle, disappointed. The entertainment had been the unervating natives.
Her most attentive companion had been Sergeant Thurston,
also a disappointment. She'd been holding out for a bigger
rank. He was shaved so closely his skin broke into a rash, and his
moustaches were stiff with too much wax. They peaked into a
gleaming pair of horns.

He stood when she did and offered his arm. The chevrons
on his sleeve shone gold on a red field. "May I interest you in a
stroll before you retire? The moon is a sight over Diamond
Head." Whiskey fumes and tobacco gushed when he spoke.

"You are kind, Mr. Thurston. But an artiste must rest her throat.
My music teacher expects me early tomorrow." – A nearly accurate
statement, her engagement was for two o'clock. "Besides, at this
hour, one would be contained to locate the moon over Diamond
Head." She rested the tip of her fan upon the ranks of decorations
on his chest. "At this hour, one would have to search for it else-
where." Here, she allowed him to find the moon in her eyes.

He insisted on escorting her upstairs, a contravention he
declared would not come to the attention of hotel management
in the general comings and goings following the breakup of the
party. He stumbled at the second elevation, victim, she was certain, of endless bottles drained on a close night. At the summit
occupied by her set of rooms, he was red-faced and perspiring
but sought to press his advantage.

She might have permitted a brush of lip to her cheek but a
native boy huddled in the corner, watching them – perhaps
reporting? She could not jeopardize her stay at the hotel. With
a smile she diverted the sergeant with her fan and turned him in
the direction of the stairwell and the lobby.

Inside her rooms, she sighed. Not much to live in, certainly nothing to impress a visitor. She unhooked her gown but heard the handle turn on her door and smiled to herself. Though built to house guests on the cheap, unlike the lower floor suites – she'd peeked – her apartment was nonetheless hotel quality, its door possessed of a sturdy lock. Still, she was flattered. Such a shame the sergeant wasn't a major or something.

Then the knocking began and she grew fearful of a disturbance. She must make a success of the kingdom. It required, as her mother wrote, a sober cup of coffee with only a judicious addition of sugar.

"I'm afraid you must go away, Sergeant Thurston," she called sweetly through the door, "or I shall have to summon the manager."

Unfortunately she could not summon the manager without unlocking the door, stepping to the end of the corridor and tugging the Third Floor bell pull.

The knocking resumed, joined by an indistinct and high-pitched voice. Had he forced himself upon a hotel guest? She could only imagine the article that would find its way into the papers. The exploits of the Honolulu Rifles were reported glee-fully like installments of a serial adventure.

She slipped into a Japanese robe gifted her by Antone Rosa.

"I am opening the door, Mr. Thurston. You really must behave yourself now."

She drew the door open and on the other side, fire in her eyes, stood the dancer from the banquet. She gasped and stepped backward. The girl pushed into the parlor and glared at her, hands on her hips.

Frightened, uncomprehending, headlines blaring scandal before her eyes, she sized up an escape route through the doorway. Then the Hawaiian boy, the one who had spied, entered and shut the door behind him. She shrank away. "I have no money, I have no jewels! What do you want from me?!"

The girl stuck out her palm and jabbered at her hideously.

Abner thought the words employed by Daughter of the High Chiefess had merit. Anyone would agree with them. "You possess the soul of the *haole* Ramsey," Daughter of the High Chiefess stated. "Release it to me, Kaka Kamahine."

The words were simple and direct. They had *pono*. He just thought they should be stated in English. But Daughter of the High Chiefess said the act of dancing before *haole* soldiers had been demeaning enough. She would not further tarnish herself through the use of words that had no spirit.

"Kaka Kamahine, *ho'oku'u i ka 'uhane o ka haole o* Ramsey!" she repeated, stamping her foot for emphasis.

He placed his cheek upon her arm. He would lend Luahine's daughter what *mana* he possessed, though none seemed required. Kaka Kamahine trembled in front of them like she would collapse in her own *kākā*.

"Kaka Kamahine, *ho'oku'u i ka 'uhane o ka haole o* Ramsey!"

Jessica shut her ears and shrieked. "All right, all right!" It was all so foreign, so sordid. "Take what I have! Take everything! Only get out, get out, please! Leave me alone!"

She rushed to her dresser and threw everything out of it: coins, wadded bills of unusual design, mementos, trinkets exchanged with cast members opening night, the disgusting fishhook from John Ramsey, her grandmothers' good ring, costume jewelry she pretended was real, a rouge stick she pilfered from makeup, a pretty little compact, and her very own Waterman pen.

Her fingers latched onto the necklace from her father. This the savages could not have, no matter what they did to her! She clutched the necklace to her robe. Breast heaving, eyes burning with tears, she turned to face her tormentors.

The Hawaiian girl stood in the center of the room, legs splayed, a hand on her hip. Her face was stern but composed. She held the fishhook on its gold chain.

"Stink Girl has returned the soul of the *haole* Ramsey," the boy said in English. He hesitated and glanced at the fierce-looking female. She spoke again and jutted her chin. "Now Ka'ahupahau is pleased. She praises Stink Girl for her *kokua*."

It was as if after a disastrous opening the curtain raised on the Second Act. Jessica recognized her, John Ramsey's horrid little heathen interpreter!

Kaka Kamahine was an Uli after all, Pua concluded as she and Abner streaked out the door, down the fire escape and out into the night. The curses of Kaka Kamahine hurtled after them, launched by her pointed tongue and darting eyes. She launched fearful weapons also, they were heard to thunder about them as the two escaped her lair and flew down the outside stairs to the wharf. They untied the canoe and hurried it into the black waters of the harbor.

Jessica shut the door behind her, face flushed, eyes blurry, hair askew. She stared aghast at her sitting room. It was a shambles.

She collapsed onto the bed to have a good cry. The company not even departed, and already everything gone wrong ... forsaken by her Navy captain, the palace closed to her, the entire town a mud hole of queer savagery, not a friend in it, and no idea what to tell her mother.

The first tear splashed onto the bedclothes, when she bolted upright again. It was clear as spring water what she must do. Of course! She found her fountain pen and addressed an encouraging letter to Lorrin Thurston, Sergeant of the Honolulu Rifles. With luck he'd become a Captain soon, couldn't he?

TWENTY-FIVE

Commander Taylor was caught off-guard by Walter Gibson's petition. Domestic turmoil, it was sucking him into the kingdom's politics. Ramsey's meddling, he knew it. Ramsey, always Ramsey.

He guided the prime minister to the settee, sat on the lip of its neighboring fiddle back chair and sought to change the subject. "I do not have it as a formal note from my government, Mr. Gibson, but have you heard? Our State Department shall be meeting with their opposite number in the governments of Great Britain and Germany. There must be an international solution to the Kingdom of Samoa."

Gibson rested his hands atop his stick. "Samoa is not the occasion of my visit, Commander. The building of the *heiau*, the temple up Pu'uloa is."

"I understand, sir. I only thought to mention it as a courtesy."

"Well I think I can express His Majesty's sentiment that no effective resolution of the Samoan question – indeed, the resolution of any Pacific kingdom – may be achieved absent the full participation of the Hawaiian government. The King said as much when he opened the year's legislative session."

"A fine speech it was, sir." Taylor's eye strayed to his desk drawer. Diplomatic discourse required effort.

The prime minister fingered his beard. "I could easily detach the kingdom's representative in Washington to the conference, Mr. Hap Carter. It will be held … ?"

"In Berlin."

"Europe, I see. Well, there is the cost of course." Gibson adjusted a glove, appearing to run through a mental list of potential sponsors. "Mr. Bishop is committed to the electrical generation plant … perhaps the Chinese … Well," he looked up brightly, "we shall find a way. The King's horoscope is magnificent this year. Now, to more pressing matters. The *heiau*. The King would toss Luahine a bone."

Taylor saw the prime minister would not be distracted. "Terrible business what she's up to." He sat back in the chair and pulled out his handkerchief. "Could she really have stopped the lava? My God."

"The chiefs claim as much. We cannot obtain independent verification. Her fleet has blockaded Hilo."

"But if it is true what they say, the natives will be unstoppable. Have you considered the effect? What's to protect American lives, American property from them?" He daubed his temples.

Gibson cautioned with his finger. "O, I should not concern myself, Commander. I know the native well. Have studied his philology, his culture. You will not find a more modest or Edenic people. It is the Occidental has visited his troubles upon the native. There is much to atone for in our western commercialism."

"But won't another temple simply spur on radicalism? I understand they have put up a shrine where she lay before the lava – damnedest feat."

He felt the walking stick tap him on the ankle. "The temple centralizes the whole thing," Gibson told him, "don't you see? That's the wisdom in it. Wolf in sheep's clothing is my King. The temple at Pu'uloa will belong to the government. It will separate the priests from the High Chiefess, keep them near Honolulu where my detectives can keep the eye on them. Defang the serpent and what do you have?"

"Yes, sir." His attention wandered to the canvas over Gibson's head, painted during a less challenging time.

"I say Commander, defang the serpent and what do you have?"

"Mr. Prime Minister?"

Gibson jabbed his leg. "It is an earthworm, do you see? *Genus lumbricus.* No teeth, no poison. So shall our Luahine be. She will return to the King with no more offense to her than the common earthworm. He will accept her back to his cultural society and she will be glad of the opportunity. – Now, as to that engineer of yours."

"Ramsey."

"Yes, like to meet the man, discuss our problems getting the temple built."

"Are you certain, Mr. Prime Minister? Ramsey can be ..."

"He's surveying out Ewa for Princess Liliu, is he?"

"He is."

"Just the chap we need. Bring him over to Government House soon as you can. Day after tomorrow, say? Take care of this Luahine affair post haste."

"Right away, sir."

Gibson gone, he shouted for his powders. He had a glass then another. He rang the bell for his aide and jotted a note to the captain of *USS Omaha,* the wood-sided screw sloop laying over in Honolulu Harbor enroute to the Orient. When the corporal of its Marine Guard reported just after the noon gun, he sent him and his men off to Ewa village to bring back Ramsey in irons.

The bearded priest could get no peace. He alone had Luahine's ear when she condescended to listen, so the movement's rival factions constantly pestered him to represent their causes. The warriors from Kauai believed they had a claim upon her. They had been loyal during the muddy moons of encampment behind Menehune Fishpond. He'd whisked Luahine there before there was a movement, after she leveled the Big Island's high chiefess with the soul-stealing curse.

The influential Big Island *ali'i* withheld their approval because of it. He did not fault them in that. But now, following the sign of Pele's fire, they could turn their backs no longer. They came forward to adopt Luahine as their own and claim the Makahiki movement. They made slit eyes at him, murmuring that he was only a Molokai priest. Luahine should transfer her headquarters to Kona District they said, on the other side of the island where Kamehameha built the temple to his war god. The great king had sacrificed his Big Island rival there then launched the campaign to unite the islands. Kona, not Hilo in Puna District, seemed the right place to launch the campaign.

The priest entered the parlor of the superintendent's house at Hilo. He wrinkled his nose. It retained the odors of her uninterrupted occupation. Rolls of discarded *kapa* were tossed about. She would only wear the red *lehua* blossom pattern now, saying she had replaced Hi'iaka as Pele's favorite sister. There were containers of *haole* food everywhere – she'd commanded that the town be looted and the food of the Whites brought to her, and she'd poked about in it, discarding most but retaining a pot of porridge for its similarity to *poi.* A meaty dog had been found still tethered to its owner's line and its roasted carcass lay before her, where she picked at it through the morning.

He prostrated and awaited her signal to approach. Even he had to observe the formalities now.

She hunched cross-legged on a stack of mats. "I am bothered by all this," she grumbled. "It is not the reason I gave myself to the goddess."

"I know, My Chiefess. But Kauai quarrels with the Big Island. We will not have unity without your ruling."

"They should each send me the entrails of their greatest warrior. I will read them."

"Yes, My Chiefess."

She sighed. *"Ke ahi a Pele,* Pele's fire consumes me. When I sleep I hear the cries of those she has eaten. I hear them as though I had eaten them. Their cries never cease. Their spirits do not rest. I also shall never find rest."

"The movement needs you, My Chiefess."

It was the wrong thing for him to say. He knew it soon as his eyes strayed to hers. Dark and empty just the moment previous, hers filled suddenly, turning in a blink *ehu* red.

"Needs me?! Needs me?!" She did not rise from her mat but appeared to engorge as she flooded with rage. "I have given everything for the movement! Everything! I murdered for you! Emptied my loins for you! Defied the goddess for you! Now my blood is lava, my heart bursts with Pele's fire! All this for you! And you demand more of me?!" She hurled the dog carcass at him. It slammed against the portal just as the door opened.

He saw Emmanuel peer through the doorway. Jellied fat and bits of flesh showered him.

"You dare enter my sanctuary?!" she roared. She rose and seized her *kapu* stick.

The man stared open-mouthed without sense enough to fall to his knees, a slender girl folded in his arms like a brown fan.

"My Chiefess!" The priest sprang up and placed himself between Luahine and the curse she was about to hurl. "Emmanuel is old family, he is our ally in Hilo."

"He violates my presence!" she cried, shifting to catch the man's eyes. She could not curse him without locking them.

Emmanuel, quickening at last to the danger, fell upon his face and pressed his daughter with his body. "Ali'i Nui," he pleaded, with his salutation ranking her equal to Kalakaua. "I do not appear for myself. Slaughter this worthless husk of a man. But I beg you, take my daughter. *Hanai* her to your royal self. She will serve you day and night."

The priest watched Luahine pause. He prayed under his breath. It was the right thing for Emmanuel to say. No one ever made a daughter *hanai* to a sorceress. No family ever wanted it said of them. But to *hanai* recognized that the chiefess now held superior rank. Emmanuel's family was Puna District. It was an act of fealty, an act of obeisance on the part of the chiefs from Pele's own home.

"You would *hanai* the girl to me?" the chiefess said.

Emmanuel raised his eyes fleetingly but continued to cover his daughter. "Aye, My Chiefess. Take my blood if you wish, but take my daughter as the covenant of Puna's *aloha* for you."

"Stand," she commanded. "Your rivals, the Kona chiefs wish me to ally with them. They wish me to link the Makahiki movement to Kamehameha's temple on the Kona side of the island."

She settled herself back upon the mats and he and Emmanuel lowered themselves to keep their heads below hers.

"I have heard, My Chiefess," Emmanuel said.

"Is that all you have to say? You would have me mother your child, you would have her suck my teat raw like a greedy pig, and that is all you say?" The color rose again in her face.

"My Chiefess! *A'ole loa!* No – I only wished to say ... that is, I did not wish to appear too bold. This is apparent already to you, My Chiefess. If you ally yourself to Kona, you state your allegiance to the Kamehameha clan."

"I am already of the Kamehameha clan."

"True, but at Kona the people will say you ally with the Kamehameha war god Ku. Your cause will be his cause."

The priest saw her ruminate over that. Emmanuel was presenting himself well. She grunted then said, "Continue."

"But if you ally with Puna then you are free. You are free to make your cause the cause of Aunty Pele."

She grunted again and swung her head in the priest's direction. He nodded back in agreement. Alliance with Puna would strengthen the movement.

"The people build me a shrine where Pele made me *hanai*."

"The people love you, My Chiefess," Emmanuel said.

"The people insult me! Pele's fire burns within me now! I cannot rest! I have sacrificed myself for them!"

He saw the Puna chief circle his daughter tighter in his arms. She still sprawled face down beneath him. The man looked confused, frightened, lost for an answer. He spoke up. "What would you have the people do, My Chiefess?"

"If Puna loves me they will build me more than a shrine. They will build a *heiau*. They will build it greater than Kamehameha built at Kona."

"But My Chiefess, Kawika Kalakaua builds you a *heiau* at Pu'uloa on Oahu island," he said.

"Am I to have just one temple? Have you so little *aloha* for Pele's sister?" Her eyes were knives.

Emmanuel spoke quickly. "You shall have your temple at Puna, My Chiefess. The people shall rejoice in the labor."

"How many courses of stone did Kamehameha lay?"

"You shall have a course taller than he," Emmanuel said. "There never shall be a temple greater on any island."

"*Hiki no,*" she said. "This is good ... Send for *awa* and dried fish. And banana, bring banana for the girl. I will forgive *kapu* this once."

The priest reverenced her, turned to fetch the food, but paused to enjoy her taking the girl into her family.

"*Hele mai, kaikamahine,*" she said to the girl, inviting her with a jowly smile and arms opened wide.

Emmanuel prodded his daughter. She hesitated then crawled forward.

"No, daughter. You may approach standing. When I *hanai* you, you are to me as my own child. Walk to me."

The girl looked at her father for help.

"My Chiefess ... my daughter ..."

"Walk to me."

"My Chiefess ..."

"What is this *ho'opunipuni*? Walk to me!"

"My Chiefess ..."

"Is the girl dumb? Walk to me! I command it!"

"... She cannot ..."

The girl, looking terrified, staggered upright on one good limb. Her second, scrawny and ill-formed, flashed beneath her *kapa* wrap. She took a step, wobbled then fell to the floor with a cry.

Luahine rose to her feet. The color turned her features purple as fresh lava. "What is this shame you bring before me! What is this defilement!"

"My Chiefess," the Puna man begged, "I brought her to you for healing."

"Healing?! Pele does not heal! She destroys!"

"I hoped –"

"You shame me! You shame the goddess!"

"Take me, My Chiefess, but spare –"

"I shall take you! Your blood shall feed the stones of my *heiau* – at Kona!"

The priest saw her withdraw her *kapu* stick before he slipped through the portal and closed the door behind him.

To say she was anxious ... well, there really should be another word for it, Jessica thought. She'd been shown the dressing room upstairs at Hale Nui, the family estate of Eliza Somers in Waikiki. She sat in it now, shoulders hunched. "Sit up, Jessica," the voice of her mother, "no man wants a slouch." She slouched anyhow.

She'd pictured her debut. The Rifles uniformed and polished, not a hair out of place. A quieter affair than the Hawaiian Hotel, dignified. The men sipping tea. When she sang, not a clink of china. Their eyes wouldn't leave her.

But the Rifles ... a detail sailed by coastal schooner from town. Hale Nui's hands brought them in wagons to the ranch. They arrived boisterous and drinking already, just as the sun aimed long rays into the windows. One of them shot his gun at it. She'd run up the stairs to the dressing room.

Noises bellied up. She blotted perspiration from her lip and peered out. Reverend Somers stood at the flag pole, the Hawaiian flag drooping above his head. The men gabbed and pushed and laughed. Then Sergeant Thurston caught her looking. He bawled at them, ordered them to straighten ranks. He'd had the idea for Hale Nui, said Reverend Somers pined to be named the Rifles' chaplain; needed the position, was without church or income. And the ranch, one of the *haole* big houses, made a prestigious location for her debut. Next to Kapiolani Park where Kalakaua raced his horses, everyone knew it. It didn't belong to Somers but to his wife, who was mistress following her brother's death from syphilis, but the Reverend was her husband and master therefore of the estate.

She blotted her lip again. She saw Eliza on the wrap-around veranda, what they called the *lanai*. Her two middle children pulled at her and squealed. Her oldest, Horace, Jr., she allowed to run barefoot. He balanced on the railing. Eliza exchanged some words with the Hawaiian nursemaid, Aunty Pauline, who cradled baby Kamuela in fleshy arms. Neither looked happy about the Rifles. Behind them hung the Chinese kitchen help, was everyone foreign? And on the lawn, the dark-skinned wranglers and field hands, a bunch of them staring blankly. Only the estate's foreman – a muscular brown immigrant from the Azores, a healthy-looking man with attractive eyes, a retired corporal in the Portuguese army, he told her when introduced – only he joined Reverend Somers in welcoming the men.

She saw Sergeant Thurston rattle off his commands. Colonel Ashford unlimbered his sword. Behind them the lawn fell away to the unpainted cabins, the outbuildings and corrals. They looked so rude. And further to the cultivated groves and trees, and even further to the low wall, overgrown, that marked the ranch's boundary. She turned away. She'd gotten herself into something, like the man who climbed too high and his arms melted. Or something else did, she couldn't remember. She'd better prepare.

Outside the window, commands repeated. Rifle bolts clicked. Sergeant Thurston ordered a salute. Gun shots exploded. She jumped and dropped her puff. Powder flew everywhere. Then cheers echoed, the thundering "Huzzah!" of the Honolulu Rifles. She thought she heard a bottle smash.

She'd made genteel appearances at the old homes of noble families. Major Rosa arranged them. The natives received her courteously. There'd been introductions in Hawaiian, she curtsied at the major's signal, and there were sandwiches and beautiful tea servings. She reprised her performance of *Hawaii Ponoi*, and following the nodding acknowledgement – everyone stood, and the uniformed men saluted – she commenced her remarks. She soon grew practiced, like a bit of dialogue, she was always quick at her lines ... the call to erect a temple at Puʻuloa ... High Chiefess Luahine an officer of Kalakaua's Hawaiian cultural society ... the need for subscriptions, all the nobles must see it as their cause. Major Rosa took care of the particulars, she hadn't an idea of the actual response, but there was no end of invitation to the better homes.

It was a privilege, she started to realize. What American was taken so deeply into titled native culture? "I do not know how to describe it, Mother," she wrote. "It is so ignobling."

When the king closed down the campaign it had broken her heart. There'd been a purse, gratefully accepted as the stipend from her father scarcely covered the milliner's bill.

But this ... this was different.

There came a knock and Eliza Somers opened the door. "I think if you want them to hear you, you ought to come down, Miss Mornay." Eliza had lost much of the baby weight from her pregnancy, but her face still looked round and generous. "I told my people only beer should be poured. But someone showed them the liquor closet. I think it was the *luna*, the foreman. There's no containing them now. My husband left, said he can't be around such ribaldry. I packed off the children and Aunty Pauline with him."

"O dear, how shall we go about this? I thought Mr. Somers would present me."

"I think Lorrin Thurston has claimed that honor. I knew him at Punahou."

"They're so ... so ... ."

"Yes they are. Why you ever wanted to do this ... ."

She gave a tight-lipped smile. "It's why they write great arias for you."

Her descent into the maelstrom of the Honolulu Rifles would have gone unremarked except the men had chosen that instant to shatter empty glasses in the wide mouth of the fireplace. Two

Chinese broke through the press of uniforms into the lounge. Missy no like, they cried, Missy no like. They stood shoulder to shoulder before the andirons, chins up. A Rifle said he'd shoot off their queues with his pistol if they did not move. Another took bets.

Lorrin Thurston, seeing her foot upon the staircase, seized the opportunity. "Men," he shouted, "put away your weapons! Put them away, I say! The moment is upon us! Our islands may boast of many a fair flower. Some among us have plucked one or two in our time." He paused for the chuckles. Pairs of eyes appraised her, a graceful stem wrapped in its red gown. "I present the fairest of them all. She is not an island bloom but a splendid import. Perhaps she may be encouraged to take up permanent residence in our garden, eh? Gentlemen, I bid you welcome Miss Jessica Mornay, *chanteuse extraordinaire!*"

"Huzzah!" roared the Rifles in their three-tiered salute. "Huzzah! Huzzah!"

> Jessica sang, her voice high and sweet:
> *Hawaii ponoi,*
> *Nana i kou, moi*
> *Kalani Ali'i, ke Ali'i.*

She followed her script. She did not know how a White audience responded to the kingdom's anthem; did not know herself that the words called on Hawaii's true sons to be loyal to their chief. But neither did the Rifles. To a man they came to attention. They maintained stiff salutes as she sang and Jessica, her command of the song having grown with renditions at the homes of Hawaiian nobles, committed her all to it. Her notes mounted to a stirring climax, the last of them clear and hanging in the air. Then Thurston commanded, "Order, arms!" and the men dropped their salutes as one. The room was hers. She thrilled to the purse that was sure to derive from it.

"My friends," she said, "brave Rifles called to the protection of King and country, I thank you for your kind attention. A sadness confuses the land like a sun half-set. It touches our hearts.

Who cannot feel it? Our King David ordered the building of a temple. Many of us heard the call. I myself responded to it. I entered the homes of the nobles and impositioned them to stand by their King."

She carried a bit of lace to keep her palms dry. She fluttered it to dramatize the role she had played for Kalakaua.

"But this King is not to build the temple. Like the David of old, he has failed. He cast me out, even as Marie was driven out in Donizetti's great opera." She daubed her eyes. "But Rifles, won't you be my regiment? Take me as your daughter. I shall take you as my Solomon, and together we shall build what David does not. What the Hawaiian cannot do, the White Man must. For the salvation of the kingdom, Solomon must come forth. Like Lazarus from the tomb, he must come forth."

She fluttered the lace like a pennant.

There was silence.

"What the blazes?" one of the men exclaimed.

A sharply sober mind might have grasped Jessica's meaning despite the scrambled allusions, but there was not such a mind among the Rifles. She stood at the foot of the stairs, statuesque and pretty, arm elevated, showing pearl-like teeth, eyes glistening with emotion.

Thurston started the applause. "Bravo!" he called. "Bravo!" Others joined in but the response was tepid.

"What the blazes?" the man repeated.

"You great bulbous arses!" Thurston shouted. "Don't you see? King David didn't build the Temple, Solomon did! Doesn't a one of you know his Bible?"

An officer of Bishop & Company spoke up, his career among the Rifles thus far undistinguished, wanting to impress. "Why, the very thing! Mr. Bishop has discussed plans – discussed them with the King himself – for a new edifice in the name of his departed wife. It's to be a bank, a bank that houses native artifacts."

Thurston, seeing it as help, clasped him familiarly. "A repository of knowledge!"

The man, inspired by the attention, clapped him on the back. "Not knowledge – wisdom!"

"The Wisdom of Solomon – well done!" Thurston cried. "How say you, Rifles, do we take Miss Mornay? Take her as the daughter of our regiment?"

The men very much wanted to take Miss Mornay. Their "huzzah's" crashed about Hale Nui until voices grew hoarse. Jessica, uncertain of what else was happening, bowed into each round as though she took her curtain at the opera. She understood an ovation. And when the hand closed over hers, she was prepared to grant Sergeant Thurston his victory.

But the hand which claimed hers did not belong to a sergeant.

Colonel Ashford lifted his scabbard. "Men, take my sword. By it you join me. We put an end to Kalakaua's temple of sacrifice in Pu'uloa. We build instead the Temple of Wisdom!"

He'd labored over the figure the while the Rifles cheered and carried on, and was pleased with it. Rifles crowded him and he released the sword, letting it be carried boisterously about the house. He did not release the hand of Jessica Mornay, however. He straightened his moustaches, looked deeply into her startled eyes and turned her back up the stairs.

To garnish the emerging stature of the Honolulu Rifles, its commander required a lady of regimental qualities.

TWENTY-SIX

R amsey had not recovered and was not strong enough to return to town. Even he admitted it. A piece of coral lodged in the pelvis. Its tip lay alongside a nerve channel and cost him control of his left foot. He would walk ably enough then suddenly lose the foot and collapse like a fool into a heap. Pua wouldn't let him out alone. He'd stumble and they'd struggle back to the tent, his arm draped about her for support.

Having fallen yet again on their evening walk, and been carried yet again on her strong shoulder into the tent, he sat on his cot in pain, in frustration and tears. He no longer cared that she saw him so; there was nothing of him she hadn't seen by this time, and little of herself that she hadn't exposed. She was a turgid explosion he couldn't keep his eyes from. White teeth, sinuous hair, endlessly expressive hands, and the fold beneath her belly still hidden by this drape of material or that fan of vegetation – and the eyes, radiating life.

When on the cot he cried then reached for her, she came to him and he buried his face in her chest. He felt her hands on his head and neck stroking him, heard her comforting tones. He felt a nipple harden against his cheek. Though he mewled disgusting like a baby, he had *mana* – great *mana*, though he was *haole*, she said. Maui's fishhook snuggled at his chest. It closed the hole in his soul and was preparing him for noble deeds. He would become *halala*, a man of majestic proportions. Then the priests would bestow a chant upon his testicles, she giggled, as they had upon the king's own.

He felt like giggling, too.

The tent was dark, she had not struck a light. He couldn't see her features, could not distinguish her duskiness from the gloom. He pulled her to her knees so her face was opposite his. Her hair smelled of the rain forest. It caressed the backs of his hands. The words she spoke now, whatever they meant, covered him like dew. They were alone, completely alone in the grandiose Hawaiian night, its poetic moon, dancing stars, symphonic sounds, its exotic perfumes and soft, sighing breeze. He brought her face close to his, a distance that finally seemed not so great after all and touched his lips to hers.

She pulled back, eyes wide at the sensation. Then she took his face in her hands and tenderly, and so sensually, laid her nose along his, first one side then the other. The thrill caused his blood to rise.

"*Honi*, Ramsey," she said gently, all her kittenish behavior suddenly gone. "*Honi honi*."

"*Honi*," he said, understanding "kiss," and softly as he was able, drew his nose alongside hers.

He touched her hair, velvet and alive. The sensation sent electricity through his entire body. It crawled out of the cocoon in which it had hibernated since the explosion, and looked in amazement at the warm, bright light which was Pua – her round shoulders, the enticing sway of her back, hips open and receptive, the mouth he ached to possess.

His hands drifted hungrily along her curves to the flimsy cord which alone defended her nakedness. He pulled her closer.

The rude noises of men, hooves and equipment shattered the night. A Marine corporal poked through the flap of the tent, Abner in tow. He struck a safety match, lit his lantern and gathered up the situation in a glance, another sailor AWOL with a native girl.

"Petty Officer Ramsey? You are under arrest. My men will conduct you in irons."

Troops crowded behind him, weapons at the ready.

When it became apparent that he could not stand, the Marines broke the cot into a travois and, Indian-style, strapped it to one of their mules. Pua screamed when they chained him at the wrists and ankles, but they pushed her aside and Abner led her out of the tent. In their eagerness to wrest their captive onto the trail back to Honolulu, they overturned the lantern, setting the tent ablaze and all its contents with it. Abner dove back in and rescued the brass tube. One of the Marines snatched it from him but the corporal ordered the man to return it.

"We'd still be rascalin' around in the bush if it wasn't for the boy," he said. "Wasn't three days enough already? The sailor don't need that contraption where he's going. Now let's shake up them mules. There's liberty and a barrel of beer waitin' back in town."

The return required the rest of the night. The Marines, accustomed to shipboard routine, had their prisoner standing tall though sleepless in the attaché's office at 0700.

"You are relieved, mister, pending court martial," Taylor told him in a strained voice. "Desertion. If this were war time, I'd have you shot."

"Yes, sir." Ramsey anticipated, given the hour, it would not go well with Taylor. The rough trail, taken at a pace calibrated to the Marines' thirst for liberty, had caused his wounds to re-open. The detail had dragged him to his quarters where he made himself shipshape in cotton bandaging and a fresh uniform, but then as he stood at attention before the attaché, the blood started to seep. He felt light-headed.

"ONI," Taylor spat. "What good is it? Not a real sailor among the lot of you."

The man smelled stale and Ramsey could see perspiration forming in his hairline.

"I had my orders, sir."

"You did, eh? Your orders were to survey upland, see to the soil conditions, develop stores for the Navy. You were discovered, illegally, at Pearl River lagoon!"

"It can be done, Commander. Pearl River ... a military base. First rate."

"I told you once, Ramsey. No more sedition. I warned you, didn't I? One war not enough for you secessionists? Didn't we give you a bellyful of Yankee blue? Regular Navy has no need of Hawaiian territory. That's official, mister. What we need is commercial treaties – the job you were sent here to do."

"But ONI ..." The blood was pinking through his uniform jacket and he lost his train of thought.

"ONI what? Knows better than Regular Navy?" Taylor's voice shook. So did his hand. "Where were you when Luahine sheeted canvas and shoved off? That's Navy talk, boy, can ONI decode it? Gone, weighed anchor, bon voyaged – did you follow that? And your commanding officer was embarrassed, looked the fool because ONI didn't follow Luahine but followed instead his native whore to the beach."

"Luahine? But I got you the information ..."

"You got me the information after the fact. That's not intelligence, it's incompetence. Gibson wants you now, but I'll be jiggered if I'll let you embarrass me again. It's court martial and the brig for you, mister. Wish it was the noose."

Taylor said more, but Ramsey did not hear it. He slumped in darkness to the floor. The blood loss was considerable and the Marine corporal, perceiving a loophole in Commander Taylor's subsequent orders, and convinced that the prisoner was now property of the United States Marine Corps rather than the Navy – and seeing a way to both aid a fellow Southerner and eliminate many hours of paperwork – returned Ramsey to his quarters, where they shackled him to the bed and left a pitcher of water an arm's length away.

"After all, the boy ain't gut shot," the corporal reasoned aloud as he led his men to his favorite barroom on Fid Street.

TWENTY-SEVEN

S ienna rushed to his bungalow soon as the story reached her ears. It had been three days, three days since the Marine guards left him, three days since their drunken tour of the waterfront barrooms and the expiation of their last hours of liberty in the arms of Sienna's girls in the Hotel Street – certainly not the King Street – wing of Madam Ho's. The Marines were gone, the corporal and his men retching over the gunwales of the liberty boat as it pulled for the *Omaha*, which weighed then steamed for the Orient, taking with it the U.S. Navy's memory of the orders for court martial of Petty Officer John Taggert Ramsey.

She wept when she found him. He reeked of urine. His cheeks were sunken and his blue eyes stared out of dark hollows, but he was alive and conscious. The manacles had rubbed his wrists raw, so the skin had festered in the heat and humidity. The enforced bed rest actually helped the stomach wounds heal, though infection had gotten to his back and legs.

She threw off her shawl and got to work. He'd stretched the water out but the pitcher had been dry since dawn. She found some in the cistern out back, but between meting it out in judicious sips and washing down his now naked body, the supply was soon exhausted.

"You arrived just in time," he croaked. "I was actually considerin' a prayer or something like. Couldn't figure how I was gonna get out of this."

"Well I am delighted to have saved you from such a gruesome turn as prayer. God forbid, John." She covered him with clean sheets.

"Would have attempted it but these chains don't let me get my hands together. Does the Good Lord hear a prayer that ain't sent up proper?"

"Afraid you're asking the wrong girl, sugar. What's this?" she asked, pulling on the bone fishhook as if to remove it.

"Leave it," he said.

She examined the manacles. The chains ran through the metal frame of his bed. By rolling to one side he had been able to reach the pitcher of water with his right hand, but it shortened the length allowed to his left. "Those boys got you locked in here real good. I'll need some help."

"Don't be gone long."

She kissed his forehead and smiled into his eyes. "You never left my side that time in New Orleans. Don't you worry, Johnny. I'm takin' good care of you."

Jessica's patience was ground to the nub. She wore her new hat, an open carriage waited to show it to advantage and it was high time to be off. It was Sunday, and fashionable Honolulu was receiving.

She had one peacock chair on the normally pleasant veranda of the Hawaiian Hotel, Volney Ashford the other. Between them on a white wicker table sat a pot of coffee and breakfast rolls on a silver tray, and distance. Birds chirruped in the bank of perfumed plumeria trees that shaded the end of the veranda, and she saw the bolder eye her before hopping over to peck at the crumbs and fly back to their mates.

The paper rustled. Ashford put down his copy of the *Gazette* then picked up the *Commercial Pacific Advertiser*. He folded the front page lengthwise and ran his finger along the divide to sharpen it.

"Really, Volney, must we wait?" She fussed with the button on her glove.

Your prospects have <u>*improved*</u>, *my dear!!!*, Mother had written back. She liked the expression. What the Rifles liked to call the Temple of Wisdom, after her, was really a campaign for subscriptions to a museum in memory of Princess Bernice Pauahi Bishop, and it made her, on the arm of the Commander of the Honolulu Rifles, a frequent guest at one of the noblest homes in the kingdom. It also made her bolder. "I want to enjoy the carriage ride before the clouds return."

Sitting relieved a puzzling physical discomfort. She thought it was nerves. Mother said to loosen her corsets. She also told her to resume her constitutionals, but walking made it worse. She was eager for the fresh air of the carriage ride. She tapped her foot. "Another story about the Rifles? Such uncompromising reviews we've had."

"No, not the Rifles. The King and Gibson. The Samoans accepted the Hawaiian embassy for God's sake. The papers have the story."

All the kingdom's newspapers ran the story, English language, Hawaiian, Chinese and Portuguese. They had it by way of *The Pacific Tattler*, a weekly published in Australia that circulated to the Pacific ports. It was more gossip than news, but its articles were seized by other publications and reproduced as space fillers, though what was reported was weeks out of date.

– Out of date, but in the first independent confirmation of *Kaimiloa's* success at Samoa, the story was boxed and embossed by even the opposition *Gazette*, and treated as one more demonstration that the palace, though it lurched from policy to pronouncement like a drunken alley cat, seemed to sustain the grace of a forgiving set of gods and land always, softly, on its feet.

"A goddamn disaster," Ashford exclaimed, and tossed the paper. "The King's emissary, J.E. Bush, what a dull oaf of a man, cannot hold his liquor – but the natives in Samoa, they accepted his credentials like he was Lord Granville."

Jessica examined her color in her mirror. "I know you do not extall the Pacific idea, Volney, though it sounds exciting enough to me. The entire ocean one kingdom, imagine."

"It's fatuous horseplay, the fantasy of an old man without sense enough to retire from office. I don't give a fig for Pacific Primacy, but *Kaimiloa* could have been outfitted as a warship. Now that's something to talk about."

"Perhaps Mr. Bishop will purchase us a new boat. He appears quite acclimating."

She caught his scowl before he replied. "The point is, the kingdom's been led down the primrose path, Jessica. It's an affront to every square-thinker in the islands."

"I see ... Well, it is only Samoa." She shook out her fan. "It's like having a bad night in Los Angeles, for goodness sake. It's not bad reviews in San Francisco."

"No it's not like having a bad night in Los Angeles – or any other theatrical venue!"

His temper frightened her. She squirmed slightly on her seat. She'd treated the aggravation with vinegar but it still flared with her nerves.

"This is real life, Jessica ... Here, read this!" He thrust the paper at her. The Senate committee had reversed itself, the article said. The kingdom had to lease Pearl lagoon to the United States or the Reciprocity Treaty would not be renewed. She didn't understand any of it, but knew John Ramsey had spent weeks with the Hawaiian girl out there when he could have been paying court to her.

"That's Spreckels' doing, I'll be damned if it isn't. He'll hold Honolulu hostage until Kalakaua calls off the Samoan nonsense. No support for Hawaiian sugar until the King regains his senses. – Here's Dole and Castle. You mind yourself, now. We'll take that drive when I'm through."

Sanford Dole and William Castle greeted her courteously, Dole bowing low over her hand. Once she'd been accepted by the Honolulu Rifles, she'd drawn close enough to the Hawaiian League to learn of the great dissatisfaction with the Kalakaua administration, and to know that changes were surely coming.

"Our apologies, Miss Mornay," Dole said. Ashford signaled for chairs. "Mr. Beckwith tarried over-long in the pulpit today. He is exercised as we over the Samoan affair. One or two of our more reserved matrons excused themselves as his opinions grew heated. His remarks were unseemly for worship, I do not fault them for retiring."

Castle helped himself to coffee and the men discussed the situation quietly. The Great Powers took umbrage at Hawaiian meddling in Samoa. King Malietoa was not acknowledged by all factions of the Samoan court, and Kalakaua's presenting him letters poked the beehive. If America retaliated by refusing the Reciprocity Treaty, thus denying the kingdom preferential treatment, it would break the Hawaiian economy. The investment of industrialists such as Spreckels in Hawaiian sugar – though Sandwich Island Pure was the world's preferred grade – would turn worthless.

"And the rest of us," said William Castle, "whose businesses depend upon the trade – the shippers, importers, factors – to say nothing of Chun Ah Fong and the Oriental merchants, what will become of us? We must do something about the King."

"If you would only arm the Rifles ..." Ashford reached for his cigarette case. The fad was not tolerated in the hotel lobby but was permitted in the casual environment of the *lanai*.

"You shall not have weaponry from the missionary party," Dole said, speaking for Castle. "The solution is to make ourselves attractive to the Americans. They must know the necessity of our friendship and renew the treaty to keep it."

"Pearl River, it's all you have." Ashford gestured with the unlit cigarette. "The hell of it is, nobody knows if it's any good. If you can't get a warship in there, the treaty's off. And if the treaty's off, your property's not worth a Chinaman's gold tooth."

Ashford patted his pockets for a match. Before he found one Jessica said, "Pardon me, Volney, but one man knows if Pearl River's any good."

"The devil you say?"

She held the newspaper out to him. In the lower corner was a boxed paragraph reporting the unusual dilemma of Petty Officer John Ramsey, USN awaiting the arrival of an American naval vessel for the execution of his court martial, and shackled the while to his own bed because the Gibson administration could propose no humane alternative to the U.S. Naval Attaché.

"This man knows, Volney, I am sure of it." While Ashford examined the article she hid behind her fan, masking the tears in her eyes.

Next day the Attorney General of the Kingdom of Hawaii deputized Colonel V.V. Ashford's Honolulu Rifles to take custody of the American sailor, who was freed from his shackles and driven out of town to Hale Nui, where he and a sentry were housed until such time as an American warship should enter Hawaiian waters and decide his fate.

Had the most recent edition of the *Tattler* not been diverted from Honolulu by Pacific storms, the men on the *lanai* of the Hawaiian Hotel would have had an up-to-date depiction of events at Samoa, not news that was a month behind. Manu had read the current edition in Samoa and concluded that his grim sad work was finally at an end. The *Tattler* declared the Hawaiian mission not just a failure but a disgrace.

Kaimiloa had been well-received initially. The Samoan court warmed itself in the glow of a Polynesian king daring to create a navy, deputize an embassy and claim Great Power standing. His Samoan Majesty, King Malietoa accorded Bush immediate status.

Manu was leaning against the ship's rail the evening the Bush delegation was received. The Hawaiians wore their dress uniforms and toted cocked hats decorated with feathers. Prince Koloa carried with great ceremony a velvet box containing the Royal Order of Oceania, a medal Kalakaua struck for the occasion. He was to present it to Malietoa.

There were but two other vessels at Apia Harbor at the time, the Japanese frigate *Tsukuba*, which reprised her acrobatic display and finished it off with a cannonade of red and white smoke, the Samoan kingdom's colors; and the mail boat, which carried the report of *Kaimiloa* to Australia.

A crewman joined Manu at the rail, a Japanese named Denzo who was a long-time pal of Kalakaua. He'd washed up in the islands as a boy in the monsoon-driven wreckage of a fishing boat and was taken into the kitchen at the Royal School where Kalakaua, an outcast and loner himself, befriended him. After *Kaimiloa*'s commissioning the king insisted he be signed on in the galley.

The two men watched *Tsukuba*'s display then the shore boat as Bush's party descended the ladderway and were rowed to the beach.

"This good for King, no?" Denzo said.

"Good for the King. Not so good for the Kingdom," Manu replied.

Denzo looked inquiringly.

"It will bring the *haole* after us. Hawaiian empire threatens their *kala*." With his fingers Manu made the universal sign for money.

Denzo nodded. His hair was cut short, his face clean save for the long gray hairs that sprang from his cheekbones. He knew from his own nation that the emperor, divine though he may be, was at times uninspired. The samurai had to take things into their own hands – even on occasion, the most disreputable warriors had to, the masterless ronin.

Denzo observed silently over the succeeding weeks as the ronin Manu went about his work. The Hawaiian mission to Samoa succumbed to drunkenness, license, even to mutiny. Its contingent of marines swam ashore after *Kaimiloa* was ordered by the government from the harbor, its conduct became the subject of letters to the Hawaiian Kingdom, and King Malietoa did everything he could to recall in March the Articles of Polynesian Confederation he had signed in February.

It was the February report of confederation which reached the kingdom. Report of the March disintegration was weeks removed.

TWENTY-EIGHT

A frightening rumor swept through Honolulu. A shipment of arms had been intercepted at the Customs House. No one seemed to know for whom it was destined: the ship's chandler E.O. Hall or Mrs. Thomas Lack's dress shop, the usual recipients of arms and uniform clothing for the Honolulu Rifles; or was the shipment intended for Luahine's warriors, who would use the weapons like the Haitian slaves had, to slaughter the White masters in their beds.

Colonel Ashford took up the cry. At nightfall he rallied Thurston's squad at the saloon entrance to the Commercial Hotel and together they led the men, armed and carrying five rounds of ammunition, down Nu'uanu Street. Businessmen poured out of the hotel in their wake and when they passed the National on Hotel Street, its saloon and billiard parlor emptied as well, so by the time he reached the Custom House, Ashford commanded an excited, swaggering crowd, some brandishing pistols of their own.

He mounted a shipping crate, drew his sword and ordered Thurston's squad to surround the Custom House. "Quiet down, men, quiet down! Nothing larger than a parasol goes in or out!"

"Nothing larger than a knitting needle!" someone shouted from the crowd.

"Nothing larger than a hat pin," came another cry. "The King cannot control his own natives!"

There was laughter and a pistol discharged into the air.

"Well, men," Ashford addressed the crowd. "Shall we learn him a lesson then? Show the King on whose brow the Hawaiian crown actually sits?"

The crowd roared in assent.

"Then follow me to the palace. Make up a torch so he can see the color of your skin!"

The mob seethed through town with stops on Merchant Street for stakes and rags dipped in oil. As the torches sent up oily smoke and leaped skyward, shopkeepers shut their doors and begged the men off the sidewalk. It was overhung with wooden slats and cloth bunting and the Chinatown fire was too recent a memory.

Report of the mob's progress had preceded it, so by the time it reached the palace the King Street gate was barricaded and two field guns served by uniformed Household Guard were pointed with unmistakable intent. Dexter Collins, Gibson's chief of detectives, stood behind them in the electric light. Ashford gesticulated, the mob shouted, shook its fists and tossed its firebrands over the fence. But no one was foolish enough to fire a pistol and all eventually retired, each to his own preferred public house.

"Next we come, you shall not stand against us!" Ashford brandished his sword at Collins.

The *Pacific Commercial Advertiser* played down the story of Ashford's demonstration, but the *Gazette* extended it across four closely-ruled columns. The editor knew what sold: outraged White men, armed mobs, secret weapons caches, the king cowering in his bed. Abdication or revolution, how soon until the American Navy intervened?

She told herself the Honolulu papers printed more fiction than fact, but Sienna Robichon was frightened nonetheless. The Navy would not be good to her John Ramsey, particularly in the charged atmosphere. She put the papers and a smoked ham in the back of her buggy, picked up Jessica Mornay and drove out to Hale Nui. When she saw him lounging on cabin steps under a faded *lauhala* hat, she could not restrain herself. She scrambled down and wrapped him in her arms. "May I squeeze you tight, John? May I? You don't hurt any longer? I must say, you look fine, sugar. Just fine. Hale Nui agrees with you."

Jessica permitted him to peck her on the cheek before she sat and removed her hat pins. "Mother inquired after you in her last letter. I simply had to see for myself," she said quietly.

"Don't you believe her, John. You'd still be rotting away in manacles if it wasn't for Miss Mornay. The way she combed my cotton on the ride out, she's still got a passing interest in your ornery old hide."

Eliza trotted down from the outdoor *lanai*. She was barefoot and wore a red patterned *muumuu* and a seed *lei*. "Jessica, *aloha*, welcome back. I was just going over the books with the *luna*." She waved up to the foreman at the house. "It's all right, Manolo. We have guests. Mr. Somers can take a tray in the study. We'll serve out here. – You will stay, won't you? The ranch always takes a large meal at lunch." She kissed Jessica on the cheek.

"Mrs. Somers, may I present ..." Ramsey took Sienna by the arm.

"Mrs. Robichon, isn't it?" Eliza interrupted. "I know who you are, of course."

"We won't inconvenience you, Mrs. Somers."

"Call me Eliza, please."

"There is such *pilikia* in town. I wanted Johnny to prepare himself." Sienna looked at him like a little boy.

"Hale Nui prides itself on hospitality. Of course you will stay. Welcome, *e komo mai*." Eliza led them onto the grounds.

The business of Hale Nui went on about them. A wrangler drove the ranch's prize bull into a corral, and the gardener cut down a watery banana trunk with a sickle. Eliza set the Chinese staff to covering a table beneath a spreading monkey pod, its flowers like spiky pink parasols. The pantry produced tea in tall glasses, cool, but no ice as there would have been in town; sandwiches, noodles, papaya and a cold rolled pork loin. They added Sienna's ham, and Aunty Pauline herded the children over for their introductions.

Sienna took a deep draft of the tea and reached for a sandwich.

"Everyone is feeling a little peckish, of course. You've had a dusty drive from town." Reverend Somers strode to the head of the table. "But please allow me to solemnize the repast." His face reflected the lassitude of life at Hale Nui. It was sunned, loose and his dark brows freshly tweezed. "You will pardon my shirtsleeves, ladies. I was at work in my study. I wasn't aware of company, my dear, but prodigiously glad of it."

"Horace, I asked Manolo not to disturb you."

"Nonsense, nonsense. What is a man without a little distraction? Mr. Ramsey knows ..."

Ramsey seized the moment. He wanted to be the one to identify Sienna Robichon to Reverend Somers. "Yes, Reverend. And may I present ... ?"

But Somers had noticed the newspapers and cut him off with a gesture.

Eliza glanced at Sienna. "Horace, there is something you should know," she began.

"Man's iniquities are never a surprise, my dear. What does the press report now? – Ah, arms smuggled into the kingdom." He struck the paper for effect. "You see? Man's iniquities never the surprise. Redeeming grace, that's the surprise."

"Yes, Horace. But let me ..." A small soiled hand grabbed the table cloth and the water pitcher toppled. "Children!" Eliza scolded. "Out from there this minute! Aunty Pauline, take them to the stream to play!"

Somers studied the paper. "Says here the King is considering abdication. Well, it is mere justice. The testament counsels submission to rulers and authorities, but rulers themselves are to submit to God. Kalakaua never has. He's pagan through and through, the great missionaries never cured him, you know. His soul's black as his skin."

"Please, husband." Eliza glanced around. "You must not inflame sentiments. The hands at the ranch ... and our guests."

"Quite right, my dear, quite right. Let us enjoy our luncheon. Enough of politics. And – where are my manners? – I have not greeted our charming visitors. You must forgive me. My head has been in my monograph."

"It is quite important," Eliza said to the table. "It describes the physiography of the volcano."

"Of the Hawaiian volcano only, my dear. Modesty in all things." Reverend Somers stood. "Miss Mornay I know, of course. Might there be wedding bells in your future, m'dear? Colonel Ashford, is it? The Chaplain of the Honolulu Rifles would be only too gratified to preside. As a courtesy to you, just a small fee." He bowed. "Military ceremony, arched swords, quite the sight. – But this delightful lady, I have not had the pleasure ..." He bent over Sienna's hand.

"Husband ..."

Somers smiled grandly at his wife. "Now, now, my dear. I am a Christian, not a Mohammedan. You know better than to distress yourself, charming as Miss Mornay and Miss ...?"

Ramsey jumped up. "May I have the honor, sir? Allow me to present my oldest and dearest friend, Mrs. Sienna Robichon."

Somers hesitated. "Robichon, do I know the name?"

"It speaks well of your profession, sir, should you not."

Sienna withdrew her hand. "John is a terrible tease, Reverend Somers. He'd bring tears to a glass eye, I swear. You can't pay him no mind."

"Husband, Mrs. Robichon is the proprietor of Madam Ho's."

Somers' finely etched brow shot up and the color drained from his face. He opened his mouth, but nothing came out.

"I tried to tell you."

He gaped again.

"Husband ..."

He turned on his heel.

"I thought you would remain in your study. Your monograph. I wouldn't ..." Eliza shrugged helplessly.

Somers marched back to the house without a word.

"I am so sorry, Mrs. Somers." Sienna reached across the table. "It was plain poor manners of me to come. It's just, in many of the homes in Honolulu ..."

Eliza poured a glass of water. "No, I should have stopped my husband at the *lanai*."

"And you were an aggravation, John Ramsey," Sienna glared.

"My husband is a proper man," Eliza said to no one in particular. "Seldom strikes the children. He's just ..."

Sienna stood. "We should be gettin' on. Don't want your husband to lose his religion. Think the government would let us take this one with us?" She gestured with her thumb at Ramsey. "I'll dress him as one of my girls, the Navy will never find him."

He snorted.

Eliza brushed hair from her forehead and grinned. "Well, he's really been no problem – no *huhu*, except his devilishness. You do like to get into things, Mr. Ramsey. I see it coming. I see it in your eyes."

Jessica tied her bonnet.

"No, please," Eliza said. "Please stay. There's all this food."

"Well I won't turn it down." Ramsey poured the tea. "Y'all usually make me eat cold in my cabin."

"You are a prisoner, Mr. Ramsey," Eliza said.

Ramsey bowed. "I am, Mrs. Somers. Therefore to eat beneath this tree is a blessing. It is evangelical, I study it from my window. It is shade and decoration all in one."

"Under your devilishness there is a certain poetry about you," Eliza said after a moment. She passed the sandwiches. "I would not want to be a young woman around you – would you, Jessica? Too confusing."

"I keep myself too busy to be confused by Mr. Ramsey," Jessica said primly.

"So I understand." Ramsey sliced off a hunk of pork. "The scuttlebutt reaches even us rustics. You're a success since quitting the opera company."

Jessica hesitated. "We have had our notices, yes."

"I regret letting you launch your career here," Eliza said, "I honestly do. The Rifles, many are local boys, *kama 'aina*, but they've turned radical. They're destroying the culture that raised us."

"Have the Rifles turned radical, Miss Mornay? Mean desperadoes now?" Ramsey gestured overhead. "They'll rob my beautiful monkey pod tree?" He leaned forward. "Or perhaps they robbed it already while I was laid up, couldn't protect my own. They harvested the flowers when I wasn't looking."

Jessica colored. "It's professional, John. I have a contract."

"Before the judge?"

"No, it's a … it's an understanding, an understanding between two people – two mature people. The kind you make when you say things to each other." Her voice charged with emotion. "And things happen, and you say things to other people, your mother for instance. You write your mother because that is the way the world is, John. You make promises to her. Everyone understands it. Everyone except you. You say things to a girl, you do things; there are certain things that are supposed to happen after that. Certain *acceptable* things, John. Certain *expected* things. But instead of what is accepted and what is expected, John Ramsey does the unexpected. He does what he wants. He gives a girl a fishhook. A *fishhook*, John!"

Sienna looked at him. "I warned you, didn't I, cher? I said, 'Treat this girl proper.' You remember?"

He nodded. "I remember."

"Let's see to the cake." Eliza started to rise. "Help me, Sienna."

"No, please, Eliza. Stay." Jessica took her hand. She began to tear, but faced him and pushed her words out. "Such mortification, John. Whatever were you thinking? What was I supposed to show people when I visit their homes? I am a guest at the Bishop home now, are you acquainted with Mr. Charles R. Bishop? Are you aware of his standing? King Kalakaua knows my name, not that I have much respect for him. He should not be the monarch. More people are saying so now. He does not have the – there's a word the natives use."

"*Mana*," Eliza said.

"Yes … The point is, John, I'm not the girl you walked out on."

"I didn't walk out on you, Jessica."

"Giving me that gruesome bone instead of asking me to marry you like an honorable man, it's the same thing!"

"Is that what Ashford's done, the honorable thing?"

Jessica blotted her tears and sipped her tea. "Colonel Ashford and I have an understanding. I told you."

"An understanding …Well, I'm no good to you or anyone if they lock me away in prison, or worse."

"That's why we came, John." Sienna touched his arm. "Excuse me, Jessica, darlin' – a warship's comin' and comin' soon. Major Rosa told me, all the ruckus with the missionary boys. What's the charge? Desertion?"

"Yes, I was at Pearl River for Stevens when I should have been at Ewa village for Commander Taylor."

"Well, I don't understand these things," Sienna said. "You were slaving in the hot sun like a Negro. But what I'm trying to say to you, none of my friends in the government can do anything for you. The town's on edge."

"Is it so bad?" Eliza asked.

"Bad enough Mr. Gibson put a curfew on the drinking houses. He stationed a constable outside my door – lock up Madam Ho's at dusk, can you imagine! Major Rosa drove the man off."

Ramsey laughed.

"It's no laughing matter, John. The Navy's putting you on trial. You'll have to defend yourself."

"You may be the devil, John Ramsey, but you don't deserve to be executed," Jessica said.

"They're not going to execute me."

"Well what are you going to do?" Sienna demanded. "I assured Jessica that the John Ramsey I know has a plan for everything."

He chuckled and nodded. Curled within the outer shell of his survey tube was a piece of foolscap on which he'd copied the salient findings, his formulae and readings. Not the complete survey of Pearl River lagoon, that had been lost when his tent went up in flames. But it was enough, a government would trade eagerly to possess the document. In the jockeying over the Reciprocity Treaty the scrap of foolscap would give its owner the upper hand.

"With the information I have they won't convict me. They'll promote me," he said.

"O, Johnny! I am so relieved! Why didn't you tell me right along?" Sienna squeezed his arm. "You've had me so worried, frightfully worried, John. And poor Jessica, how could you treat her so cruelly. You really are the most unspeakable reptile, you know."

"What is this information, Mr. Ramsey?" Eliza asked.

"I'm afraid I must decline, ma'am. There are certain things, if they fell into the wrong hands ..."

Sienna used a toothpick. "I swear, John. Sometimes you ain't got the sense you was born with. My sit-down picked up a mess of splinters drivin' out here, and you don't want our help?"

"I just need to get to Abner – him or Pua, or both. They got what I need."

"I thought you lost everything in the fire."

He shook his head. "My tube, Abner ducked in and fetched it. It would have withstood the heat. It's brass. I smelted the copper myself with a high quality of zinc ore. Abner has it, good lad. Him or Pua, I'm certain of it."

"Why, John, that ain't nothing at all. Pua is back with me at Madam Ho's. I shall see her at once."

"Would you mind, Sienna?" Jessica reached for a sandwich, a movement that masked her face as she spoke. "That is, if it would not trouble you, I should like to speak with the girl. I should like to express my personal gratitude for taking good care of Mr. Ramsey's tube."

"Why, of course, dear." Sienna caught Eliza's eye. The pun, if it was one, was not lost upon either woman, nor the trace of malevolence which underlay it.

"Well it is getting late." Sienna collected her things and stood up. "Jessica and I should head back. We've a long drive and the countryside is not safe these days. Some of the *kanaka* have gone off the deep. The Rifles are patrolling, but you ask me, they're worse than the highway men. Eliza darlin', you've been a dear. Can you keep this one here 'til we find this tube of his?"

Eliza kissed her on the cheek. "*Aloha*, Sienna. I'll discuss it with Horace. I think he will accept another week."

It was while they were waiting for their horse to be led between the carriage trees that Jessica fainted. Ramsey went to her immediately and called for water. "Poor child, all the excitement," Sienna said, but Eliza felt Jessica's brow and observed her pallor. She did not think it was merely nerves, or the heat. She had her placed in an upstairs bedroom then herded everyone into the big room with the empty fireplace. She sent Aunty Pauline to sit with Jessica and noticed that Pauline called for Noelani, her brother's lover, retained as part of the household after his death from syphilis-induced dementia.

After a supper taken cold in the bungalow, Ramsey was allowed upstairs to visit Jessica. She was sipping a beverage served her by the Hawaiian women. Burning leaves scented the room.

"Thank you for keeping me company, John. I feel so silly."

He took the chair next to her. "Plenty of folks have sat up with me these last weeks, I know how it helps."

"Yes, it does. – Will you truly be safe, John? The tube, I mean."

"Hush, now. You should be resting."

"I will retrieve it for you, John, I truly shall – that little witch … A promotion, you say? Mother shall be so proud."

TWENTY-NINE

After a night's rest Jessica felt well enough to travel. The nagging sensation had diminished. Even had it not, she would have thrown off Eliza's entreaties to remain another day. Her father always prescribed motivation for his patients, and she had motivation aplenty to return to town speedily as transportation could be arranged. Ramsey suggested the coastal schooner instead of the long buggy ride. The fresh shock of salt and sea was just the tonic, everyone agreed.

"Would I could accompany you, darlin'," Sienna said, "but it's my most popular buggy and I must return it to town. You don't mind? Some of our gentlemen prefer it to their own when they come calling."

She made appropriate response, but her attention was already fixed on the task ahead.

"You must take my traveling cloak," Sienna insisted. "Keep yourself from the chills during your passage." She wrapped her in the velvet cape. "Just return it to Carl. I shan't reach town 'til hours after you do."

In the event, an April cloudburst drove Sienna's carriage off the road, further delaying her journey, whereas Jessica's passage was marred by nothing more than a moist wind that wet her hair until she remembered to draw the hood about her.

After the schooner docked she hiked the mile from the wharf to Madam Ho's, her mind empty save for a single thought. She strode briskly, cosseted by the cape, the velvet hood covering her face as the clouds formed and the rain descended in patches. She did not notice.

The Hotel Street door opened to her touch. No one was about. She called for Carl.

"Yes, miss? Everyone's at their supper. What may I do for you?"

"Send me the girl Pua."

Carl recognized the cloak belonging to his mistress.

"You sure are wet, miss. Through and through."

"Sienna told me to ask for you. First send me the Hawaiian girl."

"Right away, miss. But you'd best step into the office, get yourself out of that draft. Let me make you a toddy 'gainst the chill. Fix you right up."

Pua, directed to the office, skipped lightly down the stairs. It was the hour before the men arrived to worship at the golden temple, the hour she most enjoyed when Sienna's priestesses had their supper. She waited on them, fetching sweet flowers from the garden and tidbits from their rooms. They talked and played with her as the girls never did at her *hula* school, and she felt part of them, though the temple precinct itself was *kapu* to her. She was not worthy, had not the *pono* to be allowed inside.

She entered the office gaily. There were *haole* words she had learned to write and she wished to share them. "*Makuahine*," she said, her respectful term for a female who was not a blood relative. "*Pehea 'oe?*" Then she stopped herself. Aunty Sienna would want to hear her use the English tongue.

The figure she saw in shadows stood in a puddle of water. Its face was shrouded. "*Makuahine?*" she asked, tiptoeing closer. Something was wrong. The hairs rose in warning on her arms.

Then the figure pulled back its hood and Pua choked. It wasn't Aunty Sienna, it was Kaka Kamahine! She tried to scream but could not. Kaka Kamahine commanded *mo'o* the water serpent, its coils tightened around her throat so she could not breathe!

The terrible Uli looked her in the eyes and grinned. Hair stuck to the sides of its face. One awful finger dripped with pond scum. It approached her face and she gagged. She tried not to let it touch her but could not move. It made a slimy trail on her cheek. "You will retrieve for me the metal *maka nui* of the *haole* Ramsey," Kaka Kamahine said.

The Uli spoke rapidly in English, but Pua was certain these were the words, or their meaning. "You will bring it to me now, before I curse you and curse this temple to the fourth generation."

The *maka nui* was Ramsey's most treasured totem. It granted him the eye of a god, how could she surrender it to the evil one? *Mo'o* the water serpent squeezed so she fell to one knee.

Kaka Kamahine spoke, the words just audible above the pounding of her heart: "You returned to Ramsey *uhane*, his soul. You counted it a victory but you did not defeat me, you have not the *mana*. By possessing his totem I shall enter him when he least suspects."

Mo'o released her only enough to run upstairs, pushing through the girls just coming from their dinner. She did not cry to them, for no matter how advanced their training they would have been helpless against the Uli's dark powers.

She prostrated herself on the floor of Sienna's office, surrendering the precious brass tube of Ramsey at the wet feet of the Uli. It spoke again. These were its words, she was certain of it, Pua recounted to *makuahine* Sienna the next day, when she, quaking from every pore of her body, relayed the tale of the awful visitation: "You have done well. You have kept the *maka nui* of the *haole* Ramsey safely for me. With the totem I shall possess him and he shall belong to me forever. You are released from obligation and fear. I shall not send my curse upon you, or upon this house. But never trouble under pain of death to seek him or to look his way again."

And when Pua lifted her head Kaka Kamahine had disappeared into the air, taking her familiar the *mo'o* with her, but leaving behind the garment by which she assumed the form of *makuahine* Sienna.

THIRTY

Ramsey got himself up with the dawn. Reverend Somers had relegated him to an empty cabin normally occupied by a pair of field hands during calving. It was spare, planked in scrubbed pine, with unfinished walls under a pitched tin roof, and to his liking. Somers chose it to make clear his status at Hale Nui. Ramsey accepted it gladly for its appreciation of the grounds, but more for Eliza Somers' frequent traverse of them in the weak morning light, a wraith in unstructured garments floating above the grass like a graceful twist of mist.

Hoof beats had awakened him, and he just caught sight of her through the cabin's rear screen door as she jogged on horseback toward the beach. He contrived to be out, dressed in his khaki and tall boots, Manu's red scarf knotted around his throat, looking innocent about the estate when she returned through the gate. She rode the horse astride, which stimulated him. He timed his stroll to be able to help her down. Though she had thrown on a cape and riding trousers, she was wet still and smelled of the ocean.

"You are out early, Mrs. Somers." Baby Kamuela got up at the cooing of the doves, a troubled infant with an arm wizened in the womb. He was accustomed to spying upon her, she looking beatific and motherly in the morning, the child cozied to her bosom, but not like this, not loosely covered, hair wet, cheeks sun scrabbled and flush from her exertions.

"As are you, Mr. Ramsey. Sentry not about?"

A *kanaka* appeared for the horse and she passed him the reins.

"'Spect he's asleep. We was up late playing cards with your *luna*. – Poor fellow's not much for a walk anyhow. Can't convince him to take me as far as that grove yonder. How's a invalid supposed to recover without fresh air and exercise?" He dimpled at her.

"You – I ..." She turned away from him – nervously, he thought, as though uncomfortable with so near a presence to him.

He liked that. He stayed close.

"I need your cooperation, Mr. Ramsey," she said over her shoulder. "*Kokua*, we call it."

She tugged the cape across her bare arms. "Please follow me onto the *lanai*. I'll have someone get your sentry out of bed. Mr. Somers pledged his word to the Attorney General, you know. We can't have you extend your walk outside the gate."

He bowed her onto the veranda. "You'll get no cause for alarm from me, Mrs. Somers. Why should I? An innocent man has no prison. And this" – he caught her eye and swept his arm across the perspective – "this is scarcely a cage."

"You really are ..." She shook her head. "Well, if Hale Nui is to your liking, Mr. Ramsey ... that is, I am glad, of course, I –"

"I trust that was a sincere remark." He squinted at her. "I am a sailor and an orphan, Mrs. Somers. I have never enjoyed a home such as this."

She faltered. "I only meant – well, we *kama☒aina*, hospitality is in our nature."

"Something else I have learned here," he said. "Mind if I smoke?" He took a chair and fished for his tobacco. He was out of cigars. "I've come to appreciate the beauty of your islands. It is quite a spectacle, you realize, what the sun does each morning. A man could ... well, a man feels things he doesn't ..." He glanced at her sheepishly, feeling suddenly genuine. "I don't know what's come over me, ma'am. Being imprisoned with you and your husband has turned me downright sentimental. Must be the good Reverend's daily Bible study." He smiled up at her and rolled a cigarette.

"Well I happen to agree with you. This is heaven on earth. It should be kept that way."

"Yes, ma'am."

She sat opposite him in the rocker she used to nurse Kamuela. "No, you misunderstand me. I mean it. Hawaii should be left alone."

"I don't quite know what you mean, Mrs. Somers."

She leaned toward him, elbows on her knees. The smoke from his cigarette lazed by her. The dried salt stood the downy hairs erect on her skin. She was close enough to smell.

"Then you are not the man I think you are. This information of yours, if it is worth your life, it will change the islands forever. I'm certain of that, and you – you have to know it. We'll never be the same again. We'll become an American outpost. The Hawaiians and Hawaiian ways will die out. Is that what you want?"

"Maybe it's progress."

"Progress?" She shook her head. "You and I must have very different ideas on that, Mr. Ramsey." She held his eyes. "Progress for me is my children growing up loving this land, seeing it as sacred, learning the traditions. What is it for you?"

"Progress? Why, I don't rightly know, I –"

"Come now, Mr. Ramsey. You wish progress on me, on my family. What is it? Is it the course of your affairs with Jessica Mornay? With the Navy? Is that progress? How about here at the ranch? How is your progress here?"

"Well I don't know, Mrs. Somers. How is it going?"

"On the ranch? I'd say the jury is still out on that, Mr. Ramsey."

He nodded and finished his cigarette. "Good to hear there is a jury. The Navy, I don't think I'll get one." He started to toss the end onto the grass, but with Eliza right there he reconsidered and crushed it on the sole of his boot. "That's why what I know, I need to know. And what I know is likely to make a big difference, you're right. A body might reckon it actually makes me look sort of good – attractive, you might say. The jury could look favorably on me because of it. What do you think, Mrs. Somers? Do I stand a chance?"

She colored and looked away. "I think you need to see my little Ruthie *hula*." She rocked in the chair.

He smiled, thinking perhaps progress had been made. "Your little girl does the *hula*?"

She nodded. "Noelani is teaching her. She was a royal dancer before she took up with my brother. It's keeping what's precious about these islands alive. No one danced when I was a girl."

"You know," he said, "folks I was raised around would be madder 'n hornets at your brother, taking up with a local gal. Separating the races is man's protection."

"Oh?" She stopped rocking. "Is that so? Tell me, what's a man need protection from, Mr. Ramsey?"

He chuckled. "Damned if I know – pardon me, ma'am."

"No, I want to know. A man's supposed to take care of his family, it's his responsibility. What's he need protection from?"

"You are the damnedest – I don't know, Mrs. Somers. Maybe himself, I don't know."

"That what you believe?"

He sighed. "Tell you the truth, I don't know what I believe anymore. Being out here, with you, the islands, it's made me – well, I don't rightly know what it's made me." He pulled the flake of white paper and tobacco strings from his pocket. "I just know this cigarette stub would have looked plug ugly tossed on your green grass."

After a moment she said, "Then maybe there is hope for you." Her eyes settled on him. "Mr. Ramsey ... John, there must be something you've loved, something you've cared about in your life enough to sacrifice for it. Or someone, someone who loved you."

He adjusted uneasily in his seat.

"Someone ... that's it, isn't it." She placed a hand on his. Her touch felt rough, a hand that worked, not dainty. "Someone loved you, I see it now under the brittleness." He looked away.

"Someone loved you, she cared about you. Did she sacrifice for you? Did she?" She squeezed his hand. "Listen, please! Would you throw away her love? Tarnish her name?"

He got up and stood against the railing.

"Her love is what we mean by *'aloha.'* It means caring about someone so much, you do something for them you would not do for yourself." She stood near him. "Maybe you do something a little foolish. My baby Kamuela – you've held him in your arms, you know he's deformed. What will become of him without *aloha?* My little Ruthie – I want you to care about them as your very own. You're an orphan? Take them as your family. These islands? Take us as your home."

He turned his head and dug blindly for his tobacco.

"Whatever you know, whatever you've found out, you must tell the King. Tell him only. Please," she said.

He stumped about the estate in the afternoon, unsettled. He could not rid himself of Eliza Somers' eyes. They'd been passionate. It wasn't passion for someone. It wasn't passion for him. It's a passion for this place, he thought, the ground I'm walking on, the wrinkled mountains, air you can feel, the way the ocean behaves in the sun.

It was love. He wanted it.

A buckboard clattered to a halt. The driver pulled too hard on the rein and the horse backed and reared in protest. Jessica was upon him before he realized. "O, John, I hired it! Did you ever? I have not driven before. They had to show me. I tore my glove on the reins. But it was so thrilling! I think I shall have to purchase a rig of my own, I've the money now. – O, but I quite drove a man off the road, what a danger I was in town!"

She greeted everyone effusively. "There is a mutton in the buggy, and a custard, if I didn't destroy it. I thought the children might enjoy it – and of course, John, your precious package!"

He took it without a word, a bundle wrapped in brown paper tied with sisal, and headed for his cabin. Behind him through the window screens of the big house eddied the noises attendant upon welcoming a visitor: the scampering of the children's feet, their voices high-pitched over the custard, the scraping of chairs, the settling of belongings, the cry for refreshment, the gabble of conversation.

The cabin door had no lock but he wedged a chair behind it and sat on the bed. The package was done up securely – by whose hand? Surely not Jessica's. Other hands had prepared this package. He had received parcels from Jessica wrapped as though she'd been called away in the midst and quite forgotten what she was about. This had method to it, and attention; appreciation, even, for a fine instrument. The tube itself was packed in cotton batting and wrapped in rolls of paper to protect it in transit. A man had prepared this package, a man of science or, more likely, a military man.

He held the tube up to the light streaming through the window. It was tarnished, the eyepiece carbon-glazed from the fire but otherwise serviceable. There were scratches at several of the seams. Some person had puzzled over it, perhaps more than one. But no one had solved it, that was evident. No one had discovered the mechanism which opened it.

He pressed the eye piece and turned the outer tube clockwise. It was the natural direction for a left-handed person, but counter to a right-hander's inclination. A catch released, he depressed a slide, and there, untouched by flame or elements or malefaction, lay nestled the foolscap, the fair copy of the notes at Pu'uloa lagoon which were his salvation.

He rolled a cigarette, making a mess of the tobacco on his bunk. His hand trembled as he held the match. Everything had been riding on the tube and its secret compartment. Without it he was imprisoned, humiliated, cashiered, all he had worked for – career, self-respect, influence over men of the world – all beached on the anonymous cruelty of a naval prison yard and endless years at hard labor. The tobacco steadied his emotions and he drew it deeply then went to the back door and pitched the butt into the bushes behind the cabin. He re-bundled the tube and placed it in a drawer under some clothing. The foolscap he hid under a floorboard he had loosened until he finished sewing its secure repository.

He checked himself in the mirror before returning. The face looked back at him with growing relief. With the foolscap he had power. Commander Taylor would not like him the more. Regular Navy would not take him to its bosom, nor, regrettably, would Eliza Somers or her little Kamuela, who would have to grow up in a different world, one far more practical. And Pua. Manu would understand of course, making the prudent choice. A man must put himself first. The foolscap spelled freedom from Stevens, escape from criminal prosecution and purchase upon world events. Manu would understand, one agent to another. On the chessboard that was the Kingdom of Hawaii he was no longer a pawn but a knight – a knight whose intelligence, he realized, had the power to topple the king.

The table that evening was set with *koa* wood shakers, the Lee family candlesticks, china and silverware, cut crystal water goblets and plumeria blossoms floating in a matching bowl – and Ramsey, universally unpopular though he was at Hale Nui, was invited to dine.

"We could scarce do less by you, Mr. Ramsey," Somers said. "From what Miss Mornay reports, this may be the condemned man's last meal."

Jessica sat across from him. "O, John, it's true. There's a warship in the harbor. They're coming for you."

"Then I shall dine hearty. What could a man want for, but company such as this? The lovely ladies, the refined Mr. Somers, and this spirited *ohana*." He spread his arms to include the Portuguese *luna* and his wife, both combed and starched in their finest, the three children struggling at the table, and Aunty Pauline struggling with them to manage dropped forks and overturned goblets.

"Don't know how you do it, Gonsalves," Somers addressed the *luna* over his plate. "Five, isn't it? And only your wife to keep them in line. Eve had just Cain and Abel. That was enough to sire all mankind. Think of it."

"Really, Horace," Eliza said. "The Gonsalves children are perfectly lovely. I said so just the other day. Children need their freedom, so good for them on the ranch. Was for me."

After another spilled milk Eliza sent the children with Aunty Pauline for their custard, and Jessica expressed her desire to have some as well-behaved as they someday.

Somers measured his beef into neat slices. "So, Miss Mornay, do you suppose the Rifles will come for our Mr. Ramsey soon?"

"Yes, very soon." Jessica pulled at her hair. "Perhaps tomorrow, John."

"Tomorrow?" said Gonsalves, his English clear but accented. "That is soon. What do you think, Reverend, will you hear his confession after supper? He'll need plenty of time for the sins he's got."

Somers smiled. "Well I am not a papist, I don't normally hear confession, but perhaps in the case of a soul truly languishing … What do you think, Ramsey, will they shoot you at dawn?"

"Sorry to disappoint you, gentlemen." He was unfazed. "Old Ned ain't left his calling card just yet."

"Too bad." Gonsalves wiped his moustaches clean of gravy. "I had my men put an edge to their shovels. They'll be *huhu*, they hoped to use them."

"Yes, Ramsey. You could be cooperative just this once," Somers said. "I've a splendid prayer for Christian burial."

He refused to be cowed. "Can't poke a polecat from the porch with a rope, Reverend. It'll take more than the Honolulu Rifles to make a pilgrim out of me."

"Well I think this is a most unsavory conversation, gentlemen," Eliza said. "Hale Nui has always practiced charity at its table."

"I apologize, Mrs. Somers," Gonsalves said. "I was just concerned the prisoner would take a fast horse over the Pali, embarrass the ranch."

"There would have to be something the prisoner feared," he said evenly.

"And you don't?" Gonsalves responded. "What's in that package Miss Mornay brought? Letters of Passage?"

"You could say that."

"See here, Ramsey," Somers said. "You've had the succor of Hale Nui. The very least, we should know your guilt or innocence."

Eliza attempted to break in on his behalf but he sloughed her off. He was in the catbird seat. Soon enough he'd be in the hands of the Honolulu Rifles.

"Guilt or innocence, Reverend? My daddy, he had this Red tick hound," he drawled, honeysuckle and grinning. "Everybody knew him, said he got after their chickens."

"I thought you scarcely knew your father," Jessica said.

"Why, whatever do you mean? That was the huntingest dog in the county." He took in the table. "He did love his chickens, though."

"Well," Gonsalves said, "once a dog gets chicken blood up its nose …"

"Yup, daddy had to shoot him, just to keep the neighbors quiet."

"You have to," the *luna* said. "I've done it."

"True enough. But the chickens kept dying,' that's the thing. Turned out wasn't my daddy's hound after all. A red fox, he was gettin' 'em. Try as they could, they never caught him, neither."

"The poor dog," Jessica said. "They killed him, and he was innocent?"

Somers looked up from his plate. "One doesn't apply guilt or innocence to the beasts, Miss Mornay. Only to men."

"So, Ramsey, you are the dog. I like this," Gonsalves said. "Innocent or not, you'll be shot. But why waste a bullet, I say. A dog, he hasn't a soul, has he, Reverend Somers? Just put him in a sack and drown him."

"Innocent? O, no, not me, Gonsalves," he said with a twinkle. "I'm the fox. And they never can catch me!"

The *luna* colored. "I think you'll find yourself dog enough when the Rifles take custody of you. I'd like to learn you a few tricks myself."

Mrs. Gonsalves put a hand on her husband's arm, and Eliza restored order by rapping the table with a *koa* shaker.

"What is all this, John?" Jessica asked hastily. "I thought you were safe now."

"He is," said Somers, "provided he's in American custody."

"But he's on Hawaiian soil," Gonsalves said. "And it's the Rifles coming for him."

"Well I don't know all the fuss over a brass tube." Jessica swallowed her glass. "O, it's water. I thought – John, anyway, the tube, I wish you'd just give it to them and be done with it."

"He gives it to them, they don't need him anymore," Gonsalves said.

"What's so important about it? Just because John made it himself? He did, you know. He's ever so clever. My father had a brass tube just like it, with his instruments. He let me look. It magnified whatever you put on the end. What looked like an old blotch turned out to have a whole world inside, like looking at the finest filigree."

Ramsey studied his plate. The others looked from eye to eye as Jessica spoke. It was the first time the contents of the package had been described.

"Sounds like a survey tube," Gonsalves remarked.

"Yes, that's what it is!" Jessica exclaimed. "John says it's the finest in the kingdom!"

"So, you've surveyed the Kingdom's treasures." Gonsalves tugged his napkin from his collar. "Don't you owe it to the Kingdom to disclose the results?"

He looked at him steadily. "I am under orders."

"Well, and to be fair about it, Ramsey is under sentence with the Navy. He must protect himself," said Somers.

"But he doesn't conceive that this government might protect him?" Gonsalves objected.

"This government?" Ramsey laughed. "Your pardon, gents, how does it protect me? It cannot protect its King. It's got no army of its own. The Rifles are the only force to reckon with, and those boys don't have the powder of a two dollar pistol."

"There is more to our King and this land than arms, Mr. Ramsey. I've spoken to you about this," Eliza said.

"We can't expect more out of an American enlisted man, Mrs. Somers," said Gonsalves. "Not one who chooses shore duty over a ship, or an embassy assignment over a man's billet."

"You are either calling me lazy or cowardly," said Ramsey.

"I'd have to put you with the field hands to know if you're lazy." Gonsalves eyed him steadily.

"I'll show you cowardice, Gonsalves!" Ramsey's chair clattered over as he stood.

"Gentlemen, gentlemen!" This time, Somers gaveled the table.

Ramsey boiled, but before he leaped across the table he mumbled an apology to Eliza and took himself out to the yard, steaming. The sky was ink with twinkling dots of white. Diamond Head loomed in the background. He cut through the shadows behind the privy and strode upslope, feeling the muscles pull behind his legs. Under normal circumstances he'd have called the *luna* out and shot him cleanly through the shoulder, an uncomplicated wound, the horse's ass should be happy it wasn't worse. But these were not normal circumstances. He was balancing on a tight rope, "making gumbo without the filé," as Sienna liked to say. No room for error. A stumble, and even Pearl River would not save him.

He stomped heavy-footed up the incline until the anger worked itself out then reversed his course and headed to his bungalow. Mounting its steps he heard the screen door at the back squeak. He did not bother to stick his head in or light the oil lamp. His room would be ransacked and the survey tube gone.

He tilted a wooden chair and sat on the porch, his boots propped on the railing, the frogs, lizards and crickets in full throat throughout the estate. The tube was gone but not the map of Pearl lagoon. That was secure and so was his future. Once he handed it over to a government, his or another, nothing native would be left to stand. The kingdom Gonsalves defended so righteously would disappear.

A man could not get sentimental about such things, or he'd be left to wind his watch stem, sip lemonade and lose his mind beneath the magnolias.

Ten years after the war he had located his father at a sanitarium on the Gulf Coast, slouched upon a bench. There were oaks overhead, no magnolias, but his father did sip lemonade and he was winding his watch. A humid wind blew off the gulf promising rain in a day, heavy, perhaps a hurricane. His father had joined the Union Army, the 50th Ohio, became wounded, was captured and interned at Andersonville, the punishing Confederate prison camp. He survived dysentery but was starved and daily tormented by the guards for betraying the Cause, until his sanity fully departed him. When the camp was opened in 1865, Sarah found him and never again left his side.

Ramsey watched them, his father blankly winding the useless timepiece that had stopped most of the minié ball responsible for the wound, Sarah cooling his face with a cloth. She'd been handled cruelly, whatever happened to them crossing north to the promised land. He saw it in her stooped shoulders and crippled hands. And Jim Crow now ruling the South, whatever his father found with her in the weathered shack back of the farmhouse was henceforth denied them. She was a nigger gal, far as the sanitarium officials knew, a freed slave who couldn't let go her master.

He told them no different. His mother had been disgraced horribly, Hanky ran off with the Blue Bellies, and he'd had to grow up fast. Nothing said would change any of that.

Standing aside watching them reprise their movements like a mechanical tableau, his father winding his watch stem, Sarah bathing his face, he could not remember why he had come. He slipped away without a word, though Sarah's eyes met his and held them, uncomfortably. All his eyes could fill with were an old man broken for his untoward beliefs. All his mind could fill with was determination. Never would he be found absently winding his watch stem, a Colored to clean the drool from his lips ...

The screen door squeaked and light footsteps tapped from the back of the bungalow through his sleeping space to the front porch. The rustling of fabric brought him to himself. He set the chair down, hopes soaring.

"John," came the voice, followed by lips wet against his ear, "what are you doing alone, when you should be putting your arms around me?"

Jessica commanded his mouth. He could smell her, lilac bath water and the sweet fumes of alcohol. "It's just the two of us, John. At last."

He carried her into the cabin. She was not the same Jessica Mornay he had known in bed just months ago. She provoked, snipped with her lips and teeth, and unhesitatingly slid her hand low across his belly. She giggled when he pressed himself firmly against her. She wore one of the missionary dresses, with scarcely anything beneath it. He could feel her breasts round on his chest, and she did not withdraw from him as he grew tumescent.

He unbuttoned the sleeves of her Mother Hubbard and slipped it over her head. She held up her arms to make it easy then threw herself eagerly back into his. He made to remove the silk chemise that covered her from shoulders to calf, but she stopped him. "No, John. Not until we are married."

He stripped to his union suit. He'd cut it down to his elbows and knees. She unbuttoned it and kissed his chest hairs. "I really like your chest," she said.

He pressed her onto the bed and kissed her lips, and she groaned. She lifted the hem of the chemise, and he fumbled with his remaining buttons. He ran both hands up her exposed thighs and she gasped. Then he sank into her, her legs open and accepting, her arms wrapped tightly around his neck, and she alternately crying or gasping with each thrust of his body, until the gasps seemed to win out, and she cried all the harder at the end. "O, John," she said, "O, John. It's you. It's always been you. O, John." Her tears drained onto his neck.

He rolled over and she lay on top of him, her body sunk completely into his. He listened to a night creature clicking somewhere for its mate and thought she dozed. His mind wandered to women, to other women, to other faces, other hands, to the gentle, passionate sort of woman he might want to have in his life, then Jessica moved. She started pleasuring herself though he had turned soft.

He wasn't committed to it, it was just pleasant, in the darkness, moving with total focus upon the genitalia, but without need for a particular result. He placed his hands on her hips, naked now, the chemise having ridden up her body, and helped her move, interested in her compulsion. The motion grew in intensity, the movements themselves shorter and driven downward into his thrusts, and her breath starting to hitch in little hiccups. She dug her nails into his chest as her body tensed. She said nothing, just clamped down on him, eyes shut, face clenched in perfect concentration as she moved atop him. She was reaching for it, he could tell. Reaching for a prick of pleasure that teased her with promise. It seemed to send out tidbits that captured and pulled her one after the other into their orbit, spinning her deeper and higher, taking over her body, launching it beyond the reach of will to involuntary, autonomic reflex, her elbows locked, fingers dumb to the damage they caused him, hips tossing forward and back in their own dance until she was thrown back, rising over him like a cobra spreading its hood in a trance. She peaked there, shuddering and expanding and crying out as wave after wave of pleasure seized and flooded her, and she was insensate to all but the autonomic which had carried her exhausted over the edge.

Jessica sat bleary-eyed before the mirror and tried to piece herself together. Morning light warmed the bungalow. The ranch was going about the new day. She watched John snore softly on the bed, twisted in the sheet like her baby brother used to. She didn't want to wake him, but there wasn't much time. "Get up, please, John. You have to help me."

He rolled over.

"Do you have a brush or something, John? I have to do some-thing with my hair. Wish I had one of my wigs."

He swung his legs off the bed and looked at her.

"We don't want everyone to talk. Not yet anyhow." She pinched her cheeks then winced. It made her head hurt more. "Help me find my things, please. You were a monster last night. What became of my reserved Navy man?"

"Who did it, Jessica?"

She looked at him in the mirror. His eyes were hollow and unblinking.

"Who sent you in here like this?"

"Did I have my straw bag with me? Look for it, John. I'm feeling a little ... Should find some pins in it."

"Was it Ashford? Had to be. Somers couldn't live with himself."

"Eliza gave me this to wear. Thank God." She smoothed the Mother Hubbard with her hands. "It covers everything. The natives wear them. O, there's my ... no need to tell you what that is, Mr. Ramsey!" She stood to retrieve an undergarment from the corner.

He stopped her with a naked shin.

"Really, John. I must get back to the house. What will people say?"

"You set there, girl. You just set there. Have a good look at yourself."

He got up, so she sat back down and poked at her hair in the mirror. She felt her heart tripping.

He loomed over her. "Who was it, Jessica? I'm about out of patience. Who's got his brand on you, you'd do anything he wants. Even this."

"I don't know what you ... you're the only –"

"Don't say it. What do you think I am? You snuck over here like a two-bit –"

"No, John, no! Believe me. I ..." Her head swam. He had to see it her way, he just had to. "Give it to them, please! Whatever it is, it's not that tube thing, is it. It's something else." She turned around to face him, tears flowing. "Give it to them. You'll be free, I'll be free. We can get on with our lives. You can quit the Navy, we could live in Honolulu. O, we could, John, we could. We'd get on very well, better than you're doing now. I'm very well thought of now, I really am. All the right circles, you should see me. You could join the government after the King steps down."

He grabbed her arms and shook her. "Nobody thinks well of you, Jessica! Nobody!"

"Don't say that, John. Don't!"

"Say the name! Say it! Was it Thurston?"

"You're hurting me!"

"Ashford, was it Ashford?" He shook her again. She thought her arms would break off. "I want to hear you say it!"

"I was trying to …"

"Tell me, goddamn it!"

"… trying to …"

"Tell me!"

"… to help you!"

His eyes bulged. "Help me?" The vein pumped in his forehead.

"They told me you'd never –"

"What? Never amount to anything?" He shook her again.

"Stop it, John! Stop!"

"Thought I needed you?"

She was blacking out. "Please, you're hurting …!"

"Say it, say what you are!"

She saw him raise his hand to strike her. She fainted and slumped to the floor.

THIRTY-ONE

A day later Eliza cut red hibiscus flowers barefoot from a
bush near Ramsey's cabin. He and Jessica weren't speaking, and she was curious. Had he got some backbone?
Some character after all? It wasn't her business certainly, still the
curiosity … She lingered at the foliage, squatting down, testing
the soil for dampness, thinking papa-san really needed to get
more water on the beds. The rattle of wagon wheels pulled her
upright.

Lorrin Thurston, dressed in sergeant's uniform, riding a
handsome nut brown gelding with long mane and white socks,
led a buckboard into the yard. Two Honolulu Rifles drove it.
One of them, a beefy, large shouldered hairless man, she recognized as a butcher in town. He lifted manacles and leg irons
from the buckboard and bellowed for the prisoner.

"See here, Mr. Thurston," her husband called from the *lanai*
of the big house, "where's the squad of infantry? I thought the
plan was to return him to the Attorney General with some
propriety."

Thurston stayed atop his horse. "Get that rig turned around,"
he ordered. "I want to bring him back with plenty of sunlight."

Her husband came down to the drive. "The kitchen can prepare a little nourishment, we want to be certain he –"

"Send your *luna* over, Reverend. Let's get the horses watered."

"Where's the prisoner?" the butcher demanded.

She dropped her snips into a basket and approached the men. "Good morning, Lorrin – gentlemen."

The driver doffed his cap, the others looked at her. She stroked the horse's nose with the back of her hand. "We really don't treat him like a prisoner, Lorrin, not exactly. He really isn't a –"

Thurston leaned across the withers. "Had the run of the place, did he? You always were too accommodating, Eliza. The city is very different from the country."

Her *luna* appeared. "Ah, Gonsalves," he said. "Take care of the horses, will you? We want to get going while the sun is still high. And Ramsey, we going to have any problem with him? You're a military man."

"My men and me," Gonsalves said, "we'll bundle him up right."

"Take my private with you, he's got the leg irons." He dismounted and handed the reins to a ranch hand.

"Really, Lorrin, leg irons?"

"Don't you think the Kingdom should demonstrate humane treatment, Mr. Thurston?" her husband said.

Thurston pulled off his riding gloves. His uniform looked dulled by red dust and his helmet had lost its garrison sheen, but he strutted cockily. "Humane treatment, Reverend? You don't know the half of what's going on. Luahine's on the rampage. Absolutely demands the new temple or lava will erupt at Punch Bowl, burn the town. People don't know what to make of it, won't go out at night. Her damned priests are everywhere acting up, scaring law-abiding citizens half to death. Kalakaua won't leave the palace. Wasn't for the Rifles patrolling the streets, no telling what we'd have. Ramsey, he's part of the lawlessness. It's time this nation showed its mettle. We won't countenance treachery anywhere – at the palace, or from a scalawag like him."

The *luna* came down the steps of Ramsey's cabin. "It's empty. He's not there."

"Empty?!" Thurston turned to her.

"I don't know … I – I thought he was asleep," she stuttered. "I was gardening right here …"

"Where's his sentry?" he demanded.

"The man's a drunk," her husband said. "He's a disgrace. Why, Mr. Ramsey had to keep an eye on him, keep him out of the liquor cabinet."

"I thought I saw the sentry earlier." She shaded her eyes and looked across the yard. "Mr. Ramsey couldn't – that is, he wouldn't …"

"Couldn't be a coward, Eliza? Wouldn't run off?" Thurston snickered. "Wouldn't you like to think so. – Gonsalves, form a search party. Take one of my men. You scour the grounds, I'll take the trail back to –"

Aunty Pauline's voice broke in. "He make *moemoe*. He stay by me," she called from the *lanai*. She was rocking Kamuela. "He sleep inside da chair."

"What's that, Aunty Pauline?" Eliza raised her voice. "Mr. Ramsey is on the *lanai*?"

"Da sentry stay on top the *lanai*. Ramsey stay wit' the *keiki* kids."

Before anyone on the carriage drive could comment further, Horace, Jr. broke from the banana grove on the *makai* end of the grounds. "We got him, mama!" he called. "We captured the prisoner! I roped him and Ruthie tied him up!"

"Ruthie?!" she exclaimed. She looked helplessly at Thurston. "You captured Mr. Ramsey?"

Thurston gestured to his big private, who with Gonsalves trotted across the grounds toward the boy.

"Not Ramsey, mama. The Indian. Big Chief Run Amok!"

She saw her little Ruthie poke through the banana trunks carrying the end of a thick rope. Her son announced, "I'm Buffalo Bill, and this is Annie Oakley. And this" – he yanked on the rope – "this is our prisoner, a real Injun!"

Ramsey, duck-walking beneath the banana leaves, stepped into the sunlight. The rope was wrapped around his arms. A peacock feather stuck out of a kerchief twisted about his head. He straightened and took in the party gathered on the carriage drive, a crooked grin on his face.

Thurston's man caught up and shoved him to the ground.

"Hey, that's our prisoner!" Horace cried.

"Our prisoner!" Ruthie echoed.

Gonsalves interceded. "All right, kids. Take your prisoner over to the wagon. The sheriff will take him from there."

"Gentlemen!" Ramsey said as he was brought over. "And madam," he bowed to Eliza.

"I didn't realize you were with the children, Mr. Ramsey," she said.

"You see, Mrs. Somers, even I can be touched by 'em. You said there was hope for me."

"And there is," she replied. "There truly is, Mr. Ramsey."

Thurston cursed. "Well, this is a comely bit of domesticity, Reverend. What sort of incarceration went on here?"

Her husband told her to take the children into the house. She shooed them before her, said a word to Aunty Pauline then stood on the *lanai*, arms crossed over her tummy, feeling heart sick. Gonsalves was uncoiling the ropes from around Ramsey. When he was free, the butcher pushed him down again. Thurston sent for the sentry, whom he dressed down for his incompetence. "Get into your uniform," Thurston ordered, "you'll march behind the wagon with the prisoner."

"Thurston," she heard Ramsey say from the dirt, "I'll just put on my uniform as well."

"You'll do nothing of the sort. You can gull the Navy, but not me. You'll march as a civilian."

The butcher grunted his approval as he pulled him to his feet and started to pass the chains around his waist.

"I am a Petty Officer in the United States Navy. I am under military jurisdiction. I demand the right to wear my uniform."

The butcher passed the chain between his legs then yanked upward so severely that he cried out.

"Just a moment, Sergeant!" Jessica descended the steps of the *lanai*. Eliza hadn't heard her come out. She wasn't fully made up for the day. A shawl pulled from the house draped her shoulders. She'd been crying.

"Mr. Ramsey is entitled to his uniform," Jessica said from the lawn. "He should wear it."

"Miss Mornay," Thurston bowed disdainfully. "You, too? The little drama is complete."

"I want him to wear his uniform."

"I see. And by whose authority, exactly?"

"I think you know." Jessica folded her arms across the shawl.

"Ah, Colonel Ashford. Or haven't you escaped from this scoundrel's web yet?"

The butcher yanked the chain again and Ramsey doubled over.

"Ashford must have been stinkingly well-seasoned to let you come out here." Thurston gestured with his riding crop. "He does know you are here?"

"His uniform, Sergeant."

Eliza felt proud of Jessica, immensely proud. The girl stood unwavering in the grass. Then she caught sight of Aunty Pauline. A file of kitchen staff followed her.

"*Kahea 'ai*, Lorrin! Come eat!" She pointed to the monkey pod. Aunty Pauline hurried toward it, the Chinese scurrying behind with tables, chairs and everything the larder could produce. They set a tall pitcher of tea under the limbs, and alongside it, two liter bottles of beer.

"*Kahea 'ai!*" she repeated.

"Let me take the prisoner, Sergeant." Gonsalves shoved Ramsey toward the cabin. "Give Hale Nui the honor of provisioning the Honolulu Rifles. I'll take care of this one, believe me."

The chains caught the cabin steps, and Ramsey stumbled.

The sun was directly overhead when Thurston got up from the shade of the tree and remounted his horse where they'd

stood Ramsey in chains, his white duck trousers and tunic as clean as Aunty Pauline and Hale Nui could make them. He wore his regulation visored hat.

"Don't you salute a superior, sailor?" Thurston demanded.

"Actually, Sergeant Thurston," the *luna* said, "he's your superior in rank. You should salute him."

Thurston, his horse skittish, eager to get away from the flies, said, "O, of course," and held his salute while Ramsey, struggling with the shackles, attempted to elevate his hand to return it. The chains tightened as he did so and impaled him in the groin.

The men laughed and the butcher knocked the hat from his head, and the horse, shying, trod it into the ground with its hooves. Thurston grinned. Ramsey now stood exposed to the direct Hawaiian sun.

Eliza watched from the table feeling helpless, wanting her husband to do something, wanting someone to do something. She heard Gonsalves order Ramsey's baggage brought from the cabin.

"Everything?" Thurston asked.

The *luna* nodded. One piece, a brown valise, he dumped in Ramsey's arms to carry. The rest he told the men to throw in the back of the rig.

Eliza gasped. She spotted Horace. He'd been hiding under the wagon. He slipped between the wheels and threw himself around Ramsey's leg. "Don't go, Chief Run Amok! Don't go!"

She ran down the lawn and got him. "Horace ..." Her eyes welled up. "Mr. Ramsey ... please, remember what I said. The King can protect you. I can –"

Thurston spurred his horse over and separated them.

Aunty Pauline pushed herself through the men, clapped Ramsey's *lauhala* hat on his brow, called Thurston "*pupule* head" and strode back to the house.

Eliza had never been so happy with the old nursemaid. "Come, Horace," she said, wiping the tears and following her up the yard.

Thurston took in Hale Nui arrayed before him: the Chinese help clustered at the detached kitchen behind the house; the field hands and Hawaiian wranglers in kerchiefs and wearing head gear styled to their various responsibilities; Gonsalves and his wife beneath the monkey pod, Somers next to them; and Eliza standing with Aunty Pauline, each of them grasping children who, for the first time since his arrival, were holding themselves still.

"As pretty a picture of Hawaiian life as I have seen, Eliza," Thurston called. "Reminds me of our days at Punahou. The whitewashed classroom. The barn we had chores in across the way. The night blooming cereus Mrs. Bingham planted. It takes me back. Maybe with what we get out of Ramsey here, we'll preserve some of it. But there must be change. No stopping that."

He touched his horse in the flanks and led the party onto the trail back to Honolulu. The two Rifles rode the buckboard, Ramsey chained behind it, and the disgraced sentry following to hoist him when he fell.

Eliza looked back at the house. Jessica stood at the upstairs window daubing her eyes.

The sun at four o'clock, if he gauged it right, its beams slanting now out of the west directly into his eyes; no sign of Honolulu, or even its proximity, after three hours or more on the trail, Thurston having led the party over uncultivated back country spiked with *kiawe* thorns, cutting sharp lava rock, and a swamp in which they'd nearly lost his sentry and his baggage – Ramsey stood now where Thurston called a halt, panting, his uniform in ribbons from being dragged behind the buckboard, bleeding everywhere, and the *lauhala* hat no longer shading him but on the head of the butcher.

The butcher took a blade to everything he had, his clothing, spare boots, books, even the satchels themselves. He shredded them then turned to Thurston and shook his head. "Nothing here, no map, nothing."

Thurston, on the stamping horse, gestured and the butcher held the blade before his nose. "Let's see what you got hid here."

He didn't take his eyes off the butcher's eyes. He felt the steel cold against his skin as it sliced through the seams of his garments. When it cut into his flesh he did not flinch. He would not give the man the satisfaction.

His clothing fell away, just enough trouser left to cover his genitals. The sun now had unbuffered access to his skin. There was no shade. He crouched to protect his chest while the men drank from their canteens. Somewhere beyond the scrub the surf boomed.

The sentry came over and offered his canteen, but Thurston stopped him. "No fraternizing with the prisoner. He wants water, he'll get it soon enough."

He looked up. He could withstand the worst Thurston gave out. Strike him, kick him, drag him behind the wagon, he was not afraid, and he knew how to take pain – provided he was on land.

Thurston kicked him to his feet. He was chewing tobacco. "You know, Ramsey, I'd just as soon drown you as come back empty-handed. Stevens promised us help, said you were the best at it. But if you're the best America has, maybe I should rethink annexation." He bent his head and expelled a clot of tobacco juice down his bare leg. "You appear to me a pusillanimous, light-heeled fag of a man. Don't know what Jessica …You won't survive what I got in mind. You ought to think again about the location of that document."

The butcher came over. Even beneath the woven hat his face had turned red. He brandished his knife. "Why don't I just open him arse-house to gullet? We'll find it."

"I don't want to cut it out of him. I want to rip it out of him." Thurston spat again.

They grabbed him under the arms and dragged him through the brush. Thorns scraped his face and sliced him further. They passed through a grove of coconut trees, their fallen limbs trapping his boots and throwing him against the chains, and there it was: below a strip of beach rocky with shells and under-digested coral, the ocean, flogging itself with bursting limbs of surf and white lashes of sea foam.

He recoiled. He had no control over himself. He twisted and pulled against the chains, terrified. The cuffs chafed his wrists and broke the skin.

Thurston yanked them to get his attention. "You're going in there, Ramsey. That's Diamond Head point. Even a strong swimmer doesn't go in when the surf is high. – Now, where is it? Where's your plans?!"

He mumbled indistinctly, unable to take in anything but the surf cannibalizing the beach.

"Take him," Thurston commanded.

The Rifles pulled him across the sand toward the waterline. He squirmed and fought but could not get his footing. He slipped on the seaweed and the chains encumbered his feet. He'd promised himself to give nothing to the Rifles. They couldn't beat it out of him, not with their fists, but the water could.

He broke free for a moment but the sand was too wet. His boots sank into it, he couldn't run. Thurston stood on one length of the chain and laughed.

Then the butcher seized a fistful of his hair and dragged him waist-deep into the water. He screamed and a wave crested and filled his mouth and lungs with salt water. It flipped him over and drove his head under the surface into the sandy bottom. He panicked, eyes open and filling with grit, the air chased out of his lungs by the water. He beat about with his legs and arms, lungs crying for air, temples throbbing. Desperate to breathe, he sucked in more water and drowned the last of his oxygen. Then the manacles tightened on his wrists and he was dragged to the beach by the Rifles pulling on the chain. He lay face down, hacking up sea water and gasping.

"And that was just a little one," the butcher said. "Wait 'til we take you into the surf!"

Thurston squatted by his head. "Where is it, Ramsey?"

"The valise," he said, coughing and spitting. "Where I lost it back at the swamp."

It wasn't there but he had to tell them something. And by Christ, he wouldn't tell them the truth, not without a fight, not if he could help it. Eliza Somers' face swam before him. He seized upon it as his brain struggled to find a way out. He wouldn't turn over the document to Thurston and the Rifles. He wasn't sure about giving it to the king, but he wouldn't turn it over to the king's enemies. That much he could do.

Footsteps crunched the sand by his face. The sentry placed the valise in front of him. It had been shredded like the rest of his baggage.

"And?" Thurston growled.

"Must have fallen out. That fat private you got is clumsy."

The butcher cursed and grabbed him again, pulled him into the shore break that skirted the beach. He panicked once more, swallowed water and was somersaulted, though he found his orientation this time more quickly. When they dragged him out he told them there was no document, it was only a ruse to get a promotion.

Twice more the butcher threw him in and in the second drubbing, by a wave that looked to him a monster, he overcame his fear. He found he could close his eyes, hold his breath and follow the chain to the bottom, which gave him a sense of security as the ocean tumbled about him. When they dragged him out, he was laughing and told them the document was under the floor boards back at the cabin. He'd be happy to lead them to it.

Lying on his back coughing hoarsely, layered in wet sand and seaweed, he could hear the four men conversing. Two of them, the driver and sentry, were for putting an end to it and heading back to town. The butcher wanted to pull him through the shore break to the reef where the surf was threatening. Thurston liked the butcher's idea.

"I'm opposed to this, Thurston," the sentry said.

"I'm the sergeant, I give the orders," Thurston said.

"You're no more a sergeant than I am a *kahuna*." The sentry threw a fistful of wet sand. "The Rifles aren't military. The Attorney General said we're supposed to provide this sailor safe conduct!"

"The American Minister said we're supposed to get out of him what we can. I put more store in the Americans than in one of Kalakaua's *hapa-haole* appointees!"

"Enough pissing around," the butcher said. He grabbed the chain and pulled him stumbling into the water.

"Ramsey!" the sentry called after him. "Duck your head when the surf breaks! Let it roll over you, don't fight it!"

Both men struggled in the surf. There was just enough bottom for them to keep their chins above water and wade out to the reef. The coral was as mercilessly cutting as lava rock, and difficult to balance upon when the current sucked out to sea, rose into a peak then came tumbling shoreward in four foot of surf. Ramsey panicked again as the undertow swept his legs out and he was dragged underwater toward open ocean. The butcher let the chain play out until he'd had a good scraping along the coral bed, then pulled him against the current until his head broke the surface, spitting water and gasping, floundering with his arms.

His boots were waterlogged and filled with sand, were a deadweight pulling him under. He reached blindly for the butcher, who had braced himself against a coral head, but the man pushed him back into the sucking belly of the next wave. He was pummeled once again and deposited bruised and bleeding, though upright on the reef. He read the rhythm of the surf this time, and before it could attack he braced himself and yanked hard on the chain, catching the butcher by surprise and forcing him over into the surf. The man stood up in the face of the next wave and he leaped onto his back and took two turns of the slack chain about his throat before the wave broke and drummed them both on the reef. He clung to his back and the butcher took the worst of it, unable to both free himself and protect his face. When they emerged coughing and spitting to the surface, he took a third turn of the chain tightly around the man's throat and rode the broad back of the butcher into another encounter with the reef. This wave, strongest of the set, pushed them across the coral toward shore. The butcher gashed his skull against the coral head and sank lifelessly. He struggled to keep the man's head above water until the three on the shore reached them and pulled them back to the beach.

Ramsey collapsed in the sand, chest heaving. He caught his breath and turned face up, propped on his elbows. A frigate bird cruised overhead. He watched it sail as the day turned quiet and prepared for evening without even an apology, as though the last hours had not happened.

Thurston came over. The wax had gone from his moustache and it drooped shaggily about his mouth. "Sentry's bandaging him with his shirt but he needs the surgeon. You all right?"

He nodded.

"Butcher always was a fool. Now he looks it. You don't look so passable yourself."

"Country livin'," he said. "Takes it out of a man."

"Tell me, would you have let him drown?"

He wiped wet sand out of his sideburns and sat up. "You'd have let him drown if you'd taken any longer to get to us."

Thurston nodded. "I guess that's right ... Look, I was just following orders."

"Orders? Whose – the Attorney General's? The Navy's? Anybody reputable?"

Thurston didn't reply.

He pressed: "Somebody told you to drown me? – or that was your idea, you thought it up yourself?"

Thurston wouldn't look at him. He flicked a shell across the beach instead. "Well, it's getting late. We better get going."

"Coward," he spat. "Piss pot. You ain't worth a bullet. Turn you out with a randy bull, let him truck with you."

The sentry knelt beside him. "Save your strength. Thurston's nothing." He had the butcher's keys and undid the shackles then addressed the other men. "Mr. Ramsey's riding in the wagon. He's my responsibility, and I won't have any more of this – here, put this on, sir." The sentry cloaked his raw torso with his uniform jacket. "I'm never wearing it again anyway."

Thurston shuffled up the beach to his horse.

John Stevens could not wait beneath the street lamp longer. He sent his driver to dinner and stepped down from the carriage. A sailor stopped him in the anteroom to Commander Taylor's office but he shoved his cloak into the man's arms and admitted himself unbidden to the attaché. Taylor straightened up, looking guilty.

"Pour me a glass also," Stevens said and settled on the maroon sofa beneath the oil of Diamond Head. He kept his hat on. "Come come, man. Pour the whiskey. The whole town knows where you keep it."

Taylor poured two tumblers and brought one over. "You don't look well," Taylor said.

He waved away the concern. "I've been seeing Gibson's physician. He's topping me up."

"Gibson's physician? So, it's leeches and opium, is it?"

He drank back the whiskey. "Just fetch me another."

"I don't think my whiskey is what you should be taking."

"What do you know about another man's pain?" Unconsciously, he pressed the photo in his breast pocket. He'd removed it from the oval frame in his rooms. It was now grimy with handling and blotched with tears. "Navy shouldn't be telling civilian authority what to do anyhow. Can't even produce your own sailor on command."

Taylor returned behind his desk. "It wasn't my idea to send the militia after Ramsey. I'd have sent a naval detachment and handled the whole affair properly."

He struck his stick. "But he's not in military custody, is he? He belongs to the Kingdom just now, and if Antone Rosa gets him before I do then it's lost, isn't it? – Everything I've worked for!"

"But what's been lost, Stevens? Does anyone know what the man knows? John Ramsey's an undisciplined, sorry excuse for a sailor. You can't count on him for a thing."

Stevens lay his finger aside his nose and cackled. "You don't know what I know, Commander. You don't know what *civilian* authority knows. You don't even know your own man. If you did, you wouldn't be so quick to dismiss him!"

Taylor hesitated. "Now see here, Stevens. Ramsey is Navy, and he is under my command ..."

"When the Rifles march him in here, they will surrender him first to me. Then I will turn him over to you, and you can hang him from a yardarm, far as I'm concerned. But I believe you will see he wants to talk to me first. Another shot of that whiskey, I said." He held out the glass.

But before Taylor could decide whether to pour the drink or protest his authority, a wagon arrived outside the office. Both men hurried out. What they saw by the gaslight stunned them: a dirty, bedraggled conveyance, much the worse for wear; two men torn and bloodied laid out in the cart, the other men drooping and exhausted, with scarcely a fixed vertebrae among them.

"Thurston, what is this?" Stevens demanded. "Where's your squad? Where are your soldiers?"

Thurston dismounted. "This is the most I could round up. Nobody wanted to hoof it out to Hale Nui on a hot day."

The sentry helped Ramsey out of the wagon. "I'm turning Mr. Ramsey over to proper authority. Where's the Attorney General? Wasn't he supposed to meet us? – And he needs a doctor. Bravest man I've ever seen."

"I am the American Naval Attaché and senior American military representative in the Kingdom," Taylor asserted. "Mr. Ramsey is in my command. I will take custody of him."

Stevens planted his stick in front of Taylor, pinning him against the door frame. He'd wrested an agreement from Thurston. Pearl lagoon was too important to his plans. He would not let Taylor get to Ramsey first. "I am civilian authority, Sergeant Thurston. You will turn him over to me."

Thurston nodded to the sentry. "That's right. This is a civil case. It'd be treason for me as a legislator to have relations with foreign military. Release the prisoner to the custody of the American Minister, Private."

Momentarily confused, the sentry relaxed his grasp. Ramsey tore out of it and thrust himself through the doorway. Taylor jumped after him, locked the door and posted his aide to guard it.

"Well Ramsey, once again in my office and a despicable sight."

Ramsey felt weak-kneed and could scarcely stand, but Taylor kept him at attention before his desk.

"You still realize who you work for, I'll give you that. But you are out of uniform and a disgrace to the service."

"Might I be permitted a glass of water, sir?"

Taylor nodded toward the pitcher on his desk. He drank, poured another and coughed. "I apologize for my uniform, Commander. I trust I will be allowed to appear seaman-like at the court martial. Would not want to disgrace your command."

Taylor, behind his desk, smiled at him. "O, shouldn't think there's much chance of that. When the board of naval officers breaks you, it will reinforce what I have maintained to the Admiral. ONI is a pack of young pups best kept on a leash held by Regular Navy. No need for all this skulking about in back alleys. It's bad for a man's character."

"Has counsel been appointed for me, sir?"

"It will be by the book, Ramsey. I am certain the Navy has arranged for an appropriately inexperienced Ensign to represent you."

He nodded. "He'll want to see the document, of course."

Taylor's brows knitted. "What document would that be?"

"Why, the one you had me prepare, sir – the chart of Pearl River lagoon." He coughed, sipped more water then looked at Taylor. "I recorded all the soundings on it, sir, even as far as the West Loch. Most of the engineering is on it too, the leverage points to blast the coral and the formulas for the various mix of chemicals."

Taylor lit a cigar. The smoke drifted appealingly into his nostrils.

"So it's true," Taylor said. "You did not lose everything in the fire."

"I tried to think like Regular Navy, Commander. Redundancy."

"And your document will show ... ?"

"Pearl River is the finest natural harbor in the Pacific. Didn't you suspect as much, Commander? Ain't that why you sent me off surveying all those God-awful weeks? Heat and bugs and bivouacking. If I may be frank, sir, I thought it more the duty of a Negro when you first give me my orders than an assignment for a Petty Officer of the United States Navy. But now I've had time to chew it over, and there's certain other governments might be curious for the results – well, sir, I think it was just a real coup on your part; an intelligence coup, that is."

"That what you think, is it?"

"Yes, sir. Naturally. Who wouldn't? Just the sort of tea leaves an attaché's office should be reading – you know, so the Navy can plot its course? The officers of that warship will think so. Not another attaché at another port that's doing it, I can tell you. Most of 'em's too busy pushing hard tack for belly timber and pocketing the difference."

"So you're going to produce this document at the court martial."

"It's Navy property, sir."

"And you want me to tell the board I ordered you to Pearl River to conduct the survey."

"It's only fitting you should receive your credit. I'm just an enlisted man. No one's going to give a hoot about me."

Taylor came from around his desk. He held a glass of whiskey in his hand. "Your demonstration that Pearl River is navigable means the United States Government will sign the Reciprocity Treaty, you know that." Taylor looked in his eyes.

"Yes, sir."

"They'll attach the rider to take possession of Pearl River in exchange for the trade preferences granted by the treaty."

"I expect so."

"And once the Navy turns Pearl River into a military harbor, these islands will never be the same. Whether there's a king or not, they'll belong to the United States. They'll be our first colony. You realize that."

Ramsey dropped his pretense. He wasn't turning the document over to the king as Eliza Somers wanted, but he also wasn't turning it over to the American Minister and his gang. Thurston had squelched any chance of that. He was turning it over to the Navy, it did him the most good. He'd won that right as the ocean mauled him along the reef, his lungs filling with salt water like a bladder. "It's power, Commander. Pure and simple. The chess game. You hold the right pieces, you control the board."

Taylor drank down the whiskey in front of him. "Of course, you are absolutely right. In my day, I believe we thought we were doing something noble, but nobility is out of fashion now. This new generation ... I just want to be convinced you realize exactly what you are doing." He gestured at his painting of Diamond Head. "You are going to change these islands and these people forever. You realize that."

His cuts and bruises had gotten the better of him and he was out of patience with Taylor's whiskey bottle morality. "What would you have me do, Commander? Hand the document over to Stevens and the missionary boys?"

"No, I'm not saying that. I'm not saying that at all. Only ... well, why turn it over at all? It wasn't my orders, you weren't conducting the survey for me. There was a fire, who's to say the document, whatever it is, didn't get consumed in it?"

He couldn't believe what he was hearing. "Let me tell you, Commander, a man gets on a horse to break him, the worst thing he can do is get off. You sit the Cayuse, you sit him all the way."

"You're going to see this thing through."

"All the way through."

"No matter the consequence."

"I think we all know the horse is going to get broke, one way or the other. Even the Hawaiians know that, the smart ones, the ones aren't chasing after Luahine."

Taylor sighed and returned to his desk and poured another drink.

He was deeply tired. "May I return to my quarters, sir? See legal counsel there?"

"You won't have need to, son. This evening I will locate my copy of the order I issued assigning you to Pearl River. Your copy burned in the fire, of course."

"Of course, sir."

"The charge of desertion will be dropped immediately. You will be returned to duty with my personal apologies and a letter of commendation stuck in your service jacket – provided the map is what you purport it to be."

"Much obliged, Commander. You won't regret it."

Taylor grunted.

"May I borrow your letter opener, sir?" He sat and struggled with his boot. Red mud and sand poured from it. He inserted the tip of the letter opener into an inner seam. It separated, and out of a waxed sleeve he withdrew the foolscap.

"Well, Ramsey," Taylor said after examining his work, "not only will you be restored to the Navy, you will be a hero in its eyes – perhaps even heroic long enough for promotion."

"I did my duty, sir."

"That you did. I on the other hand, in doing mine, am the most miserable wretch. For I have permitted you and the shop-keepers and plutocrats like Colonel Spreckels to pull the chocks on the cart wheels. It can have only one result, and as I said to you before, I fought a war against anarchy and sedition. Yet here I am, setting the cart in motion that leads irreversibly to revolution and annexation of these islands."

Taylor wiped his eyes, suddenly an old man inside and out. "For heaven's sake, clean yourself up. I'll send the surgeon in the morning. You will bring esteem to my command when I present you, or I'll hang you myself."

THIRTY-TWO

"Toast of the Town" – that's how Jessica described herself in letters to her mother. And after the queen's *luau*, she had been.

Now the accolade belonged to John Ramsey. He had saved the Reciprocity Treaty, William Castle informed her in his loudest, most disturbing courtroom voice – right in front of Volney Ashford and Lorrin Thurston, both of them together. Everyone sat in peacock chairs, taking the afternoon sun on the Hawaiian's airy veranda, and he'd taken liberties with her, poking her arm and laughing. "That rascal's the toast of the town. What a turn of events! Toast of the town! He'll be received in any big house in the Kingdom, mark my words. Best for you to stay on his good side now, eh?"

She fanned herself vigorously – the fan was a real Eugene Rimmel – and said it was no concern of hers, and why did Mr. Castle think to discuss the kingdom's politics with her? She was an artiste.

She spoke rather convincingly she thought, for the benefit of Volney primarily, but also Lorrin Thurston.

Castle sat back, harrumphed and chomped down on his cigar, declaring himself misinformed. She nodded graciously, and assured him that when it came to Mr. Ramsey, anyone could mistake her courtesy for enmity – she was certain she'd gotten the phrase accurately, she'd overheard it at tea at the home of Mr. Charles R. Bishop, who was now a widower, she liked to remind herself, and she always delivered her lines correctly.

Before she could measure the effect, the bellboy interrupted them with a parcel on his tray. Mr. Castle, rather than retire with it, slit it open with his pocket knife right there on the veranda. She hid her expression behind the fan. Such ill manners on the part of the local men of worth, but let her put three lumps in her tea and Volney would be a merciless harlequin that night.

She busied herself with thoughts of the letter she'd write next – "I anguish for <u>real</u> Culture, Mother, it is my fate. Opera has relegated me so." – but was yanked from her reverie by Castle. "Now we've got Kalakaua right where we want him!" he roared, waving a sheaf of papers. "Here, Lorrin, take a look. It's finally arrived, the little farce we commissioned in San Francisco. It will skewer the King before the world!"

Thurston sat up with the manuscript. "Look at page three," Castle urged. "It's Gibson through and through. They've captured him like a photograph, don't you think? – 'Nosebig' – ha!"

"Should be 'Assbig'," Thurston said.

"No, he sticks his nose into everything, that's the joke. You see it, don't you, Ashford?"

"I like 'Assbig'," Ashford said.

"No, too obvious," Castle insisted. "We save our direct thrusts for the King. 'Gynborn Duke,' we call him. Clever, eh? He anointed himself king at that monstrous coronation of his – no one of rank would do it. So in our farce we only allow him a dukedom – of gin, do you see?!"

Thurston paged through the script. "This has possibilities."

"Possibilities? Why, he'll be a laughing stock. We won't need your bayonettes, Ashford. Kalakaua will be laughed out of town."

"It needs an attraction," Thurston said. "We need an audience."

Castle blew a large plume of cigar smoke. "Why Lorrin, I'm surprised at you. Have you no manners? Miss Mornay is our attraction. Who better than she to play low farce? She shall be the *kiawe* thorn that cripples the royal lion!"

The Gynborn Duke was a smash. As Jessica applied makeup in her dressing room at the Music Hall – her own dressing room! – she had to admit it. Originally charted for two nights, the production had been extended for two weeks. The audience poured in from everywhere, Castle informed the cast, even as far away as the Big Island, and the diplomatic community. People stayed with relatives in town and made a holiday of it.

It was not the sort of theatrical event she could describe to her mother but it did bring her a degree of recognition. If not Toast of the Town, it earned her a table with Volney any time at The Commercial, though not at the Hawaiian Hotel.

It had not brought John Ramsey backstage, however.

She heard the laughter upstairs and got into costume. It was heavy, but the Chinese dresser helped her into it. "Missy no sit da *okole*, okay?" she said at each performance, and patted her own behind. Jessica shouldn't sit, there wouldn't be time to press out the wrinkles.

The Music Hall audience could not control itself when the Duke of Gynborn made his entrance. A portly veteran of the music halls in London, he knew how broad a role should be played to retain a ticketholder's interest, and he relished impersonating a reigning monarch without the censorship imposed upon the British stage. He made up in a shimmering tube of side whiskers and, after American minstrel shows, a coal black face and great circles of mouth and eyes exaggerated by white grease paint. The catcalls flew, and from the balcony rained the common jibes demeaning Kalakaua as the son of a blacksmith. With each performance the Duke extended his business with asides and physical comedy of all sorts and his number, sung in a stentorian bass, became a hit with the *haole* around town.

> De coco-nut am good to eat
> (I cannot climb de tree)
> Dey come in pairs, so good and sweet
> (I cannot climb de tree)
> I show my pearls. What do I see?
> (I cannot climb de tree)
> Dat coco-nut am bend to me
> Push me up de tree!

The tune, *Carve Dat Possum,* was a popular one taken from the minstrel shows, and sung before a coconut trunk striped red, white and blue, it was gotten by all: Kalakaua would whore after anyone, even the famously feral President Grover Cleveland.

Nosebig attracted a less enthusiastic following. The actor conceived his role as the voice of conscience, so delivered his speech,

> My nose is large and crooked
> Shaped like a grasping hand
> It rules what's overlook-ed
> I'll plant it where I can

straight on to the audience, though a voluptuous Emily Chow Ling – charactered after one of Chun Ah Fong's twelve daughters – stood alongside his inflated proboscis.

He was told where to plant it at each performance.

Jessica's solo was accorded center stage, which pleased her. The problem was her entrance. It came just when the audience had exhausted its own repertoire. The ladies stifled a yawn behind their fans and the men slumped in their chairs, victim to fatty beef, dark gravy and rounds of brandy.

She played Lady Columbia, too abstract a character to lift an eyelid. Not even the Duke's increasingly accurate groping of her costume could stir the air. She shook him off and launched into her number, cribbed from Yum-Yum's popular aria in *The Mikado*. It fit her range.

> The sun, whose rays are all ablaze with ever-living glory,
> does not deny His majesty – He deigns to tell a story!
> Command o'er all the earth He gives, to me He shan't deny:
> Columbia's orb is here below as His th' celestial sky.
> O, Dusky Duke, of kingdom dimmer,
> from Columbia's blaze may grasp a glimmer.
> At last you'll shine with light so holy
> If lips you'll press to my ...

Jessica's number woke the slumberers and brought down the house.

John Ramsey did not attend. Would not attend, even if he'd been able, unless he carried a barrel of lamp oil and a torch to fire it, he announced.

"I have to," Sienna told him. "I'd druther take care of you, darlin', but it's business. I must appear neutral." She tried on a new hat for the show's close. "What do you think of it? Cute, ain't it?"

He groaned noncommittally.

"Well a girl must do something to make the occasion special." She'd attended three other times, the companion of gentlemen from the outer islands. "Do you even want to know how the audience likes her? It's the last night."

He groaned again.

"I didn't think so, cher." Sienna patted him on the cheek. "I think it's your pride much as anything else."

He was embarrassingly incapacitated. The rash appeared exactly one month after his complete exoneration at court martial. Because of Pearl lagoon's significance for the treaty negotiations with the United States, he was at the top of his game, in command even of Taylor and Stevens. He consulted *Dr. Gunn's* and treated the rash confidently as all eruptions of the skin, by sweating and determined scrubbing with birch and herbs.

A nondescript aching in the knees and pelvis soon joined the rash and ended his bicycling, and was accompanied by flare-ups in the neck and head. He submitted to the examination of a ship's doctor who immediately produced lancet, cup and bowl to reduce intemperance of the blood, but he refused. *Dr. Gunn's* was unyielding about such heroic measures.

"I don't know a pustule from a boil," Sienna told him in his quarters, "but I guess I do know Old Joe. I can spot it on a dark night with no moon." She sent for Carl and one of her more experienced girls, and they allayed the symptoms with rubs and oils and a noxious Hawaiian potion, but she was direct with him: comfort was possible, there was no cure for syphilis.

His mouth dropped open. "No cure? My God, Sienna, what the sam hill you mean? What about mercury, or that arsenic treatment they got now?"

She took his hand. "They'll likely kill you before they'd ever help you, darlin'. Believe me."

Scarcely comprehending, he just nodded. *Dr. Gunn's* prescribed salt baths and abstinence in the event of syphilis.

"You'll just have to live with it, cher." She rubbed his shoulder affectionately. "Many young rakes have – old ones as well. You'd be surprised the pox I've laid my eyes on, and the top hats I've had to turn from my door. No man wants to believe Venus carries any red flower that ain't a rose. But she surely does."

"I can't believe it, Sienna. I won't believe it. I'm not the man to have this ..." He could not finish. Syphilis was a common enough scourge, but scourge it was. It did not fit his picture of himself. He was not common.

"Now John darlin', don't you go and fret. You're feeling poorly but it will pass. You'll get on with things."

"But how ever did I catch it?"

"That's what I'd like to know." She turned all business. "What houses you been visitin'? You ain't been down to the waterfront, have you?"

"You know better."

"Well you must have picked it up somewhere, John. The pox don't grow on trees."

He looked at her. "Sienna Robichon! Do you expect me to reveal my dalliances to you?"

"I don't think you realize how serious this is, John. If Mr. Gibson suspects an outbreak, he'll close me down, me and all the other houses, and he should. It's my reputation at stake. You didn't pick it up at Madam Ho's, did you?"

"I couldn't have."

She looked at him. She would not be deterred, and he knew it.

"All right then. Damn it all to hell, Sienna. I've only been with one female the last six months. The Navy's been working me so hard, I haven't had the time."

"Who is it, John? Who was the fortunate girl?"

"Jessica. Jessica Mornay."

Her eyes grew round. "The sweet little chanteuse. You certain, John?"

"I regret to admit I am."

"Well, seems the girl's had the last laugh on you, Johnny-boy. Can't say as that's happened before."

"But how did she pick it up?"

"That's easy," Sienna said. "From the Commander of the Honolulu Rifles, fine upstanding citizen that he is."

"She got it from him?"

"Without a doubt. You didn't really expect the girl to be faithful without a ring, did you? – And he, well you don't need a bloodhound to catch his scent. Volney Ashford picked up his case from me."

He straightened up.

"Remember that Portagee I had to get rid of? He couldn't get enough of her."

THIRTY-THREE

At the moment the cast of *The Gynborn Duke* took its final curtain and missionary-baked Honolulu rose to its feet elated by the public broadcast, even though farcical, of its grievances against the king, the king's own navy made landfall southwest of the Big Island's Kona coast.

Kaimiloa had burned through most of her coal on the return from Samoa and was scarcely making headway when the night watch made out Mauna Loa's shield-like curve against the garden of white stars. Gibson had filled out the crew with six boys from the Oahu Reformatory. It was a great economy but the boys, even after months aboard, still were not seamen. The one on watch sounded every alarm he could reach and everyone on board leaped from sleep to fire and rescue parties. But the panic subsided, the boy was quickly forgiven. Theirs had been a long, tumultuous sojourn in the South Pacific and Hawaii had never looked so attractive, even just the sailor's promise of her.

Prince Koloa put his arm around the boy and stood with him at the rail. He carried a letter from the Samoan court buttoned inside his jacket pocket. J. E. Bush, Kalakaua's envoy, possessed the official document, the instrument King Malietoa signed February 17, 1887, by which the Kingdom of Samoa entered into "the installation of confederation" with the Kingdom of Hawaii. The letter Koloa carried, thrust upon him by the Samoan Secretary of State just as *Kaimiloa* cast off, registered an official protest with Walter Gibson. It did all within the constraints of diplomacy to rescind the February agreement.

The Samoa mission sickened his soul. He dearly wanted to be done with it. He wanted to be done with Honolulu politics and with Honolulu. He wanted to find Pua and flee to his estate on Kauai.

He patted the boy and went below.

"*Kali i ka makani 'olu 'olu*," Manu said to him. It was a sailor's expression: tarry for the fair winds.

Koloa shook his head. "Another day's steaming, I make it. We'll reach Honolulu tomorrow afternoon."

"Didn't the lookout say something about the Big Island?"

"He did, but you'll never see it. Next dry land you'll see is Iwalei. I'll turn you over to Gibson's constables and they will happily inter you in one of its humid jail cells forever."

Manu ran his hand across the metal grate of *Kaimiloa's* cargo hold. It separated him from Koloa and freedom. "Does the coconut growing behind the wall think itself in jail?"

"*Hiki no*, certainly you will have time to ponder such questions. Perhaps you will also ponder why you felt called to humiliate Father Kalakaua."

"Pacific empire," Manu snorted. "Someone had to stop it. You wouldn't."

"I wouldn't because he is *mo'i*, sovereign."

"We have no sovereigns, only chiefs," Manu said. "That is our way. And the chief must seek the *pono* of the people or we are no different than the *haole. Pau ka pono, pau ka mana* – without righteousness, there is no strength."

"Do you think the people care whether their king is chief or emperor? They care only that there is *poi* at the end of a hard day."

"Do you care, Koloa?"

He considered Manu quietly. "Yes," he said after a moment. "Yes, I do care."

Kaimiloa's rudder went over and Koloa, with a glance back at
Manu, bounded up the ladderway. The captain had decided to
steer for Kona and await a tow to Honolulu Harbor. But Koloa
was adamant: *Kaimiloa* represented the crown, she could not be
brought in under tow. She must enter the harbor on her own,
the people must be made proud of their navy and the comple-
tion of its first official mission.

At daybreak the captain spread a little sail though the crew
were inept at it, and the vessel huffed toward Honolulu. Luahine's
ocean-goers flocked about her, the crews raising their paddles,
blowing the conch and trading loving greetings with the
Reformatory Boys, some of whom sobbed at the rail for dry land
and home.

As she neared Fort Street wharf, *Kaimiloa* made out a great
crowd. The Hawaiians ashore could not contain themselves but
dived in with fresh coconuts, cane sugar stalks and flower *lei*, and
were pulled aboard dripping wet and into the arms of the crew.
In a moment the decks spilled with joyful, keening Hawaiians,
and all the official party were circled with garlands and welcomed
with kisses and tears.

In the commotion Denzo slipped below and pried open the
cage. Manu sprang for the arms locker, from which they removed
four big navy revolvers and two boxes of ammunition in oil cloth.
Rifles stood in racks, but those would have to wait. They scrambled through the galley then out the scullery's garbage hatch
and into the water astern of the vessel.

"Well, Prince, *aloha no!*" Kalakaua welcomed Koloa into his
study with a generous wave. "Look, Gibson, the young Prince
feared he would be ill-served by the embassy to Samoa. Was he
not well-advised to invest his faith in his Father and his King?"
Gibson, balanced atop his customary settee, nodded
obligingly.

The king turned to the Articles of Confederation with Samoa. Koloa thought he blinked away tears. He understood what the document meant to the king and to the kingdom. It was a declaration of independence, independence from foreign governments and from foreign commercial interests. Kanaka Maoli would dwell in freedom and prosperity, the modern Nineteenth Century values, and would do so with their identity intact. He hesitated, uncertain how to begin. "Majesty, I am returned, but I …"

"I know, my boy, I know. You wish to go home to your beloved estate. Of course I give you leave, of course. And with my fondest *aloha*. Just one thing more your King requires of you – the Kamehameha Day festivities."

Kamehameha Day was the kingdom's own holiday. Kapiolani Park would be alive with horse racing, vendors and every class of denizen that inhabited the capital.

"I shall stroll among my people openly, *al fresco*, the Venetians say. Gibson will print up the handbills. We shall announce the merits of empire – directly, that is, without the hoarse cavil of the newspapers to frighten them. And you must join us, Prince. You will bear King Malietoa's tidings to the Hawaiian people. He is the first splinter to mold into our grand Pacific paddle."

"The King makes you the people's guardian," Gibson said, a kindly smile parting his white beard. "You, not Mr. Bush. I see many years of faithful service in you."

"Majesty, I …" Koloa hesitated then sighed. There was no other way but the truth. Malietoa signed the confederation but the mission to the Samoan kingdom had failed wretchedly. With Minister Bush daily in his cups the delegation lost all sense of itself. The Samoan government quarantined the crew and Malietoa attempted to seize the treaty document. "I carry a letter of protest to Mr. Gibson."

"To me?" Gibson said, surprised.

Kalakaua motioned for him to read it.

The Hawaiian Envoy, Mr. J.E. Bush is the most dissipated man who has held a high position at this place for many years. His associates are mostly the lowest kind of half-castes and whites.

The letter went on to catalog the "disreputable conduct" of the mission. In blatant disregard for the decorum demanded by Malietoa's court, *Kaimiloa's* officers had laid siege to the young ladies of Apia. Its crew were the source of public drunkenness, lewd displays, fights and debauchery. There was insubordination aboard ship and the loss of all order and decency.

"I did what I could, Your Majesty, but I could not prevail. Only the Reformatory Boys listened to me and were a credit to our Race."

"Who knows about this letter?"

"Just I ... maybe a member of the crew, one of the Hawaiians. Hard to tell. It looked as though my belongings had been ransacked. I had him imprisoned in the hold."

Kalakaua stood up and paced the room. Gibson swirled the tonic in his glass. There was silence.

"Just give me weeks!" the king exploded. "Weeks is all I ask! A month or two, is that too much to expect?" He raised his arms to heaven. "I have fought too hard, come too close! I need more time, do you hear? I demand more time!" He whirled upon Gibson. "Help me, man! Do you sit there? What news of the Queen?"

The prime minister shrugged. "Only what the newspapers have carried. The Queen was well-received in Washington, though Secretary Lamar refused to see her – he is a Confederate from their Mississippi, of course. Her address concerning your remarkable reign was reported widely, as were her triumphs in Boston and New York."

"Yes, yes. And London? What of London?"

Another shrug. "Nothing, Highness."

"She must secure that loan! My tenancy depends on it! I have won the leniency of the Americans, but Reciprocity is only a profit to the business community. I must have specie for the Crown!"

Koloa caught a sidelong look from Gibson before the prime minister cleared his throat and spoke. "Highness, the matter of Reciprocity is still ... delicate, I should say. It is well you have not signed the treaty papers. Luahine's man made known her disinclination to part with Pearl River, an opinion I share –"

The king cut him off. "I shall not bargain with Luahine! Specie is at issue here, credit for the Crown. We must have solvency until Pacific Primacy is realized!"

"Nothing more for us then." Gibson's voice was scarcely a whisper. "I shall approach the Colonel."

"Never! Never though the gods take me! He shall not have the last laugh on me! Do you recall the interview he gave the San Francisco papers? He made me out a popinjay and a marionette – his marionette! If I turn to him now, it is the doom of my people. If their King cannot outwit the *haole*, what chance have they? The Kalakaua dynasty shall not be our last! I shall not be remembered so!"

He watched Kalakaua swing for the sideboard. The king swallowed a tumbler of gin, appeared to meditate for a moment then downed another. "Prince Koloa," he said, approaching him, the bottle in one hand, glass in the other. "Prince Koloa, you are to swear on your sacred honor: you are to forget this matter of the letter and the poor report from Malietoa. He is a monarch, he understands a king is underserved by his emissaries. Do you understand?"

He nodded.

"You will attend the holiday in our box and give a proud report of your nation's achievement. Proud."

The king threw back another tumbler and took him in, then Gibson, eyes beaming. "Fear not, gentlemen. Time is in our favor. That spiritualist from San Francisco – Rosenburg? You know him, Gibson. He has the gift. He gave me a very favorable reading. Very favorable, eh? Take heart, my friends!"

Hale Nui's extended family fanned over the bleached grasses of Kapiolani Park on Kamehameha Day. The fair June sky, the anticipation of flights of horses at the races, and the promise of food, music and dancing invigorated spirits. The Gonsalves herded the children, Aunty Pauline supervised the kitchen, and Eliza visited acquaintances with her husband. The talk was of Samoa and the surprising coup engineered by the king and, following upon the Reciprocity Treaty, the friendly sun that seemed to prosper the islands just now.

Manolo Gonsalves showed Eliza one of the handbills. "They say the King is walking about the grounds."

"He is seeing to his horses already? He must feel confident about his entry."

"No, it's the *Kaimiloa*," Gonsalves said. "The King is shaking hands and telling everyone how the Pacific federation will free them."

"Well I don't know about that. But bless the man, he's been so put upon. That awful play of the Rifles? I am glad he can enjoy himself today."

Her bonhomie soon guttered like a candle, for Kamehameha Day was vulnerable to greater circulation than the palace handbill. The rumor began as a whisper but swelled into a roar of dismay. Its source was a *Kaimiloa* crewman, it was said; a *kanaka*, round-faced, no one could quite describe him. Ugly as the story sounded – vulgarity, incontinence, disgrace – it rang with truth. Then fast on its heels whisked the claim that the American Minister possessed independent verification via *USS Adams*, just arrived in harbor.

Her husband crowed that the pagan hadn't the backbone of a Chinese noodle so nothing surprised in the news, but she shook her head and walked away. "I don't believe it," she said to Gonsalves. "That new man you hired, the Oriental, he sailed with *Kaimiloa*. Bring him to me."

Denzo confirmed the worst, and she could not be consoled. She left Horace with the children and had the *luna* drive her back to the ranch where she climbed into bed and pulled the covers up, sobbing. She loved Kalakaua. He was her liege, her country's father. He filled her with confidence in the survival of *aloha*. She shrank from the vigilantism of the Rifles, many of them her Punahou classmates. But the stench of scandal trailing *Kaimiloa*'s wake revolted her.

THIRTY-FOUR

V olney Ashford strutted about the parlor of the Commercial
Hotel. Anyone could hear him, he wasn't guarded. His
boot heels thumped the floor boards. Flagons of ale
sailed into their meeting, then a cold roast so the Committee of
Thirteen, the executive board of the Hawaiian League, was pro-
visioned. "I say put a rope around Kalakaua's neck. Don't waste
a bullet on him. The whole thing's an indictment of respectability." He called for another glass.

Sanford Dole turned round from the sandwich board – laid
beneath the knothole and easily spied upon therefore, as well as
heard. "We'll have no more talk of violence. Weapons were pilfered from *Kaimiloa's* armory. Rifles, pistols, ammunition. We
must not provoke an uprising."

"An uprising? Hah!" Ashford again. "Do you see this message from F.A. Schaefer?" A paper rustled. "He has promised
the Drei Hundert from Maui. They are well-drilled and fero-
ciously armed. – Then won't we have an army!"

"Well Schaefer needs to come *wikiwiki*." Lorrin Thurston's
reedy voice. "Did you see the San Francisco papers? Chun Ah
Fong is after Kalakaua. I gather he bankrolled Samoa and now
he wants his due." He read aloud:

Passengers who have arrived by the steamer San Pablo *report that there is great excitement at Honolulu over the threatened revolution against King Kalakaua. It is said that the Germans and Chinese are at the bottom of the trouble, and that the latter will wage a war of extermination with the Hawaiians during which the Europeans will gain control. Ah Fong, the millionaire Chinese operator is fostering the insurrection. A watch is being kept for a schooner said to be equipping in this city to carry 300 men, with arms and ammunition, to capture Hawaii.*

The men were quiet. Ramsey heard a chair scrape then Dole's voice again. "Sad, the San Francisco press feels no greater obligation to veracity than our own papers. Ah Fong would not bring insurrection, he has no cause and no profit. Can there actually be a schooner outfitting for war?"

"God help us." That was William Castle. "War, it'd be our ruin."

"Far more likely the Chinese than the Germans." Thurston. "Kalakaua has permitted 30,000 Chinamen to enter these islands, they would overwhelm the Christian forces in an instant."

"If Ah Fong allied with Luahine ..." Castle did not complete the thought.

"The Chinese were barbaric to their own kind." Thurston once more. "Taiping was a bloody slaughter. Can you imagine here, the Chinese united with the Hawaiian?"

Ramsey heard murmurs. None of them wanted to admit the possibility. The Taiping Rebellion, a bloodbath, he couldn't blame them.

"I say we take the armory." Ashford, probably waving his sword, or prancing about. "Geld the stallion before he has the chance to bite."

"My squad could be ready in a day." Thurston, eager, maybe wanting to make up for Hale Nui. "The men are all local. I can send word tonight."

Ashford: "No, we'll wait on Schaefer's men. That's the way to do it. The armory first then arrest Gibson, the King, and Liliu. A hat trick!"

Ramsey shook his head. He played billiards in the adjoining room and eavesdropped through the knothole. It had cost him a gold piece to have it drilled. His opponent was one of Sienna's customers, a middle-aged architect from Sydney who was good but not nearly as skilled as he. He missed shots, leaving the architect the table so he could sit at the knothole and keep up. It was eating into his pay, but he was under orders from ONI to produce an intelligence estimate of the missionary party's intentions. A boat departed next day for San Francisco, he'd place the details in its diplomatic pouch.

He sipped his beer, watched the architect rack up points and imagined the faces in the next room. Volney Ashford was growing erratic, a serious concern as the Honolulu Rifles became better equipped and drilled. But Castle and Dole were allied in opposition to his extremism. The swing vote was Thurston's. Would he align with the moderates, or would he throw himself behind Ashford?

Thurston was weak, conflicted. He'd seen it in his face that day at Diamond Head, man with his finger on the trigger, never pulled it before. Kind of man might do anything then say he hadn't, kind of man someone could sway.

"We'll stretch three necks as one, save the government the executioner's purse."

"The three of them – really, Volney?" William Castle. "You would hang a woman, and a noble one at that? You'd lift her in her skirts, bare-legged before the world? ... Gentlemen, this is the counsel of the man we have placed over the Honolulu Rifles."

"I cannot be party to such atheism." The voice of Horace Somers.

"Nor I." Castle again. "I will not tolerate the red-shirted sentiment of this ... this immigrant. He owns neither property nor lineage here, yet he'd risk all of ours in civil war. His antecedents did not sail the Horn. Ours did. Why give him ear."

The businessman's reasonable voice.

"You give me ear because I am the only among you who is a man of action!" He heard Ashford slam something to the table. "I am as warm a patriot as any of you. And I will do my duty!"

317

"Calmly, friends, calmly." Dole now. He pictured his arms flapping, as if conducting a band. "The pudding is but half baked, let us proceed soberly. Give no cause for intervention, eh? If Britain landed her tars or Germany her marines, should we ever gain our country back?"

Somers spoke. "Gentlemen, brothers – if I may be permitted a word. I entered the Rifles with some reluctance, I confess. It is not an ecclesial assembly after all. But I have felt so welcome in it, and so grateful of your company. Your fathers and your grand-fathers, what they have meant to the mission field – its finest hour. To stand with you is to stand with them ..."

The architect missed his shot, he had to take his turn, but he felt confident in leaving the knothole. The moderates would prevail. They'd wait and watch, and let Kalakaua sink under his policies.

His opponent left him a delectable bank shot. "Just miss it," he said to himself, "return to the knothole." But it was too inviting. He could even the score and show up the rube. He executed with a flourish and ran the table.

By the time he pocketed his winnings and returned to his post, the meeting's atmosphere had changed. He could sense it as if he sat among the men himself. John Stevens had taken the floor.

"... then, gentlemen, what could be more democratical, more Christian that is to say, than to turn the matter over to the people?" Stevens had lathered up his creaky voice so it oozed like an orator's. "The *vox populi*, can the King dispute it?"

He heard consternation in the room. Ashford feared the proposal blunted the bayonet of the Rifles. Dole and Castle feared it surrendered the Hawaiian League to mob rule.

Stevens soothed them. "The mob? Nay, you must insulate yourselves, gentlemen, as the hoarfrost o'erlays the common stubble." Host a meeting, he told them, but a meeting only of the propertied class. The voices of men of worth must be registered, their influence in the government must be extended. "A meeting of the propertied, it prospers the poor man and the rich, and it prospers good government. Each of you shall benefit. An assembly of your peers – even as my country at its nativity in Philadelphia. The propertied men, responsible men, men of reputation, the men who build government and are its rightful beneficiaries."

The scraping of chairs signaled the meeting's end, but he remained at the knothole, deflated.

He had delivered Pearl lagoon to his government. It nearly cost his life but it was the best deal he could make. It put the islands under America's wing. It didn't give the government to the carpetbaggers and it kept the king safe. But Stevens undid him with a mouthful of words. Undid weeks of sunburn and sweat at Pearl lagoon. Undid humiliation at the hands of the Marines. Undid near drowning. Stevens' words, the direct appeal to greed. Not intellect, not careful strategy, not moving pieces on the chessboard, but greed. Just a single speech. He talked the missionary party into a mass meeting. It would unstop all the hysteria that had bottled-up in respectable Hawaii during the Kalakaua years. There'd be bedlam.

A man had rights, and he had the right to defend them with a gun. But if every fool was armed then you had a mob … you had the White League Riots. The resentful gray men pulled their CSA rifles out of hiding, he'd been there. The Republican officials fired back, Reconstruction in Louisiana disappeared in a firestorm of bullets. So did Negro office holders and militia men, and so, nearly, did Sienna Robichon, caught in the middle.

He shook his head. Bedlam played directly into Stevens' hands. He'd use it to take over. Get Taylor involved, Taylor had no backbone. There'd be an incident, he'd bring in the Navy and that would be it. Stevens would take over the palace, Thurston, Ashford swinging in behind him.

Too much government, and men used guns to tyrannize. Too little government, they used guns to murder. But solitary, a man used his gun to protect.

He settled the bar bill and hurried to his quarters to clean his revolver.

THIRTY-FIVE

The kingdom in turmoil, Commander Taylor ordered Ramsey to stay where he could find him. The attaché had built an alcove off his inner office. He intended it for a code room once the U.S. concluded a treaty to lay a submarine cable between San Francisco and Honolulu. The room was used now to manually decode documents but as there were few of them, Taylor stuck him in it at a wobbly desk on an unpadded chair. There was no window and no relief.

There also was no secrecy. The wall was thin and Ramsey could hear everything the attaché said.

He heard his voice now, him and John Stevens. Taylor was staying away from drink, so he was not in good shape. Ramsey wasn't certain the attaché could hold his own. And if he couldn't, only one direction a boulder rolled.

"Should American lives be threatened, Mr. Stevens, I will authorize *Adams'* captain to take action. I, the Attaché. But it shall be appropriate action, appropriate. Appropriate as military protocol prescribes it. Only."

"And the Marines?"

"As I said, to protect American lives – only." He heard the attaché close his office windows. Rain, he guessed. "Now, if that will be all …"

"No, Commander, not all, not all by half. Come an uprising, by the natives or by the Honolulu Rifles, they put American lives at risk. But more than American lives, they put American property at risk. American property, their businesses, their homes, the tools of industry they have imported at great personal cost."

He saw where Stevens was headed. First he fired up the businessmen. Then he leaned on the Navy. If he caused lightening to strike, the Marines would have to land and once they did, there'd be no turning back. He'd make himself governor de facto before Washington knew any different.

"You imperil American property, you imperil American lives. They are the same. That is why the Navy sent *Adams* to us."

That comment seemed to stiffen Taylor's backbone. "*Adams* is a military vessel. I will remind you of that, sir. She was not sent 'to us.' She was sent to me. To me, sir."

He thought he caught Stevens chuckle before saying, "I forget myself, Commander. I have no intention of contravening your precious chain of command. But do not forget you have an obligation to the flag. It flies over a mud hole, it is your sacred duty to –"

"I have shed blood for the flag, sir, shed blood! You needn't remind me of my obligations, to God or country!"

He thought the attaché had probably held out long as he could.

"… natives have weapons, you know," Stevens was saying, "stole them off that tub of Kalakaua's. The armory meeting, they could turn them upon American citizens –"

Looking smart in uniform of the day, he rapped three times on the open door. "Commander Taylor, I have that dispatch."

Taylor looked at him, blank. "Dispatch?"

"The one you was expecting, sir."

"O, yes."

"The priority dispatch, sir."

"Priority ..." Understanding dawned. "Priority, yes." Taylor glared pointedly at the U.S. Minister.

"Well ..." Stevens looked him up and down. "Ramsey. Still a meritless Petty Officer, without medals or distinction, and still with us, I see. But not for long. Once Washington reads my next report ..."

"Commander, I'll need to escort you to the code room," he said to Taylor.

"Wait a minute." Stevens stopped him with the end of his stick. "No dispatch case? I know enough about these matters. Is that protocol, Commander?"

Ramsey saw Taylor shift on his feet, not quick enough for the game, and so he spoke up before Stevens smelled the rat. "The message is in cipher, Mr. Minister."

"I see. Well ... my dispatch won't be. Easy reading so Washington makes no mistakes. I'll see you hang yet, Ramsey."

He shut the door behind the minister and heard the attaché exhale. "Thank you, Ramsey. The man was at Eden when Eve bit the apple, I am convinced of it."

"Yes, sir."

"He won't be satisfied until Marines occupy every corner and rifle fire spits through the capital. – Every man's a warrior who hasn't been to war, remember that."

"I'll leave you to your work, Commander."

"... Goes for you, too."

"Yes, sir."

"...Just like him. Thoughtless, underhanded. Undisciplined."

"I'll be in my office, Commander."

"And just what would happen if I landed the Marines? Does the thought occur to him?" He paced, massaging his temples. "The Imperial German Fleet, that's what. A pair of dreadnoughts, modern, put little *Adams* in a tea cup. Or the Royal Navy – hell, they'd steam from India before granny dried her drawers. Then we'd have an incident. O, we'd have an incident! I'd have to beg Kalakaua for reinforcements, can you see that? – Or Luahine, for God's sake!"

Taylor plopped beneath his painting of Diamond Head and placed his face in his hands. "Have my aide bring me my powders," he said after a moment. "My powders, Ramsey."

When he re-entered, Taylor turned a purplish face upon him. "I warned you about all this. The intelligence work, doing Stevens' bidding, ONI, all of it – well, you call it intelligence work. I call it spying." Taylor stood and resumed his pacing. "Where is that damned sailor with my powders?"

"He had to send out for more, sir. Apparently you used the last dose."

"Blast! He should have known!"

"Let me pour you a glass of water, sir. You'll feel better."

"No, you won't pour me a fucking glass of water! And it won't make me feel any fucking better! Is that clear? 'Cause if it's not, you can just fuck yourself inboard!" The attaché's beard quivered with emotion.

"Yes, sir. I'll see to the aide."

"No, you won't see to the aide! That's just like you ONI ducks, swim away from the fight, your little duck tails aloft. Regular Navy stays for the fight. You little ONI ducks swim away from it. You rile up the water with your little duck feet, don't you, Ramsey?!"

Taylor approached him, perspiring. "You rile up the water and you leave the mess for Regular Navy, don't you, Mr. Intelligence Agent. Well how do you like the mess you've made – here, on my watch! How do you like it? This government is falling around Kalakaua's ears. I doubt he'll keep his throne. It's insurrection and anarchy. Could be another civil war and Stevens is backing the revolutionists! The man posted to His Majesty's government by our Commander in Chief wants to overthrow the government! And you made it all possible, Ramsey! You! How grand you must feel! Letter of commendation for the Reciprocity Treaty, and a second letter for bringing down constitutional authority in these islands. ONI must be so proud!"

"If you will excuse me, Commander."

Taylor swept a cloth across his face. "No, I will not excuse you." He pulled open the door. "Where are those powders?!" he shouted at the sailor at the desk. "Ramsey," he said, turning back into his office, "you are responsible, you understand? Stevens' crowd could bayonet Kalakaua on his throne. They'll tar and feather

Gibson, drive every Chinaman into the sea. You know what it's like when a people gets its spirit broken, I know you do. Well, you'll see it here. The natives, they'll be the lame, the sick, the blind, dancing for a penny and bowing to ole massah. That's what you've done, Ramsey. Feel downright proud. Tell your children about it. Tell them about that girl you raped, that Hawaiian girl."

"You are mistaken, sir, I never forced myself upon any female."

"You raped her, Ramsey. What was her name? Poloa? You got her to help you at Pearl River. You got her to betray her country. If she's ever smart enough to understand what she did, it will destroy her. It will break her heart."

Ramsey turned steely. "Her name is Pua. And I never touched her!"

"You raped her, same as you raped her country!"

The sailor appeared with the packet of headache powders. He stepped between them then pulled back as though scalded.

"It's about time, sailor! Where the hell you been?!" The vein pumped on Taylor's forehead. "Now get out of here, Ramsey, get out before I find my gun. Get out and leave me alone!"

Late that night, on his back clothed upon the bunk in his quarters, pistol shots from drunken men cracking the air on streets to either side of him, and unsuccessful at sleep, he heard the floor board creak in the next room. He slipped his heavy Navy service revolver from under the pillow and waited. The Colt was cumbersome but its muzzle flash and explosive report would stop a target dead even if the bullet missed in the dark. The floorboard creaked again and he pulled back the hammer.

"Ramsey?" The voice sounded timid, higher, less confident, but he recognized it.

He slid the Colt under the sheet and lit a lamp. There in its yellow glow stood Pua. Her hair was coiled and worn up the way Hawaiian women in town did their hair, though strands of it hung down as if they'd been tugged out of the bun. On the same side the sleeve of her blouse was torn at the shoulder. The blouse was tucked into a very plain, full black skirt. Her feet were bare.

"Ramsey?" she said again and curtsied. "Manu like me fetch you. *Wikiwiki*, he say."

Her English and her manner had improved measurably under Sienna's hand. The native girl he'd last seen had turned into a fawn-colored young woman, graceful as the flower petal for which she was named. But like a petal in the breeze, she trembled before him.

"Pua, what happened to you?"

"Manu say *wikiwiki*. Please Ramsey, you hurry."

A shot went off and she cowered.

He got out of bed and went to her, but she shied away from him.

"What's happened to you, Pua? What happened to your blouse?"

She looked back at him, eyes large in the lamp light. "The *haole* men, they like hurt me, I scared."

"Someone put his hands on you?"

She nodded and began to weep. Her shoulders hunched protectively, hands clasped to her bosom.

"O Pua, darlin'," he said softly and offered his arms to her, but she looked at him big-eyed again, and danced away.

"No, Ramsey, you come."

"Are you afraid of me, Pua? I won't hurt you. I won't hurt you, *ku'uipo*." He used the word for sweetheart, the tenderest word he knew in Hawaiian. "I ..."

Another pistol shot made her jump. Her eyes pleaded with him.

"Bastards!" he exclaimed and slipped his boots on. "Cowardly, godforsaken bastards! Any man comes near you, he'll sleep in the bone yard!" He flourished the Colt revolver and stuck it in his belt then threw on a coat.

His preparations seemed to relax her. She regained a trace of her pluck. "Ramsey fix hair. No look like porkypine."

"Porkypine!" He grinned. "Ever see one?"

"No, Sienna teach me. Now I teach you. Porkypine get hair like *wana* sea urchin. You fix, Ramsey." She licked her fingers and mushed down his hair.

They stepped into the night. Honolulu proper, normally an early town soon to bed, had taken on the character of its waterfront. Men lingered on corners and lurched in clusters down the alleyways. Odors of sweat, tobacco and beer draped the streets, trapped by the humidity. Three Russian merchant seamen accosted them, sizing up Pua as his whore. "*Blyadischa!*" one of them leered and grabbed at her. She screamed and he stuck his pistol between the man's eyes. He motioned for her to come to him, but she scurried off in the direction of Chinatown. With a backward glance at the men he hurried to follow.

Pua led him to the original Hotel Street entrance of Madam Ho's. Her room was in the older wing on the second floor, and when they reached her door she said, "Manu wait inside." She curtsied, gave him a swift glance and turned back downstairs.

Inside was a sitting room just large enough to accommodate two parlor chairs and a writing table. A door connected to an equally small sleeping chamber. Manu got up from the bed and approached him. "What took you so long?" he asked.

"I actually thought I'd try a little sleep. I read somewhere that's what night is for."

"You look thinner."

"You look fatter."

"I am." Manu patted his belly. "We ate good in Samoa. Better than the swill aboard ship."

Manu pointed to a chair, but he refused it. The window was open and through it floated strains from the brass band located on the King Street side of the establishment. "You're a wanted man now, you must be proud," he said. "Didn't you steal every loose gun in the Kingdom? You and some Chinaman?"

"A Jap. You westerners never could tell us apart."

"Coloreds, what's to know? Y'all crooked as snakes at a blind chicken dance."

Manu snorted then looked at him. "I heard about Ashford's demonstration at the palace."

He shrugged. "All powder, no shot."

"True, but they'll be back."

"They'll be back," he agreed. "And Stevens will use it to stir things up."

"I get *po'o nui* – unease."

"Manu, last time we had a heart-to-heart I committed the gravest error of my career."

"You think getting me aboard *Kaimiloa* was a mistake?"

"Have you seen your island? It's bedlam out there." He went to the window.

"If the confederation had gone through, it would be worse. Luahine would declare herself dictator."

"As I said, your problems with your mother are not my problems."

Manu made a face and nodded. "So, you know. What else do you know?"

"I know it's late and you used your sister to get me here. Now that I am here, you have wasted my time. You know some corn-cracking sodomite forced himself upon her? Tore her clothing, scared her to death."

Manu's eyes narrowed. "Is she all right?" he asked.

"Yes, but she's skittish as a colt around me." He sat. "I suppose she's afraid of White men now."

"Could be, but that's not why she's afraid of you. She thinks you've lost your soul – *uhane ole*. That makes you a demon in her eyes."

"Well I've been called many things. Where'd she get that idea?"

"I might have mentioned something about it."

He cocked his head.

"Look, my mother threw a curse on you."

He snorted.

"She's Kahu," Manu said. "Everybody's afraid of her, and they should be."

"You believe all that? No wonder that movement of yours is going nowhere."

"I believe enough of it. And you should, too. Why you think you had so much trouble at Pu'uloa?"

"Pu'uloa?" Ramsey yawned. "You mean …?"

"I mean everything. All your accidents. All your injuries. The fire burning your tent. Everything."

"The fire was the Marines knocking over a lantern."

"So you *haole* say. We know better. Pearl River is sacred, Ramsey. It nests in a spirit world you know nothing about. And you'll never know anything about long as –"

"What are you saying, Manu. The faeries bit me?"

"No. I'm saying Luahine cursed you. She's responsible for the sacred locations on each island. She couldn't let you discover too much."

"But why did Pua …?"

"Unlock the entrance to the lagoon?" Manu shrugged. "My idea, actually. Luahine thinks I went too far. But we had to give my people something to fight for. You proved the lagoon is valuable. Kalakaua giving it away, giving away sacred Pu'uloa, that's fat in the fire. My people will crawl out of their grass huts to oppose that."

He shook his head, chagrined. "You used me."

Manu stretched his round belly. "*Mahalo*, boss. You one *aikane*, one friend of the people. *No ka 'oi* – da best!"

"And Pua thinks I'm a demon. What does she think about you?"

"I guess she doesn't know me that well," Manu said. "But maybe you and I, we're demons together. No souls."

"Well, not an association I intend to continue, pard." He stood up.

"Something else you don't know," Manu said.

He hesitated.

"The King is asking Gibson to resign."

He whistled softly and sat back down. "Sacrificing his bedfellow. First Spreckels, now his Prime Minister." He pulled out a cigar, spit out the end and lit it. "He's all alone. He couldn't be considering roping in with Luahine."

"No."

"Who's he putting up for Gibson?"

"Antone Rosa."

"The part-Hawaiian? Think he can get away with it?"

"Not a chance."

He agreed. "The missionary boys have their blood up. They won't tolerate it."

"So, what do we do?"

"O, no, Manu. I lay down with you once and come up full of fleas. What does it matter to me who Kalakaua puts in his cabinet."

"I'm begging you, boss."

"Not my problem, Manu. You work it out."

"You're cursed, boss. You want your soul back, don't you?"

"If your mother has my soul, tell her to keep it. I'm getting along fine without it."

"Well, if not your soul, how about something else?"

"Nothing I want from you, Manu."

"You're lying."

He looked hard at him. "Where I come from, Manu, those words –"

"Where I come from those words are true and you know it. You want something from me, admit it."

He looked away.

"Admit it, Ramsey."

"All right, damn your black heart, Manu. Yes, I want ... that is, if your sister ... I cannot ..."

"Pua's right about your soul, you know. Got a hole in it the size of a plantation drainage ditch. You want me to speak to her. Put in the good word. Tell her you're not entirely evil."

"Something like that."

"And for what reason, exactly?"

"What do you mean?"

"For what reason, Ramsey? Who is my sister to you?"

"I don't know what you're talking about."

"You *haole* and your attitudes toward nature. We don't understand them but we are grateful for them, makes you vulnerable to us. – Who is my sister, she's a study to you? You've changed your field, you're a scientist now … an anthropologist? She's your subject?"

"No, of course not. She's …"

"What are your feelings for the girl, Ramsey?"

"Feelings? She's a native."

"Do you love her, Ramsey? Do you love my sister?"

"Love? Where'd you get that idea? Love, why … no, I –"

"Well what is it then? Why should I speak to my sister for you?"

"… *Aloha*, that's what it is. It's *aloha*. Tell her that. Say I'm not a demon, or whatever she thinks I am. I … what's that paddle law?"

"Splintered Paddle?"

"That's it. Take care of each other, or the weak, or however you put it."

"You think my sister is weak, Ramsey?"

"No, goddamn it! Not that way, not weak. What you being so dull for? I swear. No, I'm just trying to say what kind of *aloha* it is. It's the paddle kind, not the …"

"Not the other kind."

"Exactly! That kind of *aloha*. Hell, Manu. If y'all would put some more words in that fool tongue of yours …"

"That's the problem with you *haole*. You divide everything with words and lines and notions, like it means something. Then you've splintered the paddle and you're dead in the water."

"You're the one dead in the water. You'd have let me sleep else wise."

Manu sat back with a grin. "Look Ramsey, I know you have an idea about the missionary boys. What is it? I'll tell my sister you're a paddle or whatever you want."

"Just tell her what I said."

Manu nodded. "What's your idea?"

He hunched forward, elbows on knees. "Well look, there are two camps in the missionary party. Ashford wants revolution, Thurston with him, most like. Castle and Dole, they're moderates, just want reform."

"That's it? That's what the Navy pays you for? My aunty on Kauai knows that."

"You have to split them."

"Like a coconut. Sure." Manu waved his hand dismissively.

"Exploit their weakness."

"That the best you can do?"

He exhaled. "Well, Manu ..." In the plume of cigar smoke he saw the chess board take shape, saw the moves, only a few needed, that would topple the king. "If I catch your fleas again, I'll just have to shoot you."

"I'm a *Lua* master, a *haole* can't shoot me. I just change my shape. – What's your plan?"

He hesitated. "I don't know, Manu. You want me to go out on a limb for you. Why should I? What's in it for me?"

"Pua ... I thought we agreed."

He waved his cigar. "Come on, Manu. This is my career we're talking about, getting me involved in local politics. Hell, even prison."

"How about your soul, Ramsey. Doing something you can tell your children about. Maybe even for love – ever think of that?"

He smiled. "A little old-fashioned, Manu. Not at all what John Stevens offered me."

"I don't know what to tell you, Ramsey. My people need help. We're singers, we're dancers, we still bathe naked in the waterfall. We don't understand the modern world. You tell me to split the coconut. I don't even have a machete to do it." He slumped, frustrated.

"Maybe that's your mistake, Manu. You're looking for a machete, you should be looking for ..."

He sat back up. "For what, Ramsey?"

"For something much more intelligent." He pulled on his cigar. "... You know they've put a bounty on the King."

Manu nodded. "The *pake* Chinese. My side can't afford it."

Ramsey's face broke into a grin as the chess pieces lined up and he saw the moves stretching before him to a king protected this time by Castles, Bishops and even a phalanx of Doles. "Here's what we'll do – who do you know in Chinatown?"

THIRTY-SIX

Luahine sailed into Honolulu Harbor aboard her war canoe. The body of her fleet still patrolled the channels between the islands, but she felt no need of them. When a dancer performed Hula Pahu the fire was contained by the ancient movements, the dancer herself was not turned. Luahine had met the goddess as a sorceress however, and her blood was now molten, her eyes fierce as the Uli, and she surged and struck and flashed as unpredictably and cruelly as Pele herself.

She engulfed Prince Koloa's Honolulu house with her retinue, brushing aside the protests of his caretaker with a flick of her *kapu* stick. She draped herself upon mats, demanded food and rested.

Without waiting for orders, Dexter Collins, Gibson's chief of detectives, took over security at the palace. He commandeered a *kanaka* work party to throw up gun emplacements and insisted the gates be locked and manned. There was a small armory in the basement which, if it fell into Luahine's hands ... Upon inspection, it proved to be dreadfully maintained. The rifle barrels were pitted and the ammunition old. He was not certain it would fire. He stuck a cavalry revolver in his belt, meaning to test it when he had the chance.

He moved Gibson to his Waikiki estate where Fred and Talula Hayselden could look after him. Kalakaua refused to quit the palace, however. His place was with his people, he insisted.

Collins grunted. "You'll find me right with you, Your Honor, me pistol in me belt, big as a carbuncle." He patted the grip of the cavalry revolver. "Give the Chiefess something to think about."

When after two days Luahine determined the omens were propitious, she summoned her bearers and they lifted her palanquin. They were soft, pudgy *kahuna*, the ones who'd wanted to sacrifice her on the Big Island, not her trim, tattooed warriors, and they grunted with the effort. After her victory with Pele, she insisted they carry her everywhere, and she chuckled as she discharged and the priests beneath her *okole* had to inhale her great eruptions of gas.

She sent her crier ahead but ordered the remainder of her retinue to stay behind. She wanted enough of a disturbance to attract a crowd, but not enough to rouse the militia. The bearded priest fell in with the procession and the crier warned bystanders out of the way.

In no time *kanaka* admirers, Dutch and Russian sailors on liberty and loafers of every sort fanned out behind her. A knot of Gibson's native constables followed at a distance.

Reporters from the Honolulu papers tagged along. They had run the story of a local movement to replace Kalakaua with young Princess Kaiulani. It was cribbed by the San Francisco press and reported as far afield as the Tyrone, Pennsylvania *Herald*:

> *Gibson is the real power behind the throne, but he is anxious to be the throne de facto and is certain to be the central figure in the coming revolution. It is possible he may more than prove a match against the combined forces who are determined to place the Princess, daughter of Archie Cleghorn, on the throne as symbol that British influences reign triumphant in Hawaii.*

The bearded priest kept an eye on the reporters. The high chiefess was easily distracted these days and when distracted, she did not control herself. When she did not control herself, bad things happened, bad for the movement. A reporter shouted questions at her. He wrote for the *Pacific Commercial Advertiser,* he said in workable Hawaiian. "Will there be a revolution, Chiefess? Will your warriors fight the Rifles?"

He wrestled the man away. "She wears the royal red *kapa,*" the reporter persisted. "Only the monarch wears – will she *hapai* the throne? Will she take it?"

He hurried up the steps into the palace and saw the *kahuna* stumble. They nearly lost Luahine from their shoulders. They had never seen anything like the interior: waxed hard woods, *haole* fixtures and colors, polished furniture. Not a calabash, not a woven sleeping mat in sight. The chiefess growled at them to keep their eyes straight.

A guard led them into a room with western floor cover and invited them to wait. He heard Luahine sniff. The guard spoke worse Hawaiian than the reporter.

He examined Kalakaua as he entered through a curtain. His hair shone, as did his whiskers, but it was not with life. All his oiling and combing could not cover the effect of *haole* gin. He greeted the chiefess with kisses and the formal words of *aloha,* but she did not stand. None of them did. She remained cross-legged on her litter, fanning with a newspaper. He'd given her the newspaper idea.

The king climbed to his throne. The priest smiled to himself. Kalakaua would not sit on the floor with the chiefess, it would place his head below hers.

He signaled the crier. A slender man, he straightened his *malo* and planted himself before the king. He had rehearsed him for this moment. The crier commanded imagery like a musician, but like a musician, he often played too long. "Kawika Kalakaua," the crier began. This was by design, the use of Kalakaua's common name. Luahine wanted it, there was no arguing with her. She wanted the king addressed commonly, as though he were anyone, not *mo'i,* not sovereign over the nation.

The crier recited her heritage – pointedly descended out of the Kamehameha line, not the king's house – and finished with her greatest achievement. "She is *kahu 'ana 'ana.* She is sorceress by way of her mother's village on Molokai island, birthplace of the dark arts. She fasted under the Lono moon at the rock which divides sorcery from dance, and there she divided herself. No more the *hula,* but only the spells, that our people's command over the spirit world not be lost during the dark season of the Whites."

A *haole* man emerged from a curtain behind the throne. The butt of a pistol protruded from his broadbelt. He was small, compact, a fighter. The priest stopped the crier and looked uneasily at the chiefess. They were unarmed, something else she insisted on. "I have Pele," she'd told him.

She urged on the crier with a grunt.

The crier raised a boney arm. "All her powers Luahine surrendered before the fire goddess, Pele-honua-mea, Pele of the sacred land. At Hilo town the Chiefess made her offerings. She poured out her libations. She displayed her gifts. Pele rose up around her, Pele-'ai-honua, she who devours the land. Her flow is so great as to retire Lord Kanaloa from the sea, her heat shrivels the mighty testicles of the pig god Kamapua'a. She drives the *haole* invaders before her like pale sand crabs.

"But before her stood Luahine-ho'opi-opi'o, she who dispatches the Flying God to collect souls. 'Lei of Mauna Loa, beautiful to look upon,' the High Chiefess of all Hawaiians sings, the love song with which Chief Lohiau courted Pele on Kauai island. And behold, the goddess pauses. '*Ka!*' Pele exclaims. '*Ka!* Is it you, my Sister?'"

The crier excelled at this, excelled at making a story come alive. To portray Pele, his bones seemed to quiver like flames, his eyes blazed. How would he inflate himself to dramatize the high chiefess? The priest leaned in with the others.

"'Aye,' responds the Chiefess. 'Your Sister, Hiᐤiaka-in-the-bosom-of-Pele. *Hanai* me to your family, Aunty Pele. Devour me for my failures or if it be your will, fill me with your fire. I offer myself to thee.'

The crier gestured. He had all eyes upon him. "Once before had Pele consumed Hiᐤiaka in flames. It was punishment for her faithlessness. Would she do so again? The Chiefess folds herself to the ground. It burns to the touch. She composes herself and recites her birth chant. There on the plain of Hilo, the goddess Pele rises up. The fiery tresses of her hair embrace the Chiefess. They draw ever tighter. The sparks mount to the sky like a spray of stars. But, lo! The embrace turns into a caress, the caress of Haumea the Mother! The Chiefess suckles. Hot fluid fills her. She arises. Pele's fire swims in her. It is *koko* her blood. She changes, like *papaʻi* the hermit crab she changes. She is Kaʻula-o-ke-ahi, she is fire itself. Hear me, Kawika Kalakaua!"

Beautifully done. The crier should receive an extra share of wherever this was heading. The priest retrieved a *ti* leaf parcel from his own wrap and tossed it at Kalakaua's feet. It parted and revealed the blue sash the king had bestowed upon the chiefess when he inducted her into his Hale Naua society.

Then Luahine spat on the floor.

That had not been talked about. She did it on her own. He could see the color rising in her face.

The White sidled in front of the king and placed his hand upon the grip of his pistol. Nothing the priest could do, the chiefess had gone too far. He stepped back from the throne and positioned himself between her and the *haole*. He signaled the *kahuna* to their feet.

The White withdrew the weapon.

The king stirred, as if crawling awake. "No," he commanded the White and started to say more, but Luahine heaved herself erect. The king shut his mouth. The White whispered something to him and aimed.

The priest put a hand on her arm, but she pushed through him and her men. The red drapery fell from the promontories of her body like lava itself. *Lehua* was in her hair and Pele's own disdain upon her face. It seemed the pathetic weapon would no more stop her than it could a caldera. She approached the throne.

The *haole* fired. Everyone saw him work the firing mechanism. It was clear as day. For a heartbeat, nothing happened. Then the ammunition rim-fired. The breech exploded and shattered the White's thumb. He cried and dropped the pistol. His knees gave and he sank to the floor.

The smoke floated upward and the report echoed through the room. The man hunched over his hand, moaning. The priest started to laugh and turned to Luahine's bearers. They laughed, too. They pointed at the *haole* and jeered.

Luahine glared at the fallen man then raised both hands for silence. She was in charge now. She was the only monarch in the room, a *keiki* child could see it. "Kawika Kalakaua, am I *okole ka'aka* that you show no regard for the Office of High Chiefess? You dare insult me with this *haole*?"

She wrinkled her face in disdain. Whites are *opae* the shrimp that shits from its head, she said. White testicles are lumps that rot like a sailor's at sea. The smell disgusts the nostrils. She held up her thumb and forefinger close together. "*Aia ho'i,* behold! The *haole* is a pinworm crawling out of my rectum." She bent over and shook her enormous posterior, and the *kahuna* roared with pleasure. He joined them. It felt good to see her deride the Whites in the king's own throne room. It undid a generation of ill treatment and shame.

"Sister!" The king spoke nervously. The White squirmed at his feet. "Sister, you dared gird yourself in the royal color –"

She cut him off. "I wear the color of the goddess, Kawika Kalakaua. What care I for royalty?" She filled as she spoke, rising up dark and menacing like a volcanic cone. The priest lowered his eyes. He'd seen her thus before.

"I am Kahu Pele," she roared, hair alive as Pele's own. "I am Priestess to the Goddess. Pele's fire burns within me. She is *koko* my blood. She is *ha* my breath. Dare to touch me, and you expire. Point your puny weapon at me, and the goddess laughs." She flourished her *kapu* stick. "Hear the words of the goddess now, Kawika Kalakaua: you steal your title like the western island steals the sun. You were to rule only as *Makua*, Father. Instead, you claimed the title *Mo'i*, Sovereign, and invoked the allegiance of the Jehovah god when you dedicated this profane place." She spat again. "It is an abomination."

The word she used suggested everything from filth to defiling the gods. The mildly ranked Kalakaua had spread a vulgar stain upon the land. Pele demanded he purify himself so the people would be made righteous. *Ua mau ke ea o ka aina i ka pono … preserve the land in righteousness.*

"You, Kawika Kalakaua, you must restore your *pono*." She made a face. She did not think the king had it in him. "No wonder the people ask for the girl Kaiulani to sit upon the throne. They have lost heart. *Kapu* is gone. They believe *mana*, strength and authority have fled to the *haole* side. But their Kahu Pele does not flee. In the days of the Kamehamehas, High Chiefess Princess Ruth protected the people. She was *ka pali*, the great cliff that shielded them from the wind. Today I am their cliff. And you Kawika Kalakaua, you will restore your *pono*, or you will fall like the warriors of Oahu when Kamehameha pushed them over the Pali."

The crier passed her a *kapa* cloth bundle. She unfolded it and the priest looked away again. In her hands was a length of *manele*, the soapberry tree. Its bark was red, it had been harvested at Waianui Gulch near her mother's village. A grotesque visage had been carved into the wood.

"Behold *akua lele*," she cried and held up the totem. "The Flying God, he who enters the accursed and destroys him. See how his skin is *ehu* red. *Ehu* now becomes the ill omen of your household, Kawika Kalakaua. I will plant the Flying God in the sacred burial cave of Kaumuali'i, grandfather to your queen and last chief of Kauai. If you have *pono* the gods will conduct you through the *kapu* protecting the cave, you will find the Flying God, you will offer him to Aunty Pele at Mauna Loa, and you will live. If you do not, the skin of *akua lele* will turn green, and you will die. In three English years you will die of the lingering curse, Kawika Kalakaua."

She snorted. "I say, send for the beaters now, O King. Order them to prepare your funeral robe, for you have not the *pono*. The Kauai gods will not serve you. You shall surely suffer long and die."

She called to her retinue. The *kahuna* staggered under her weight.

"*Hiki no*, it is good," the bearded priest thought to himself. The chiefess kept her fire under control. Just one last gesture, his idea …

From the palanquin, Luahine tossed the newspaper at the feet of the king. It reported the movement to place Princess Kaiulani on the throne. "Faagh! This *hapa-haole* child is not the line of descent. It is not through the Kalakaua lineage that *pono* travels. It is through Kapiolani, the Queen. Through her sisters on Kauai, consorts of the dark *menehune*, that is how *pono* is fed; that alone is where royalty can be claimed.

"*Ho'ohiki wawe ia*," she ordered the bearers and was rushed out of the palace.

He lingered for a moment. The injured White got to his feet and wrapped his bleeding hand. The king stood on the steps of his throne and gazed after the chiefess.

She had told the king, *pono* travels from Kauai. He agreed. If not from the *menehune* to Luahine the sorceress, then from the *menehune* to her daughter, the dancer. "*Hiki no*, it is good."

He followed her party out.

THIRTY-SEVEN

T he Honolulu newspapers speculated that Tong Kee was "the Hakka Chinee" rumored to have placed a bounty on King Kalakaua's head. The king had granted his favor to the Punti Chinese Chun Ah Fong, an insult guaranteed to turn Tong Kee "recklessly choleric," as one paper put it.

Tong Kee mused about it as he crossed through carriage traffic and mounted the steps to the *Hawaiian Gazette*. The papers were wrong. If he wanted the king murdered he would save the expense of an assassin and slip a knife under Kalakaua's ribs himself.

He had sliced open Punti landlords with a pole axe during the Taiping Rebellion in his native Canton Province in 1861. That's where he first encountered Occidentals and their strangely immodest ways. They comprised the Officer's Corps of the Imperial Army, and would have seemed unremarkable except careless sprays of their bullets felled even the fiercest swordsman. Later during the Second Opium War he encountered Occidentals again. He ruminated over what he'd observed and buried his pole axe. Then he organized gangs of boatmen to ferry the Occidental opium chests from their squat India merchantmen to landed distributors, who injected the product into the commercial arteries of Manchu China.

As a consequence he'd been able to study Occidental business practices closely. Despite being immodest, they were strikingly effective.

He determined that his own business practices should be equally effective, though they were not so immodest as the Occidental, not so immodest at all. More was to be gained through subtle manipulation than by immodesty. Much more.

He called at the editor's office. He wore a bowler hat for the occasion, striped waistcoat and pearl gray spats fastened over his ankle boots. A shower had swept across Honolulu just before he set out, so the leggings were spattered with grit from the street, but his walking stick, lacquered and topped by a solid gold knob, gleamed. He carried it in both hands across the mud so it would not become soiled.

A pressman, garters restraining his sleeves and an ink-stained apron about his neck, stopped him. The editor was getting out the next edition and could not be bothered, the man said. But Tong Kee put a hand on his chest and shoved him aside then located the largest office on the floor. He placed his walking stick upon its desk, which was littered with papers.

"Gibson no buy for me," he said of the stick. He did not remove his hat. "The King no buy. I buy. Him tell much lie."

The editor of the *Hawaiian Gazette* recognized the makings of a front page story and cleared off a chair.

"Gold," he added, pointing to the knob as the editor sent for a stenographer then poured two tumblers of brandy and unlocked the cabinet where he kept his good cigars.

He drank the brandy but refused the cigar. "I no coolie."

"The coolie traffic is truly reprehensible," the editor said. "These islands received shipments enough from the barracoons of Macau. It is a stain upon our labor policies."

He frowned, rolled a cigarette and lit it. "I business man," he said through the smoke. "Do much business. Send money home. King no friend. Him make friend with Chun Ah Fong. Then he want money, he come to Tong Kee."

"The King asked you for money?"

"Him sell me opium license."

"But the legislature awarded the license to Chun Ah Fong."

He snarled and crushed his cigarette on the underside of the desk. "No! I pay money first! I pay Gibson! I pay Kaae! I pay first!"

"What did you pay for the license?"

"I pay dollars one time twenty thousand, ten thousand, thirty thousand. I go nighttime. Then I pay eleven thousand and one pig!"

"You went to the palace?"

He nodded.

"With a live pig?"

"Dead. I cook first, like my village. *Char siu,* King like very much."

The editor exchanged a look with the stenographer. "Where is the money now?"

He shrugged. "King want more money for Luahine temple. I say, first you send me from Hawaiian Empire to China Empire, yes? Ambassador – I dress good. Like this." He indicated his attire.

"Kalakaua promised to make you his minister, from the Hawaiian Empire to China?" The editor swallowed another brandy.

"I go Peking, first Hakka from my village to enter palace of Son of Heaven. Chun Ah Fong the Punti never go. His son Chun Lung never go. Tong Kee go. But Hawaiian Empire no good. *Pau* finish – See? I talk good Hawaiian. This my cane, these my clothes for Son of Heaven. Now Emperor never see."

"It's been rumored there is a price on the King. He does not leave the palace. Gibson has placed bodyguards around him."

He looked at the editor. "Why I kill Kalakaua? He not Chinese."

The editor had the stenographer transcribe her notes on a Remington then read the affidavit aloud. Tong Kee listened carefully, nodded occasionally and placed his name at the bottom.

"You print, yes?"

The editor said he was particularly taken by the detail of the pig and the darksome transactions at the palace. "I print, yes," he added with a smile.

Tong Kee left the newspaper office. He was immensely pleased with himself. If you killed a man he died only once. If you humiliated him he died many times, and his family, too. He learned this from the Occidentals who looted the Palace of Perfect Clarity in Peking, seized the emperor's favorite dog as a gift for the barbarian queen Victoria, and forced the Son of Heaven to cede Hong Kong and then Kowloon. It was humiliation enough to bow the head of every Chinese around the world.

He collected his rig from the blacksmith and drove back to Waipahu. As the red dirt of Honolulu flaked from the carriage wheels, he held his head high.

Honolulu society – local and foreign born, *haole* and native – mutated into a sleek, sinuous, wounded beast, surprised, shamed and outraged at its hurt and turning with lethal intent upon its perpetrator, barricaded now behind the palace gates. Its frustration swelled into the howl of indignation that echoed Ewa Point to Diamond Head, *mauka* to *makai*, and quickly over the plains and volcanic escarpments to encompass Oahu, whence it carried in short order to the outer islands.

The *Hawaiian Gazette*'s special edition did not contain its customary number of pages. As word flew around town and the small telephone exchange was overwhelmed, Honolulu's reading public had interest only in the close-ruled columns which carried the story. The paper laid out the opium case in considerable detail, making much of the "nocturnal assignations" and the baked pig. In an opinion column the editor added:

These are incontrovertible facts. They are backed up by sixty odd pages of sworn affidavits, by fourteen persons, establishing them beyond a possibility of a doubt. The only question is whether Kaae got any of the money, or whether the King kept it all.

Honolulu's other papers and the Hawaiian language press each brought out their own versions, which were reprints of the *Gazette* story colored by hastily assembled opinions and the slimmest of new facts concerning the case. Together the news pages fanned the embers of discontent scattered about the kingdom. Knots of people appeared in the streets of the various towns and plantation communities, the barrooms overflowed and the story was masticated and embossed into the wee hours.

The next edition of the *Gazette* carried a letter to the editor:

Men who lived here from the time of the Kamehamehas have seen a constitutional government changed into an absolute despotism and military rule. Some of the descendants of the men who forced King John to give the English people the Magna Carta are here. The descendants of those who fought on Bunker Hill are with us, and also Germans, who love liberty and right.

Let us then act unitedly, firmly, judiciously, and the right will prevail, and we shall have the approval of the civilized world.

THIRTY-EIGHT

H*eʻe nalu* – it meant wave sliding – had suffocated in the whalebone corset the missionaries tightened upon native culture, but a handful of Hawaiians kept surfing alive at various beaches around the islands. From one of them Manu borrowed a board and paddled out to the reef on a mother-of-pearl sea tinted in pinks and golds.

The hour after daybreak before the wind came up, the ocean surface was smooth, the white sandy bottom visible. Away to the east he could see the waves break viciously at the foot of Diamond Head, but here opposite the Waikiki beach house of Princess Lilu Dominis they unrolled like green, frothy carpets.

He attacked five, caught two and managed to keep his balance for one, his feet parallel, arms akimbo, and remained upright through the break until the wave petered out. He pushed his hair back and shook out the water. One for five, about the same chance he had of convincing the Punahou wife of Reverend Horace Somers to help him.

Eliza joined him on a wide redwood board and they paddled together toward the reef.

"Long time," he remarked with a grin.

"Me, too," she said. "They say you don't forget."

"You don't forget, but the waves forget you. *Nalu* don't like me so good."

"Did you make a little sacrifice on the beach? We always did when I was a girl. Some seaweed or something in a mound of sand. You could use tobacco but we were afraid to sneak any out of the house."

They were outside the reef where the swells lifted the boards but did not suck them toward shore, and he sat up, legs overlapping the rails. He was shirtless and wore khaki shorts secured over his navel by a broad seaman's belt. Eliza remained prone, leaning on her forearms. She wore a bathing costume with a skirt to mid-thigh. Beneath it her legs were firm. *Kukui* nuts encircled one ankle.

"It's good to get away from things," he said, surveying the horizon from Diamond Head toward Honolulu. The spars of an outbound schooner sank below the curvature. Other than that, they were completely alone as the day yawned awake.

"Yes," she said and dipped her face in the water to push back her hair. "There is far too much going on. I am supposed to be a society matron and mother of four *keiki*. 'Red Shirted Revolutionary' I did not anticipate."

"I am sorry about all this. But your *kokua* – well, without your help we'd have been found out, and well ..."

"You may yet. Mr. Somers is Chaplain of the Honolulu Rifles. They are forever drilling at Hale Nui. And the *luna*, he's a sympathizer. Poor Denzo. He's become a cadaver, he is so anxious. He didn't know what I'd do when I found out. – I didn't, either."

"The weapons, are they safe?"

"Lord willing. Long as I can keep Gonsalves from fixing the privy. I told Aunty Pauline to break the water pump, should keep him occupied the week ... What do you plan to do with those rifles, Mr. Manu?"

"Forget the 'Mister,' just 'Manu,' please. Here, want to catch this one?"

They paddled, the water feeling cool but not cold. The swell lifted both their boards just before the wave crested and broke into a comb, and they were off, angling right, away from the break. The salt spray flew in their faces and coated their lips. After their boards slid along the front of the wave to the shoulder, they drifted to a stop.

"You should try standing up," he said. "*Wela ka hao,* we say. Fun!"

She laughed. "I know what you Hawaiians say. I'm *kama☐aina,* you know. *Wela ka hao* – that's why the missionaries put a stop to surf riding. The Hawaiians were having too much fun with one another. Too many mothers without husbands."

He looked her over. She was lively and attractive. He liked the way her hair stayed off her face when wet. It made her eyes appear large and clear in the morning light. "True," he said, "but it was a different time back then. The people were stronger."

"Is that what the rifles are for? To take us back to those days?"

He shrugged and watched the break. They were out of the surf line. Suddenly he did not want to talk about the movement or the politics of the kingdom.

"I don't really think you can go back, do you?" she said. "If you go back to the days of the Kamehamehas, what becomes of families like mine? We were all born here, even though we are *haole.* My baby, little Kamuela – Sam Parker is his godfather. Sam's *aliʻi,* descendant of Kamehameha the Great. Does Luahine expect us to leave, abandon our homes, all we have?"

The current caused their boards to bob close together. He reached out and held her board alongside his.

"What are the rifles for?" she repeated. "You folks *hana make,* Manu? You kill people?"

She sat up so she was staring him in the eye. He looked aside.

"I am *kuʻi a lua,*" he said, "'hand fighter.' I use my wits – deception, feints. I don't use the *haole* weapons."

"Then get rid of them, Manu. Tell Denzo to destroy them."

"You don't understand. There's a problem." He returned her direct gaze.

"Of course there's a problem. If you use the *haole* rifles, you admit you've lost your *mana* – isn't that what you call 'soul?'"

"Something like. *Uhane* is closer to soul."

"To think of that, Manu ..." She shivered. "No, too terrible. Like in *Frankenstein*, they made us read the book. Scared me for days."

"Don't worry about us, Miss Lee. We don't have all the categories you do. We flow, like *wai*, the water."

"The men you'd have to fight, Ashford's men, they don't flow. There's not a thing watery about them. I've seen them all around the ranch. They're drilling, shooting, practicing. They would love human targets, Manu."

"I know. And we have to sneak around in the shadows, in our own land. But the warriors are here, they're here ... Kauai, Oahu, now Maui."

"But why fighting, Manu? Why killing? Isn't there another way?"

"That's the problem. We need the warriors. Otherwise it's in the hands of the *kahuna*. If they come to power, they'll take Hawaii back to Kamehameha the Great, or even before. They'll take it back to *kapu*, no matter what the people say. You will be driven out because you are *haole*. It won't matter who your baby's godfather is. They'll try to make the land pure again."

"But that's ... it's crazy, Manu. *Pupule!*"

He shrugged.

"How do they think to do such a thing? Back to *kapu*? How could they ever ...?"

"How could they succeed? – Look at Pele. They think she's on their side. You can't argue with that."

Eliza nodded. No one argued with Pele.

"Our movement began in Kauai as cultural reform," he said. "The warriors began it. We only wanted to break up the Three Kings, get Kalakaua away from Gibson and Spreckels. We've accomplished that. Now Luahine wants more. It's Pele's fire. Pele's good for us, she gives my people backbone. But Luahine, she's different now, like she's gone mad. No reasoning with her. – And the priests, they've been out of favor so long, they see a way back."

They were silent for awhile, bobbing on the floating boards, looking at one another.

"I'm scared, Manu," she said at last.

He nodded. "Me, too. *Pono* has gone out of my people. No wonder there's trouble."

"What are you going to do?"

"To be frank, I don't know. – Can I tell you something? Luahine is my mother."

She blinked. "You're the son of the High Chiefess?"

He nodded. "And I find I cannot do her bidding longer. I – I don't know. She cursed the King, you know."

She covered her mouth. "My God, Manu. I hadn't heard."

"Her worst curse, from Molokai. He'll never survive it."

"My God ... What can be done?" The current pushed the surfboards together so their bare legs rubbed against each other. The touch felt natural and companionable.

"Only one thing I know of, the *menehune*. They have powers she doesn't."

"The *menehune*? They'll let you ...? I mean, you can approach them? They never ..."

He shrugged. "They taught me my hand fighting. Luahine's son, you see. I can approach them. I must stabilize things here first. You know about the meeting at the armory?"

She nodded. "My husband is attending. It's disgusting, it will get out of hand."

"I don't know. We've put some contingencies in place. Denzo and I need to take the weapons tonight."

"You're not going to the meeting, Manu, please. You'd be risking ..." She touched his arm.

"No, we need the weapons – so the *kahuna* don't make things worse."

"Sounds like bloodshed. On my island. I don't like that."

He sighed and nodded his head. "Sometimes you have to stick your hand in the calabash, no matter what's in it ... Miss Lee, you realize if you speak of any of this, I'll have to curse you myself, real bad. I'll have to come in person, make eye contact."

She held his eyes as they made contact then cocked her head. "Call me Eliza ... And if you're going to curse me, you'll have to catch me first!" She paddled hard into the surf line, caught a wave, stood up and rode it to shore, arms spread wide.

That night, the town quiet for the first time in days, as though the hotheads were saving their powder for the meeting at the armory, Ramsey prepared supper. *Gunn's Domestic Physician* advised young men to eschew foods served too warm or overly seasoned. Such stimulation of the gastric organs should be put off until a man grew longer in the tooth and his humors turned sluggish. His supper consisted of a piece of boiled fowl and a single boiled potato. He added pickled cabbage as an aid to digestion, and a glass of white wine.

He put a match to the lamp and took a book from the shelf, *On War*, Clausewitz' study of Napoleon's campaigns. A handful of copies existed in English. There had not been time for reading and he looked forward to it. He unbuttoned his shirt and hung it in the wardrobe, and opened the top of his union suit to get comfortable. He heard the creak just as he started the book. This time he recognized the tread.

"If it's another meeting Manu wants, tell him I am occupied."

Pua entered. She was dressed as before but wore a polished *kukui* nut *lei* and a flower in her hair. Its fragrance drifted pleasantly to his nostrils.

"Sit down, Pua. I was just having my supper."

"O, Ramsey like I wait?"

"No, no, darlin'. Sit with me, please."

He stood and held a chair. "First time," she said as she sat. "First time sit with the man."

"O? Are you sure then?"

"I like try *haole* style."

"Well, I am honored. Had I known you was coming, I'd have laid the cloth and picked up a bouquet. Shown you a proper supper, New Orleans style." He lit a candle and placed it between them. "Pour you a glass of wine?"

She held up her hand. "Sienna tell me no drink the English *awa*. I too young."

"Sienna is right, Pua. Don't drink the English *awa* especially with the English man. But this? This is French I think, or perhaps German. I'll have to look. Anyhow, you are with me, and you are safe."

He poured the wine and they drank. She wrinkled her nose at its flavor, but drank again.

"You like?" he asked.

"*Ono*," she said then put her fingers to her lips. "I mean, good. I like. Sienna tell me speak *Amelika*."

They drank again and he refilled her glass.

"What you eat, Ramsey? *Limu*? Seaweed?" She took a pinch of sauerkraut in her fingers and munched it. "Faagh! This seaweed *nui lepo*! What you eat, Ramsey?"

She drained the glass to chase the taste from her mouth.

"Now you mention it, it's not what you'd call a high-button repast, but care to join me?"

She scrunched up her face and shook her head.

"Come now, you don't mean to say fish and that god-awful *poi* is more attractive?"

"No, Ramsey. I like casserole now. Sienna make. Very *ono*."

He laughed. "Casserole! Yes, Sienna is formidable in the kitchen!"

"I like casserole, Ramsey. Eat plenty. Get big *opu* now, see?" She stood and pulled the waist of her skirt down to show him. Her bare flesh pooched out below the navel, lending her a generous, womanly profile. "Plenty *opu* now, Ramsey," she said and laughed with unrestrained pleasure. The wine had made her tipsy.

"Plenty *opu* now, Pua," he echoed, joining her laughter. "My God, you're a young woman now, aren't you? You're growing up!" He savored the look of her, so free, her belly a luxurious brown curve, her breasts not seen but imagined: full, fertile and warm. "Upon my soul, you're growing up!"

Her face fell and she sat back down. She leaned toward him across the table. "You no get soul, Ramsey. Bad man. *Uhane ole.*"

His face hung with hers. "You'll get no argument from me, gal. Not tonight."

"What you do with soul, Ramsey? Why you *hemo?*"

He drank. "Maybe I never had one. Some of us just missed out."

"No, Ramsey. You have! Ka'ahupahau give you at Pu'uloa!"

"The shark goddess. Yes, I see what you mean. She gave me a soul."

"You *hemo*, Ramsey, you take away. Now you *make*. You dead." She started to weep.

"I'm a old tow shirt, darlin'. Don't waste your tears on me. Koloa's the better man."

"Why you give *uhane* to Kaka Kamahine?" She grabbed his arm, knocking over her wine glass. "Why, Ramsey? You like lovey her?"

"What? Why, Jessica doesn't have the fishhook. I do. It's here, around my neck, just where you put it."

He undid his union suit. There on the black curly hair of his chest lay the bone fishhook, suspended on its gold chain. "I wouldn't take it off for the world. *Pau hemo.* Why, you put it on me, remember?"

Maui's fishhook! Still around his neck! Ramsey was not rejected by the gods, he was chosen! Chosen still! Her heart burst open. Sensations quickened her from the top of her head to the bottom of her feet. She wanted nothing more than to worship – to worship fully and completely *haole* style.

Before he knew it she was upon him, shedding enormous lumps of tears, flooding his chest with kisses, her hair falling out of its bun and cascading against his face and shoulder. She sat on his lap and sobbed, patting *makau* the fishhook with her fingers and cooing into his ear Hawaiian words he could not follow. Her lips were wet, her breath warm and perfumed with the wine.

"Ramsey, you not *hemo!*" Her eyes shone with love. "You keep *uhane*. You not one Uli!"

He stroked her beautiful face with his fingers. "I may be the devil sometimes, darlin', but I'm no demon."

"*Honi*, Ramsey," she said. "*Honi honi.*" And she drew her nose gratefully, tenderly, lovingly alongside his.

He grew tumescent and her hazel eyes enlarged. "Ramsey! Get *ma'i* big like King Kalakaua!" She giggled.

He pulled her against his bare chest so he could savor her breasts and her turgid nipples through the cotton cloth. She felt so good and so willing. Then he kissed her, his way, long and hot until she melted and was pliant against his body. It had never seemed so right.

"Pua," he whispered softly. "Pua, darlin'." If the moment were being orchestrated by the puckish Hawaiian night – its breezes rustling the palm trees, the moonlight catching the crashing surf, Diamond Head's rakish profile a bulwark for young lovers – if it was, he had no need of it. No need and no awareness. He was a man being pulled by his heart over a crevasse so wide and so deep that all his life he believed it was insurmountable. But now, in his spare rooms with no more atmosphere than a candle could cast, he was halfway across.

Her arms were about his neck. They were naked to his touch, smooth and firm, as though he passed his hands across satin. Her hair was liquid, falling in a black river down her shoulders. He wanted to drown in it.

"Pua, gal." Almost there.

Her eyes were lit. He gazed into their wells, the flame of the candle magnified a thousand times. He had seen their light before, but now there was more and other – the heat of passion and love. His eyes drank hers. It was like brandy pouring into his cold, numb body. He wanted to drink them forever.

Almost there. Almost.

He slid his hand slowly up her belly to her breast. It fell naturally into his palm, luxuriating there while he explored her nipple with light touches of his thumb. She sighed and sank against him.

Almost …

"No!" he gasped. "No!" The realization broke upon him.

Pua was hiked up close, legs akimbo, the skirt pushed back to her hip, no pantaloons, her strong brown thighs exposed and naked. She was panting softly, eyes gauzy, ready for him.

"Pua, I cannot. I should not." He pressed her into a standing position.

She seemed unsteady, had to catch herself by the edge of the table. "Why, Ramsey? Why?"

He strode to the basin and splashed his face with water. "I should not," he said again, hoarsely.

Her face was twisted. Tears ran freely. "Because I *kanaka* girl? You no like me, Ramsey?"

"No, that's not it at all." He rubbed his face with a towel. He had to think. The mixture of feelings, the confusion of his childhood, his present pain, all seemed to peel away into the nap of the towel. If ever he were going to lay claim to a soul, it was now. "Not at all," he said again, rubbing vigorously until his face was burnished like a knob. "Pua, I don't know how to tell you this. I'm angry about it. Haven't got used to it myself. But you see I've got ..."

He wanted to look into her beautiful eyes and tell her face to face. But when he turned, she was gone.

THIRTY-NINE

Tuesday, June 28, 1887

At ten o'clock in the morning Walter Gibson and the cabinet submitted their resignations. Kalakaua embraced the men in turn before they left, kissing them on both cheeks as the Europeans did. He loved each of the Hawaiians, and with Walter Gibson had spun the gossamer of dreams, many of which had materialized, though not enough of them to keep this moment at bay. The business called for an affecting set of words. Words had been his livelihood. With the words of two and three and four languages he had held the kingdom together. They dropped from his tongue like colored gum drops. But increasingly, his tongue had soured. He no longer wrote music, his step had lost its spring, and each morning he felt compelled to dig his spirit out of a ruddy hole. He could manufacture no words for the occasion at all.

"I am only grateful the Queen did not have to witness this day." He wiped tears from his eyes with a lace handkerchief.

Gibson, seated, hands atop his walking stick, nodded gravely.

"I shall ask Rosa to form the next cabinet."

"He shall do well by Your Majesty."

"He is loyal. – And you? What of you? Retire to Lanai? You are well set there, you and your son-in-law. And you'll have Talula to care for you. Such a faithful daughter she is."

Gibson's eyes twinkled. For a moment the sly look of the Pacific adventurer returned to his face. "O, I shan't be a bother to my dear Talula. Not a bother a-tall. I believe I shall be quite kindly provided for, quite kindly indeed."

His interest quickened. "Ho-ho, Gibson! What have you up your sleeve, eh? Not the Queen of Hearts is it?"

"Indeed, indeed! And if Your Majesty will allow, this old knave shall become her King of Hearts."

"Gibson! You don't mean the matter has been resolved! You have settled the breach of promise affair!" The lawsuit had been one more embarrassment to his reign. "You shall make Mrs. Saint Clair your wife!"

Gibson recoiled. "Majesty, it is not Mrs. Saint Clair, that reprehensible widow! Heaven forbid! Why, it is my own Marianne!"

The king, on his way to the buffet to pour a toast, stopped without another step. "Marianne, you say? Mother Marianne?"

Gibson nodded, beatific.

"But look here, have you … that is, has she … She is a nun, after all, she's a religious."

Gibson held up a hand. "Majesty, I learned it first from Rosenberg. I saw him before he departed Honolulu. Such a reading of the cards he gave me! He showed me the souvenir you made him, the gold medal. So fanciful, Majesty, a delight in itself. Can you guess what the dear man told me? He turned over the Queen of Hearts and none other than the King of Hearts – and the red three, which was the very month we met. March, la, la. '*He wana kau lani, wana 'ao.*' What say you, eh? 'The streaks in the heavens mean a new dawn.'"

"But Gibson, Mother Marianne is ordered by Bishop Koeckemann to Molokai. She is to join Father Damien at the leper colony. She is obliged."

"Tosh! She has never yet departed, have you noted her delay? Do you know what I had incised on the inner band of the ring I presented her, a ring she accepted – rather graciously, I might add. It was a heart, our initials and a heart. We are paired, Majesty, it is fated. Rosenberg said as much himself. Said he had never seen the cards so unmistakable in their intent."

He fixed his drink, not to raise Gibson a toast but to provide time to think.

"Gibson, old fellow," he said, taking a chair across from him and leaning forward with brotherly affection, "what's she going to do with herself? That is, she will care for you, of course. I am quite certain as a Mother of the Church she is more than learned in matters of home and family. You intend to wed her? She would make an upstanding mate, how could she not. But after all, she is a nun. The religious are obliged to care for the indigent. It is their cross. They have such *aloha*, haven't they? – But whatever would Mother Marianne do on Lanai, Gibson? Such a small island. Without your sheep on it, there's scarcely foot, hoof or wing to be found."

"La, la, my king. Lanai's size is what commends it. Could Eden itself have been larger? O, I think not. There shall my Lady Eve join me, bounded by our Tigris and Euphrates, our Pishon and Gihon. There shall we plant and harrow our Land of Cush. This old Adam may yet produce seed, nothing is beyond the compass of the Almighty. But in the mean, she may fulfill herself in caring for my Scottish crofters, they are ripe for the harvest. She may yet bring their protestant souls to Mother Church, even as she has brought mine, the dear."

Kalakaua sat back. He finished his drink. There seemed nothing left to say, as man or monarch.

"I have writ it all out here. It is quite plain." Gibson removed a piece of writing paper from the breast pocket of his coat. His close, even handwriting covered both sides. "She will take my meaning without doubt. Perhaps you will have need of a colony for lepers on Lanai. Eh, my King? You will find your two devoted missioners there ahead of you, laboring side by side, preparing the soil. What say you, eh? La, la. What say you?"

He said nothing aloud. Privately he expressed relief that the man before him was no longer in government. It was sad, but a relief.

"I go to take her this missive. It shall change both our lives, of course." Gibson folded the letter in his kerchief then glanced up at him. "Would you give me the grace of your blessing upon it? I confess I am timorous. You are my liege and my lord."

As Gibson turned out of the palace gate, James Wodehouse, senior British diplomat to the kingdom, hailed him. He paused to watch the prime minister, as oblivious to the commotion around him – the mad convergence of horses, drivers, vehicles and a panicked urgency to reach the wharf – as he was to the call. Perhaps Kalakaua was not so far gone, he mused. Perhaps he had given Gibson the sack, in which case he might save his administration, even the monarchy itself.

Wodehouse was admitted into Kalakaua's presence. He reverenced the king and mentioned seeing the prime minister.

"No, not Prime Minister any longer," Kalakaua confirmed. "Just a fool, on a fool's mission."

"I see. Then Your Majesty shall form a new government."

The king nodded. "I have asked Major Rosa to name the cabinet."

"Rosa? The Hawaiian chap?"

"The Attorney General, yes. *Hapa-haole*, we say. Part Hawaiian."

"Quite. But the business community shall recognize in him only the Hawaiian. Is this the wisest course, Majesty?"

"I need a man I can trust, a man with his feet on the ground."

"But if I might point out, the British government shall be interested that Your Majesty protects the rights and interests of British citizens. We have always enjoyed a favored, and might I say, enlightened interest in the Sandwich Islands. We must know that the Saxon peoples may be safeguarded."

Kalakaua lit a cigar. "I must protect my flank, Wodehouse. This is not the Crimea. 'Into the Valley of Death rode the six hundred.' Do you know your Tennyson? It is not a wasteful frontal attack. I have Luahine on my flank. I must toss her a sop or I'll have her *kahuna* demonstrating on Punch Bowl in addition to Ashford's Rifles on King Street."

"You already have Honolulu Rifles at the intersections. They are attempting to clear the traffic, every foreigner in the capital anxious to send his family out of town. Your Majesty must reassure the populace."

"There is a vessel departing? I had not realized."

"Japanese flag. Sailing to America."

Wodehouse watched the king ruminate for a moment, as if he fancied himself upon the ship and well quit of the kingdom and its measureless problems.

"*Maika'i loa!*" Kalakaua exclaimed brightly. "Returning to normal! You'll soon see, Mr. Minister. We'll come out of this crisis. – By the way, I have confirmation that my lady Kapiolani embarked out of New York. She sailed to make landfall at Liverpool in good order for Queen Victoria's Jubilee. She and her party were quite the thing in all the American cities: Chicago, New York, Boston. Quite the thing."

"Yes, quite so, Your Majesty, quite so. Not surprised in the least. Quite the lady, your Queen. The real article. And your sister, of course. They could not fail to impress. But Majesty, not to prolong the point, Luahine isn't the concern, is she. It's vigilantism, you can't have it. Not at all. This Ashford fellow, he's Canadian you know. Not the thing, is he? Flighty chap, solicitor, can't really understand him. 'Volney,' you can't be certain of a name such as that. The brother Clarence is the more reliable. But Volney's got the militia behind him, hasn't he? Long as he has, you don't want to give him an excuse."

"What are you driving at?"

"Far be it from Her Majesty's government to provide advice to so noble and independent a regime as the Hawaiian Kingdom. But if I might suggest – informally, you understand: Mr. William Green."

"Green."

"Good chap. Merchant, head on his shoulders. The deuce with figures, just what you need. And an Englishman, of course."

The king pondered his cigar. "I see," he said at last. "An Englishman in my cabinet. And while he's there ..."

"Her Majesty's government would not permit anything untoward occurring to the Hawaiian government."

"Protecting British citizens."

"Quite right. Must protect them from the Germans or the Americans, or the Chinese, for that matter. Any respectable government would."

"I see," said the king.

As he departed the palace gate, hopeful but not convinced in the success of his mission, Wodehouse caught sight of a barefoot Hawaiian boy near the gatepost. The sentry was wrestling with him, and the child in twisting free lost his shirt to the sentry's grasp and the sheaf of papers under his arm to the pavement. The boy ran off and Wodehouse got a look at what he carried: handbills, yellow paper with black lettering. The British Minister held one with his stick to keep it from blowing away. "$500 BOUNTY PAYED," its headline read, beneath which were the Hawaiian Coat of Arms, the words "David Kalakaua" in block print, and details about collecting the reward for assassinating the king.

Various clues pointed to a Chinatown origin for the handbill. The bounty was to be paid in Kalakaua dollars – a giveaway because no Chinese would pay off in gold – and an advice appeared in its bottom corner for Soong Kee-yun's restaurant.

But to the observant its Chinese origins were not conclusive. The misspellings were so obvious as to suggest intentionality, as was the tortured grammar: "Head Detachd From Most Dispickible Body" sounded like a line from *The Mikado.*

Wodehouse thought the handbill a fake. He spotted its mates fluttering, nailed to every post and tree along King Street. This was a plot on the part of the White business establishment, he was certain. By making out that the Chinese wanted Kalakaua's head, they hoped to raise such a hullabaloo as to require the militia to keep order. The Honolulu Rifles would command the street corners and take over the government – under the noses of the Great Powers, with not a shot fired.

Wodehouse swore aloud. What a time for Kalakaua to be without sensible men at the palace. Played wrong, the next move would commit the islands to the control of American annexationists. William Green had to form the new cabinet, Kalakaua had to agree. Wodehouse turned on his heel and re-entered the palace grounds, gazing the while in the direction the former prime minister had walked. Gibson will see the handbills, he thought, he will rally to the king one last time.

Walter Gibson only had eyes for the wimple-haloed visage of Barbara Kopp, a Franciscan who, as Mother Marianne with four other Sisters, had care of two hundred lepers at Kaka'ako. For the selflessness of her work Kalakaua had awarded her the Royal Order of Kapiolani.

Gibson hoped to have her assume her Christian name once more. His step felt elastic, his stoop less evident, the hand upon the knob of his stick lighter as he approached the convent door. He had traversed the route countless times. This would be his last until he returned with a carriage and a boy for her luggage. He unwrapped a peppermint and pulled the bell.

The door opened and he swept the hat from his head. "Ah, Sister, good morning. Please announce me to Mother Marianne."

"I am afraid Mother cannot see you just now, Mr. Gibson. She left explicit orders."

"Cannot see me? What, pray? She has not taken ill?"

"No, quite strong, strong as usual, *Deo gratias*. She is not to be disturbed, she said."

"She said I was not to see her?"

"Yes, Mr. Gibson. She said she was not to be disturbed, not by you or by anyone. Only the King."

"Not to be disturbed? But does she understand? I believe my enemies wish to kill me. They are about to carry out their threats of these many years. – She will not see me?"

"Mother Marianne is in prayer, Mr. Gibson. She has not eaten save the precious body of Our Lord received from the hand of the Bishop himself. It is three days now. She worries for the nation. She fasts and prays for our dear Kalakaua, and for you, of course. All the Sisters do."

"Prays for me? But I wanted … I thought …" His hand slipped to the pocket containing the letter blessed by Kalakaua.

"Is there a message for her? Something you would like me to give her?"

"No, nothing to give her," his thoughts suddenly wooden. "No cake this time. Another time. – She will not see me? My Marianne will not see me? How can it be?"

He replaced his hat and returned on the worn path. "Can such a thing be?" the Sister heard him remark as he left. When she entered the visit in her diary, she recorded his frailty:

> … *his bowed white head, drooping shoulders and snow white beard, his thin hands clasped as in prayer.*

FORTY

"You should have seen Ashford's face!" Manu was still laughing. "He turned so warm I thought his moustaches would melt!"

"How many men did you say *Kinau* carried?" Ramsey asked. They met in Pua's room once again, shade drawn, door locked.

"Thirty."

"Not three hundred."

"No. Turns out 'Drei Hundert' is just the unit's name."

"After the Spartans," Ramsey said.

"They wanted a name sounds inspiring."

"Yes, the three hundred who held at Thermopylae. – O, but that's a good joke. Ashford must have been warm!"

"And no baggage. Drums, trumpets, a tuba, but not one weapon. A few sabers, that's all." Manu laughed again. "Ashford said he'd send them back to Maui, said they had embarrassed him in front of real soldiers."

Ramsey shook his head. "Ashford's a dog has lost the scent. He'll be casting around now, figuring which way the wind's blowing."

Manu grunted. "Wodehouse wants William Green to form the government. You know him?"

Ramsey nodded. "Played cards with him. What do you make of him?"

"We'd prefer Rosa of course. But we can live with Green – *akahele ka noho*, we'll just live cautiously."

Ramsey took a deep breath and coughed on the exhale.

"You turning ill, boss?"

"No I'm not. I've not been exercising, Manu, that's the problem. I've been a cat's paw, hell if I know why, pulling your chestnuts from the fire."

"The Hawaiian nation is beside itself with gratitude."

"Kindly impose upon the British next time the monarchy needs saving – or better, the Japanese. They're pesky little gnats."

"So do you think we've done it? The handbills were all over town. Cost me two Kalakaua dollars."

Ramsey chuckled. "Scared the daylights out of Commander Taylor. He come close to having *Adams* land the Marines. 'Won't have a king assassinated on my watch,' he says."

"I saw the Marines on deck. They're ready. But as long as the moderates keep Thurston and Ashford out of government, I think it's a victory."

"Tomorrow will tell."

"What do the English say, 'The pen is mightier than the sword'? The handbills split the *haole* coconut, boss."

"The pen was not mightier than the sword for the Confederacy. Our boys had more prose than Grant had troops. We'll see how it pans out for you, Manu."

They parted warmly. But Manu did not mention he had sent a pigeon to Koloa on Kauai and begged him to let bygones be bygones, mobilize the warriors. To his relief, the *menehune* came out in favor of it.

Some things you kept from a *haole*, even one you liked.

FORTY-ONE

Thursday, June 30, 1887

On the morning of the mass meeting at the armory, Attorney General Antone Rosa addressed a letter to Colonel Volney V. Ashford. He wanted to send it with a member of the Household Guard but the men had been deserting their posts the greater grew the tension in the capital. A Guardsman might take the letter and melt into the countryside, uniform and all. Rosa had more confidence in a boy who would run to Ashford's for a coin of any size and minting.

The boy sped through a town holding its breath. Ashford kept his suite at the Commercial. He'd moved Jessica Mornay from the Hawaiian into rooms across the corridor. The boy found him easily and delivered the king's request: only the Honolulu Rifles had the ability to maintain order.

Sanford Dole watched as Thurston issued the Rifles ten rounds each and the troops deployed along Beretania Street. It brought his heart to his throat. He feared the day was already out of control. Earlier, placards had gone up around town in English, Chinese and Portuguese. He assumed Stevens was behind them, despite his assurances of a gathering only for the propertied. The result would be predictable: not a sober assembly, but an ungovernable meeting of the masses.

Inside the wood framed armory a speaker's platform had been erected on the Beretania side of the hall. Behind the platform hung the Hawaiian flag flanked by the British, American and Portuguese flags. Not his idea, could they not even agree upon the sovereignty of the kingdom's colors? Below the platform, the table for the press. He saw their scribes already there, pencils and notebooks at the ready to record every twist, every flub: *Pacific Commercial Advertiser, Gazette, Bulletin, Chinese News* and *Elele* the Hawaiian language paper.

Businesses shut down at one o'clock and thankfully, the town marshal closed the saloons. Soon, fifteen hundred boisterous men of all costume and station surged through the line of militia and filled the building to the eaves. The temperature grew with the tide of bodies, and with the temperature, the crowd's irritation.

He whispered a prayer and called the meeting to order.

Horace Somers' invocation was long and figurative – he'd counseled otherwise – but the minister labored nonetheless over his metaphor. David was Israel's king, he said, until he transgressed the sacred compact and the prophet Nathan chastised ... foot stomps drowned him out. Dole placed his hand on the minister's arm. The crowd were impatient for the speeches, eager as Parisians at the guillotine to discover the bloody lengths to which their leaders would go.

Dole took a deep breath and loudly introduced Peter Cushman Jones. Jones would set a proper tone. A Massachusetts man long resident in the islands, trustee of Punahou School and manager of C. Brewer & Company, a downtown sugar factor, he was well-respected.

They were gathered in view of "the present mal-administration of public affairs, and to consider means of redress," Jones began. Before him, every seat was occupied. The aisles and doorways were thick with humanity onto Beretania Street. He pleaded for a dignified conduct of proceedings.

Someone hooted, then another and another, Jones waved his arms, flummoxed, and Dole lost control of the meeting.

Lorrin Thurston sprang into the breach. He saluted members of the Hawaiian League, who cheered his uniform in the three-tiered huzzah of the Honolulu Rifles. They raised such a din that he could not be heard. He bowed from the podium, held up his hands for silence and when he could, complimented the gathering for its size. Then he said:

> *I remember reading somewhere of a man who was going to shoot a coon, and the coon said: "Don't shoot; I'll come down." Well, the King is the coon and this meeting is the gun!*

The king at gunpoint! This was the style of oratory for which the crowd had turned out. It whistled and stomped and chanted its approval. Riding its tide, Thurston called for the "overthrow of the King and his government!"

Volney Ashford shouldered through, determined to be more pointed than his sergeant. At his cue Rifles sidled along the hall and occupied the walls. The king had encouraged a dangerous and growing nationalism, he said. Luahine was his doppelganger. Such a movement, combined with Kalakaua's prostitution of the kingdom to the Chinese, endangered every right thinking man in the islands. "If we have to fight, by the name of heaven, we will!" His voice cracked in the emotion of the moment. Kalakaua and Gibson should be executed for their numberless crimes.

Ramsey, disguised in the tunic of the Honolulu Rifles he'd been wrapped in coming from Hale Nui, exchanged glances with Manu, who was standing near an exit. The chess game played out before them. They had gambled that the moderates would influence the assembly. Castle and Bishop and Dole, they'd protect the king. If they could not, the crowd would turn into a mob and the palace would fall beneath the knives of Thurston and Ashford and the White insurrectionists.

But only Dole stood before the assembly, no Castle or Bishop on the board. Manu edged toward the door.

Dole demanded order and called upon William Hyde Rice. Rice was missionary-born at Punahou but grew up on Kauai where he fell in love with the Hawaiian people and culture. At one time he spoke more Hawaiian than English. "You must quell the crowd," Dole told him as he took the podium.

"Hawaiian citizens from the Big Island to Niihau," Rice began,

> *the roads are wasting and groaning from one end to another of the land. Where is the money for the roads? Sent on an exploration with the* Kaimiloa.

It was a promising start. "The ship of this movement has been launched," he continued, for which he was cheered. The cheers grew, then he glanced at Dole and declared S.S. Reform had been launched, not S.S. Revolution. A new constitution was required, not the head of the king.

The crowd shouted him down. They clamored for more men of Ashford's temperament. More seized the podium in quick succession. Kalakaua was condemned for his "vigorous attempt to establish a State Church," which was the king's Hawaiian-only Hale Naua society and its "disreputable practices," the *hula* and "invidious games" of a sexual nature. He had "secured elections by using liquor taken from the Custom House duty free," and had buttressed himself with halfwits "promised offices under patronage."

When the crowd roared agreement over the suggestion that the common native had not the capacity for self-government, Dole rose again to straighten the meeting away from revolution. A series of resolutions was read. They required the appointment of a *haole*-favored cabinet and the repayment of the bribe money to Tong Kee.

A howl erupted from the throat of the citizens knitting at the guillotine. The measures were piddling, too piddling by half.

He tried to explain that a new ministry would write a new constitution that hamstrung the king, but the crowd were not satisfied. Constitutions did not entertain, bloodshed did. Ashford signaled his men onto the streets. The beast was about to migrate out-of-doors where it could feed unhindered.

Charles R. Bishop pushed through the hall waving his arms. "He has just come from the King!" Dole announced and had him brought onto the stage.

Bishop addressed them:

I see before me mechanics, merchants, professional men. They are not here for amusement, but because they feel the course of affairs calls for prompt and determined action. We have found out during the last four years that our constitution is defective, partly on account of bad advice to the King, but largely on his own account. The King has encroached upon our rights.

Dole chewed his moustache, anxious. Bishop was going wrong. Noble by virtue of his marriage to Princess Pauahi, rich as a consequence of her lands, he did not understand this crowd. It had no patience for prose, it wanted hyperbole. He cast about the audience. Who could he bring up to stop the tide?

Then, strident-sounding, Bishop: "Friends, the King has invited William Lothian Green to form the government!"

The beast halted in mid-shuffle to the door. It swung its head around. William Green. Conservative. White. Certain to invite White men into government.

Ramsey caught Manu's eye. It was exactly the compromise they had strategized. Green was foreign but he was not a radical. Perhaps now the center could hold against the extremes.

Most in the crowd agreed. Green would bring respectability to government. The beast grumbled but gradually lost its appetite for blood.

Dole wondered how to dismiss the meeting. Did he dare invite Somers back for the benediction?

Radicals in the Hawaiian League did not wait. They stirred up the working men. "We've been Bishop'd!" a rudely garbed man roared into Ramsey's ear. The phrase meant getting fleeced in a horse trade, but the pun brought laughter and more cries. "We've been Bishop'd," clusters of men called, armed with clubs and broken plantation tools, and they pushed out of the armory into the late afternoon light.

Volney Ashford raced to their lead. Kalakaua had saved himself by appointing Green to the government. Nothing protected Gibson, however. He directed his men to surround Gibson's residence across from the palace. "He'll not flee his many crimes!" Ashford promised. "Should anyone attempt his rescue, you have orders to shoot on sight!"

Unattached men moiled about the streets. Their watchword was "We've been Bishop'd," or "We've been Bishop'd again," by which they meant their perennial manhandling by the rich. As darkness came on, they lit torches and collected in the business district. Proprietors spent the night in armchairs outside their establishments, shotguns across their laps. The saloons remained closed.

From his lampless upstairs window Walter Gibson watched the torches swarm, cluster and parade. Jeers of the most vile nature assaulted the blank side of his house. He was alone, a prisoner, in mortal terror.

To console himself he read and reread the letter composed to Mother Marianne. By daybreak he could recite each word, despite the tender condition of his nerves.

FORTY-TWO

Friday, July 1, 1887

F red Hayselden rode in early from Waikiki to his father-in-law's home in town. He found Gibson upstairs, staring out the window.

"Are you arrested, Fred?" his father-in-law asked.

"Arrested, sir? What do you mean?"

"The guard. They have been about the house this entire night. I am to be executed, sure."

"Whatever do you mean? There are no guard. The streets are quiet. The government is restored. Mr. Green is to form the cabinet."

"Green, not Antone Rosa?"

"No. The businessmen would not hear of it. I understand Green will invite Godfrey Brown into government."

"Brown? He is a sensible man."

"Yes. The King could have done far worse. But come, sir, have you broken fast? Talula is packing. She will come to town this morning. We shall escort you to the ranch on Lanai."

"The ranch? O, I could not depart quite yet," Gibson said as Hayselden lifted him to his feet. "The Sisters, you know. They will be lost without me. These are parlous times."

"Parlous indeed," Hayselden said sternly. "More for you than for they. We must get you away. The city is quiet, but it is far from resolved."

He cajoled Gibson into washing his face, brushing his hair and straightening his cravat. His father-in-law had not shifted his clothing, but he was concerned for the hour.

They descended the stairs and in the pantry he found bread and a cheese. He put these out with a jug of buttermilk. It had not turned, though the ice upon which it sat had melted into water. He cut the bread, as Gibson's eye had sealed closed with infection.

Hayselden attempted to occupy him with talk of the ranch, what needed to be done, an enclosure to be erected. But talk of Lanai brought Gibson to the subject of the crofters and a dreamy soliloquy upon the merits of Mother Marianne and the material blessing she should bring to their labors.

A ruckus at the front door cut him short. The door was thrown open and Colonel Ashford burst in. Four armed men accompanied him.

"The possum and her kit!" Ashford exclaimed. "I had not hoped to snare both in their den!" He directed Hayselden and Gibson to put on their hats.

"Now see here, Ashford," Hayselden said, "by what authority do you enter here? You cannot break into a man's house. It isn't done."

Ashford had been awake all night. His eyes were bloodshot, his nerves frayed. "By what authority? By what authority? By the authority of Justice herself! Rule of law, boy-o – did you think to escape your crimes?!"

Hayselden was a sturdy man and began to struggle. During the scuffle Gibson pulled out the letter to Mother Marianne, mottled from a night's worth of tears, and chewed it down.

Ashford noticed, but too late to stop him. "What?!" he shrieked. "Destroy evidence, do you?! The court shall have you now, old man! The court shall have you now! Put on your hats while you still have heads to support them!"

The two were shoved out the door and quick-marched in the direction of the Pacific Navigation Company's warehouse. The early risers fell in, and those who could get a hand on the prisoners, or aim a clod at them, did their best to make the procession a miserable one.

Ramsey caught up, looking to break the two away. Dressed in a foreign uniform and taking sides in local affairs, he risked everything if identified. It meant prison for certain. He'd pilfered a pistol in the crowd then discovered it had just one live round in the chamber, and saw that Gibson, when he got close to him, was too played out to run. He thought to steal a wagon at the wharf but when they arrived, an ugly cluster of men was standing at the far end of the warehouse. Its doors were open to the dock and from the yardarm of a ship two ropes hung.

Ashford pounded his sword hilt on a hollow water cask to call to order his court, the loafers, Rifles and hangers-on who thirsted for more than the armory meeting had produced. "Men, we strung two nooses, one for Kalakaua and one for his Prime Minister," he declared. "Dole and the businessmen cheated us of the one, but we have found another candidate. The rope is a ring that shall not be jilted. If she loses one lover, she takes another!"

The court made plain its approval.

A party of men – one of them the *luna* from Hale Nui – bound the two and marched them to a chorus of jeers onto a platform of packing crates. The nooses drooped like quiet plumb lines centered upon their heads. A uniformed Rifle read a summary of charges. Most were directed at Gibson – malfeasance, embezzlement, abuse of power – but Hayselden in his capacity as Health Minister was accused of employing "Crown and State money" for personal gain.

Gibson's knees failed him and he had to be held upright. Hayselden faced forward unblinking.

Ashford invited a popular missionary son to argue for the prosecution. "We need to stall for time," he confided to the men around him, Ramsey listening in. He'd dispatched fast riders to Gibson's Waikiki house to collect evidence.

The man rose to the occasion, pacing before the accused and declaiming wildly, and finished by striking Gibson's top hat from his head. "You are overdressed for your interview, Mr. Prime Minister!" he crowed.

He was slapped on the back and cheered, but Ramsey saw one of the riders return and sidle up to Ashford. They'd broken in, the household still asleep, he breathed into Ashford's ear. They assaulted Talula Hayselden, placed a noose around her neck and forced her to watch as they ransacked the premises for evidence. They came up empty.

Ashford waved him off. "He has concealed the indicting papers at the government offices," he judged and straightened his moustaches. Evidence absent, the court of public opinion could yet be swayed. What stood close-packed before him was the cub of the animal which he'd commanded the day before at the armory, but it was lethal still, and it was eager.

He mounted the packing crates and stood alongside his prisoners. "No matter the nationality, you and I, we approached these islands with the anticipation of good and of gain," he began. "We brought the accumulated wisdom of civilization to a tropical land that roiled in the hands of the pagan and the indigent. We were received indifferently. We expected as much from the dark-skinned man. But to be betrayed by two of our own!"

He was interrupted by shouts of outrage. "Vile! ... Despicable! ... Judas!"

Hayselden attempted to speak but was shouted down.

"How it rankles, how it humiliates," Ashford continued. "To know that the man who is the product of your own hearth and home is nonetheless the basest viper of Cleopatra's own nest." Ashford's voice softened. He was the older brother of every man before him. "Friends, I have heard of a statue lately erected in an American harbor. She stands tall, I am told; she is proud. She holds aloft the torch of liberty. How she would cry, how she would rail did she know of liberty's demise in these islands. Did she know, friends, she would wrest her feet from their concrete impediment. She would stride across mountain, across plain, through sea itself. Nothing would stop her. She would plant the torch of liberty in the hand of every suffering man captive to the greed and machinations of the Hawaiian King and his odious henchmen."

"Let them die of the hempen fever!" someone called out. "Hang 'em both!"

"Are you sons of liberty?!" Ashford cried. "What say you?"

"Hang 'em!" the mob shouted back.

Ashford drew his sword. "Our proceedings shall be democratical. We shall vote, men, vote openly and proudly. Cast your ballot then. What say you?"

He swung his saber in an arc left to right across the heads of the assembly, and every segment called out with a single voice: "Hang 'em!"

A noose was draped about the neck of each man. Ramsey found a handcart and rolled it casually behind the gallows, as though he were graves detail.

Ashford stepped down and considered the prisoners. "The condemned shall be accorded their last words."

There was silence. The crowd leaned in. This was a moment to be detailed accurately.

"O, come now," Ashford said impatiently, "it shall not be said we did not scragg 'em fair. Speak up, men. Your words shall be conveyed to your loved ones. We are honorable fellows."

Words began to tumble off the lips of Walter Gibson. They fell fast as pebbles over a cliff and were as difficult to follow. They were the words he had memorized, words that sloughed like atoms from his soul.

"What?" Ashford said. "Slow down, old man. We cannot catch you."

"O, father!" Talula Hayselden pushed her way through the crowd to the foot of the gallows. She'd driven quickly as a team could be harnessed. "O, father! O, Fred, husband! What do they do to you?"

Hands reached out to turn her away from the scene.

"O, you cannot!" She implored the faces near her. Hair askew, sleeve torn, she showed signs of her earlier rough handling. "Surely you cannot do this. My husband, my father – O, please!"

Ramsey drew his pistol. One shot, a bullet in Ashford, it might be enough …

A breath heavy with whiskey pressed his ear. "I thought I made you out, Ramsey." It was Gonsalves. "You, uniformed like a Honolulu Rifle had me confused. But you preparing to shoot a man in the back, I recognized the coward right away."

There was commotion as men at the front of the gallows seized Talula and pulled her sobbing to the side.

"Surrender your weapon, and I'll let you walk out," Gonsalves said. "Maybe you'll save your pitiful little soul after all."

Ramsey snarled and smashed him in the face with the butt of his pistol. The *luna* crashed unconscious to the ground.

A hand grabbed his sleeve. He yanked himself away and straightened his tunic. "This man is drunk. He's disgracing the proceedings. You there," he summoned two Rifles.

Ashford demanded order. "We must be juridical. Remove that man. We want none among us who cannot hold his liquor. You men —"

"What is the meaning of this!" The indignant voice of James H. Wodehouse overrode him.

The British Minister was the only authority Talula had thought to call upon. He waded into the crowd, pushing men aside with both hands until he could mount the platform.

These men are British subjects!

Wodehouse's words cracked like a whip. The crowd stirred as though its barbed end had licked each in the face. One after the other, the taxpayer and the scalawag recovered himself from the precipice of blood thirst and lawlessness.

"You shall not wield your provincial insubordination here, Ashford!" Wodehouse declared.

Ramsey sprang to the prisoners. He slipped the nooses from their necks and ordered their bonds cut. Gibson could not walk unaided so he put his arms about him and guided him down. Talula threw hers around her husband and sobbed. Ramsey commanded her rig be led over and Hayselden helped Gibson into it.

Ashford thought quickly to regain control of the situation. "These men are criminals. They shall stand trial. — Incarcerate them at Oahu Jail!" he called out.

Ramsey hesitated. In jail they would be safe from further mob violence and protected from further derangement on Ashford's part.

"Jail it is, Colonel."

It seemed at first a matter to celebrate. He met Manu at Madam Ho's, and Sienna poured three glasses. She saluted them. They'd split the Hawaiian League and kept the radicals out of government. Green and Brown were moderate business-men, British subjects who valued monarchy and wanted to hold the center. Dole worked up a new constitution with Castle and Bishop. It was consistent with the kingdom's legal tradition and respected Hawaiian monarchy. It merely clipped Kalakaua's wings and corrected his excesses. Manu thought the more con-servative *ali'i* would actually welcome it.

"*Hana hou!*" Sienna said and drank. "Well done, John."

Only a few days later, and their self-satisfaction quickly eroded. The Hawaiian League had escaped its pen. It had tasted the streets. It was not satisfied with moderation. It coerced Green and Brown into inviting Lorrin Thurston into govern-ment as Minister of Interior, raising him to cabinet level.

The radicals demanded a second representative from the League's Committee of Thirteen and proposed Volney Ashford. Moderate Honolulu quaked but was able to insert an alternate from the Committee, the Colonel's brother, Clarence Ashford. He was named Attorney General. The town, *haole* and Hawaiian, breathed prayers of gratitude.

Convinced the armory meeting conferred a mandate, Thurston and the radicals tore into Dole's proposed constitu-tion. They wrote feverishly, erecting eighty-two articles into a new legal framework. It left Kalakaua his title as king but stripped him of his powers as head of government. It cut him off from his supporters by making it impossible for most native Hawaiians to vote. It delivered the kingdom to the downtown business establishment and gave White property owners control over policy, whether they were citizens or not.

Humiliated, fearful, bargaining for a patina of native presence in government, Kalakaua did what no other Hawaiian ruler had. He signed away his sacred position as chief and father of the people, validating the document on July 6, 1887 with his signature:

Kalakaua Rex

The newspapers dubbed it "The Bayonet Constitution."

FORTY-THREE

uahine struggled upright on her mats. It was quiet after the storm passed, quiet in the camp. Her warriors had not stirred out of their huts. Why should they? They had their women. They had their children. They had their comforts.

What did she have? She had the body she'd sacrificed for them. It ached so severely it snatched her breath when she tried to move. Pele hadn't taken it, but the Flying God had.

She picked at a platter of roast dog. The bearded priest brought it earlier. "*'Ono ka pu'u.*" He made the sign for eating. "Your favorite. The Kauai chiefs sent it. They love you."

She could not eat. Maka Ana Ana the Seeing Eye flickered in and out like a stuttering fire. Sometimes it flared brightly, and for a moment she saw. But mostly her powers were charred coals, difficult to ignite. They'd been cooling ever since she tore her heart from Pele and laughed in the goddess' face. She sighed a deep groaning sigh that caused her sentry to stick his head through the doorway. "*Hapai* this one," she said of the dog meat. "Give it to the children in camp."

The fire had flared just brightly enough before the storm broke. She saw. She saw, finally, what *pe'a* the brown bat signified. The *menehune* had sent *pe'a* as a warning. But she misread it, misread it badly. She sought Pele. Then she cursed the king.

"You do not eat again, My Chiefess." The bearded priest entered and reverenced her.

"*Hele mai*, come to me," she said.

He glanced over his shoulder.

"Come ... please."

She opened her arms to him and he entered them, but something didn't feel right. She pushed him back then settled herself against his chest. He sagged with her weight but she didn't care. He must know, he had to know. She didn't want it any longer. None of it. She was empty inside like an old bleached coconut. Her milk had seeped away. Just ask me, she yearned to say. I will go with you to Molokai. My mother's village still stands. Take me. Let me end my days with you – let me end them a woman.

"... My Chiefess?" He sounded hesitant, uncertain. "Pakalana is here."

She lifted the hair from her eyes.

He pointed over her shoulder with his chin. "Pakalana. You sent for her."

She recognized her old teacher's dry cough behind her and shot him a searing look.

He shrugged. "I only sent the pigeon yesterday. She arrived today."

She turned toward her teacher. Every movement required effort. When she breathed it hurt.

"I took the overnight steamer," Pakalana said. "*Haole* things, sometimes ..."

Luahine pushed the priest aside and straightened her whale tooth pendant, trying to recover her dignity. She looked from under her brow. Her teacher plucked the sleeve of her Mother Hubbard and studied her. She knew what she must look like: indirect, flighty gaze, faded coloring, bones protruding where she used to display splendid cushions of flesh.

The priest tried to back toward the doorway, but Pakalana stopped him and turned to her again.

The silence made her uncomfortable. "*He aha, tutu?* Why do you stare?"

Her teacher grunted and shook her head. "You know why. *Akua lele*, the Flying God – you invoked him against the King."

She heard the challenge and she wanted to say something back, wanted to defend herself. Wanted to pull her *kapu* stick and curse Pakalana and every one of her teachers into the previous generation, and every one of Pakalana's students into the next. But she couldn't. She'd been so wrong about *pe'a*. She had nothing.

Her teacher snorted. "You are the elder after too many shells of *awa*. But you have taken too many shells of Pele. Her *awa* empties your head."

"I do not want it longer, *tutu*! I want Aunty to leave me!"

"But you made yourself *hanai* –"

"I must break it! I must break my bond to the goddess!"

There, the words were out of her mouth. She had said them. *Makani* the wind could take them now. It could ferry them to Pele's ear for all she cared.

Her teacher said nothing for a moment. But her eyes were very large and unblinking. She turned to the priest. "What do the *menehune* say about this?"

"I have gone to the *menehune* many times," Luahine hurried to say. "Many times."

"Yes? And what do they say? They have no *aloha* for Aunty ... but to break a vow to her ..."

"Many times, *tutu*. I –"

The priest broke in. "Their signs were unclear, *tutu*."

Pakalana looked from him to her. "Unclear? What were the signs?"

"It came at the dark of the moon," he said. "There was a salt water fish found inside the fishpond. I found it myself. It breathed the fresh water and still lived."

Pakalana sucked her teeth. "There was no sign, was there. The *menehune* have withdrawn from you, haven't they."

"No," the priest said, but Luahine stared at her feet and nodded.

"This is bad," her teacher said. "Who knows?"

"No one. We dare not let the people know," the priest said. "The movement will fail."

"The *menehune* want unity. Kauai must reach to the Big Island. There must be wholeness among the people. That will save the movement." Pakalana looked sternly at her.

"I do not wish to save the movement!" Luahine cried. "I am tired, *tutu*!"

"What do you expect? You cursed the King."

"He disgraced us."

"You cursed the Father of the Land."

"But I am its mother!"

"Yes, and what mother is it who causes harm for her children?"

She hung her head again.

"You sought Pele's fire. You ignored my counsel. You haven't the *pono*. A dancer, she has the *pono*. But not you, not Kahu the Sorceress."

"Then let a dancer lead the movement, *tutu*! Let my daughter lead it! Let me go!" Her eyes flickered over the bearded priest. If only he ... but he sat back on his heels. He was shocked. She could tell. So was her teacher.

"You would send your daughter to Pele?" her teacher said after a moment.

"She dances the Hula Pahu, *tutu*. I never could."

"You abandoned your training. You cursed your better, the Big Island chiefess. You made trouble for us. You curse the King and make trouble for us again."

"The black blood boiled too eagerly in me. I am the daughter of a Molokai sorceress."

"Your daughter is granddaughter of a Molokai sorceress. I tell you, the blood is more eager for her than ever for you."

Luahine released a long slow breath of air and eased onto her mat. The Flying God combed with sticky fingers through her body searching for the hidden place where *uhane* dwelt. He would trap her soul in his web and fly it back to the twilight land. From the pain, he was drawing nearer. Kalakaua alone could save her by going to Kauai island, but he'd not even left Oahu. She could tell.

"Find the girl, *tutu,*" the priest said. "Work with her again. Prepare her for Pele. Meanwhile, I —"

"In her, Kauai comes to the Big Island," her teacher considered. "Aunty should be pleased."

"She cannot go alone," he said. "She is young. She needs training. Aunty would eat her like morning mist."

Luahine nodded. She was feeling sleepy. Her eyes drooped.

"Meanwhile, I will gather the warriors," she heard the priest say. "We must protect the King from the *haole.*"

"Yes, Manu has contacted Prince Koloa," her teacher responded.

"Manu? He strays from me," Luahine yawned from her mat. "His eye roves to the *haole.* He cannot have the warriors."

"Cannot have the warriors? Cannot have the warriors?" She was aware of the priest's breath hot upon her, his face just above hers. She had not given permission for familiarity, her teacher was in the hut.

"Your son fights for the people," he said, "as you should – not the girl!"

"*Aue,*" Pakalana said, sounding disgusted with her.

She saw the priest jump to his feet. His thighs were muscled, his chest firm, his face hard and unloving. "I go to bring the warriors to him now," he told Pakalana.

She reached for him. "I cannot lose you. *I'ini o ka na'au,* you are my heart's desire. Molokai island, let us go together."

No man had given her such a stare and lived. Her hand did not even reach for her *kapu* stick, did not even quiver. "*I'ini o ka na'au,*" she mouthed as he stooped and slipped out the doorway, not looking back.

"*Aue,*" her teacher said, shaking her head.

She slumped back on the mat. She had nothing more to say, not to Pakalana, not to the priest. Seeing Eye had flared, she finally understood the prophecy. It was senseless to go to Pele. Senseless to protect the king. Fate could not be changed. Who understood the gods? She gazed at the palm which had crushed the twin kits into smears of blood and bone. Kalakaua would die ignobly and horribly, and alone. That was the meaning behind the sign. But so would she … and by the same hand. Her own.

On Friday, July 8th Gibson and Hayselden were escorted before the new attorney general, Clarence W. Ashford. He was as uncompromising as his brother but believed firmly that the new administration could not deviate from rational observance of the law. As much as passion told him that Gibson was the mastermind of Kalakaua's schemes, thorough searches of his office, residences, his records and ledgers produced no evidence of financial misdeeds.

The most ignominious of schemes was the opium scandal. If Gibson could be tied to it he could be marched post-haste back to the gallows. The attorney general fanned himself and dozed through the early stages of the inquiry while the marshal documented his dogged if fruitless efforts to discover a transaction damning the former prime minister. No matter. Tong Kee was expected after lunch, his testimony would put the noose around Gibson's neck.

But the marshal's long-winded recital was cut short. A court official appeared ashen-faced and signaled for the attorney general's ear. Tong Kee had been found in his Waipahu home, poisoned. He was dead.

Denied a case, Clarence Ashford angrily dismissed the charges. He chastised Gibson and Hayselden and ordered them to quit the islands. A ship was scheduled to embark for San Francisco the following week and they were both to be aboard.

FORTY-FOUR

O n July 10ᵗʰ, Honolulu was quiet. Pairs of Honolulu Rifles patrolled the business district. The king's Household Guard manned its posts on the palace grounds, though Kalakaua was at his Waikiki beach house. Most of the capital was at its Sunday dinner or slumbering in the heat of a close afternoon. The Rifles, though on their feet, walked dumbly. Nothing of interest had occurred since the discovery of Tong Kee's body, turned blue when the toxin constricted his lungs. Cyanide, was the general talk, introduced into almond cookies to mask the poison's distinctive odor.

The pair of Rifles responsible for the King Street gate had not progressed beyond the Punch Bowl corner. They disposed of the current news in short order and turned to what really interested them. Both men were baseballers and were fascinated with the cards newly introduced into cigarette packages by American manufacturers. One man owned a particularly fine Icebox Chamberlain, the St. Louis Cardinals pitcher, which had arrived in his packet of Old Judge Cabinets. He also had an Admiral Schlei and a Monte Ward, the New York Nationals shortstop.

"Here, smoke these," he said to the other as they examined the slender cards. "I don't really like the Turkey Red cigarette. But you are obliged to purchase them to get the cards. My sister ships them from Cleveland."

They paid no attention to the *kanaka* workmen with the wheelbarrow sweeping up horse dung on King Street. And they did not notice the other pairs of Hawaiian men appear from several directions, all arriving at the gate just as the church bells began to ring in succession throughout the town. At four o'clock the guard changed at the palace. As there were few men remaining on duty, it was the moment of greatest vulnerability. The bearded priest and his men uncovered their weapons from the wheelbarrow, burst through the gate and overpowered the sentries. They seized the gun positions and rounded up the Guards on roving patrol without a shot. Five of the Guards joined the conspirators on the spot. The rest surrendered their uniform jackets, were escorted out the gate and drifted off to watch the action.

The priest attached the Hawaiian flag to a bamboo pole and Denzo helped him drive it into the ground, where it fluttered over the Hale Akala bungalow. He sent out patrols dressed in the hijacked uniforms and consolidated the position.

Thus far everything was according to plan. Their small detail was the bait. After Koloa's force arrived the trap would be sprung, they only had to hold out until dawn.

The boy Abner scampered across the grass. Three men remained in the palace, he reported, one of them *haole*. They were guarding the weapons room.

The priest took Denzo and they peered through a basement window. He recognized Kalakaua's *haole*, his gun hand in a plaster from the throne room shooting. The White gestured animatedly at the two native guards. They seemed reluctant. The priest leaned too near, the *haole* spied them, they ducked and started running back. Glass shattered behind them and they heard a pistol shot.

More shots issued from the palace basement. The bullets tore through the croton bushes outside the window, but were not well aimed. They seemed to crack high overhead.

The priest directed the men at the bungalow behind cover. They returned fire, splattering the palace's thick walls with .44 caliber rounds. He joined them. It was exhilarating to shoot and see the puffs erupt from the masonry or hear the glass shatter. They were fighting for the land at last.

The crack of small arms shook the Rifles on patrol and they ran to the gate in no particular order and without leadership. The priest called to his men to stand strong in their positions and aim carefully, fire slowly. They needed to hold out.

Volney Ashford heard the report of weaponry through the fog of a dream and pulled himself awake. He and Jessica were feuding again and he had taken to his rooms with a cold chicken and a warm pail of beer. The chicken remained uneaten but the pail scuttled empty across the floor when he swung his feet heavily from the bed. He was dressed and reasonably alert by the time the private rapped on his door.

He rallied the Rifles at the armory. Thurston was in government now, so he had to take direct control of the men. He mustered and armed a full platoon and marched to the palace. He positioned them across the street in squads and surveyed the situation and in a moment, ruled out a frontal attack.

The men inside the grounds found that fighting was thirsty work. They had guns and ammunition enough but no one had brought water or rations. During the lull the priest took Abner and investigated Hale Akala for provisions. It was disappointing. There was plenty of alcohol – he broke all the bottles as a precaution – but only two pitchers of water on nightstands. He found some fruit and a container of dried nuts, and nothing else. Not enough to sustain the men until morning. They needed to get into the palace.

As they walked out of the bungalow a round cracked overhead and drilled into the door behind them. It could not have come from the palace basement. The priest shielded the sun with his hand and looked for its origin. A round cracked again, closer this time, shattering a window. Shards of glass cut his bare arm and the shock drove him to the ground. Abner dove after him, spilling the water.

One of the Hawaiians collapsed with a cry. Another man dropped at a gun emplacement guarding the gate.

"They shoot up!" Denzo cried. He pointed to figures on the roof of the Music Hall.

The priest signaled the men away from the gate back toward the bungalow. He was proud of them. No man broke. They picked up their wounded comrades. Denzo knew about defensive positions, and they established themselves so they could still command the gate but were not vulnerable to the overhead fire.

John Ramsey's symptoms had subsided so he had wheeled exuberantly away from his quarters on a new bicycle. It was a dark green Burger's Rover with a front wheel smaller than the rear for handling. The machine was sold with a lantern box on the yoke but he removed it as an unsightly obstruction. He wore the bicycle jockey strap for male convenience manufactured by Sharp & Smith of Chicago, and pulled on his tobacco-colored, wool exercise costume with pantaloons that buckled at the knee. He added high brown socks, a jacket and cap to match, and worked up a satisfying perspiration after escaping town on the carriage track and pedaling west. The gunshots brought him to a halt. Their report echoed off the mountain range to his right, but there was no doubt as to their origin. He reversed himself and wheeled back to town quickly as he could.

A knot of spectators had collected on the corner of King and Richards streets. William Castle and Sanford Dole were among them. Ramsey stopped. A band of *kanaka* renegades had seized the palace, he was told. He could see Ashford with his men across the street. Sharpshooters had been mounted in the bell tower of Kawaiahao Church and on the rooftop of the Music Hall. The riflemen were methodically delivering rounds into the palace grounds. The fire was not rapid, but it was accurate.

Ramsey pedaled to Commander Taylor's office, reported to the attaché and rushed back to the scene. "Bring me information, Ramsey!" Taylor shouted as he raced away. "Do I land the Marines?"

The most advantageous perspective would be afforded by the east facing dormers of Sienna's attic rooms. Ramsey was shown upstairs and discovered he was not alone in thinking of Madam Ho's. Antone Rosa stood at the open window studying the disposition.

"Major," Ramsey said. "By your leave, sir."

"Come in, come in. Join me. I was beginning to feel uncomfortable as a spectator. Some of those men have been wounded, perhaps even killed."

Ramsey squinted through the window. It was difficult to make out the details.

"Here, this should help," Rosa said. "I believe you are familiar with its operation." He handed Ramsey his own brass survey tube.

The palace grounds sprang to life before him. There was a downed man, and he saw Hawaiians attempting to reach him through the sniper fire. The position was also taking sporadic fire from the palace basement, but the insurgents had erected barricades and most appeared to have withdrawn into the bungalow for safety.

"Why don't they shoot?" Rosa asked. "They've got ammunition. They were shooting earlier. Why don't they defend themselves?"

"Which side, sir?"

"The Hawaiians. Why aren't they shooting?"

Ramsey studied the situation with the glass.

"Do you see, sir? They cannot. Ashford has allowed civilians to gather about him. They're skylarking. If the *kanaka* was to fire, they'd like as not hit the bystanders."

Rosa smiled ruefully. "That's my people, principled to the last drop of their own blood."

Ramsey examined their position carefully. He needed to discover who was leading them. Seizing the palace was a dramatic but foolhardy move. He supposed it was Koloa. It was just the kind of romantic but ultimately disastrous gesture of which he was capable.

He focused his glass upon a figure which seemed to be in heated conference with one of the larger Hawaiians. He was a little squirt, straight black hair, an Oriental. Another crawled over to join them ... Abner!

He took the glass from his eye.

"Had enough, Ramsey?" Rosa asked him.

"I see what you mean, sir."

"It is affecting to see a wounded man struggling to reach safety."

He handed Rosa the tube. It was affecting to see Abner under fire.

Two explosions in quick succession rolled across the palace grounds. He snatched back the tube. Ashford's men were running in turn at the fence with lighted explosive and hurling it over.

"What the devil?!" Rosa exclaimed.

"It's Ashford – man's inventive, I'll give him that. No artillery pieces, but he does have dynamite. Plenty of it. I can see the cases. Enough to scare up a monsoon in the desert." He laughed.

"What are you laughing at, man? It's a massacre. The Hawaiians will have to shoot into the crowd!"

He handed him the tube. "No, Major, it's all for show. It's all falling short, do you see? The Rifles haven't got a pitcher among 'em. His boys don't have the throwing arm!"

As night fell the positions hardened, Ashford and his men outside, the Hawaiians inside the palace perimeter. Spectators remained on the street corners, so neither side wanted to throw much ammunition around. It was a standoff.

Antone Rosa picked up his hat. "I'd better get to Wodehouse," he said. "Don't want you Americans advantaging yourselves by our situation."

"Don't go and beat the devil on my account, Major."

"Not you. Stevens."

"Stevens," Ramsey agreed.

"God knows what he'll try to make of all this," Rosa said as he departed.

As darkness arrived and the snipers lost their profit, the Hawaiians crept back to the forward positions. Ramsey did not believe there would be further changes to the disposition over-night, but he was immensely curious about what the morning held. He was certain the *kanaka* would not cage themselves inside the palace without a plan for escape ... or for victory. The night turned cloudy and windy. There appeared to be a storm making up offshore. He had Sienna send supper up and pre-pared for a long night.

He dozed. The floorboard creaked and Pua came to him once again. She appeared naked as she did when they worked together at Pearl River, just the narrow cloth around her hips. Her breasts were golden, her shoulders round and firm. But her hair was coiled up and a white flower shone in it like the moon. Her face was older. She was saying things to him he could not understand, but he thought they were deeply important. He wanted to understand them. He begged her to speak more clearly but his words could not escape. His lips were stitched together.

"Eh, Ramsey, no scared, yeah?" Manu shook him awake by the shoulder. "The Night Marchers nevah like hurt you. You nevah get one soul, remember? *Uhane ole.*"

Light had etched the craggy outline of Diamond Head but the coastal plain with its seraglio of graceful coconut trees was still predawn gray. Cocks crowed in the town outside Madam Ho's and soon the doves would awaken and coo.

"Why do I have the feeling you could pass for one of them, Manu?" Ramsey stretched himself. He was still clothed in his bicycling costume.

"A Night Marcher?" Manu made a face. "Well, I have been up all night."

"How did you find me?"

"That machine of yours. I'd kiss the gunner's daughter before you'd get me on it. You want to sweat, you should hire out to the plantation."

He grabbed Ramsey's tube and leaned through the window.

"You won't pick out the men at the palace. It's still too dark."

"Not where I'm looking." Manu aimed the glass at the point where Diamond Head cleaved the sea. The ocean was still rough from the storm that swept through during the night. He could see the angry breakers thrashing the volcano's stark lava rock, the plumes of their death dance illumined in the dawning rays of sun.

But he saw nothing else, no fleet of war canoes and no collection of flotsam telegraphing their sudden demise.

"Who's behind this?" Ramsey asked. "Reminds me of the glorious, heroic and prodigiously asinine things my people did during the war."

"I couldn't tell you."

"Well it's either you or Koloa."

Manu sat down to the remains of his supper.

"Let me see if I can cogitate which of the two of you would strand a fistful of men inside the palace compound with no way out. Which of you is such a brilliant tactician, you mount an operation with a boy in the ranks."

"A boy? What are you talking about?" Manu said.

"I'm talking about Abner, the Ewa boy. What's he doing there?"

"I didn't know about that. Really?" Manu was working his way through the carcass of cold duck. Its fat had congealed and he wiped his fingers on his trousers. "We didn't get as many men as we thought. Maybe – I don't know. My mother didn't see the point. And no one can argue with her anymore."

"Well he worked with me at Pearl River. I don't appreciate Ashford making him a bulls eye."

Manu laughed. "You starting to care, Ramsey? Danger, boss. Much *pilikia*. No good for our profession. You start to care then you turn weak, maybe even get back your *uhane*."

"What's your Bonnie Prince Charlie done, sold his to the devil? I don't see him out there. I see lesser men putting their lives at risk. Where's Koloa?"

"I wish I knew."

"Last I heard he was pruning trees on Kauai."

"Your sources never were worth a damn. – O, by the bleeding wounds of Christ!" Manu had trained the glass once more out the window. There was light enough to reveal movement. He stared with his mouth ajar.

Ramsey seized the tube and put it to his eye. The palace grounds were still caught in the dew of sleep but far out along King Street, where it branched from boulevard into the trail that led through Waikiki to Diamond Head, he detected a clutch of men. They were bedraggled and spiritless, and as he focused the glass, he made out torn clothing and cuts across their torsos. There were a dozen at most, some carried spears and clubs, but most were empty handed. A few paces in front strode Prince Koloa. His tunic, though soiled, was decked with braid and fancy piping. Thaddeus hunched along beside him.

"Koloa promised three canoes of warriors," Manu said. "Last night – they were supposed to paddle into the harbor last night." He shook his head. "I waited for them. But the storm – did you hear it? I'll bet it caught them in Maunalua, or rounding Diamond Head point. I feared … that's all that's left. They swamped, must have drowned, lost their guns."

He took the glass back and studied what remained of Koloa's invasion force. "The plan was a good one – Koloa's, not mine. But a good one. Take Ashford from the rear. It's been done before, a proven maneuver. The warriors at the palace hold them by the nose and the invaders strike from the rear. My job was to meet them at the beach, guide them into position. We had a watchword: *I mua, e na koa.*"

"Three canoes, Manu? How many men?"

"Not enough, but we had courage. You might even say *pono.* It was supposed to be more. It was supposed to be my mother's flotilla of sailing canoes. There'd have been hundreds of men. They all wanted to come. They'd have fought Ashford hand-to-hand and relished telling the tale to their grandchildren. Just like the days of Kamehameha. But she wouldn't commit herself."

A series of explosions shattered the dawn. Four dynamite sticks flew like sparkling pinwheels over the fence toward the bungalow. Two found their mark. They exploded on the roof of the structure, sending tiles in all directions and beams and rafters plunging inward.

Whoops erupted from the loose line of Honolulu Rifles along King Street. Some men had gone home at night to their families and not yet returned. Those who remained were still uniformed but had lost all sense of order. The overnight bivouac took the starch out of them. They stood and gawked, watching the show.

Flinching with the explosions, Ramsey swung the glass from Abner taking cover at Hale Akala to the street, where two men in civilian attire limbered up. One was tall and rangy. "What the hell? I know that man! It's William Wall, best pitcher the Whangdoodles ever had!"

He watched as the men were handed two lighted sticks of dynamite each. They charged the palace barricade like javelin throwers and launched their missiles. They had the arms and their projectiles soared with murderous effect, three landing squarely on the roof, the fourth hitting the wall and bouncing off. Abner broke from cover and scrambled for it. It was almost too painful to watch. He lifted his arm to toss it back, and the four charges detonated nearly simultaneously.

A chastened silence engulfed the scene as the explosion played off the surrounding buildings. Bystanders on King Street turned away. Ramsey sank to the floor. "My God," he whispered.

He locked eyes with Manu, his growing increasingly sharp and accusing until Manu turned his head.

"I never actually knew the boy," Manu said.

"I did."

Manu grunted and turned back to the window. Ramsey placed his head in his hands. Pua's fishhook swung on its chain from his neck.

"*Ka make mau loa!*" he heard Manu exclaim. "This can't happen! This just can't happen!"

He jumped up and pointed the glass where Manu was looking. Koloa and his men had broken into a trot and were heading in formation along Beretania Street toward Iolani Palace, spears and clubs swinging at their sides. They had heard the explosions. They concluded it meant trouble for their men in the compound.

Manu made for the door. Ramsey grabbed him.

"What do you think you're doing, Manu?"

"They'll be slaughtered! What you think I'm doing?!"

Manu was heavy and strong. He was fit and wiry. It was a struggle to keep the Hawaiian inside the room. "You can't go out there. Those boys will kill you!"

"I can't let Koloa run into a trap. I've got to stop him!"

"You won't stop him, it's Koloa!"

"Well if I can't stop him, I'll join him!"

"Goddamn if you will! I just lost Abner. I'm not losing you, Manu!"

"I can't stand up here and watch!"

They were panting now, hands on knees, faces close together.

"But that's what we do, Manu. We're supposed to. We're spies. We watch."

"That's what you do, Ramsey. You watch. You watch the Ewa boy blow himself up. I'm not watching anymore ... I guess I'm not the agent you are after all."

Manu utilized a release hold from his *Lua* fighting and broke loose. They looked at one another for a moment.

"Be careful, Manu."

"Shuah t'ing, boss." He dashed down the stairs.

FORTY-FIVE

In his glass, Ramsey found Manu and Koloa. They had settled on a diversionary attack. If Ashford could be turned from the gate, he saw there might be opportunity for the men inside the palace compound to escape.

Koloa's troop threw itself headlong into the flank of the Honolulu Rifles. The Rifles had been gadding about, pointing and laughing over the dynamite explosions and shouting encouragement to the Whangdoodles' pitchers. They were taken by surprise and the shock of the assault carried deep into their formation. The privates did not have time to ready their rifles; grim-faced *kanaka* were on them, swinging clubs and overmatching their cumbersome firearms with effective hand fighting.

Ramsey followed the battle. Koloa directed the attack with his sword. Manu fought at the center of the melee. He struck like a wild beast, impressively light and quick for a man his size.

He swung his glass to the royal bungalow. If the men inside charged now, the day might be carried. They had only to reach the gate and lay down a curtain of flanking fire. Koloa would break the back of the Honolulu Rifles.

But there was no charge. He saw the Oriental emerge from the ruins of the bungalow bearing a white flag. Behind him followed the Hawaiians, bleeding, stumbling, carrying three makeshift stretchers with figures on them. He focused his tube. One was Abner's shattered body. The second was the big bearded Hawaiian. The third he did not recognize.

Pistol shots rang out. He turned back to the skirmish. Half the Rifles had broken and run from the onslaught of Hawaiians. But Ashford had rallied two men armed with revolvers, and they were firing into the lines. He saw Hawaiians fall and the surge begin to turn. The fleeing privates halted and, urging each other on, ran back to administer the coup de grace. Then Ashford threw himself upon Koloa, saber drawn. The blade flashed with force enough to behead the prince, but Ramsey saw Manu move with the power of an ocean wave. He absorbed the blow himself, deflected Ashford's sword arm with a subtle move then fell beneath its edge.

Ramsey cried aloud. Koloa stood straight up when Manu fell. He opened his mouth again to yell out, tell the prince to cover, as if he could hear. Then a pistol barked and Koloa collapsed.

He flew down the stairs to the street. The smell of cordite lay upon the morning air. He saw the Hawaiians panting, blood stained, a crumpled train of bodies behind them, white and brown, to show how remarkably far they had progressed. The privates faced them, Winchesters now aimed unwaveringly, clearly alarmed at how thin a line stood between the warriors and victory.

Spectators appeared out of doorways and offices. He pushed through them to the palace gate. A rank of brown bodies lay side by side on the grounds, victimized by falling roof beams or flying shards of glass, or decimated by a blast. Hawaiians kneeled and wailed beside them. He touched Abner's body on the shoulder. Only its youthfulness made him recognizable. Then he tore himself away, choking a sob. Abner's face was gone.

He searched for Manu. Ashford's men were cordoning the area and disarming the remaining Hawaiians. The butcher who'd tried to drown him stopped him then backed down. "The big Hawaiian, where is he?" Ramsey demanded. The butcher didn't know.

He found Koloa. Blood leaked through a wound to his chest. Thaddeus stooped over him, weeping. They pulled him into a sitting position against the fence.

"Ashford," he called, "for God's sake, get the wounded out of here. They'll die in the sun!"

Thaddeus located a tin cup of water and Ramsey poured it over Koloa's wound, swabbing it out with his red scarf. The lung was filling with blood. He could hear it gurgle as the prince struggled to breathe.

"I may not get my harvest in, Ramsey," Koloa groaned. "Too bad. A big one. Used those methods."

"Don't talk, Koloa." He gave him a sip from the cup, but he coughed it up.

"Go to my ranch on Kauai. Take the girl with you. Do what I couldn't."

"You're talking crazy. *Pupule* brains. Crazy as attacking the palace."

"Had to do something, Ramsey. You put us in a bad way, you know." Koloa coughed up blood, and his wound spit out again.

"Put you in ... What do you mean, Koloa?" He straightened him up by the jacket lapels. "What do you mean?"

"Pu'uloa ... you splintered the paddle. First time since ..."

The Oriental came over with a wet compress. "No talk, Prince."

"Ah, Denzo. Friend, my *aikane. I mua, e na koa.*"

"Ashford, where's the surgeon?!" Ramsey called out. Then he turned again to Koloa. "Splintered ... what? What do you mean?"

Koloa's mouth showed red. "Sleep safe in the highway. Remember? I told you." He wiped bloody drool from his lip. "My ranch ... take the girl. Take ... others, more."

"Ashford!" he called again and tried to shift Koloa, but the Oriental stopped him. The prince coughed one last time. His eyes fixed, he hemorrhaged and expired inches from him. "Koloa!" he cried, "Koloa!"

Denzo closed the prince's eyes. "Honor," he said, pressing his forehead to the blood-soaked grass, "much honorable man."

Two privates stood Denzo to his feet. "This one's just an Oriental," one said, and ordered him to lift wounded men onto the carts Ashford had summoned. They shoved Thaddeus to the middle of King Street, where the Hawaiians sat under guard. Though corralled by Ashford's troops, the natives looked primitive and frightening, blood stained and naked beneath their wraps, and proud in ways not seen since the early days of the missionaries. They looked like warriors.

A crowd gathered and there was much crying and pushing and carrying on. It was not a scene Colonel Ashford felt particularly called to manage. He summoned three men to join him, ordered the captives marched to Oahu Jail, and announced his intention to retire to the saloon of the Commercial Hotel. His heroic defeat of native insurrection had been accomplished.

Ramsey sat by Koloa's body. The horseflies descended and he chased them off with a helmet dropped by one of the Rifles. Much as he swung it, he could not keep them away. He drove them from the chest and they settled on the hands. He attacked them there and they went for the prince's face. He did the best he could, finally covering Koloa's body with his, his hands over the prince's bloody ones, his legs stretched atop the dead man's own, and screamed at the flies to get away.

The graves detail found him and tried to pull him off. "No!" he cried, stained with gore and looking wounded himself. "No, goddamn it! I'm keeping him safe, safe in the highway, goddamn your godforsaken eyes! Don't you see?"

The privates jabbed him with their bayonets until he surrendered Koloa. Then he searched frantically through every stretcher and every wagon for Manu until a reporter from the *Commercial Pacific Advertiser* approached him for an interview. "You were in the battle, mister? What was it like, them warriors bearing down on you?"

He struck the man to the ground then tore off for Madam Ho's.

FORTY-SIX

Princess Liliu stood at the rail as the steamer broached Diamond Head point and coasted the perimeter of Waikiki. At this distance nothing appeared to have changed. She fancied she could make out the beach home where she passed so many pleasant, languid days. Farther on would be Kawaiahao Church, its stately walls mined from the coral reefs the ship paralleled. She looked forward to her first return there, to clasping her hands in its cool interior and bowing her head. She taught Sunday School and played the organ, but her only thought was for the prayers she would say: gratitude at seeing her beloved islands again, gratitude for the safe journey, and intercessions as well for her brother.

Once the vessel nosed into Honolulu Harbor it became evident that the worst rumors were true. The queen's party had been bothered at the stops along the homeward route from London. The newshounds would not be put off their insufferable urgency to record monarchy in defeat. She had refused comment and the queen had replied with dignified assurances of the Hawaiians' love for their sovereign.

But Honolulu Harbor awaited their arrival somberly. Onlookers thronged the wharf, sailors crowded the rigging of parked ships. They looked like dark birds spectating a funeral.

The cabinet of the Bayonet Constitution met them at the landing: Green, Brown, Thurston and Clarence Ashford. Not one man Hawaiian by blood, she noted. The Royal Hawaiian Band made to strike up in salute, but she silenced them with a cut of her fan.

Kalakaua waited in the private rooms of the palace. He and the queen clung to one another. Liliu's heart broke at the sight of him. He had prepared himself carefully to welcome them home but no effort could efface the corrosion of the last months. It had eaten away his appearance like one of the western diseases and he had not the inner fortitude to put it off.

He turned and greeted her then gestured at his cravat. "Forgive the bow, won't you? I could not render it properly. My wrist has become arthritic."

She curtsied. Her brother was her king.

"I signed a new constitution," he said, raising her by the hand. "The sorrow weighs heavily upon me."

She nodded gravely.

"I had no choice. It was that, or the Calvinists take all. I would not turn our people over to them." He faltered. "There was blood on King Street. Our own people's blood, staining the front of the palace. It was horrible. They shot at them from the clock tower of your church, did you know?"

"Kawaiahao? The minister gave ...?"

He blotted his brow. "I don't know. From the tower riflemen could look into the palace grounds. Horrible. Our faithful came to me when they heard. All the next day I had them scrub to get rid of it, the blood. It was everywhere. I forced myself to stand behind the tree and watch them. People saw me, I made a spectacle of myself, but what did it matter? Blood had been shed for me, brave blood. Braver blood than ever I deserved."

"Brother, do not say that. You are the noblest –"

"No, I have done wrong. I led our dynasty down paths ..." He could not finish. "Luahine has ... *Ka i ka 'ino*, she has cursed me. The flying curse. I ..."

She dropped her eyes behind her fan.

"You do not fear her, Sister, I know you do not."

"As you should not, Brother."

"As you should. Our ancestors knew what the ancients of every high culture knew."

She would not dispute the king.

"I consulted the *kahuna*," he said, "the ones working on the *heiau*. They are learned but they can do nothing. Even Rosenberg – he found the pages of his testament scorched and he fled."

"Is there no remedy?"

"It is on Kauai. I must go there to find it."

"And Luahine?" she asked.

"She waits on Kauai. She watches, she suffers as I do ... We are bound now, by the curse. My fate is hers."

"I shall pray for you, Brother. Give me leave, I shall retire immediately to church."

Kalakaua shut the doors to the family apartment. "I must confide in you," he said.

Surprised, she sat without being invited. The king never unburdened himself to her.

"You must watch over the government for me. I'll take Rosa. We will leave next week."

She nodded. Her brother always appointed her regent in his absence, though he made plain he did not trust her beyond ceremony.

"I don't know how long ... or if ... I weaken, Liliu. Some days my breath, and my bones – I feel the curse working in me."

"But Brother, it is some ailment, surely."

"It is Luahine. My only hope is Kauai."

She fanned herself, not knowing what to say.

He sat next to her. "Listen to me closely. I was ambitious, I thought like the *haole*."

"*I mua*, you leaned too far forward," she replied.

"Aye, as Kamehameha did, the time the paddle splintered."

"We must provide for the people," she said. "It is our calling as Christians and our duty as *ali'i*."

"No, Sister. Not as Christians. That is why I would speak to you. *Kiku*: you must learn to lean back, lean back into the arms of the ancestors. The kingdom must belong to the Colored

Races. Only then will the ball pass through the hoop." He started to demonstrate, but gripped his wrist and winced with pain. "Lili'uokalani – I grant you your exalted title now: pray for me, Sister, but not to Jehovah. You must forego Kawaiahao forever."

"Brother!" She fanned herself.

"Listen," he insisted. "This is the sacrifice you must make – for The People. You will not set foot in Kawaiahao. Your monarch orders you. It is an abomination. You will pray for me at the *heiau* we build at sacred Pu'uloa. Let the people see you. God willing, you will restore the balance, *pala'ie*. I cannot."

She fanned herself and stared into his eyes.

"Pray hard for me at Pu'uloa, that I shall live."

Her fan ruffled the air between them.

"Make a public ceremony of it."

She scratched her throat.

"I command you, Sister."

Epilogue

P ua put her head on Sienna's lap and cried for hours over the deaths of beautiful Koloa and her dear brother. She cried until she was numb. When the tears stopped she shut herself in her room, looked out the window as the sun rose and fell many times, and waited for someone to come for her, tell her what to do next. But no one came. No one told her. For the first time she was truly on her own.

Her *waimaka lehua* came, mocking her with its promise of fertility, so the seclusion seemed to have a purpose, and after the pain stopped she sighed, pulled herself together and started a batch of dye in a pot she found at the cook house back of Madam Ho's. The tears still leaked but she'd chosen *olena* to match the golden color of Sienna's temple, and tears of mourning seemed a proper addition to the mixture. She planned to submit herself and train in the worship style of Sienna's other girls.

She was just composing a letter, laboring over such *haole* words as would please the Chinese cook and cause him to release the pot of dye he had seized so angrily from her, shouting the pot was his best, what did a *kanaka* girl know? – when pebbles struck her window. It was Thaddeus! She ran barefoot down the Hotel Street staircase and out the rear door. Manu was alive, he told her. He was weak but recovering out Ewa.

She shrieked, tore off the cumbersome *haole* skirt and rode astride in bloomers, following Thaddeus to the village. She ducked into the grass lodge and ran to embrace her brother, babbling in soft, loving Hawaiian. The village elder was with him, and also the *haole* priest's woman. She'd brought him medicine from her ranch, Manu told her. In the confusion after Ashford quit the field for the saloon, Denzo had hurried him away in a buckboard to the village. When fever struck, Denzo begged Eliza at Hale Nui and she had returned with him unquestioningly.

"She departs now, Little Sister," Manu said in Hawaiian. His voice was low but clear. "The wife of the *Iesu* priest goes to see if her husband will be father to their youngest child."

As Manu spoke, she watched the *haole* woman. She was divided as the forked tail of the frigate bird. She was obliged to the healing of her child, but her heart wanted to be satisfied in Manu. She departed with a potion fermented from the organs of the great pig Ramsey brought down.

Pua saw her brother's face as the *haole* woman left. His yearning displeased her. "Brother, do you not remember that night at the *luau?* I thought you would take me, as our mother commanded." She placed her hand on his arm. "I was frightened, but I was also …"

"Pua-lani," he said, his familiar name for her. "Some practices need to be buried with the ancients. A brother and sister should not be mated just to enhance the *mana* of their mother. Our mother has *mana* enough. Any more, and it is not *mana* she builds up. It is the *haole* power." He used the English. "I instructed you to learn about this word."

She turned away. "I know the word well. The *haole* Ramsey taught it to me," she said bitterly. "There is no *pono* to it. And no *aloha.*"

"You must return to him, Pua-lani."

She was taken aback. "I cannot! Who will care for you? Pakalana will play the drum, and I will summon the *aumakua* deities to heal you."

"No, you must go. I have a task for you."

"But Brother, I must care for you."

"Thaddeus will tend to me. You must find Ramsey."

"Faagh! Brother, do not ask me this! Ramsey has no *aloha* for me. I am *kanaka* girl to him. He has *aloha* for the *haole*, Kaka Kamahine."

"You must be our ears with him now, Pua-lani, I am too weak. We must be warned of what *Amelika* intends."

"Brother, Ramsey has the *haole* soul. Not even Maui's fish-hook healed him – and neither can I!" Tears rolled down her cheeks.

"Do you fear, Pua-lani?"

She nodded and wiped her face. "He will contaminate me, Brother. He is Uli, I will never be pure to dance again. Lono will never accept me."

She felt his thick fingers stroke her face and comb the hair behind her ears. "Sister," he said, "it is much to ask of you ... It is too much. Our mother commanded it, but our mother commanded wrongly. I see it now, to live with a divided heart." He gripped her shoulders. "You are right. Leave this, leave Oahu island."

"But where do I go?"

"You return to Kauai island. *A'a i ka hula* – just dance!"

She hesitated. "But Brother, our mother inhabits Kauai."

"Our mother weakens from her own curse. Pay her no heed, Pua-lani."

"But to be near her. She is Kahu, she will know."

"She moans in the mud to the *menehune*. She knows nothing." He started coughing. "Now go, go with my *aloha*. *Hele aku!*"

Kauai! He was freeing her from Ramsey's hook! She ran from her brother's side. She leaped upon her horse and headed out of the village. She would have to ride through the night creatures to get back, but she would say her prayers. In the room Sienna gave her she kept the *haole* coins in a coconut shell. With them she could mount the next day's steamer to the outer islands.

Ramsey lined up the three pieces of paper. It was hard to keep them separate. He swallowed the rest of the whiskey and tiptoed with the bottle to the foot of his bed. The other empties seemed to stand to, if he approached them carefully. Order was important. It helped keep things ordered. He steadied the bottle alongside them then returned with long slow steps to the problem.

The three pieces of paper on his desk. Frustratingly similar, that was the problem. He arranged them in sequence: from the Admiral, summoning him to San Francisco to receive his promotion; to the Admiral, his report on the kingdom in the ten days since the Bayonet Constitution – but it was unfinished. He put his eye closer to it and saw another terrible word that had to be scratched out. Terrible. Then he picked up the third: his note, a secret, to Antone Rosa, who was not his friend, but who on this stinking island was? Koloa was dead, so was Manu, Sienna had closed her doors to him – "You overplayed your hand, John, and good people got killed" – and Rosa was the only person he could think of to get a message to the king.

He rearranged the papers. First came the promotion. Second came the secret … He would tell the secret! The king must not sign the Reciprocity Treaty. If he did, the United States would take Pearl River. Then it would take something else. Then something else. "Let the British Minister protect you. Wodehouse is a good man," the note said.

All in order. He stood to offer a toast, but found there was no more whiskey. No matter. He was American power in the kingdom now. Taylor was a drunk, and little Stevens took more opium than a Chinaman. Soon as word of his promotion leaked out, he had credit with every merchant in town.

He pulled on his jacket and stepped wincing into the sunlight. He found his sea legs after a bit and made his way to the grocer's, where he was successful, and to Madam Ho's, where he was not.

"If I let you in here, it would be my hide, Mr. John." Carl blocked the Hotel Street door. He had known better than to try the fancied up King Street side.

"Got to get this note to the King. Very important. Secret."

"You know what Miz Sienna told you."

"Well, how 'bout the girl. Pua. Will she see me? She must know the King."

"She lit out this mornin' like a house afire. I think she's gone, Mr. John. Tore off her fine clothes. Miz Sienna's mad at her as she is at you."

"Gone? She can't be." The sun and the whiskey were suddenly too much, and he stumbled into Carl's arms. "Got to sit down a minute, Carl."

"You sick, Mr. John?" Carl sat him in the alcove. "No shave, hair a mess. What's that, ink all over your fingers? What's wrong with you?"

Ramsey slipped into stupor and Carl pulled the curtain then made up coffee and a ham sandwich in the pantry. The food sobered him up a bit. "Can you bring me a basin of water, Carl?"

"I can't bring you nothin' more, suh. You got to go."

"But the girl?"

"I told you, she's gone. Probably went back to her people, as you should go back to yours."

Back to his people ... Carl was right. Back to his people, pick up his promotion. He forgot his bottle of whiskey, remembered to stop for another, and returned to his bungalow to finish the report to the Admiral. He wanted it done before shipping out the next day.

He pulled out fresh paper and worked into the night. He took pride in terse, analytical reports and aimed for a sharp summation of the kingdom's position following the near coup executed by the businessmen. The government would not survive, he wrote, not ruled by a native. Not because it couldn't, but because it wouldn't. It wouldn't be allowed to. The White elites had had enough.

Fair enough, he thought, and swallowed his whiskey. Most government wasn't worth surviving.

He thought to stop right there but the new attaché-designate, he could not leave the subject of Stevens unaddressed. He picked up his pen and it wrote. Then it kept writing, words piling upon words. He drank to slow it, but the pen gushed onward sheet after sheet until he ran out of paper. The lamp dried up, and he was astounded to discover that daylight had replaced it and his report had inflated into a gabby justification of intervention on behalf of monarchy – his intervention, and the intervention the Navy ought to ready for the future. There was more to government than government, he'd written. There was – it astonished him what he'd written. "There was *pono*."

A Hawaiian word in official correspondence. He scratched it out. He'd have to redo the report aboard ship.

He finished the bottle, started folding his clothing precisely according to regulation then gave up and stuffed it and his possessions into his bag, and found a *kanaka* loitering at the Hawaiian Hotel to carry it to the wharf. Returning bleary-eyed, head swimming to the bungalow to shave, he realized he had sent everything off with the boy.

Pua slipped off the horse. She felt nervous. It became clearer through the night as she rode from Ewa. She needed refuge, and only one person could she think of with *mana* to protect her. Who understood the gods?

Her dream had been to find her prince, fair as the god Lono, and dance for him in the moon shadows of Mount Waialeale on her beautiful Kauai island. She thought her light-skinned prince was Koloa; it struck her as one of the mirthless tricks of Maui that it should be the *haole* Ramsey. The fishhook seemed not to have stitched together his soul, but it had caught her heart. When he pulled she felt such things as she'd never known. Her body danced beneath his touch. Her female place warmed and pulsed. Their hearts beat together like twin drums, *ha* their breath met like lava met the wild sea.

Molokai girl desired more of Ramsey's touch, much more. Kauai girl cried to be unhooked, but Luahine lived there. The daughter of a sorceress became a sorceress herself. This was talked about, this was known, it was seen. She could not return to Kauai island.

She crept into the bungalow. The screen door closed behind her. The floor creaked under foot, mid-morning lighting its boards. She ran through her English words, not knowing what she'd say.

She saw the small box with the heavy door. It was empty. She saw the tall box that held the stink words of Kaka Kamahine. It also was empty. She saw the table where she had eaten with him, and the bed where she thought she would lie with him. Bottles stood alongside it, the kind that carried the dangerous *haole awa*. More bottles lay upon it, and the faded khaki shirt he wore at Pearl lagoon. But Ramsey was gone.

She clutched the shirt to her nose, breathed him deeply into her, and sobbed and sobbed, her heart breaking. She felt completely lost, totally alone, abandoned once more. She shut her eyes and buried her face in Ramsey, her tears and his odors the one way they ever would be joined, and realized that without him she had to *hanai* herself, and a single destination, a single destination only remained to her.

It was Steamer Day. *S.S. Alameda* anchored in port bound for the Orient, and the barkentine *J.D. Spreckels* prepared to sail for San Francisco. Both ships belonged to Colonel Claus Spreckels. *Alameda* discharged her Honolulu passengers, tourists who had engaged rooms at the Hawaiian Hotel for the summer season. They descended her gangway timidly, as reports of unrest in the capital had put the blue on many plans for rest cures and diversion in the Sandwich Islands. But Honolulu had turned out in showy spectacle. Vendors parked their carts and hawked exotic wares. The Royal Hawaiian Band assembled in martial costume, and turning the bells of brass instruments to reflect the sunlight, it welcomed the newcomers with familiar marches and airs. Soon each visitor was encircled in fragrant necklaces of island flowers, and carters were busying themselves with trunks and cases.

Society was arrived also. The fashionably dressed milled side by side with the fustian, purchased a stick of cane sugar from a cart or a refreshing cone dispensed by Mr. H.J. Hart's Elite Ice Cream Saloon. In their profusion of color, class and demeanor they were a bawdy demonstration of the cornucopia emptied upon the Kingdom of Hawaii.

They were not arrived for the benefit of *Alameda* however, but for the departing *J.D. Spreckels*. Ramsey caught his breath among them.

"So, the cat with nine lives, or the chameleon who changes sides. Which is it?" John Stevens, drawing alongside him, hunched trembling on his stick, shorter than ever.

He shoved his hands into his trousers and said nothing.

Stevens poked him in the side. "Or is it the skunk, so arrogant he thinks he's a house cat? Look at you, unshaven, uncombed. You smell like liquor. You're a disgrace."

"You got no hold on me." Ramsey jabbed himself with his thumb. "I saved the treaty. I'm a hero to two governments. They're making me an officer."

Stevens snorted. "Commission changes nothing, Ramsey. You're still a murderer. Now you're a drunk. I just have to prove it."

"And what're you? Just another lotus eater. Kingdom's full of 'em, you're like coconuts. Only difference, you wear a top hat. Or did you pawn your daddy's beaver to pay the Chinaman?"

"You're a fool, Ramsey, to make an enemy of me and the men I represent. We're the future of these islands. The future of the goddamn Pacific."

"I ate your future twenty years ago, Minister. It was hog piss. I got the power to do somethin' about it now."

He pushed through the crowd and boarded *J.D. Spreckels*.

Behind him a carriage arrived. Only the most observant tourist would have noted the extreme attention accorded its occupants: a frail man, fully-bearded as from an earlier day, accompanied by a stouter man, more vigorous, who helped him out of the carriage and onto the wharf. The older fellow – could he have been in the islands taking a rest cure? – halted and stood a moment, leaning upon his stick. His eyes swept the panorama from Diamond Head to Ewa, taking in the lush green vales that disappeared into the sensuous folds of the Koolaus, the steeple at Kawaiahao Church, the stout towers of Iolani Palace and the crystalline sky broken only by white puffs that gamboled like playful lambs on a ranch at Lanai island. He raised his topper and held it a moment in quiet salute. The Hawaiians on the wharf, white and brown, paused just as quietly. Then taking the arm of his son-in-law, Walter Murray Gibson boarded the San Francisco ship and quit the Hawaiian kingdom for the last time.

Ramsey glowered from the railing. Since word of his promotion, businessmen tipped their hats and politicians reached for his hand. He went nowhere without recognition. But no one invited him for a drink, no society matron asked him to tea for her daughter, the crowd hadn't come to see him off. Gibson escaping sentence was more one of them than he was. He was still a Taggert from the hills.

The porter took him by the arm to his cabin and offered to unpack his bag. "Just bring me a bottle," he said.

He collapsed onto the bunk and woke when the porter, tired of knocking, opened the cabin door, not wanting to miss his tip from the next attaché.

Ramsey poured a tumbler of whiskey and spread the report on the little writing desk. He started reading and poured another drink. The first page stood up. The second led him astray. So did the next and next. He scratched out two offending words, then phrases, then cursed and slashed through whole paragraphs, then tore up the report and dumped the pieces on the bunk. He'd made his bones, the Admiral didn't need his palaver.

The cabin was sweltering. The ship was still tied up. He pushed the porthole open then sloughed off his jacket. He tore open his shirt and paced, trying to stir up some air. Then he decided to rid himself of what was really irritating him. He jerked Pua's fishhook from his neck. The filthy thing, he had the power, what the hell did he need with *pono*?

He staggered against the bulkhead as the ship lurched and began warping from the harbor. He emptied the bottle and stuck his head out the cabin door.

"Porter!" he yelled.

J.D. Spreckels was spreading sail. To his deep surprise, Jessica Mornay paraded the deck, watching the canvas bloom from beneath a red parasol.

"Another bottle, Mr. Ramsey?"

He changed his mind. "No, not another bottle. Send the barber. I want a shave. And porter, that little steamer over there?" He pointed to the barkentine's leeward side.

"A sightseer, sir, bound for the Big Island. Folks want to see Pele, all that hullabaloo."

"That what it is?"

"Never seen it myself, a volcano. They say it's a reg'lar fire-storm when it cuts loose."

"She's steering a little close, that steamer." He rubbed his eyes, blurred from drink.

"And overcrowded, too," the porter said. "They put the native passengers on the deck. See? There's one, a female looks like. Long hair. She's wearing khaki."

He looked but could see nothing. "Yeah, well, shake up the watch. Don't want a collision, do we."

The End

Historical Note

Kalakaua's scheme for Pacific empire … Walter Gibson's amorous entreaties to Mother Marianne … the opium bill, Tong Kee's sudden death before testifying … opposition of Thurston, Dole, Castle, who were missionary heirs, Punahou men and businessmen … Bayonet Constitution … Whangdoodles baseball club … dynamite attack by Honolulu Rifles upon native insurgents dug in at the palace – all true, though John Stevens arrived a few years later, and the native attempt to restore Kalakaua's power also occurred later.

Luahine is fictional, though she is modeled after High Chiefess Ruth Keelikolani, who did offer herself to Aunty Pele, arresting the lava flow threatening Hilo town in 1881 – as I learned many years after graduating Punahou School.

Also true, the endless wrestle of sea with land, in whose embrace we were, growing up, just children together, brown, yellow, white and black.

Watch for *Goddess Revenge* in print soon.

 # Acknowledgements

I thought writers worked alone. Maybe they do, but authors require a village and I've been blessed with a wonderful village of readers, resources and friends.

My buddies Paul and H. James, who always encourage my ventures. Early readers from down South Jamie and Suzanne, and Stuart in New York. Ku'uipo, my sistah. Ellen Conley's writers group. Kilian who helped my breakthrough. Cynette and Alex for their detailed feedback. Noelani, for support calls. Neal ... always. Lilikala for welcoming me onto the beach. Kainoa for sharing his expertise on language and culture. My Hawai'i *ohana* in New York, Star and Leslie; and in the islands, Lauren and Laurel. And Paula at the Brooklyn VA, who said, "Women like sex. Put in plenty."

My gratitude to Patrice, my partner in the publishing process. Gratitude for the mysterious turns that brought us together. And to Mickie, who "feels" Hawai'i in her heart.

To the Hawaiian institutions that nurtured my own heart: Holy Nativity Church, Punahou School, Outrigger Canoe Club, and the louche, insouciant beaches where we surfed.

And the great Herb Kawainui Kane, a family friend back in the day, whose art inspired life and the Polynesian Voyaging Society and the arc of my series, The Goddess Stories.

But mostly, my family, especially my brother Robert, who called it "best book ever." Big sister Georgia, always only a phone call away. My son Josh and his wife Kim, who gave me their hearts and two beautiful *keiki* girls, Alex and Kaitlyn. My mother Jeanne, who tolerated rewrite after rewrite and insisted the original title was wrong – and she was right.

And my wife Cynthia, my Creole New Orleans girl and best copyeditor, who daily creates the safe space for me to be old and young.

Mahalo nui loa.